Given in Memory of

Cecelia Covington Dicks Winslow

by

J. Brian Scott

Then Came You

Then Came You

Lisa Kleypas

LARGE PRINT

This large print edition published in 2004 by
RB Large Print
A division of Recorded Books
A Haights Cross Communications Company
270 Skipjack Road
Prince Frederick, MD 20678

Published by arrangement with HarperCollins Publishers, Inc.

Publisher's Cataloging In Publication Data
(Prepared by Donohue Group, Inc.)

Kleypas, Lisa.
    Then came you / Lisa Kleypas.

    p. (large print) ; cm.

    ISBN: 1-4025-7938-1

1. Large type books. 2. Historical fiction. I. Title.

PS3561.L456 T456 2004b
813/.6

Printed in the United States of America

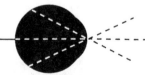

**This Large Print Book carries the
Seal of Approval of N.A.V.H.**

To my grandmother, Ethel Kleypas
With Love

Then Came You

CHAPTER 1

London, 1820

"Damn, damn . . . there it goes, the frigging thing!" A stream of curses floated on the gust of wind, shocking the guests at the water party.

The yacht was anchored in the middle of the Thames, the guests assembled in honor of King George. So far the party had been dull but dignified, everyone dutifully complimenting His Majesty's magnificently fitted yacht. With its brocaded furniture, fine mahogany, chandeliers of clustered crystal droplets, gilt sphinxes, and carved lions poised in every corner, the yacht was a floating pleasure palace. The guests had all been drinking heavily in order to attain the mild euphoria that would substitute for a real sense of enjoyment.

Perhaps the gathering would have been more entertaining had the king's health not been so poor. The recent death of his father and a taxing ordeal with gout had taken their toll, leaving him uncharacteristically morose. Now the king sought the company of people who would provide laughter and amusement to relieve his sense of isolation. That was why, it was said, he had specifically requested the presence of Miss Lily Lawson at the water party. It was only a matter of time, a languid young viscount had been heard to remark, until Miss Lawson would stir things up. As usual, she did not disappoint.

"Someone get the deuced thing!" Lily was heard to shout between lilting bursts of laughter. "The waves are moving it away from the boat!"

Grateful for the reprieve from ennui, the gentlemen rushed in the direction of the commotion. The women protested in annoyance as their escorts disappeared to the bow of the ship, where Lily hung over the railing and stared at some object floating in the water. "My favorite *chapeau*," Lily said in reply to the chorus of questions, indicating it with a sweep of her small hand. "The wind blew it right off my head!" She turned to her crowd of admirers, all of whom were ready to provide consolation. But she didn't want sympathy—she wanted the hat back. Grinning with mischief, she looked from one face to another. "Who will play the chivalrous gentleman and retrieve it for me?"

Lily had tossed the hat overboard on purpose. She could see that some of the gentlemen suspected as much, but that didn't stop the torrent of gallant offers. "Allow me," one man cried, while another made a show of doffing his own hat and coat. "No, I insist that I be afforded the privilege!" A rapid debate ensued, for each one of them wished to gain Lily's favor. But the water was rather turbulent today, and cold enough to cause a health-threatening chill. More importantly, it would be the ruination of an expensive, perfectly tailored coat.

Lily watched the controversy she had caused, her mouth curving with amusement. Preferring argument to action, the men were all posturing and making gallant statements. If anyone were inclined to rescue her hat, he would have done so by now. "What a sight," she said under her breath, staring at the bickering dandies. She would have respected a man who would step forward and tell her to go to hell, that no ridiculous pink hat was worth such a fuss, but none of them would dare. If Derek Craven were here, he would have laughed at her, or made a crude gesture that would have sent her into a fit of giggles. He and she both had similar contempt for the indolent, overperfumed, overmannered members of the *ton*.

Sighing, Lily switched her attention to the river, dark gray and choppy underneath the heavy sky. The Thames in springtime was unbearably cold. She lifted her face to the breeze, her eyes slitting as if she were a cat being stroked. Her hair was temporarily straightened by the wind, and then the shining black curls sprang to their usual buoyant disorder. Absently Lily pulled off the jeweled ribbon that had been tied around her forehead.

Her gaze followed the ridges of waves as they broke against the side of the yacht.

"*Mama . . .*" she heard a little voice whisper. Lily shrank from the memory, but it wouldn't disappear.

Suddenly she imagined she felt downy baby arms encircle her neck, delicate hair brush against her face, a child's weight settle in her lap. The Italian sun was hot on the nape of her neck. The quack and bustle of a duck procession crossed the glassy surface of the pond. "*Look, darling,*" Lily murmured. "*Look at the ducks. They're coming to visit us!*"

The little girl wriggled in excitement. A chubby hand lifted, and a miniature forefinger extended as the baby pointed to the parade of self-important ducks. Then she looked up at Lily with dark eyes, and a grin that revealed two tiny teeth. "*Dah,*" came the exclamation, and Lily laughed softly.

"*Ducks, my darling, and very handsome ones, too. Where did we put the bread to feed them? Dear me, I think I'm sitting on it . . .*"

Another whisk of wind came, chasing away the pleasurable image. Moisture seeped beneath her lashes, and Lily felt a painful twisting in her chest. "Oh, Nicole," she whispered. She tried to breathe away the tightness, willed it to disappear, but it refused to go. Panic built swiftly inside her. Sometimes she could numb it with liquor, or divert her mind with gambling or gossip or hunting, but the escape was only temporary. She wanted her child. *My baby . . . where are you . . . I'll find you . . . Mama's coming, don't cry, don't cry . . .* The desperation was like a knife twisting deeper every moment. She had to do something at once, or she would go mad.

She startled the men nearby with a high, reckless laugh, and kicked off her heeled slippers. The pink plume of her hat was still visible in the water. "My poor *chapeau*'s nearly sunk," she cried, and threw her legs over the railing. "So much for chivalry. I see I'll have to rescue it myself!" Before anyone could stop her, she leapt off the yacht.

The river closed over her, a wave smoothing over the place where she had been. Some of the women screamed. Anxiously the men scanned the rippling water. "My God," one of them exclaimed, but the rest were too astonished to speak. Even the king, informed of the goings-on by his grooms-in-waiting, waddled forth to take a look, pressing his massive bulk against the railing. Lady Conyngham, a large, handsome woman of fifty-four who had become his latest mistress, joined him with an astonished exclamation. "You know I've said it before—that woman is mad! Heaven help us all!"

Lily stayed underwater a moment longer than was necessary. At first the coldness was a shock, paralyzing her limbs, making her blood turn to ice. Her skirts turned heavy, pulling her down into the mysterious cold darkness. It wouldn't be difficult

7

to let it happen, she thought numbly . . . just drift downward, let the darkness overtake her . . . but a pang of fear impelled her hands to make a finning motion, propelling her to the dim light above. On the way up, she grasped the lump of sodden velvet that brushed her wrist. She broke the surface of the water, blinking the stinging salt from her eyes, licking it from her lips. Needles of intense cold stabbed through her. Her teeth chattered violently, and she regarded the shocked assemblage on the yacht with a shivering grin.

"I've got it!" she chirped, and held the hat aloft in triumph.

A few minutes later, Lily was pulled from the river by several pairs of willing hands. She emerged with her wet gown clinging to every curve of her body, revealing a slim, delectable figure. A collective gasp went through the crowd on the yacht. Women watched her with a mixture of envy and dislike, for no other female in London was so admired by men. Other women who behaved just as disgracefully were regarded with pity and contempt, whereas Lily . . .

"She can do anything, no matter how abominable, and men adore her all the more for it!" Lady Conyngham complained out loud. "She attracts scandal just as honey draws flies. If she were any other woman, she would have been ruined a dozen times over. Even my darling George won't abide any criticism of her. How does she manage it?"

"It's because she behaves like a man," Lady Wilton replied sourly. "Gambling, hunting, swearing, and politicking . . . they're charmed by the novelty of a woman with such masculine ways."

"She doesn't *look* very masculine," Lady Conyngham grumbled, observing the dainty form sheathed in wet fabric.

Assured of Lily's safety, the men crowded around her erupted into laughter and applause at her daring. Pushing the sodden curls back from her eyes, Lily grinned and gave a dripping curtsey. "Well, it *was* my favorite hat," she said, regarding the ruined clump of material in her hands.

"Good Gad," one of the observers exclaimed in admiration, "you're absolutely fearless, aren't you?"

"Absolutely," she said, causing them to chuckle. Rivulets of water ran down her neck and shoulders. Lily wiped at them with her hands and turned away to shake her wet head vigorously. "Would one of you dear, *dear* gentlemen fetch me a length of towel and perhaps a bracing drink before I catch my death of . . ." Her voice trailed away as she caught sight of a still figure through the curtain of wet tendrils.

There was movement around her as the men scattered to find towels, hot drinks, anything to serve her comfort. But the one standing several feet away did not move. Slowly Lily straightened and pushed her hair back, returning his bold stare.

9

He was a stranger. She didn't know why he stared at her that way. She was accustomed to men's admiring gazes . . . but his eyes were cold, emotionless . . . and his mouth was taut with contempt. Lily stood without moving, her slender body shivering.

She had never seen immaculate golden blondness combined with such satyric features. The breeze blew the locks of hair back from his forehead, revealing the intriguing point of a widow's peak. His hawklike, aristocratic face was strikingly hard and stubborn. In his eyes, so brilliantly pale, there was a bleakness that Lily knew would haunt her for a long time afterward. Only someone who had experienced such bitter despair would be able to recognize it in another.

Profoundly disturbed by the stranger's gaze, Lily turned her back to him and beamed at her approaching admirers, who were laden with towels, cloaks, and steaming hot drinks. She banished all thoughts of the unknown man from her mind. Who gave a damn about some stuffy aristocrat's opinion of her?

"Miss Lawson," Lord Bennington remarked with a concerned expression, "I'm afraid you'll catch a chill. If you wish, I would be honored to row you ashore."

Discovering that her teeth were chattering against the rim of a glass, making it impossible for her to drink, Lily nodded gratefully. She reached her blue-tinged hand toward his arm and tugged in order to make him lower his head. Her icy lips came near his ear. "Hurry, pl-please," she whispered. "I th-think I may have been a little t-too imp-pulsive. But don't t-tell anyone I s-said so."

Alex, Lord Raiford, a man known for his self-discipline and remoteness, was battling an inexplicable anger. Ridiculous woman . . . risking her health, even her life, in order to make a spectacle of herself. She had to be a courtesan, one known in a few select circles. No one with a shred of a reputation to preserve would behave like that. Alex unclenched his hands and rubbed his palms on his coat. His chest felt tight and banded. Her high-spirited laughter, her lively gaze, her dark hair . . . dear God, she reminded him of Caroline.

"You've never met her before, have you?" he heard a scratchily amused voice nearby. Sir Evelyn Downshire, a fine old gentleman who had known his father, was standing nearby. "Men always have that look when they see her for the first time. She reminds me of the marchioness of Salisbury in her day. Magnificent woman."

Alex tore his gaze away from the flamboyant creature. "I don't find her all that admirable," he replied coldly.

Downshire chuckled, revealing a carefully constructed set of ivory teeth. "If I were a young man I'd seduce her," he said reflectively. "I would indeed. She's the last of her kind, you know."

"What kind is that?"

"In my day there were scores of them," Downshire mused with a wistful smile. "It took skill and cleverness to tame them . . . oh, they required no end of managing . . . trouble, such delightful trouble . . ."

Alex looked back at the woman. Such a delicate face she had, pale and perfect, with fiery dark eyes. "Who is she?" he asked, half in a dream. When there was no reply, he turned and realized that Downshire had wandered away.

Lily climbed out of the carriage and made her way to the front door of her Grosvenor Square terrace. She had never been so uncomfortable in her life.

"Serves me right," she muttered to herself, walking up her front steps while the butler, Burton, watched from the doorway. "What an idiotic thing to do." The Thames, in which all of London's refuse was dumped, was not an advisable place to swim. Her leap into the water had left her clothes and her skin tainted with a distinctly unpleasant odor. Her feet squeaked inside her wet slippers. The odd noise, not to mention her appearance, caused Burton's brow to furrow like a millstone. That was unusual for Burton, who usually greeted her calamities without expression.

For the past two years, Burton had been the dominant figure in the household, setting the tone

12

for servants and guests alike. When welcoming visitors into her home, Burton's starched manner conveyed that Lily was a person of consequence. He overlooked her follies and adventures as if they didn't exist, treating her as an impeccable lady although she rarely acted like one. Lily knew full well that she would not be respected by her own servants if it were not for Burton's imposing presence. He was a tall, bearded man with a solid girth, his neat iron gray beard framing a stern face. No other butler in England had his precise combination of haughtiness and deference.

"I trust you enjoyed the water party, miss?" he inquired.

"A smasher," Lily said, trying to sound animated. She handed him a wad of soggy velvet, adorned by a straggling pink feather. He stared blankly at the object. "My hat," she explained, and squeaked into the house, leaving a wet path in her wake.

"Miss Lawson, a guest is awaiting your arrival in the parlor. Lord Stamford."

"Zachary's here?" Lily was delighted by the news. Zachary, Lord Stamford, a sensitive and intelligent young man, had been a dear friend for a long time. He was in love with her younger sister, Penelope. Unfortunately he was the marquess of Hertford's third son, which meant that he would never inherit sufficient title or wealth to satisfy the Lawsons' ambitious plans. Since it was clear that Lily would never marry, her parents' dreams of social advancement were centered on Penelope. Lily felt sorry for her younger sister, who was betrothed to the earl of Raiford . . . a man Penelope reputedly did not even know very well. Zachary had to be suffering.

"How long has Zachary been here?" Lily asked.

"For three hours, miss. He claimed to be about urgent business. He stated that he would wait as long as necessary in order to see you."

Lily's curiosity was awakened. She glanced at the closed door of the salon, positioned between the arms of the double-sided staircase. "Urgent, hmm? I'll see him right away. Er . . . send him to my upstairs sitting room. I must get out of these wet things."

Burton nodded without expression. The sitting room, attached to Lily's bedchamber via a small anteroom, was reserved for Lily's closest acquaintances. Few were allowed up there, although an untold number had angled for invitations. "Yes, Miss Lawson."

Zachary had found it no hardship to wait in Lily's parlor. Even in his agitation, he couldn't help noticing that something about No. 38 Grosvenor made a man feel extraordinarily comfortable. Perhaps it had something to do with the color schemes. Most women had their walls done in the fashionable pastel colors—cool blue, icy pink, or yellow, ornamented with white friezes and columns. Uncomfortable little gilt chairs with slick cushions were the mode, those and sofas with dainty legs that looked incapable of bearing any real weight. But Lily's terrace was decorated in rich, warm colors, with solid furniture that invited a man to put his feet up. The walls were covered with hunting scenes, engravings, and a few tasteful portraits. There were frequent gatherings of writers, eccentrics, dandies, and politicians at her home, although Lily's liquor supply was undependable—sometimes abundant, sometimes perplexingly sparse.

Apparently Lily was amply stocked this month, for one of the housemaids brought Zachary a decanter of good brandy and a glass on a silver tray. She also offered him a copy of the *Times*, ironed flat and stitched down the seam, and a plate of sweetened biscuits. Enjoying a feeling of well-being, Zachary asked for a pot of tea and relaxed with the paper. As he finished the last of the biscuits, Burton opened the door.

"Has she arrived?" Zachary asked eagerly, jumping to his feet.

Burton regarded him implacably. "Miss Lawson will see you upstairs. If you will allow me to show you the way, Lord Stamford . . ."

Zachary followed him up the curving staircase, with its intricately turned balusters and highly polished banister. He entered the sitting room, where a lively blaze cast its light from a small marble fireplace, and illuminated the green, bronze, and blue silk wall hangings. After a minute

15

or two, Lily appeared at the doorway that connected to her bedchamber.

"Zachary!" she exclaimed, rushing forward and seizing his hands. Zachary smiled as he bent to brush her soft cheek with a perfunctory kiss. His smile froze as he realized that she was clad in a robe, her bare feet peeking out from beneath the floor-length hem. It was a circumspect robe, heavy and thick, the neck trimmed in swansdown, but it was still a garment in the category of "unmentionable." He stepped back in a startled reflex, but not before he noticed that her hair was drying in spiky clumps, and she smelled rather . . . peculiar.

In spite of that, Lily was still strikingly beautiful. Her eyes were as dark as the center of a sunflower, shadowed by a thick sweep of lashes. Her skin had a pale, polished glow, and the line of her throat was delicate and pure. When she smiled as she did now, her lips had a singularly sweet curve, as if she were an angelic little girl. Her innocent appearance was deceptive. Zachary had seen her trade the subtlest of insults with rarefied dandies, then shout vulgarities at a pickpocket who had attempted to rob her.

"Lily?" he asked tentatively, and he couldn't help wrinkling his nose as he got another whiff.

She laughed at his expression and waved at the air in front of her. "I would have bathed first, but you said your concern was urgent. Pardon me for reeking of *eau de poison*—the Thames was rather

16

fishy today." At his uncomprehending stare, she added, "My hat was blown into the river by a gust of wind."

"While you were still wearing it?" Zachary asked in confusion.

Lily grinned. "Not precisely. But let's not talk about it—I'd rather hear about the matter that brought you to town."

He gestured to her attire, or rather her lack of it, uncomfortably. "Shouldn't you like to dress first?"

Lily gave him a fond smile. There were some things about Zachary that would never change. His soft brown eyes, his sensitive face, the neatly groomed hair, all of it reminded her of a little boy dressed for church. "Oh, don't blush and carry on. I'm perfectly well covered. I wouldn't have expected such modesty of you, Zachary. After all, you did ask me to marry you once."

"Oh, yes, well . . ." Zachary frowned. The proposal had been made and rejected so quickly that he had almost forgotten about it. "Until that day Harry was my best friend. When he jilted you in that dastardly manner, I felt the only gentlemanly thing to do was to act as his second."

That provoked a snort of laughter. "His second? Good Gad, Zachary, it was an engagement, not a duel!"

"And you turned down my proposal," he remembered.

"Dear boy, I would have made you miserable,

the same way I made Harry miserable. That was why he left me."

"That is no excuse for him to have behaved so dishonorably," Zachary said stiffly.

"But I'm glad he did. If he hadn't, I never would have traveled 'round the world with my eccentric Aunt Sally, and she never would have left me her fortune, and I would be . . ." Lily paused and gave a delicate shudder, "*married.*" She smiled and seated herself before the fire, gesturing for him to do the same. "At the time, all I could think about was my broken heart. But I do remember your proposal as one of the nicest things that ever happened to me. One of the few times a man has acted unselfishly on my behalf. The only time, actually. You were prepared to sacrifice your own happiness and marry me, just to save my wounded pride."

"Is that why you've remained friends with me over the years?" Zachary asked with surprise. "With all the elegant, accomplished people you know, I've always wondered why you bother with me."

"Oh, yes," she said dryly. "Spendthrifts, wastrels, and thieves. Quite an assortment of friends I have. Obviously I don't exclude royalty and politicians." She smiled at him. "You're the only decent man I've ever known."

"Decency's gotten me far, hasn't it?" he said glumly.

Lily looked at him in surprise, wondering what

had made Zachary, a perennial idealist, look so woebegone. Something must be very wrong indeed. "Zach, you have many wonderful qualities. You're attractive—"

"But not handsome," he said.

"Intelligent—"

"But not clever. Not a wit."

"Cleverness is usually born of malice, which I'm glad to say you don't have. Now stop obligating me to praise you, and tell me why you've come." Her gaze sharpened. "It's Penelope, isn't it?"

Zachary stared into her fire-lit eyes. He frowned and gave a long sigh. "Your sister and your parents are staying with Raiford at Raiford Park, making preparations for the wedding."

"It's only a few weeks away," Lily mused, warming her bare toes before the crackling blaze. "I wasn't invited. Mother is terrified that I would make some sort of scene." The sound of her laughter was tinged with melancholy. "Where would she get such an idea?"

"Your past doesn't quite recommend you—" Zachary tried to explain, and she interrupted with amused impatience.

"Yes, of course I know that."

She hadn't been on speaking terms with her family for some time. Those ties had been cut years ago by her own careless hands. She didn't know what had driven her to rebel against the rules of propriety her family held so dear, but it didn't matter now. She had made mistakes for which she would never be forgiven. The Lawsons had warned her that she would never be able to come back. At the time, Lily had laughed in the face of their disapproval. Now she was well acquainted with the taste of regret. Ruefully, she smiled at Zachary. "Even I wouldn't do something to embarrass Penny. Or heaven forbid, endanger the prospect of having a wealthy earl in the family. Mother's fondest dream."

"Lily, have you ever met Penelope's fiancé?"

"Hmm . . . not really. Once I caught a glimpse of him in Shropshire during the opening of grouse season. Tall and taciturn, that's how he appeared."

"If he marries Penelope, he will make her life hell." Zachary intended the statement to be shocking, dramatic, spurring her into immediate action.

Lily was unimpressed. Her dark, slanting brows drew together, and she contemplated him with almost scientific detachment. "First of all, Zach, there's no 'if' about it. Penny is going to marry Raiford. She would never disobey my parents' wishes. Second, it's hardly a secret that you're in love with her—"

"And she loves me!"

"—and therefore you may be apt to exaggerate the situation for your own purposes." She raised her eyebrows significantly. "Hmm?"

"In this matter I *couldn't* exaggerate! Raiford will be cruel to her. He doesn't love her, whereas I would *die* for her."

He was young and melodramatic, but it was clear he was sincere. "Oh, Zach." Lily felt a surge of compassion for him. Sooner or later everyone was driven to love someone they could never have. Fortunately, once had been enough for her to learn that particular lesson. "You will remember, I advised you long before now to coax Penny to elope with you," she said. "Either that or dishonor her so that my parents would have to consent to the match. But it's too late now. They've found a fatter pigeon than you to pluck."

"Lord Raiford is no pigeon," Zachary said darkly. "He's more like a lion—a cold, savage creature who will make your sister miserable for the rest of her days. He isn't capable of love. Penelope is terrified of him. Ask some of your friends about him. Ask anyone. They'll all tell you the same thing—he doesn't have a heart."

Well. A heartless man. She had met her share of those. Lily sighed. "Zachary, I have no advice to offer," she said regretfully. "I love my sister, and naturally it would delight me to see her happy. But there's nothing I can do for either of you."

"You could talk to your family," he begged. "You could plead my cause."

"Zachary, you know I'm an outcast from the family. My words carry no weight with them. I haven't been in their good graces for years."

"Please. You're my last hope. *Please.*"

Lily stared into Zachary's anguished face and shook her head helplessly. She didn't want to be

21

the source of anyone's hope. Her own small supply had been exhausted. Unable to remain sitting, she sprang up and paced around the room, while he remained deathly still in his chair.

Zachary spoke as if he feared that one ill-chosen word would be his ruin. "Lily, think of how your sister feels. Try to imagine what it is like for a woman without your strength and freedom. Frightened, dependent on others, helpless . . . oh, I know that is a feeling utterly foreign to someone like you, but—"

He was interrupted by a caustic laugh. Lily had stopped pacing and was standing near the heavily draped window. She rested her back against the wall, one leg bent until the point of her knee showed through the thick ivory robe. Regarding him with bright, mocking eyes, she gave him a smile shadowed with irony. "Utterly foreign," she repeated.

"But Penelope and I are both lost . . . we need someone to help us, guide us to the path we were meant to walk together—"

"Dear, how poetic."

"Oh God, Lily, don't you know what it is to love? Don't you believe in it?"

Lily turned away, pulling at a few strands of her short, matted hair. She rubbed her forehead wearily. "No, not that kind of love," she said in a distracted manner. His question troubled her. Suddenly she wished he would go, and take his desperate gaze with him. "I believe in the love a mother has for her child. And the love between brothers and sisters. I believe in friendship. But I've never seen a romantic match that lasts. They're all destined to end out of jealousy, anger, indifference . . ." She steeled herself to look at him coolly. "Be like every other man, my dear. Marry advantageously, then take a mistress who will supply all the love you need for as long as you're willing to keep her."

Zachary flinched as if she had slapped him. He stared at her as he never had before, his soft eyes accusing. "For the first time," he said unsteadily, "I can believe some of the things that others say about you. F-forgive me for coming here. I thought you could provide some help. Or at least comfort."

"Damnation!" Lily exploded, using her favorite curse. Zachary winced but remained in his chair. In astonishment, Lily realized that his need was that great, his hope that stubborn. And she, of all people, should understand the hell it was to be separated from the one you loved. Slowly she went to him and pressed a kiss to his forehead, smoothing his hair back as if he were a little boy. "Forgive me," she muttered remorsefully. "I'm a selfish wretch."

"No," he said in confusion. "No, you're—"

"I am, I'm impossible. Of course I'll help you, Zachary. I always repay my debts, and this has been long outstanding." Suddenly she leapt away and strode around the room with renewed energy, chewing on her knuckles as if she were a cat frantically grooming itself. "Now let me think . . . let me think . . ."

Dazed by her swift change of mood, Zachary sat there and watched silently.

"I'll have to meet Raiford," she finally said. "I'll assess the situation for myself."

"But I've already told you what he's like."

"I must form my own impression of him. If I find that Raiford is neither as cruel nor as horrid as you paint him, I'll have to let the matter alone." Her small fingers laced together and she flexed them up and down, as if making them more limber before seizing the reins of a palfrey and charging off on a hunting course. "Go back to the country, Zach, and I will notify you when I've made a decision."

"What if you discover that I'm right about him? What then?"

"Then," she said pragmatically, "I'll do whatever I can to help you get Penny."

CHAPTER 2

The lady's maid entered the room with an armload of evening finery. "No, Annie, not the pink gown," Lily said, gesturing over her shoulder. "Tonight I want something more dashing. Something wicked." She sat at her dressing table, peering into a gilt-framed oval mirror and running her fingers through her unruly sable curls.

"The blue with the slash-and-puff sleeves and the low neck?" Annie suggested, her round face wreathed in a smile. Born and reared in the country, she had a fascination for all the sophisticated styles to be found in London.

"Perfect! I always win more when I wear that one. All of the gentlemen stare at my bosom instead of concentrating on their cards."

Annie chuckled and went in search of the gown, while Lily tied a silver and sapphire *bandeau* around her forehead. Artfully she coaxed a few curls to fall over the sparkling ribbon. She smiled into the mirror, but it looked rather like a grimace. The daring grin she had once used to great effect had disappeared. Lately she couldn't seem to manufacture anything but a poor imitation. Perhaps it was the strain she had been living with for so long.

Lily frowned at her reflection ruefully. Were it not for Derek Craven's friendship, she would have become far more bitter and hardened by now. Ironic, that the most cynical man she had ever known had helped her to retain her last few shreds of hope.

Lily knew that most of the *ton* believed that she was having an affair with Derek. She was not surprised by such speculation—Derek was not the sort of man who had platonic relationships with women. But there was no romantic attachment between them and there never would be. He had never even made an attempt to kiss her. Of course, it would be impossible to convince anyone else of that, for they were seen together, cup-and-can, in their favorite haunts, places that ranged from the most prized seats at the opera to the dingiest Covent Garden drinking establishments.

Derek never asked to visit Lily's London terrace, and she did not invite him. There were certain lines they did not cross. Lily liked the arrangement, for it kept other men from making unwanted advances to her. No one would dare intrude on what was considered to be Derek Craven's territory.

There were things about Derek that Lily had come to admire over the past two years—his strength and utter lack of fear. Of course, he had his faults. He was lost to sentiment. He loved money. The clink of coins was music to him, sweeter than any sound a violin or piano could produce. Derek had no taste for paintings or sculpture, but the perfect shape of a die—that he appreciated. As well as his lack of cultural refinement, Lily also had to admit that Derek was selfish to his very marrow—the reason, she suspected, that he had never fallen in love. He would never be able to put another's needs before his own. But if he had been less selfish, if he had possessed a sensitive and kind nature, his childhood would have destroyed him.

Derek had confessed to Lily that he had been born in a drainpipe and abandoned by his mother. He had been raised by pimps, prostitutes, and criminals who had shown him the darkest side of life. In his youth he had made money by robbing graves, but found his stomach was too unsteady for it. Later he had turned to laboring on the docks—shoveling dung, sorting fish, whatever would yield a coin. When he was still just a boy, a highborn lady had caught sight of him from her carriage as he carried boxes of empty bottles out of a gin shop. In spite of his unkempt and filthy appearance, something about his looks had appealed to her, and she had invited him into her carriage.

"It's a lie," Lily had interrupted in the middle of that particular story, watching Derek with wide eyes.

"It's the truf," he countered lazily, relaxing before the fire in his apartments, stretching his long legs. With his black hair and tanned face, and features that were neither chiseled nor coarse but somewhere in between, he was handsome . . . almost. His strong white teeth were slightly snaggled, giving him the appearance of a friendly lion when he smiled. Nearly irresistible, that smile, although it never reached his hard green eyes. "She took me in 'er carriage, she did, an' brung me to 'er 'ome in London."

"Where was her husband?"

"Away to the country."

"What would she want to do with a dirty boy she had just plucked from the streets?" Lily asked suspiciously, and scowled as he gave her a knowing smile. "I don't believe this, Derek! Not a bloody word of it!"

"First she 'ad me take a bath," Derek reminisced, a thoughtful expression on his face. "God . . . the 'ot water . . . hard soap, an it smelled so sweet . . . an the rug on the floor . . . soft. I washed my arms an elbows first . . . my skin looked so white to me . . ." He shook his head with a faint smile and sipped some brandy. "Afterwards I was shiwerin' like a newborn pup."

"And then I suppose she invited you into her bed and you were a magnificent lover, beyond anything she had experienced before," Lily said sarcastically.

"No." Derek grinned. "The worst, more like.

28

'Ow did I know to please a woman? I only knew as to please myself."

"But she liked it anyway?" Lily asked skeptically. She was experiencing the same confusion she always had concerning such matters. She had no idea what drew men and women together, why they desired to share a bed and engage in an act that was so painful, embarrassing, and joyless. There was no doubt that men enjoyed it far more than women did. Why would a woman deliberately seek out some stranger to couple with? A blush came to her cheeks and her gaze fell, but she listened intently as Derek continued.

"She taught me what she liked," he said. "An' I wanted to learn."

"Why?"

"Why." Derek hesitated, drinking more, staring into the dancing fire. "Any man can rut, but few knows or cares to please a woman. An' to see a woman like that, going soft an eazy underneaf me . . . it gives a man power, y'see?" He glanced at Lily's perplexed face and laughed. "No, I s'pose you don't, poor gypsy."

"I'm not poor anything," she retorted, wrinkling her nose in distaste. "And what do you mean by 'power'?"

The smile he turned to her was faintly nasty. "Tickle a woman's tail right, an' she'll do anyfing for you. Anyfing."

"*Th*ing," Lily said distinctly, and shook her head in bemusement. "I don't agree with you, Derek.

I've had my . . . I mean, I've done . . . *that* . . . and it wasn't at all what I expected. And Giuseppe was known everywhere as Italy's greatest lover. Everyone said so."

Derek's bright green eyes filled with mockery. "Sure 'e did it right?"

"Since I conceived a child from the act, he must have done *something* right," Lily retorted.

"A man can father a thousand bastards, an' still not do it right, lovey. Plain as a pipe stem—you don't know nofing about it."

Arrogant male, Lily thought, and gave him a speaking glance. She didn't care *how* someone did it, there was no possible way it could be pleasant. Frowning, she remembered Giuseppe's wet mouth on her skin, the suffocating weight of his body, the pain that had driven through and through her until she had gone rigid in silent misery . . .

"*Is this all you have to give?*" he had demanded in his fluid Italian, his hands roving over her body. She had flinched from the intimate groping that had brought only embarrassment, the rough probing that brought pain. "*Ah, you're like all the English . . . cold as a fish!*"

Long before then, she had learned that men could never be trusted with her heart. Giuseppe had taught her not to trust anyone with her body, either. To subject herself to that again, from any man, would be more degradation than she could bear.

Reading Lily's thoughts, Derek stood up and approached her chair. He braced his hands above her head and stared down at her with glinting green eyes. Lily shifted uncomfortably, feeling trapped. "You do tempt me, lovey," Derek murmured. "I'd like to be the man what shows you the pleasure it can be."

Disliking the threatened feeling that was coming over her, Lily scowled at him. "I wouldn't allow you to touch me, you wax-nosed cockney."

"I could if I wanted to," he returned evenly. "An' I'd make you like it. You needs a good tumble, worse than any woman I ever knew. But it won't be me that does you over."

"Why not?" Lily asked, trying to sound bored. Her voice held a nervous quaver that made him smile.

"I'd lose you then," he said. "That's what always 'appens. An' the devil will go blind before I loses you. So you'll find some other man to lift your 'eels for. An' I'll be 'ere, when you come back to me. Always."

Lily was quiet, her wondering gaze locked on his purposeful face. Perhaps, she thought, this was as close as Derek could ever come to loving someone. He saw love as a weakness, and he despised weakness in himself. But at the same time, he depended on their odd friendship. He didn't want to lose her . . . well, she didn't want to lose him, either.

She gave him a glance of mock scorn. "Was that supposed to be a declaration of affection?" she asked.

The mood was broken. Derek grinned and rumpled her short hair, pulling at the silky curls. "Whatewer you wants it to be, lovey."

After her meeting with Zachary, Lily went to Craven's in search of Derek. Certainly he would know something about Raiford. Derek knew the financial worth of every man in England, including past bankruptices and scandals, future inheritances, and outstanding debts and liabilities. Through his own intelligence service, Derek was also aware of the private contents of their wills, which men kept mistresses and how much they paid for them, and what marks their sons made at Eton, Harrow, and Westfield.

Dressed in a pale blue gown, her small breasts emphasized by a scoop-necked bodice edged with sparkling cream lace, Lily strolled through Craven's unaccompanied. Her presence attracted little attention, for by now she was a familiar sight, an accepted oddity. She was the only woman Derek had ever allowed membership at Craven's, and in return he had demanded complete honesty from her. He alone knew her darkest secrets.

Peering into room after room, Lily took in the sights of early evening at the gambling palace. The supper rooms were filled with guests partaking of fine food and drink. "Pigeons," she said softly, smiling to herself. That was Derek's word for his guests, although no one but her ever heard him use it.

First the "pigeons" would dine on the best cuisine in London, prepared by a chef to whom Derek paid the unthinkable salary of two thousand pounds a year. The supper would be accompanied by a selection of French and Rhenish wines, which Derek furnished at his own expense, ostensibly out of the goodness of his heart. Such an appearance of generosity encouraged the guests to spend more at the tables later.

After supper, the club members would proceed through the building to the game rooms. Louis XIV would have felt entirely at home here, surrounded by stained glass, magnificent chandeliers, acres of rich blue velvet, dazzling and priceless artwork. Set at the center of the edifice, like a precious jewel, was the hazard room with its domed ceiling. The air was filled with a quiet buzz of activity.

Skirting the edge of the octagonal-shaped room, Lily absorbed the rhythm of ivory dice rattling in the box, the crisp shuffle of cards, the hum of voices. A shaded lamp hung directly over the oval-shaped hazard table, concentrating brilliant light on the green cloth and yellow markings. Tonight several German embassy officials, a few French exiles, and a number of English dandies were grouped around the central hazard table. A wry, pitying smile touched Lily's lips as she saw how absorbed they were. Bets were placed and dice tossed with hypnotic regularity. Were a foreigner to come here, someone who had never seen gambling before, he would assume that some sort of religious rite were taking place.

The trick of winning was to play with detachment, taking calculated risks. But most of the men here did not play to win; they played for the thrill of casting themselves on the mercy of fate. Lily played without emotion, winning moderately but consistently. Derek called her a "rook," which was for him a term of highest praise.

A couple of the croupiers at the hazard table, Darnell and Fitz, nodded discreetly as Lily passed by. She was on excellent terms with Derek's employees, including the kitchen staff. The chef, Monsieur Labarge, always insisted that she sample and praise his latest creations—lobster patties covered with breadcrumbs and cream, miniature potato souffles, partridge stuffed with hazel-nuts and truffles, omelets filled with jellied fruit, pastries, and mouthwatering custards layered with crushed macaroons.

Lily glanced around the hazard room in search of Derek's slim, dark form, but he was not there. As she headed toward one of six arched doorways, she was aware of a light touch at her gloved elbow. Turning around with a half smile, she expected to see Derek's lean face. It was not Derek, but a tall Spaniard wearing a golden insignia on his sleeve that designated him as an ambassador's aide. He bowed to her perfunctorily, then reached for her with insolent familiarity. "You have attracted de notice of Ambassador Alvarez," he informed her. "Come, he weeshes you to sit with him. Come weeth me."

Jerking her elbow away, Lily looked across the room at the ambassador, a rotund man with a thin mustache. He was staring at her avidly. With an unmistakable gesture, he motioned her to come to him. Lily returned her gaze to the aide. "There's been a mistake," she said gently. "Tell Señor Alvarez that I am flattered by his interest, but I have other plans for this evening."

As she turned away, the aide took her wrist and jerked her back. "Come," he insisted. "He weel pay for hees pleasure."

Obviously she had been mistaken for one of Craven's hired women, but even they were not subjected to this sort of treatment, as if they were whores procured from a street corner. "I'm not one of the house wenches," Lily said through her teeth. "I'm not for sale, do you understand? Now let go of me."

The aide's face darkened with frustration. He began to chatter in Spanish, trying to force her toward the hazard table where Alvarez was waiting. Several guests paused in their gambling to observe the commotion. As embarrassment joined her irritation, Lily shot a murderous glance at Worthy, Derek's factotum. He stood up from his desk in the corner and began toward them. Before Worthy reached the aide, Derek miraculously appeared from nowhere.

"Well, now, Seny'r Barreda, I see as you've met

35

Miss Lawson. A beauty, ain't she?" As he spoke, Derek deftly extricated Lily from the Spaniard's grasp. "But she's a special guest—*my* special guest. There's other women we 'as for the ambassador's convenience, an' sweeter to the taste. This one's a sour little apple, she is."

"You know what *you* are," Lily muttered, glaring at Derek.

"He wants thees one," the aide insisted.

"'E can't 'ave 'er," Derek said, his voice pleasant. The gambling palace was his own private kingdom, his word the final one in all matters.

Lily saw the flash of uneasiness in the Spaniard's gaze. Having once attempted to face down Derek, she knew exactly how daunting he was. As always, Derek was dressed in expensive garments—a blue coat, pearl gray pantaloons, and an immaculate white shirt and cravat. But in spite of his exquisitely tailored clothes, Derek had the rough, seasoned look of someone who had spent most of his life in the streets. Now he rubbed elbows with the cream of society, knowing as everyone else did that his elbows had originally been meant to occupy far less exalted places.

Derek motioned to his two most beautiful house wenches, who sped efficiently to the frowning ambassador, sporting lavish displays of cleavage. "No, I azure you, 'e'll like those two better . . . see? 'Appy as a mouse in cheese."

Lily and Barreda followed his gaze and saw that with the women's expert attentions, Alvarez's frown had indeed cleared away. Giving Lily one last frown, the aide retreated with a few mumbled words.

"How dare he," Lily exclaimed indignantly, her face flushed. "And how dare *you*? Your *special guest*? I don't want anyone to think I need a protector. I'm completely self-sufficient, and I'll thank you to refrain from implying otherwise, especially in front of—"

"Easy, settle your temper. I should've let 'im 'ave a go at you, is that it?"

"No, but you could have referred to me with some respect. And where the hell have you been? I want to speak with you about someone—"

"I respects you, lovey, more than a woman should be respected. Now come 'ave a walk with me. My ear—what's left ow it—is yours to chew."

Lily was unable to prevent a short laugh, and she slipped her hand into the crook of Derek's wiry arm. He often liked to take her on his strolls through the gambling palace, as if she were a rare prize he had won. As they crossed the main entrance hall and went to the magnificent gold staircase, Derek welcomed some of the arriving club members, Lord Millwright and Lord Nevill, a baron and an earl, respectively. Lily favored them with a bright smile.

"Edward, I hope you'll indulge me later with a game of cribbage," Lily said to Nevill. "After I lost to you last week, I've fretted for the chance to redeem myself."

Lord Nevill's pudgy face creased with an answering smile. "Most assuredly, Miss Lawson. I look forward to another match." As Nevill and Millwright headed to the dining room, Nevill was heard to say, "For a woman, she's quite clever . . ."

"Not too much ow a scalping," Derek warned Lily. "'E touched me for a loan yesterday. 'Is pockets aren't long enow to please a little rook like you."

"Well, whose are?" Lily asked, causing him to chuckle.

"Try young Lord Bentinck—'is father takes care of 'is debts when 'e plays too deep." Together they ascended the magnificent grand staircase.

"Derek," Lily said briskly, "I came to ask what you know about a certain gentleman."

"Who?"

"The earl of Raiford."

Derek recognized the name instantly. "The nob what's betroved to your sister."

"Yes, I've heard some rather disturbing speculation on his character. I want your impression of him."

"Why?"

"Because I fear he is going to be a cruel husband to Penelope. And there is still time for me to do something about it. The wedding is only four weeks away."

"You don't give an oyster for your sister," he said.

Lily directed a reproving glare at him. "That shows how little you know about me! It is true that we have never been much alike, but I adore Penny. She is gentle, shy, obedient . . . qualities I think are very admirable in other women."

"She doesn't need your 'elp."

"Yes, she does. Penny is as sweet and helpless as a lamb."

"An you were born wi' claws an teef," he said smoothly.

Lily lifted her nose. "If something is threatening my sister's future happiness, it is my responsibility to do something about it."

"A bloody saint, you are."

"Now tell me what you know about Raiford. You know everything about everyone. And stop snickering like that—I don't intend to interfere in anyone else's affairs, or do anything rash—"

"Like 'ell you won't." Derek was laughing, envisioning yet another scrape she might land herself into.

"*H*ell, Derek," she corrected, enunciating the word. "You didn't see Mr. Hastings today, did you? I can always tell when you've missed a lesson."

Derek gave her a warning glance.

Lily alone knew that for two days every week Derek employed a special tutor who tried to soften his cockney accent into a more genteel one. It was a hopeless cause. After years of devoted study, Derek had managed to elevate his speech from the level of Billingsgate fish vendor to that of . . . well, perhaps a hackney driver, or a Temple Bar merchant. A slight improvement, but hardly remarkable. "His *h*'s are his downfall," the tutor had once told Lily in despair. "He can say them if he tries, but he always forgets. To him I'll be 'Mr. 'astings' until he draws his last breath."

Lily had replied with a mixture of laughter and sympathy. "That's all right, Mr. Hastings. Just have patience. He will surprise you someday. That *h* won't stop him forever."

"He doesn't have the ear for it," the tutor said glumly.

Lily had not argued. Privately she knew that Derek would never sound like a gentleman. It didn't matter to her. She had actually come to like the manner of his speech, the mixed up *v*'s and *w*'s, the imprecise consonants that fell rather pleasantly on the ear.

Derek led her to the carved, gilded balcony overlooking the main floor. It was his favorite place to talk, for he could watch every move at the tables, his mind never ceasing its intricate calculations. Not a farthing, cribbage-counter, nor a card flicking through nimble fingers ever escaped his vigilant gaze. "Lord Raiford," he murmured thoughtfully. "Aye, 'e's shook the elbow 'ere a time or two. Not a pigeon, though."

"Really," Lily said with surprise. "Not a pigeon. Coming from you, that's quite a compliment."

"Raiford plays wise—follows runs but never goes

40

deep." Derek turned a smile on her. "Even you wouldn't be able to rook 'im."

Lily ignored the taunt. "Is he as wealthy as the rumors claim?"

That produced an emphatic nod. "More."

"Any family scandals? Secrets, trouble, past affairs, any misdeeds that would reflect badly on his character? Does he seem like a cold, cruel sort of fellow?"

Derek folded his long, well-tended hands over the balustrade, looking down at his small kingdom. "'E's quiet. Private. Especially since the woman 'e loved was knocked off a year or two ago."

"Knocked off?" Lily interrupted, both amused and appalled. "Must you be so vulgar?"

Derek ignored the reprimand. "Miss Caroline Whitmore, Whitfield, somefing o' the sort. Broke 'er neck on an 'unt, so they say. Damn little fool, I say."

"*H*unt," Lily said, irritated by his meaningful glance. She loved to ride to the hounds, but even Derek didn't approve of such a dangerous activity for a woman. "And I'm not like other women. I can ride as well as any man. Better than most."

"'Tis your neck," he replied casually.

"Precisely. Now, that can't be all you know about Raiford. I know you. You're keeping something from me."

"No." Lily was caught by Derek's steady gaze, transfixed by the cool depths of green. His eyes

41

contained a spark of humor, but also a warning. Once again she was reminded that despite their friendship, Derek would not be there to help her if she landed herself in trouble. His voice was shaded with a quiet force that was as troubling as it was rare. "Listen to me, gypsy. Let it be—the marriage, ewerything. Raiford's not a cruel sort, but 'e's no rum cull. Stay clear ow 'im. You 'as problems enow to 'andle." His lips twisted wryly, and he corrected himself. "*H*andle."

Lily considered his advice. Derek was right, of course. She should be preserving her strength, thinking of nothing but getting Nicole back. But for some reason, this question of Raiford's character had taken root inside her, nagging until she would not have peace without seeing him. She thought of how docile Penny had always been, never misbehaving or questioning their parents' decisions. God knew Penny had no one to help her. The image of Zachary's pleading face came before her. She owed this to him. Lily sighed. "I must meet Raiford and see for myself," she said stubbornly.

"Then go to the Middleton *h*unt this week," Derek said, taking special care with his vowels and consonants. Suddenly he almost sounded like a gentleman. "Most likely *h*e'll be there."

Assembling at the stables with the others, Alex waited while a small army of grooms brought the horses out to their masters. There was excitement in the air, for all participants knew it would be an exceptional day. It was cool and dry, the course would be challenging, and the Middleton pack was renowned for its quality, reputedly worth more than three thousand guineas.

Alex glanced at the brightening sky, his mouth twisting with impatience. The hunt had been scheduled for six o'clock. They would be late getting started. More than half the hunting party hadn't mounted their horses yet. He considered walking over to someone and striking up a conversation. Most of the men here were familiar to him, some of them old classmates. But he wasn't in a sociable mood. He wanted to ride, lose himself in the chase until he was too tired to think or feel.

He looked across the field at the cool mist that hung over the yellow grasses and edged the dark, gray-green woods. The nearby covert was thick with spiny, gold-flowered gorse. All at once a flash of memory assailed him . . .

"Caro, you're not going on the hunt."

His fiancée, Caroline Whitmore, laughed and pouted playfully. She was a lovely girl, with peach-colored skin and bright hazel eyes, and hair the dark amber of clover honey. "Darling, you wouldn't deprive me of such fun, would you? There's no chance of danger. I'm a superb rider, a clipping one, as you British would say."

"You don't know what it's like, riding to a leap in company. There are collisions, refusals,

43

or you could be thrown or ridden down—"

"I'll ride with the utmost discretion. What do you suppose, that I'll ride neck-or-nothing across every hurdle? I'll have you know, dearest, that common sense is one of my strongest virtues. Besides, you know it's impossible to change my mind once I'm set on something." Caroline sighed melodramatically. *"Why must you be so difficult?"*

"Because I love you."

"Then don't love me. At least not tomorrow morning . . ."

Alex shook his head roughly, trying to clear away the haunting memories. God, would it always be like this? It had been two years since her death, and still he was tormented by it.

The past engulfed Alex in an invisible shroud. He had tried to move beyond it, but after a few futile attempts, he had realized he would never be free of Caroline. Of course there were others like her, women of spirit, passion, and beauty, but he did not want that kind of woman anymore. Caroline had told him once that she thought no one would ever be able to love him quite enough. There had been too many years in which he had been bereft of a woman's nurturing care.

His mother had died in childbirth when Alex was a boy. Her death was followed a year later by the passing of the earl. It was said that he had willed himself to death, leaving behind his two sons and a mountain of responsibilities. Since the age of eighteen Alex had been occupied with managing business interests, tenants and land agents, household staff and family. He had property in Herefordshire, set among fertile wheat and corn fields and rivers filled with salmon, and a Buckinghamshire estate poised on a tract of harshly beautiful land that included steep Chiltern chalk hills.

Alex had devoted himself to caring for and educating his younger brother, Henry. His own needs had been neglected, put aside to be taken care of at some future date. When he had found a woman to love, the feelings he had pent up for so long were overwhelming. Losing Caroline had nearly killed him. He would never subject himself to such pain again.

That was why he had deliberately sought Penelope Lawson's hand. A demure blonde girl, quintessentially English, she had attracted him with her gentle manner at many of the society balls in London. Penelope was what he needed. It was time to marry and produce heirs. Penelope couldn't be more different than Caroline. She would share his bed, bear his children, grow old beside him, all in safety and peace, never becoming a part of him. Alex found ease in Penelope's undemanding presence. There was no spark or vivacity in her pretty brown eyes, no sharp wit in her comments, nothing that threatened to touch his heart in any way. She would never think to argue with him or contradict him. The distant friendliness between them was something she did not seem to want to bridge any more than he did.

Suddenly Alex's thoughts were interrupted by a remarkable sight. A woman was riding past the edge of the crowd, a young woman mounted on a high-strung white palfrey. Alex dropped his gaze instantly, but the vision blazed across his mind. A frown knotted itself between his brows.

Exotic, hoydenish, startling, she had appeared from nowhere. She was as slim as a boy, except for the gentle rise of her breasts. Her short, curly black hair was held back from her forehead with a ribbon. Incredulously Alex saw that she straddled the horse the way a man did, that she was wearing breeches underneath her riding gown. Breeches the color of *raspberries*, for God's sake. Yet no one seemed to find her as astonishing as he did. Most of the men seemed to be acquainted with her, exchanging laughing comments with her, everyone from the fresh-faced Lord Yarborough to crotchety old Lord Harrington. Alex watched expressionlessly as the woman in raspberry breeches rode around the clearing where the bagged fox was to be loosed. There was something strangely familiar about her.

Lily suppressed a satisfied smile as she saw that Raiford had fastened an unblinking gaze on her. He had definitely noticed her. "My lord," she said to Lord Harrington, a robust older gentleman who had been an admirer of hers for years, "who is that man staring at me so rudely?"

"Why, it's the earl of Raiford," Harrington replied. "I would have assumed you had made acquaintance with him before, considering that he is soon to wed your delightful sister."

Lily shook her head with a smile. "No, his lordship and I move in quite different circles. Tell me, is he as boorish as he appears?"

Harrington gave a hearty laugh. "Would you like me to introduce you, so that you may judge for yourself?"

"Thank you, but I believe I will present myself to Raiford unaccompanied." Before he could reply, Lily walked her horse toward Raiford. As she drew closer to him, she was conscious of an odd sensation in the pit of her stomach. She caught a glimpse of his face and suddenly realized who he was. "My God," she breathed, stopping her horse beside him. "It's you."

His gaze was as piercing as a rapier. "The water party," he murmured. "You were the one who jumped overboard."

"And you were the one with the disapproving stare." Lily grinned at him. "I was an idiot that day," she admitted ruefully. "But I was slightly foxed. Although I suppose you wouldn't consider that an acceptable excuse."

"What do you want?" His voice caused every fine hair on her spine to rise in awareness. Low, gravelly, it sounded as if he were growling.

"What do I want?" she repeated, laughing softly. "How direct you are. But I like that in a man."

"You wouldn't have approached me unless you wanted something."

"You're right. Do you know who I am, my lord?"

"No."

"Miss Lily Lawson. Your fiancée's sister."

Concealing his surprise, Alex studied her closely. It didn't seem possible that this creature was related to Penelope. One sister so fair and angelic, the other dark and smoldering . . . and yet, there was a resemblance. They had the same brown eyes, the same fine features, the same unique sweetness in the curve of the lips. He tried to recall what little the Lawsons had revealed about their eldest daughter. They had preferred not to speak of her, except to say that Lily—or Wilhemina, as her mother called her—had gone "a little mad" after having been jilted at the altar when she was twenty years old. She'd gone to live aboard after that. Under the lax chaperonage of her widowed aunt, Lily had led a wild existence. Alex had been only mildly interested in the story—now he wished he had listened more closely.

"Has my family ever mentioned me to you?" she asked.

"They described you as an eccentric."

"I wondered if they still bother to acknowledge my existence." She leaned down and said conspiratorially, "I have a tarnished reputation—it's taken years of dedicated effort to acquire. The Lawsons don't approve of me. Well, fate chooses our relatives, as they say. Too late to prune me from the family tree." Lily paused in her friendly chatter as she stared down into his closed face. Heaven knew what was going on behind those silver eyes. It was clear that he was not going to indulge her with small talk and smiles, reverting to the game that sociable strangers played.

She wondered if bluntness were the best way to deal with him. "Raiford," she said briskly, "I want to talk to you about my sister."

He was silent, watching her with icy gray eyes.

"I know more than anyone about my parents' ambitions of making an exceptional match for Penny," Lily remarked. "She is a lovely and accomplished girl, isn't she? And it would be a brilliant marriage. Miss Penelope Lawson, the countess of Raiford. No one in my family has ever ascended to such a title. But I wonder . . . would it be in her best interests to become your wife? That is, do you care for my sister, Lord Raiford?"

His face was impassive. "As much as necessary."

"That hardly sets my mind at ease."

"What is your concern, Miss Lawson?" he asked sardonically. "That I'll mistreat your sister? That she's had no choice in the matter? I assure you, Penelope is quite content with the state of affairs." His eyes narrowed, and he continued softly. "And if you're about to delight everyone with one of your theatrical displays, Miss Lawson, I warn you . . . I don't like scenes."

Lily was taken aback by the veiled menace in his tone. Oh, she didn't like him at all! At first she had considered him vaguely amusing, a large, slightly pompous aristocrat with ice water in his veins. But something warned her that his nature was not only cold, but cruel. "I don't believe your claim that Penny is content," she replied. "I know my sister, and I have no doubt my parents have bullied and prodded her every step of the way to get what they want. You must terrify Penny. Does her happiness matter to you at all? She deserves a man who truly loves her. My instincts tell me that all you want is an obedient, fertile girl who will produce a string of little blond heirs to carry on your name, and if that's the case you could easily find a hundred other girls to—"

"Enough," he interrupted harshly. "Go interfere in someone else's life, Miss Lawson. I'll see you in hell—no, I'll *send* you there—before I let you meddle with mine."

Lily gave him an ominous look. "I've found out what I wanted to know," she said, preparing to leave. "Good day, my lord. You've been most enlightening."

"Wait." Before Alex was aware of what he was doing, he reached out and caught one of her reins.

"Let go!" Lily said in surprised annoyance. His actions were outrageous. To take hold of any rider's reins without invitation, removing control of the horse—it was a demeaning act.

"You're not going to hunt," he said.

"You don't think I came out here to wish you well, do you? Yes, I'm going to hunt. Have no fear, I shan't slow anyone down."

"Women shouldn't hunt."

"Of course they should, if they wish to."

"Only if they happen to be wives or daughters of masters of hounds. Otherwise—"

"A mere accident of birth won't prevent me from hunting. I am a bruising rider, and I insist that no allowance be made for me. I'll top any fence, no matter how high. I suppose you would like me to stay inside with the other women, tatting and gossiping."

"There you won't pose a danger to anyone. Out here you'll be a hazard to others as well as yourself."

"I'm afraid your opinion is in the minority, Lord Raiford. No one but you takes exception to my presence here."

"No man in his rational mind would want you here."

"Now I suppose I should go away meekly," Lily mused, "my gaze cast down in shame. How dare I interfere in such a *manly* occupation as hunting? Well, I don't give *this*—" she made a snapping motion with her gloved fingers, "—for you and your self-righteous opinions. Now let go!"

"You're not riding," Alex muttered. Something broke free inside him, driving him beyond rational thought. *Caroline, no, Oh God—*

"I'll be damned if I'm not!" Lily jerked at the

51

reins, while the white palfrey sidestepped uneasily. Alex's grasp remained unbroken. Shocked, Lily stared into gray eyes as reflective as mirror glass. "You're mad," she whispered. They were both still.

Lily was the first to move, lashing out with her whip in a stroke of rebellious rage. It caught Alex underneath the jaw, leaving a streak of red that ended at the tip of his chin. Spurring the palfrey forward, Lily used the burst of motion to free the reins from the snare of his fingers. She rode away without looking back.

The confrontation had been so quick that no one had noticed. Alex wiped the smear of blood from his jaw, barely noticing the sting of pain. His mind was whirling. He wondered what was happening to him. For a few seconds he hadn't been able to separate the present from the past. Caroline's light, far-away voice came to his ears. *"Darling Alex . . . then don't love me . . ."* He flinched, his heart beginning to pound as he remembered the day she had fallen . . .

"An accident," one of his friends said quietly. "Unseated. I knew when she fell—"

"Get a doctor," Alex said hoarsely.

"Alex, it's no use."

"Damn you, get a doctor or I'll—"

"Her neck was broken by the fall."

"No—"

"Alex, she's dead . . ."

His groom's voice abruptly recalled him to the present. "My lord?"

Alex blinked and focused his gaze on the shining chestnut gelding, chosen for its combination of power and suppleness. Taking the reins, he mounted the horse easily and glanced across the clearing. Lily Lawson was chatting and smiling with the other riders. To look at her, one would never guess there had been a confrontation between them.

The pack of foxhounds were set loose, covering the field with their frantic snuffling. Then a scent was found. "Reynard is out!" came the call as a fox broke cover. A rich note pierced the air as the master blew the horn and the riders set out on the chase.

The hunters rode to the copse in a fever of exultation, shouting madly. The field fairly shook under the onslaught of horses and dogs, hooves tearing at the ground, eager cries renting the air.

"Gone away!"

"Tallyho!"

"Halloo!"

As the congregation spurred their mounts onward, the hunt took on the expected formation, the huntsman riding close to the foremost hounds, the whippers-in following the dogs and keeping the occasional stragglers in pace with the pack. Lily Lawson rode like a woman possessed, rushing at the highest obstacles and taking them as if she had wings. She seemed to have no concern for her own safety. Usually Alex would have ridden ahead with the others, but for now he held back.

He was driven to follow Lily, watching her take suicidal chances. The course was filled with noise and revelry, while Alex went through a living nightmare. His horse strained over the jumps, hooves biting into the ground with every surge. *Caroline* . . . Long ago he had closed it all away, stored every recollection in the back of his mind. But he had no defense against the thoughts that came without warning, the feel of Caroline's mouth beneath his, her silky hair in his hands, the sweet torment of holding her close. She had taken away a part of him that would never be restored.

You fool, he told himself savagely. He was making the hunt into a macabre reprise of his past. A fool chasing after lost dreams . . . and still he followed Lily, watching her leap through gaps and over reinforced hedges. Although she did not look back, he sensed that she knew he was there. They rode for nearly an hour, crossing from one county to another.

Lily spurred her horse onward in determination, her nerves crackling with excitement. She had never cared much for the end of a hunt, being in at the kill, but the riding . . . oh, there was nothing like it. Gleefully she approached a towering "double oxer," a quickthorn braced on each side with an ox rail. In a split second she realized it was too high and too much of a risk to take, but some devilish urge impelled her forward. At the last moment, the palfrey refused to jump. The arrested motion of the horse threw Lily out of the saddle.

The world seemed to spin, and she was suspended in mid-air. Then the ground came rushing up at her. Shielding her face with her hands, Lily felt her body slam into the mossy earth. The breath was forced from her lungs. Writhing on the ground, she gasped for air, while her hands clutched reflexively around bits of leaves and mud.

Dazedly she felt herself being turned and her shoulders lifted. Opening her mouth, she fought to pull in air. Red and black danced before her eyes. Slowly the mist cleared away to reveal a face above her. Raiford. The golden glow of his skin was infused with ashen gray. Lily stirred against him, discovering that she was held securely in the lee of his muscular thighs. She was as limp and helpless as a doll.

Her breasts rose and fell rapidly as she tried to regain her breath. His hand was tight on the back of her neck . . . too tight . . . hurting her . . .

"I told you not to hunt," Raiford snarled. "Were you trying to kill yourself?"

Lily made a small sound, looking up at him with hazy confusion. There was blood on his collar, a splotch of scarlet from the wound she had given him earlier. His hand was powerful on her neck. If he chose, he could snap her bones if they were twigs. Lily was aware of the weight and sinew of him, the sheer power lodged within his body. There was a primitive expression on his flushed face, a mixture of hatred and something else she couldn't identify. Through the roaring of her ears, she thought she heard a name . . . Caroline . . .

"You're a madman," she gasped. "Good God. You belong in Bedlam. Wh-what's going on? Do you know who in the hell I am? Get your hands off me, do you hear?"

Her words seemed to bring him back to awareness of what he was doing. The murderous gleam left his eyes, and the contorted shape of his mouth softened. Lily sensed an enormous tension leaving his body. He dropped her abruptly, as if the touch of her had burned him.

Falling back among the leaves and dirt, Lily watched with a glare as he stood up. He did not reach down a hand to assist her, but he did wait until she struggled to her feet. Assured that no serious harm had come to her, he hoisted himself onto his horse.

Finding that her knees were weak, Lily braced herself against a tree. She would wait until she felt stronger before mounting her palfrey again. Curiously she stared at Raiford's expressionless face. She took a few steadying breaths. "Penny is too good for you," she managed to say. "Before I was afraid you would only make her miserable. Now I believe you'll cause her bodily harm!"

"Why do you pretend to give a damn?" he sneered. "You haven't seen your sister or your family in years. And obviously they want nothing to do with you."

"You know nothing about it!" she said hotly. To

think of this monster crushing all the happiness from Penelope's life . . . it would make her sister old before her time. Outrage leapt inside her. Why should an ogre like Raiford be allowed to marry Penelope, when someone as dear and gentle as Zachary was in love with her? "You shan't have Penny," Lily cried. "I won't allow it!"

Alex regarded her with contempt. "Don't make an even bigger fool of yourself, Miss Lawson."

Swearing, dredging up the foulest language she could think of, Lily watched Raiford ride away. "You won't have her," she vowed under her breath. "I swear it on my life. You won't have her!"

CHAPTER 3

Upon his arrival at Raiford Park, Alex went to bid good morning to Penelope and her parents. By anyone's standards, The Lawsons were an odd pair. Lawson was a scholarly man, occupying himself with books of Greek and Latin, closeting himself in a room for days at a time with his texts and having all his meals sent in. The squire had no interest in the outside world. Through sheer carelessness he had badly mismanaged the estate and fortune he had inherited. His wife Totty was an attractive, fluttery woman, all round eyes and bouncing golden curls. She adored society gossip and parties, and had always set her heart on a splendid wedding for her daughter.

Alex could see how the two of them could produce a child like Penelope. Quiet, shy, pretty—Penelope was the best of them combined. As for *Lily* . . . there was no accounting for how she had emerged from the Lawson family. Alex didn't blame them for casting Lily out of their lives. Otherwise there would have been no peace for any of them. He had no doubt that she thrived on conflict, that she would meddle and torment until those around her had been driven insane. Although Lily had left the Middleton estate after their encounter on the course, Alex hadn't been able to stop brooding about her. He was grimly thankful that she was estranged from her family. With luck he'd never have to abide her presence again.

Happily Totty informed him that the wedding arrangements were progressing nicely. The vicar would be coming to visit later in the afternoon. "Good," Alex replied. "Inform me when he arrives."

"Lord Raiford," Totty said eagerly, gesturing to a place on the sofa between her and Penelope, "won't you take tea with us?"

Wryly Alex noted that all of a sudden Penelope looked like a small rabbit in the presence of a wolf. He declined the invitation, having no desire to endure Totty's chatter about flower arrangements and wedding fripperies. "Thank you, but I have business concerns to attend to. I'll see you at supper."

"Yes, my lord," both women murmured, one in disappointment and the other in poorly concealed relief.

Closeting himself in the library, Alex regarded a pile of documents and account books that required his attention. He could have allowed his estate manager to handle most of it. But since Caroline's death he had taken on more work than was necessary, wanting to escape from the loneliness and the memories. He spent more time in the library than in any other room of the house, enjoying the sense of peace and order to be found there. Books were categorized and grouped together neatly, furniture was carefully arranged. Even the decanters of liquor on the Italian corner cupboard were placed with geometrical precision.

There was not a speck of dust anywhere, not in the entire mansion at Raiford Park. An army of fifty indoor servants saw to that. Another thirty took care of the outside grounds, gardens, and stables. Visitors had always exclaimed with pleasure over the mansion's domed marble entrance hall and the great hall with its barrel-vaulted ceiling and exquisite plasterwork. The mansion possessed summer and winter parlors, long galleries filled with artwork, a breakfast room, a coffee room, two dining salons, countless sets of bedchambers and dressing rooms, an immense kitchen, a library, a hunting room, and a pair of drawing rooms that were occasionally combined into a massive ballroom.

It was a large household, but Penelope would be capable of managing it. Since early childhood she had been reared to do exactly that. Alex had no doubt that she would be able to take her place as lady of the manor without difficulty. She was an intelligent girl, albeit quiet and docile. She had yet to meet his younger brother Henry, but he was a well-behaved lad, and it was likely they would get along quite well.

The silence in the library was broken by a tiny *tap-tap* on the door.

"What is it?" Alex asked brusquely.

The door opened a crack, and Penelope's blonde head appeared. Her overcautious manner annoyed him. For God's sake, it seemed as if she considered visiting him to be a dangerous undertaking. Was he really so fearsome? He knew his manner was abrupt sometimes, but he doubted he could change even it he wanted to. "Yes?" he demanded. "Come in."

"My lord," Penelope said timidly. "I-I wish to know if the hunt was successful? If you found it enjoyable?"

Alex suspected that her mother Totty had sent her to ask. Penelope never sought his company of her own accord. "The hunt was fine," he said, setting aside the papers on his desk and turning toward her. Penelope shifted nervously, as if his gaze made her uncomfortable. "Something rather interesting happened on the first day."

A vague expression of interest crossed her face. "Oh, my lord? Was there an accident of some sort? A collision?"

"You could call it that," he said dryly. "I met your sister."

Penelope gasped. "Lily was there? Oh, dear . . ." At a loss for words, she closed her mouth and looked at him helplessly.

"She's quite extraordinary." Alex's tone was far from complimentary.

Penelope nodded and gulped. "There is usually no middle ground with Lily. One either likes her tremendously, or . . ." She shrugged helplessly.

"Yes," Alex said sardonically. "I'm of the latter persuasion."

"Oh." Penelope's forehead puckered in a dainty frown. "Of course. Both of you are rather decided in your opinions."

"That's a tactful way of putting it." Alex stared at her closely. It was unnerving to see the echoes of Lily in Penelope's sweet, gentle face. "We talked about you," he said abruptly.

Her eyes turned round with apprehension. "My lord, I should make it clear that Lily does not speak for me or the rest of the family."

"I know that."

"What was said between you?" she asked timidly.

"Your sister claimed that I must frighten you. Do I?"

Underneath his cool appraisal, the color rushed to her face. "A little, my lord," she admitted.

Alex found her sweet shyness somewhat irritating. He wondered if she was capable of snapping back at him, if she would ever take him to task when he did something to displease her. As he stood and walked over to her, he saw her flinch involuntarily. Coming to stand next to her, he put his hands on her waist. Penelope bent her head, but Alex was aware of her quickly indrawn breath. Suddenly he couldn't rid his mind of a disturbing image—picking Lily up from the ground, holding her lithe body in his arms. Although Penelope was taller, more voluptuous than her older sister, she gave the impression of being much softer and smaller.

"Look at me," Alex said quietly, and Penelope obeyed. He stared into her brown eyes. Exactly like Lily's. Except these eyes were filled with startled innocence, not dark fire. "There's no reason to be uneasy. I'm not going to hurt you."

"Yes, my lord," she whispered.

"Why don't you call me Alex?" He had asked it of her before, but the use of his name seemed to be difficult for her.

"Oh, I . . . I couldn't."

With great effort, he suppressed his impatience. "Try."

"Alex," Penelope murmured.

"Good." He bent his head and touched her lips with his own. Penelope didn't move, only brushed his shoulder with her hand. Alex prolonged the kiss, increasing the pressure of his mouth. For the first time he sought more than docile acceptance from her. Her lips remained cool and still beneath his. All at once Alex was puzzled and annoyed to realize that Penelope considered his embrace a duty she had to endure.

Lifting his head, he looked down at her placid face. She looked like a child who had just obediently downed a spoonful of medicine and was suffering the aftertaste. Never in his life had a woman considered kissing him to be a chore!

Alex's tawny brows drew together in a frown. "Dammit, I won't be *tolerated*," he said gruffly.

Penelope stiffened in alarm. "My lord?"

Alex knew he should play the gentleman and treat her with tender respect, but his full-blooded nature demanded a response from her. "Kiss me back," he commanded, and crushed her against his body.

With a surprised squeak, Penelope twisted away from him and slapped his face.

Not exactly a slap. He would have welcomed a vigorous, hearty slap. This was more like a reproving pat on his cheek. Penelope retreated to the door and regarded him tearfully. "My lord, are you testing me in some manner?" she asked in a wounded voice.

Alex looked at her for a long time, keeping his face expressionless. He knew he was being unreasonable. He should not expect something from her that she was not able or willing to give. Silently he cursed himself, wondering why he was in such a devilish mood. "I beg your pardon."

Penelope gave him an uncertain nod. "I suppose you are still excited from the hunt. I have heard that men are very affected by the primitive atmosphere of such events."

He smiled sardonically. "That's probably it."

"May I be excused now?"

Wordlessly he waved her out of the room.

Penelope paused at the door, looking back over her shoulder. "My lord, please don't think badly of Lily. She is an unusual woman, very brave and headstrong. When I was a child, she used to protect me from everyone and everything that frightened me."

Alex was surprised by Penelope's little speech. It was rare that he heard Penelope put more than two sentences together. "Was she ever close to either of your parents?"

"Only to our Aunt Sally. Sally was an eccentric in the same way my sister is, always seeking adventure and doing unconventional things. When she passed away a few years ago, she left her entire fortune to Lily."

So that was how Lily had obtained her means to live. The information hardly improved Alex's opinion of her. Probably she had deliberately courted the old woman's favor, and then danced upon the deathbed at the thought of the money she had inherited.

"Why hasn't she ever married?"

"Lily has always said that marriage is a dreadful institution devised for the benefit of men, not women." Penelope cleared her throat delicately. "Actually, she hasn't a very high opinion of men. Although she does seem to enjoy their company . . . going hunting and shooting and gaming and so forth."

"And so forth," Alex repeated sardonically. "Does your sister have any 'special' friends?"

The question seemed to perplex Penelope. Although she didn't quite understand his meaning, she answered readily. "Special? Well . . . er . . . Lily keeps company quite often with a man named Derek Craven. She has mentioned him in her letters to me."

"*Craven?*" Now the entire sordid picture was clear. Alex's lip curled with disgust. He himself was a member of Craven's club. He'd met the proprietor on two occasions. It only made sense that Lily Lawson would choose to associate with such a man, a cockney who was disdainfully known in polite circles as "flash-gentry." No doubt Lily had the morals of a prostitute, for a "friendship" with Craven could mean nothing else. How could a woman who had been born into a decent family, provided with education and all her material wants, sink into such degradation? Lily had willingly chosen it, every step of the way.

"Lily is merely too high-spirited for the kind of life she was born to," Penelope said, guessing at his thoughts. "Everything might have been different for her, had she not been jilted all those years ago. The betrayal and humiliation, being abandoned like that . . . I believe it led her to do many reckless things. At least that is what Mama says."

"Why hasn't she—" Alex broke off, looking toward the window. He had been alerted by a sound outside, the grating of carriage wheels upon the graveled drive. "Is your mother expecting callers today?"

Penelope shook her head. "No, my lord. It could

be the dressmaker's assistant, come to do some fittings for my trousseau. But I thought that was tomorrow."

Alex couldn't explain why, but he had a feeling . . . a very bad feeling. His nerves sparked with a sensation of warning. "Let's see who it is." He sent the library door swinging open. Striding to the gray- and white-marbled entrance hall with Penelope at his heels, he brushed past the elderly butler, Silvern. "I'll take care of it," he said to Silvern, and went to the front door.

Silvern sniffed in disapproval at his lordship's unorthodox behavior, but did not voice a protest.

A magnificent black and gold carriage with no identifiable crest had come to a stop at the end of the long graveled drive. Penelope came to stand by Alex, shivering in her light gown as the breeze touched her. It was a misty springtime day, cool and fresh, with billowing white clouds overhead. "I don't recognize the carriage," she murmured.

A footman dressed in splendid blue and black livery opened the carriage door. Ceremoniously he placed a small rectangular step on the ground for the convenience of the passenger.

Then *she* emerged.

Alex stood as if turned to stone.

"Lily!" Penelope exclaimed. With a cry of delight she hurried to her sister.

Laughing exuberantly, Lily reached the ground. "Penny!" She flung her arms around Penelope and hugged her, then held her at arm's length. "My goodness, what an *elegant* creature you are! Ravishing! It's been years since I've seen you— not since you were little, and now look at you! The most beautiful girl in England."

"Oh, no, *you're* the beautiful one."

Lily laughed and hugged her again. "How nice, to flatter your poor spinsterish sister."

"You don't look at all like a spinster," Penelope said.

In spite of Alex's amazement, his emotions rallying to battle-readiness, he had to agree. Lily was beautifully dressed in a dark blue gown and velvet cloak edged with white ermine. Her hair, unconfined by a ribbon, curled prettily around her temples and lay in wisps in front of her dainty ears. It was difficult to believe she was the same outlandish woman who had dressed in raspberry breeches and straddled a horse like a man. Pink-cheeked and smiling, she looked like a well-to-do young wife on a social call. Or an aristocratic courtesan.

Lily saw him as she looked over Penelope's shoulder. Without shame or even a trace of discomposure, she disentangled herself from her sister and walked up to the circular steps to where he stood. Extending a small hand to him, she smiled impudently. "Straight into the enemy camp," she murmured. The sight of his thunderous scowl caused her dark eyes to gleam in satisfaction.

Wisely Lily restrained herself from grinning

outright. It wouldn't do to send Raiford into a rage. He was angry, though. Certainly he hadn't expected her to come sailing up to the door of his country estate. Oh, she hadn't expected to enjoy this so much! She had never felt such pure delight in provoking a man. By the time she was through with Raiford, his entire world would be turned upside down.

She felt no remorse for what she planned to do. It was an outrage, this pairing of Raiford and her sister. The wrongness of it was evident just in glancing at these two. Penny was as fragile as a white-petaled anemone, her golden hair shining with the soft gleam of a child's. She had no defense against those who would bully and intimidate her, no recourse except to bend like a delicate reed in the face of a violent storm.

And Raiford was ten times worse than Lily had remembered him. His features, so harshly perfect and remote, with those clear, pale eyes, and the stern jut of his chin . . . there was no compassion, no gentleness in that face. The brutal power of his body, all muscle and sinewed tension, was evident in spite of his civilized attire. He needed a woman who was as cynical as he was, insensitive to his barbs.

Alex ignored Lily's hand. He stared at her coldly. "Leave," he growled. "Now."

A chill scattered over her back, but Lily smiled demurely. "My lord, I wish to see my family. It's been far too long."

Before Alex could reply, he heard Totty and George's exclamations behind him.

"Wilhemina!"

"Lily . . . Good Gad . . ."

There was silence, all of them forming a frozen tableau. Their gazes centered on Lily's petite form. Rapidly the cockiness and self-assurance on Lily's face faded, until she resembled an uncertain little girl. Nervously her white teeth pulled at her delicate lower lip. "Mama?" she asked softly. "Mama, will you try to forgive me?"

Totty burst into tears and came forward, holding her chubby arms wide. "Wilhemina, you might have come before. I've been so afraid I would never see you again!"

Lily flew to her, laughing and crying. The two women embraced and talked at the same time.

"Mama, you haven't changed at all . . . and how splendidly you've done with Penny . . . she's the toast of the season . . ."

"Dear, we've heard such dreadful tales of your carryings-on . . . I always worry, you know . . . merciful heavens, what have you done to your hair?"

Self-consciously Lily raised a hand to her short, curly locks and grinned. "Is it too dreadful, Mama?"

"It suits you," Totty admitted. "Rather becoming, actually."

Lily saw her father and hurried to him. "Papa!"

Awkwardly George patted her slender back, and

pushed her away gently. "There, there, no need to carry on. Gad, such scenes you cause, Lily. And in front of Lord Raiford. Are you in some sort of trouble? Why have you come here of all places? And now of all times?"

"I'm in no trouble at all," Lily said, smiling at her father. They were of similarly small stature, standing nearly face-to-face. "I would have come sooner, but I was uncertain of my reception. I want to share in the joy of Penny's wedding. Naturally if my presence displeases the earl, I will leave immediately. I've no wish to cause trouble for anyone. I just thought that I might be allowed to stay for a week or so." She glanced at Alex and added cautiously, "I would be on my best behavior. I would be a veritable saint."

Alex's gaze bore through her like an icicle. He was tempted to shove her back into the ornate carriage and tell the driver to head straight for London. Or a far hotter place.

Confronted with his silence, Lily appeared to be perturbed. "But perhaps there isn't enough room for me here?" She craned her neck up to stare at the towering mansion, letting her gaze travel across the endless rows of windows and balconies.

Alex gritted his teeth together. It would have been the greatest pleasure of his life to throttle her. He understood what she was doing. To refuse her now would paint him as an inhospitable black-guard in her family's eyes. Penelope was already regarding him with anxious dismay.

"Alex," Penelope beseeched, coming up to him and placing a hand on his arm. It was the first time she had ever voluntarily touched him. "Alex, there is enough room here for my sister, isn't there? If she says she will conduct herself well, I am certain that she will."

Lily clucked affectionately. "Now, Penny, let us not embarrass his lordship. I will find some other occasion to see you, I promise."

"No, I wish you to stay," Penelope cried, her fingers tightening on Alex's arm. "Please, my lord, please allow her to remain here!"

"There's no need to beg," Alex muttered. How could he refuse his fiancée when she was pleading with him in front of her family, the butler, and every servant within earshot? He glared at Lily, expecting to see a gleam of triumph in her eyes, a smug tilt to her lips. But she wore a forbearing expression that would have become Joan of Arc. Damn her! "Do whatever you want," he said to Penelope. "Just keep her out of my sight."

"Oh, thank you!" Penelope whirled in delight, hugged Lily and then Totty. "Mama, isn't it wonderful?"

In the midst of Penelope's torrent of gratitude, Lily approached Alex calmly. "Raiford, I'm afraid you and I have got off to a bad start," she said. "It was entirely my fault. Can't we forget the bloody hunt and begin again?"

She was so sincere, so frank and appealing. Alex didn't believe any of it. "Miss Lawson," he said with deliberate slowness, "if you do anything to undermine my interests . . ."

"You'll what?" Lily smiled at him provocatively. There was nothing he could do to hurt her. The worst had been done to her long ago. She wasn't afraid of him.

"I'll make you regret it for the rest of your life," he said softly.

Lily's smile faded as he strode away. Suddenly Derek's warning came to her ears . . . *Listen to me, gypsy. Let it be . . . Stay clear ow 'is path . . .* Lily pushed the words out of her mind, shrugging impatiently. Lord Raiford was only a man, and she could run circles around him. Hadn't she just gained herself an invitation to stay right underneath his roof for the next few weeks? She looked at her mother and sister and laughed quietly.

"I asked Raiford if he loved you."

Lily had taken the first opportunity to steer Penelope to a private room where they could have, as she put it, a "sisterly chat." Immediately she had launched into an account of the Middleton hunt, determined to make Penny understand what manner of man she was engaged to.

"Oh, Lily, you didn't!" Penelope put her hands over her eyes and moaned. "But why would you do such a thing?" Suddenly she surprised Lily by bursting into giggles. "I can't imagine how his lordship replied!"

"I don't see what is so amusing," Lily said with

perplexed dignity. "I am trying to have a serious conversation with you about your future, Penny."

"My future is well in hand! Or was, rather." Choking with dismayed laughter, Penelope covered her mouth with her hand.

Indignantly Lily wondered why the story of her meeting with Raiford at the hunt was causing her sister amusement, instead of making her properly alarmed. "In response to my perfectly straightforward question, Raiford was rude, evasive, and insulting. In my opinion, he is not a gentleman, and is far from worthy of you."

Penelope shrugged helplessly. "All of London recognizes him as a splendid catch."

"I beg to differ." Lily paced back and forth in front of the canopied bed, repeatedly slapping a kid glove in her palm. "What are the qualities that make him a good catch? His looks? Well, I admit he could be considered handsome—but only in a bland, cold, *unremarkable* sort of way."

"I . . . I suppose that is a matter of taste . . ."

"And as to his fortune," Lily continued vigorously. "There are many other men who have the means to take care of you and keep you in a fine style. His title? You could easily land someone with even bluer blood and more impressive lineage. And you can't claim you have any great liking for Raiford, Penny!"

"The arrangement has been made and settled between Papa and Lord Raiford," Penelope replied softly. "And while it is true that I do not love him, I never expected to. If I am fortunate, that sort of feeling may come later. That is the way of things. I am not like you, Lily. I have always been very conventional."

Lily uttered a garbled curse and stared at her in frustration. Something about her sister's prosaic manner was making Lily feel much as she had during her rebellious youth, when everyone had seemed to have an understanding of the world that she could not share in. What was their secret? Why did a loveless arranged marriage make sense to everyone else and not to her? Clearly she'd enjoyed too much freedom for too long. She sat on the bed next to Penelope. "I don't see why you're so agreeable to the prospect of marrying a man you don't care for." Lily tried to sound brisk, but her voice came out plaintive.

"I am not agreeable, just resigned. Do forgive me for saying it, Lily, but you are a romantic, in the worst sense of the word."

Lily scowled. "Not at all! I have quite a hard-bitten, practical nature. I've been dealt enough knocks to develop a realistic understanding of the world and its workings, and therefore I know—"

"Dearest Lily." Penelope took her hand and pressed it between her own. "Since I was a little girl, I've always thought of you as the most beautiful, most courageous, most *everything*. But not practical. Never practical."

Lily withdrew her hand and regarded her younger sister in amazement. It seemed that

Penelope wasn't going to be as cooperative as she had expected. Well, the plan still had to be carried out. It was for Penny's own good, whether or not she admitted that she needed to be rescued. "I don't want to talk about myself," she said abruptly. "I want to talk about you. Of all the swains in London, there must have been someone you preferred over Raiford." She arched her brows meaningfully. "Such as Lord Stamford. Hmm?"

Penelope was quiet for a long time, her thoughts seeming to drift to some faraway place. A wistful smile appeared on her face. "Dear Zachary," she whispered. Then she shook her head. "My situation is settled. Lily, you know that I have never asked you for anything. But I am asking you now, from the depths of my heart, *please* do not take it into your head to 'help' me. I am going to abide by Papa and Mama's decision and marry Lord Raiford. It is my obligation." She snapped her fingers as if a new idea had occurred to her. "Why don't we direct our attention toward finding a husband for *you?*"

"Good God." Lily wrinkled her nose. "I have no use for men. Of course, they can be great fun on the hunting field and in the gaming room. But other times . . . oh, men are too bloody inconvenient. Greedy, demanding creatures. I can't abide the thought of being at someone's beck and call, and being treated as a forward child instead of a woman with her own opinions."

"Men are useful if one desires a family." Like

all proper young girls of her station, Penelope had been taught that bearing children was a woman's most laudable role.

The words gave Lily an unpleasant sensation, stirring up painful emotions. "Yes," she said bitterly. "They're certainly helpful in producing children."

"You don't wish to be alone forever, do you?"

"Better that than to be some man's pawn!" Lily didn't realize she had spoken aloud until she saw the confusion on Penelope's face. Giving her a quick smile, Lily fumbled for a shawl draped over a chair. "May I borrow this? I believe I'll go exploring, perhaps take a stroll outside. It's rather stuffy in here."

"But Lily—"

"We'll talk more later. I promise. I-I'll see you at supper, dear." Hurriedly Lily left and strode through the hall and down the ornate staircase, not caring where she was going. Ignoring her sumptuous surroundings, she kept her head down. "My God, I've got to be careful," she whispered. Lately her self-control had been stretched to its limits, and she wasn't guarding her words carefully enough. Wandering through the great hall, she found herself in a gallery at least one hundred feet long, illuminated with the light from a row of glass doors. Through the well-polished glass she could see a formal garden with smooth green lawns and bordered paths. A brisk walk was just what she needed. Flinging the shawl around her shoulders, Lily went outside, relishing the cool bite of the breeze.

The garden was magnificent, dignified and lush, divided into many sections by precisely trimmed yew hedges. There was a chapel garden with a tiny stream and a small round pool filled with white lilies. It opened into the rose garden, a multitude of flowers surrounding a large and rare Ayrshire rose bush. Lily walked along a garden wall covered with vines and climbing roses. She ascended a series of weathered steps that led to a terrace overlooking an artificial lake. Nearby was a fountain surrounded by a pride of a dozen strutting peacocks. There was an aura of absolute serenity in the garden. It seemed like an enchanted place, where nothing bad could ever happen.

Her attention was drawn by a planting of fruit trees on the east side of the estate. The sight of them reminded Lily of the lemon garden of the Italian villa where she had lived for two years. She and Nicole had spent most of their time in the garden or in the many-columned *loggia* at the back of the little house. Sometimes she had taken Nicole for walks in the shady wooded *bosco* nearby.

"Don't think of it," she whispered fiercely. "*Don't.*" But the memory was as clear as if it had happened yesterday. She sat on the rim of the fountain and gathered the shawl more closely around her body. Blindly she turned her face toward the distant woods beyond the lake, remembering . . .

"Domina! Domina, I've brought the most wonderful things from the market—bread and soft cheese and good wine. Help me gather some fruit from the garden, and for lunch we'll . . ."

Lily stopped as she became aware of the unnatural silence in the casetta. Her cheerful smile faded. She set the basket down by the door and ventured into the little house. Like the local women, she was dressed in a cotton skirt and a full-sleeved blouse, her hair covered with a large kerchief. With her dark curls and her flawless accent, she was often mistaken for a native Italian. "Domina?" she asked cautiously.

Suddenly the housekeeper appeared, her wrinkled, sun-weathered face covered with tears. She was in disarray, her gray hair escaping from the narrow braid coiled around her head. "Signorina," she gasped, and began to speak so incoherently that Lily couldn't understand her.

She put her arm around the elderly woman's round shoulders and tried to soothe her. "Domina, tell me what's happened. Is it Nicole? Where is she?"

The housekeeper began to sob. Something had happened, something too dreadful for words. Was her baby ill? Had she been hurt? Terrified, Lily let go of Domina and raced toward the stairs that led to the nursery. "Nicole?" she called. "Nicole, Mama's here, it's all—"

"Signorina, *she is gone!*"

Lily froze with her foot on the first step, her hand gripping the banister. She looked at Domina, who was trembling visibly. "What do you mean?" she asked hoarsely. "Where is she?"

"It was two men. I could not stop them. I tried, Dio mio . . . *but they took the baby away. She is gone."*

Lily felt as if she were in the middle of a nightmare. Nothing was making sense. "What did they say?" she asked in a queer, thick voice. Domina began to sob, and Lily swore at her, rushing forward. "Damn you, don't cry, just tell me what they said!"

Domina stepped back, frightened by Lily's contorted face. "They said nothing."

"Where did they take her?"

"I do not know."

"Did they leave a note, a message?"

"No, signorina."

Lily stared into the elderly woman's streaming eyes. "Oh, it's not happening, it's not . . ." Frantically she ran to the nursery, stumbling to her knees and bumping her shins, not feeling the pain. The little room looked the same as usual, toys scattered on the floor, a ruffled dress draped over the arm of a rocking chair. The crib was empty. Lily pressed one hand over her stomach and the other up to her mouth. She was too frightened to cry, but she

heard her own voice in a wrenching scream.
"No! Nicole . . . Nooo . . ."

With a start, Lily recalled herself to the present. It had been more than two years since then. Two years. Bleakly she wondered if Nicole still remembered her. If Nicole were even still alive. The thought caused her throat to tighten until she could hardly breathe. Perhaps, she thought miserably, this was to be the punishment for her sins, to have her baby taken from her forever. But the Lord had to be merciful—Nicole was so innocent, so blameless. Lily knew that if it took the rest of her life, she would find her daughter.

Alex had never seen one small woman eat so heartily. Perhaps that was the source of her unflagging energy. With dainty precision, Lily downed a plateful of ham and madeira sauce, several spoonfuls of potatoes and boiled vegetables, pastry, and fresh fruit. She laughed and chattered all the while, the warm light casting a glow over her animated face. Several times Alex was chagrined to find himself staring at her. It bothered him greatly, his fascination with her and the puzzle she presented.

No matter what the subject of conversation, Lily had something to add to it. Her knowledge of hunting, horses, and other masculine subjects gave her a certain rough-and-tumble appeal. But when she exchanged society gossip with Totty, she sounded as sophisticated as any woman in the *beau monde* could ever hope to be. Most perplexing of all, there were moments—brief, to be sure—when she displayed an artless charm that far eclipsed her younger sister.

"Penny will be the most exquisite bride London has ever seen!" Lily exclaimed, causing her sister to giggle modestly. Then she glanced at Totty wryly. "I'm glad that you'll finally have the grand wedding you dreamed of giving, Mama. Especially after the years of torment I've caused you."

"You haven't been *completely* tormenting, dear. And I still haven't relinquished my hopes of giving you a wedding someday."

Lily kept her expression bland, but inwardly she laughed. *May the devil take me before I become someone's wife*, she thought grimly. She glanced at Alex, who appeared to be absorbed in the plate of lukewarm food before him. "The kind of man I would consent to marry is difficult to find."

Penelope regarded her curiously. "What kind is that, Lily?"

"I don't know if there's a particular word to describe him," Lily said thoughtfully.

"Milksop?" Alex suggested.

Lily glared at him. "From what I've observed, this business of marriage is far more advantageous for the man. The husband always has the whip hand, legally and financially, whereas the poor wife spends her best years bearing his children and seeing to his welfare, and then discovers herself to be as burnt out as an old candle."

"Wilhemina, that is not so," Totty exclaimed. "Every woman requires a man's protection and guidance."

"I don't!"

"Really," Alex remarked, his steady gaze pinning her to the chair. Lily writhed in discomfort as she returned his stare. Apparently he had heard about her relationship with Derek Craven. Well, his opinion of her didn't matter a damned bit. And it was none of his business whether she had an "arrangement" with someone or not!

"Yes, really," she said coolly. "But were I to marry, my lord, I would only have a man who doesn't equate strength with brutality. Someone who considers a wife a companion rather than a glorified slave. Someone—"

"Lily, that is enough!" her father said, his face darkening. "Above all I desire peace, and you are creating a disturbance. You will keep your silence now."

"I'd like her to continue," Alex said calmly. "Tell us, Miss Lawson, what else do you want in a man?"

Lily felt her cheeks begin to burn. There was a strange sensation in her chest—tautness and warmth and turbulence. "I don't wish to continue," she muttered. "I'm sure you all have the general idea." She put a bite of chicken in her mouth, but the succulent morsel suddenly had the texture of sawdust, and it was difficult to swallow. All seated at the table were silent, while Penelope's distressed gaze flickered back and forth between her financé and her sister.

"Although," Lily said after a moment, lifting her gaze to Totty's pink face, "I'm becoming more settled in my advanced age, Mother. It's possible that I could find someone willing to make certain allowances for me. Someone tolerant enough to endure my wild ways." She paused significantly. "In fact, I think I may have found him."

"What are you talking about, dear?" Totty asked.

"I may be receiving a caller in a day or two. An absolutely delightful young man—and a neighbor of yours, Lord Raiford."

Totty registered immediate delight. "Are you teasing, Wilhemina? Is it someone I'm familiar with? Why haven't you mentioned him to us before now?"

"I'm not certain how much there is to tell," Lily said coyly. "And yes, you are familiar with him. It's Zachary."

"Viscount Stamford?"

Her family's astonishment caused Lily to grin. "None other. As you know, I began a friendship with Zach after Harry and I left off. Through the years we have cherished a certain fondness for each other. We get along famously. Lately I have suspected that the feelings between us may have ripened." Perfect, she thought with pride. She had delivered the news in just the right tone—casual, pleased, a touch bashful.

It was on the tip of Alex's tongue to ask what

her paramour Derek Craven thought of the situation, but he bit the words back. He considered what kind of pair they would make. Stamford was a harmless pup without much of a spine. Lily would lead the poor fool around by his refined little nose.

Lily smiled at Penelope apologetically. "Of course, dear Penny, we all know that Zach entertained an interest in you for a while. But of late Zach has begun to view me in a light he never has before. I hope you would not be disconcerted by the prospect of a match between us."

There was a strange expression on Penelope's face—amazement battling with jealousy. Penny had never looked at her sister in such a way before. She managed to produce a valiant smile. "It would please me if you were to find someone who could give you happiness, Lily."

"Zach would be quite a good husband for me," Lily mused. "Although we'd have to work on his marksmanship. He's not quite the sportsman I am."

"Well," Penelope said with wan enthusiasm. "Viscount Stamford is a gentle and thoughtful man."

"Yes, he is," Lily murmured. Penny, bless her, was easy to read. She was in shock at the thought that the man who had courted her so ardently was now considering marriage with her older sister. Everything was going to fall into place nicely. Glowing with satisfaction, Lily looked at

Alex. "I trust you have no objections to my receiving visitors, my lord?"

"I wouldn't dream of interfering with any matrimonial prospect that comes your way, Miss Lawson. Who knows when there might be another?"

"You're too kind," she replied sourly, and leaned back as a servant ventured forth to remove her empty plate.

"Miss? Miss, shall I fetch something from the kitchen? P'raps a cup o' tea?"

There was the sound of curtains being pulled. Lily stirred and groaned, climbing up from the soft depths of sleep. The glare of daylight was in her eyes. As she turned her head, she winced at the ache of sore muscles in her neck. What a wretched sleep she'd had, filled with strange dreams, some of them about Nicole. She'd been chasing after her daughter, trying to reach her, stumbling through endless hallways in unfamiliar places.

The maid continued to pester her with tentative questions. Probably his odious lordship had sent his servants to wake her at some ungodly hour, just for spite. Cursing Raiford silently, Lily rubbed her eyes and struggled to a sitting position. "No, I don't want any tea," she muttered. "I just want to stay in bed and—"

Lily broke off with a gasp as she saw her surroundings. Her heart thumped in fright. She was not in bed. She wasn't even in her room. She was . . . oh God, she was downstairs in the library, curled uncomfortably in one of the leather armchairs. The maid, a young woman with a wealth of red curls stuffed under a white cap, was standing in front of her, wringing her hands. Lily looked at herself, realizing she was dressed in her thin white nightgown, no robe or slippers. She had gone to sleep last night in the guest room provided for her, and somehow she had ended up here.

The problem was, she had no recollection of getting out of bed or coming down the stairs. She didn't remember any of it.

It had happened again.

Disoriented, Lily ran her palm over her sweat-beaded forehead. She could understand the situation if she had been drinking. Oh, she'd done quite a few foolish things when she'd "bought the sack," as Derek called it when she was tipsy. But all she'd had to drink last night was a few sips of liqueur after dinner, and that followed by a cup of strong coffee.

It had happened on two other occasions. Once, when she had gone to sleep in the bedroom of her London terrace and had awakened the next morning to find herself in the kitchen; and the time after that, Burton, the butler, had discovered her asleep in the parlor. Burton had assumed that she had been under the influence of strong drink or some other intoxicant. Lily hadn't mustered the nerve to tell him she'd been as sober as a judge. Good Lord, she couldn't let anyone know that she roamed the house in her sleep—that wasn't the behavior of a sane woman, was it?

The maid was watching her, waiting for an explanation.

"I . . . I was feeling restless last night and . . . came here for a drink," Lily said, twisting the folds of her nightgown in her fists. "H-how silly of me to fall asleep right in this chair." The girl glanced around the room, obviously wondering about the absence of a glass. Somehow Lily manufactured a light laugh. "I sat here to think about . . . something . . . and then I went to sleep before I even got the bloody drink!"

"Yes, miss," the maid said doubtfully.

Lily ran her fingers through her tousled curls. A headache pounded in her temples and forehead. Even her scalp was sensitive. "I believe I'll return to my room now. Have some coffee sent up, would you?"

"Yes, miss."

Gathering her nightgown around the front of her body, Lily crawled out of the large chair and left the library, trying not to stagger. She went through the entrance hall. There were clinking sounds of dishes and pots from the kitchen, voices of servants engaged in their early-morning tasks. She had to get to her room before she was seen by anyone else. Clutching the hem of her nightgown in her hands, she flew up the stairs, her feet a pale blur.

Just as Lily neared the top, she saw a dark, imposing figure. Her heart sank. It was Lord Raiford, going for a morning ride. He was dressed in riding clothes and gleaming black boots. Defensively Lily pulled at the front of her gown, trying to conceal herself as much as possible. Raiford's assessing gaze seemed to shred her thin nightgown and detect every detail of her body underneath.

"What are you doing, traipsing through the house like that?" he asked curtly.

Lily was tongue-tied. On a sudden inspiration, she lifted her nose and stared up at him as haughtily as possible. "Perhaps I was consorting with one of the servants last night. Shouldn't one expect such behavior from a woman like me?"

There was silence. Lily endured his unfathomable gaze for an eternity, then tried to look away. It was impossible. Suddenly it seemed to her that instead of icy glints, his eyes were filled with sparks of intense heat. Although she stood there motionless, she had the sensation of the world careening around the two of them. She swayed slightly and placed her hand on the banister.

When Raiford spoke, his voice was more gravelly than usual.

"If you're to stay under my roof, Miss Lawson, there'll be no displays of your well-used little body, for the benefit of the servants or anyone else. Do you understand?"

His contempt was worse than a slap in the face. *Well-used?* Lily drew in a quick breath. She couldn't recall ever hating anyone more in her life. Except, of course, Giuseppe. She wanted to fling a scalding retort at him, but suddenly she was overwhelmed with the urge to flee. "Understood," she said briskly, and rushed past him.

Alex did not turn to watch her go. He descended the stairs with nearly the same speed as she had gone up them. Instead of walking toward the stables, he strode into the empty library and closed the door with such force that it shook in the doorjamb. He allowed himself several long, searing breaths. From the moment he had seen her in the filmy white gown, he had wanted her. His body was still rigid, trembling with arousal. He'd wanted to take her right then on the steps, bear her down to the carpet and push into her. Her hair, those damnable short curls that enticed his fingers to wind through them . . . the delicate whiteness of her throat . . . the small, tempting points of her breasts.

Alex cursed and rubbed his shaven chin roughly. With Caroline his desire had been mingled with tenderness and love. But this kind of wanting had nothing to do with love. He felt as if the surge of arousal had been a betrayal of his feelings for Caroline. Lily was more dangerous than he had suspected. He managed to stay in control of himself and everything around him, except when she was near. But he wouldn't yield to the temptation she presented . . . he wouldn't, by God, even if the effort killed him.

CHAPTER 4

"Zachary! Dear, *dear*, Zachary, how nice of you to call!" Lily strode forward and clasped his hands, welcoming him into the mansion as if she were the lady of the manor. Standing on her toes, she lifted her face, and he kissed her cheek dutifully. In his black silk cravat and elegant riding clothes, Zachary was every bit the handsome country gentleman. Discreetly the butler took Zachary's coat, gloves, and hat, and withdrew. Pulling Zach to a corner of the entrance hall, Lily whispered in his ear. "They're all taking tea in the parlor—Mother, Penny, and Raiford. Remember to act as if you're in love with me—and if you make eyes at my sister, I'll pinch you! Now come—"

"Wait," Zachary whispered anxiously, tightening his hold on her. "How is Penelope?"

Lily smiled. "Don't look so worried. There's still a chance for you, old fellow."

"Does she still love me? Has she said so?"

"No, she won't admit it," Lily said reluctantly. "But she certainly doesn't love Raiford."

"Lily, I'm dying of love for her. Our plan *must* work."

"It will," she said with determination, slipping her hand into the crook of his arm. "Now . . . off to battle!"

Together they strolled out of the entrance hall. "Have I called at too late an hour?" Zachary inquired, loudly enough that the occupants of the parlor could hear.

Lily winked at him. "Not at all, dearest. Just in time for tea." With a broad smile, she pulled him into the parlor, a beautiful and airy room with pale yellow silk walls, carved mahogany furniture, and large windows. "Here we are," she said lightly, "all familiar with each other. No need for introductions—how convenient!" Fondly she squeezed Zachary's arm. "I must tell you, Zach, that the tea at Raiford Park is excellent. Almost as good as the blend I serve in London."

Zachary smiled as he regarded the room in general. "Lily does serve the best tea I've ever tasted—she orders a secret blend that no one else can quite reproduce."

"I encountered it during my travels," Lily replied, seating herself in a delicate claw-foot chair. She sneaked a glance at her sister, and was delighted to witness a brief but intense glance between Penny and Zachary. For just a moment, Penny's gaze was filled with sadness and hopeless longing. *Poor Penny*, Lily thought. *I'll make everything right for you. And then perhaps you and Zach can prove to me that true love does exist.*

In a courtly manner, Zachary went to the settee,

where Penelope and Totty were situated. Sensitive to Penelope's deep blush, he did not speak directly to her, but addressed her mother. "Mrs. Lawson, it is a pleasure to see you and your lovely daughter. I trust all is well with you?"

"Quite well," Totty replied in mild discomfort. In spite of her objections to Zachary's courtship of her daughter, she had rather liked him. And she had been aware, as everyone else had, that Zachary's love for Penelope had been sincere and honorable. But a family of limited financial means had to be practical. Lord Raiford was by far a more advantageous match for their daughter.

Alex stood by the marble mantel of the fireplace and lit a cigar as he surveyed the proceedings. Lily glared at him. How impossibly rude he was. Gentlemen usually reserved their smoking for when they congregated to discuss masculine subjects of interest. Unless he were an irascible elderly gentleman puffing on a dignified pipe, Raiford should have smoked in private, not in the presence of ladies.

Warily Zachary nodded to Alex. "Good afternoon, Raiford."

Alex nodded and brought the cigar to his lips. As he exhaled a stream of smoke, his eyes narrowed into gleaming slits of silver.

Surly beast, Lily thought darkly. He must feel threatened by the presence of a man so different from himself, a charming, gentlemanly fellow whom everyone liked. Raiford couldn't make himself likeable even if he tried for a hundred years. She scowled at him and then directed a smile to Zachary. "Come sit down, Zach, and tell us the latest happenings in London."

"Unbearably dull without you, as always," Zachary replied, taking the chair next to hers. "But I did attend a large dinner party recently, and observed that Annabelle is looking quite splendid since her marriage to Lord Deerhurst."

"Glad to hear it," Lily rejoined. "She deserves to be happy after enduring ten years of marriage to Sir Charles, the randy old goat."

"Wilhemina!" Totty gasped in dismay. "How could you call Sir Charles, may he rest in peace, such a *dreadful* name—"

"How could I not? Annabelle was only fifteen when she was compelled to marry him, and he was old enough to be her grandfather! And everyone knows that Sir Charles wasn't kind to her. Personally, I'm gratified that he passed on in time for Annabelle to find a husband of more suitable age."

Totty gave her a disapproving frown. "Wilhemina, you sound quite heartless."

Zachary reached over to pat Lily's hand as he came to her defense. "You are rather forthright, my dear, but anyone who is acquainted with you knows that you have the most compassionate of hearts."

Lily beamed at him. Out of the corner of her eye she saw that her sister looked dumbstruck.

Penelope could scarcely conceive that the man she loved was calling Lily "my dear." Sympathy and amusement battled within Lily's chest. She wished she could tell Penelope that this was all a sham. "I shall try to curb my tongue," Lily promised with a laugh, "if only for this afternoon. Do go on with your news, Zach, and I'll refrain from spouting my shocking opinions. Let me pour your tea. Milk, no sugar, correct?"

While Zachary entertained them with his tales of London. Alex drew on his cigar and watched Lily. He was forced to concede there was a possibility the two were contemplating marriage. There was an easy familiarity between them that bespoke a long friendship. It was clear that they liked each other and were comfortable together.

The advantages such a marriage would present were obvious. Zachary would certainly be appreciative of Lily's fortune, more sizeable than what he would stand to inherit. And Lily was an attractive woman. In the sea green gown she was wearing today, her skin took on a faint rosy glow, and her dark hair and eyes were strikingly exotic. No man would find it a chore to bed her. Furthermore, in the view of society Lily would be fortunate to land a man of such good family and character. Especially after she had strayed along the edge of the *demimonde* for so long.

Alex frowned at the thought of the two of them together. It was all wrong. For all his thirty years, Zachary was still a guileless boy. He would never be the man in his own home, not with a wife as headstrong as Lily. Zachary would always find it easier to obey her wishes rather than argue with her. As the years passed by, Lily would come to feel contempt for her callow husband. This marriage was misery in the making.

"My lord?" Lily and the others were looking at him expectantly. Alex realized that his thoughts had wandered, and he had lost track of the conversation. "My lord," Lily said, "I just asked you if the hole has been dug in the garden yet."

Alex wondered if he had heard her correctly. "Hole?" he repeated.

Lily looked extremely pleased with herself. "Yes, for the new pond."

Alex regarded her in dumbfounded silence. Somehow he regained his voice. "What in hell are you talking about?"

Everyone seemed startled by his profanity except for Lily. Her smile remained unaltered. "I had a lovely conversation with your gardener Mr. Chumley yesterday afternoon. I gave him several ideas to improve the garden."

Alex stubbed out his cigar and threw the butt into the fireplace. "My garden doesn't need improvement," he snarled. "It's been the same way for twenty years!"

She nodded cheerfully. "Precisely my point. I told him that the style of your landscape is sadly outmoded. All the *really* fashionable gardens have several ponds all around them. I showed Mr.

Chumley exactly where a new one must be dug."

A flush of scarlet crept up from Alex's collar to his temples. He wanted to strangle her. "Chumley wouldn't overturn a spoonful of dirt without asking my permission."

Lily shrugged innocently. "He seemed enthusiastic about the notion. I wouldn't be surprised if he's already begun digging. Really, I think you'll adore the changes." She gave him a fond, sisterly smile. "And whenever you walk by that dear little pond, perhaps you'll always think of me."

Raiford's features contorted. He made a sound that resembled a roar as he stormed out of the parlor.

Totty, Penelope, and Zachary all stared at Lily.

"I don't think he appreciated my idea," she remarked, looking disappointed.

"Wilhemina," Totty said faintly, "I know your efforts were well intentioned. However, I do not think you should attempt to make any more improvements about Lord Raiford's estate."

Suddenly one of the cook-maids, clad in a white apron and ruffled cap, appeared at the door of the parlor. "Ma'am, Cook wants to speak wi' ye about the weddin' feast, as soon as yer lady-ship 'as the time. She don't know what to make o' what, from the soup to the trifle."

"But why?" Totty asked, perplexed. "She and I already agreed on those preparations, down to the last detail. There's no reason for confusion."

Lily cleared her throat delicately. "Mother, it's

possible that Cook wants to discuss the changes I suggested to the wedding menu."

"Oh, dear. Wilhemina, what have you done?" Totty stood up and rushed from the room, her curls bouncing agitatedly.

Lily smiled at Zachary and Penelope. "Well, why don't the two of you pass the time together while I try to undo some of the havoc I've caused?" Ignoring Penelope's weak protests, she slipped out of the parlor and closed the door. She rubbed her hands together and grinned. "Well done," she said to herself, restraining the urge to whistle as she strode through the back gallery. Opening the French doors, she went out to the garden.

Wandering around hedges and well-tended trees, Lily enjoyed the clear day and the feel of the breeze in her curls. She took care to keep out of sight, especially when she heard the sound of voices. The ominous rumble of Raiford's tone resembled thunder. She had to hear what was going on. It was too great a temptation to resist. Lily sneaked closer, drawing behind a concealing yew hedge.

". . . but my lord," Chumley was protesting. Lily could picture his round face turning pink around his whiskers, the sunlight shining off his balding forehead. "My lord, she did make the suggestion, but I would never undertake such a significant project without consulting you."

"I don't care what she suggests, significant or trivial, *don't do it*," Raiford commanded. "Don't so much as clip a twig or pull a weed at her request! Don't move a pebble!"

"Yes, my lord, I certainly agree."

"We don't need any more damned ponds in this garden!"

"No, my lord, we do not."

"Inform me if she tries to instruct you in your duties again, Chumley. And notify the rest of the staff that they're not to make any changes in their usual activities. I'm afraid of setting foot off my own estate—next she'll have the entire mansion painted pink and purple."

"Yes, my lord."

It seemed that Raiford's ranting had come to an end, the conversation concluded. Hearing the sound of footsteps, Lily shrank further into the protection of the yew. It would not do to be discovered. Unfortunately, a sixth sense must have alerted Raiford to her presence. Lily made no movement or sound, but still he looked around the hedge and found her. One moment she was smiling and silently congratulating herself, and the next she was staring into his scowling face.

"Miss Lawson!" he snapped.

Lily used her hand to shade her eyes. "Yes, my lord?"

"Did you overhear enough, or should I repeat myself?"

"Everyone within a mile could not help over-hearing you. And if it reassures you, I would never *dream* of painting the mansion purple. Although—"

"What are you doing out here?" he interrupted.

Lily thought rapidly. "Well, Zachary and I had a . . . a slight altercation. I came out here to take the air, and let my temper cool, and then—"

"Is your mother with Stamford and Penelope?"

"Well, I suppose she must be," she replied innocently.

Raiford stared into Lily's eyes as if he could see past her carefully blank expression and read every thought. "What are you up to?" he asked in a murderous tone. Abruptly he turned and walked away from her, following the path to the house.

Oh, no. Lily went cold, thinking that he might possibly catch Zachary and Penelope in some compromising situation. Everything would be ruined. She had to find some way to stop him. "Wait," she cried, hurrying after him. "Wait! W—"

All at once her foot was caught in something, and she went flying to the ground with a shriek. With an oath, she twisted to see what had stopped her. A twisted tree root, arcing out of the ground. She tried to get to her feet, but a stab of pain went through her ankle, and she collapsed to the grass. "Oh, bloody hell—"

Raiford's voice cut through her extravagant cursing. "What is it?" he demanded, having come back a few steps along the path.

"I turned my ankle!" she said in furious surprise.

Alex gave her a speaking glance and turned away.

"Damn you, I *did!*" she shouted. "Come and help me up. Surely even *you* must be enough of a gentleman to do that—surely you have the *teaspoonful* of breeding required for that."

Alex approached her, making no effort to reach down for her. "Which leg is it?"

"Is it necessary for you to know?"

Sinking to his haunches, Alex flipped the hem of her skirts up to her stockinged ankles. "Which one? This?"

"No, the—*ow!*" Lily yelped in pain. "What are you trying to—*ow!* That hurts like the devil! Take your blasted hand away, you big, hatchet-faced sadist—"

"Well, it seems you're not shamming." Alex seized her elbows, lifting her to her feet.

"Of course I'm not! Why hasn't that deuced root been cut out of the ground? It's positively hazardous!"

He responded with a scorching glare. "Are there any other changes to my garden you'd like to suggest?" His tone was humming with suppressed violence.

Prudently Lily shook her head and kept her mouth closed.

"Good," he muttered, and they started back to the house.

Awkwardly Lily limped along beside him. "Aren't you going to offer me your arm?"

He shoved his elbow at her. She took his arm, leaning her weight on the solid support. Lily did her best to hamper Raiford as they made their way back through the garden. She wanted Zachary and Penelope to have as much time alone as possible. Discreetly Lily glanced at her companion. Some time after he had left the parlor, Raiford must have raked his hands through his golden hair, for the usually immaculate smoothness was ruffled and disordered. The humid air was making it curl on the back of his neck. A stray lock or two had fallen onto his forehead. Really, he had beautiful hair for a man.

Walking so close to him, Lily became aware of the pleasant scent that clung to him, the mixture of tobacco and crisp starched linen and some appealing, underlying fragrance she couldn't quite identify. In spite of the throbbing of her ankle, she was almost enjoying her stroll with him. That disturbed her so profoundly that she was compelled to stir up another argument.

"Must you walk so fast?" she demanded. "I feel as if we're in a frigging footrace. Blast it! If this worsens my injury, Raiford, I'll hold you accountable."

Alex scowled but slowed his pace. "You have a foul mouth, Miss Lawson."

"Men talk the same way. I don't see why I can't. Besides, all of my gentlemen friends admire my colorful vocabulary."

"Including Derek Craven?"

Lily was glad that he was aware of her friendship with Derek. It was good for him to know she had a powerful ally. "Mr. Craven has taught me some of the most useful words I know."

"I don't doubt it."

"Must we plow ahead like this? I am not some obstinate mule to be dragged forth at such a relentless pace. Could we slow to a more reasonable speed? Incidentally, my lord, you reek of cigars."

"If it offends you, make your own way back."

They continued to quarrel as they entered the house. Lily made certain that her voice was strong enough to echo through the gallery and the marble hall, alerting Penelope and Zachary to their return. As Raiford opened the parlor door and yanked Lily inside with him, they saw the star-crossed lovers sitting respectably far apart from each other. Lily wondered what had transpired between them during their moment of privacy. Zachary appeared to be in his usually good humor, while Penelope looked pink and flustered.

Alex surveyed the two of them and spoke dryly. "Miss Lawson mentioned something about an argument?"

Having risen to his feet at their entrance, Zachary gave Lily a bewildered glance.

"My quick temper is legendary," Lily interceded with a laugh. "I just had to dash out and clear my head. Am I forgiven, Zach?"

"There's nothing to forgive," Zachary said gallantly, coming over to kiss her hand.

Lily switched her hold on Alex's arm to Zachary's. "Zach, I'm afraid you'll have to help me to a chair. I turned my ankle while I was strolling through the garden." She waved a hand disdainfully in the direction of Raiford's immaculately groomed landscape. "A root was protruding from the ground, nearly as thick as a man's leg!"

"A slight exaggeration," Alex said sardonically.

"Well, it was quite large, nonetheless." With Zachary's help, she limped dramatically to a nearby chair and eased herself into it.

"We'll have to make a poultice," Penelope exclaimed. "Poor Lily—don't move!" She rushed from the room and headed toward the kitchen.

Zachary began to question Lily in concern. "How bad is the injury? Is the pain limited solely to your ankle?"

"I'll be perfectly fine." She gave an exaggerated wince. "But perhaps you would return tomorrow, to check on my condition?"

"Every day, until you're better," Zachary promised.

Lily smiled over his head at Raiford, wondering if the grating sound she heard was his teeth gnashing together.

By the next day, Lily's ankle felt almost like new, with only a twinge of discomfort as a reminder of having sprained it. The weather was unusually warm and sunny. In the morning Zachary arrived to take her for a carriage ride, and Lily insisted that Penelope accompany them. Brusquely Alex declined Penelope's halfhearted invitation to join them, electing to stay behind and attend some business about the estate. Needless to say, Lily, Penelope, and Zachary were all silently relieved at Alex's refusal. Had he participated in their outing, it would have made things rather tense.

The threesome set off in an open-air carriage. Zachary handled the ribbons expertly, occasionally looking over his shoulder and grinning at the comments made by his two passengers. Lily and Penelope sat together, their smiling faces shaded by straw bonnets. They came to a fork in the road. At Zachary's suggestion they took the less-traveled avenue, until they reached a particularly beautiful section of country. Zachary pulled the carriage to a stop. They admired the wide green meadow before them, fragrant with violets, clover, and wild geraniums.

"How lovely!" Penelope exclaimed, pushing an errant blonde curl away from her eyes. "Might we go for a walk? I'd love to pick some violets for Mother."

"Hmm." Lily shook her head regretfully. "I'm afraid my ankle still pains me a little," she lied. "I'm not up to tromping through fields today. Perhaps Zachary would volunteer to escort you."

"Oh, I . . ." Penelope looked at Zachary's serious, handsome face and blushed with confusion. "I don't think that would be proper."

"Please," Zachary entreated. "It would be my great pleasure."

"But . . . unchaperoned . . ."

"Come, we all know Zach's the perfect gentleman," Lily said. "And I will keep my eyes on the two of you the entire time. I'll chaperone from a distance. Of course, if you don't wish to walk, Penny, I would be delighted for you to sit here with me and admire the view from the carriage."

Faced with the decision to walk unchaperoned through the meadow with the man she loved or sit in the carriage with her sister, Penelope bit her lower lip and frowned. Temptation won out. She gave Zachary a small smile. "Perhaps just a short walk."

"We'll return the very moment you desire," Zachary replied, and leapt eagerly from the carriage.

Lily watched in fond amusement as Zachary helped Penny to the ground and the two began a slow trek across the meadow. The two of them were perfect for each other. Zachary was an honorable young man, strong enough to protect her, yet boyish enough that he would never intimidate her. And Penny was exactly the sweet, innocent sort of girl that he needed.

Putting her slippered feet up on the velvet-upholstered seat, Lily reached for the basket of fruit and biscuits they had brought. She bit into a strawberry and tossed the green stem over the side of the carriage. Untying her bonnet strings, she let the sun shine on her face, and reached for another strawberry.

Once, long ago, she and Giuseppe had partaken of a picnic lunch in Italy, reclining in a meadow very much like this one. It had been in the days just before they had become lovers. At the time Lily had thought herself to be quite sophisticated. It had been only later that she realized how stupidly naive she had been . . .

"The country air is splendid," she had declared, leaning her bare elbows on a blanket and biting into a buttery, ripe pear. "Everything tastes better out here!"

"So you tire of the jaded pleasures of the city, amore mio?" Giuseppe's beautiful eyes, long-lashed and liquid black, regarded her with sensuous warmth.

"Society is as much a bore here as it is in England," Lily said reflectively, staring at the hot green grass. "Everyone striving to be witty and sought-after, everyone talking and no one listening . . ."

"I listen, carissima. *I listen to evert'ing you say."*

Lily turned and smiled at him, resting her weight on her elbow. "You do, don't you? Why is that, Giuseppe?"

"I am in love with you," he said passionately.

She couldn't help laughing at him. "You're in love with every woman."

"Is that wrong? In England, per'aps. Not in Italy. I have special love to give every woman. Special love for you." He plucked a succulent grape and held it to her lips, while his eyes bore into hers.

Flattered, feeling her heart beat faster, Lily opened her mouth. She took the grape between her teeth and smiled at him as she chewed. No man had ever pursued her with such ardent gentleness. There were impossible promises in his gaze, promises of tenderness, pleasure, desire; and while her mind refused to believe them, her heart desperately wanted to. She had been lonely for such a long time. And she wanted to know about the mystery that everyone else seemed to take for granted.

"Lily, my beautiful little English girl," Giuseppe murmured. "I can make you 'appy. So very 'appy, bella."

"You shouldn't say that." She looked away from him, trying to hide her flushed cheeks. "No one can promise such a thing."

"Perchè no? Let me try, cara. Beautiful Lily, always with the sad smile, I make it all better." Slowly he bent to kiss her. The touch of his lips was warm, pleasant. It was in that moment Lily had decided that he would make a woman of her. She would give herself to him. After all, no one would expect or believe that *she was a virgin. Her innocence mattered to no one.*

Looking back now, Lily had no idea why she had thought of men and love as such an alluring mystery. She had paid for her mistake with Giuseppe a thousand times over, and she would continue to pay the price for her sins. Sighing, she watched her sister walk with Zachary. They were not holding hands, but there was an air of intimacy about them. *He's the kind of man who'll never betray you, Penny,* she thought. *And that, believe me, is a rarity.*

After Zachary had taken his leave, Penelope was radiant. However, something changed in the hours afterward. During supper the sparkle was gone from her eyes, and she was pale and subdued. Lily wondered at her thoughts and feelings, but they had no opportunity to talk until late evening, when they were preparing for bed.

"Penny," she said, unhooking the back of her sister's gown, "what is the matter? You've been so quiet all afternoon, and you barely touched your supper."

Penelope walked to the vanity table and pulled the pins from her hair until a golden cascade fell to her waist. She looked at Lily, her gaze shadowed with misery. "I know what you're been trying to do. But you must not arrange any further meetings between Zachary and me. It can lead to nothing, and it is wrong!"

"Are you sorry for having been with him this afternoon?" Lily asked contritely. "I placed you in an awkward position, didn't I? Forgive me—"

"No, it was *wonderful*," Penelope exclaimed, and then looked shamefaced. "I shouldn't have said that. I don't know what is the matter with me! I'm so confused about everything."

"It's because you've always obeyed Mother and Father, and done what's expected of you. Penny, you've never done a selfish thing in your life. You're in love with Zachary, but you're sacrificing yourself for the sake of duty."

Penelope sat on the bed and lowered her face. "It doesn't matter whom I'm in love with."

"Your happiness is the *only* thing that matters! Why are you so upset? Has something happened?"

"Lord Raiford took me aside this afternoon," Penelope said dully. "After we returned from the carriage drive."

Lily's gaze sharpened. "What? What did he say?"

"He asked questions . . . and he implied that Zachary is not really your suitor. That Zachary is behaving dishonorably in trying to court me by pretending an interest in my sister."

"How dare he say such a thing?" Lily demanded in instant fury.

"It is true," Penelope said miserably. "You know it is."

"Of course it is—I'm the one who thought of the plan in the first place!"

"I thought so."

"But how dare he insult us by making such an accusation!"

"Lord Raiford said that if Zachary had once been intent on marrying a girl like me, he would never want to marry one like you."

Lily's frown deepened. "One like me?"

"'Seasoned' was the word he used," Penelope said uncomfortably.

"*Seasoned?*" Lily paced around the room like a tigress. "I suppose he doesn't think I'm desirable enough to catch a husband," she fumed. "Well, other men find me quite attractive, men who have more than ice water running through their veins. Oh, he's a fine one to criticize when he's got more faults than I have time to list! Well, I'm going to fix everything, and by the time I'm through—"

"Lily, please," Penelope entreated in a small voice. "All this trouble distresses me terribly. Can't we let things be?"

"Certainly. After I bring his lordship some much-needed enlightenment!"

"No!" Penelope held a hand to her forehead, as if the situation were too much for her to bear. "You must not make Lord Raiford angry! I would be afraid for all of us!"

"Did he threaten you?" It was fortunate that Penelope could not see Lily's eyes, for there was a vengeful glow in them that would have frightened her.

"N-not precisely, no. But he is such a powerful

man, a-and I don't think he would tolerate any sort of betrayal . . . he is not a man to be crossed!"

"Penny, if Zachary asked you to—"

"No," Penelope said quickly, tears springing to her eyes. "No, we must not discuss this any further! I won't listen . . . I can't!"

"All right," Lily soothed. "No more talking tonight. Don't cry. Everything will be fine, you'll see."

Alex strode rapidly down the grand staircase. He was dressed in traveling clothes—a coat of fine blended wool, a tan poplin waistcoat, and cotton trousers. In response to a message he had received from a carrier the day before, it was necessary for him to travel to London. His youngest brother Henry was being expelled from Westfield.

Feeling equal parts of anger and concern, Alex wondered what incident had prompted the expulsion. Henry had always been an energetic boy, full of mischief, but possessed of a good-natured disposition. There had been no explanation in the short note from Westfield's headmaster, only that the boy was no longer welcome at the school.

Alex sighed heavily, thinking that he hadn't given the boy enough guidance. Whenever it had come time for discipline, he'd never had the heart to punish Henry for his misdeeds. Henry had been so young when his parents had died. Alex had been more of a father than a brother to Henry. He wondered if he had done well by the boy.

Guiltily Alex thought that he should have married years ago in order to provide a kind, maternal woman in Henry's life.

Alex's thoughts were interrupted by the sight of a small figure clad in a nightgown, hurrying up the staircase. Lily again, scampering through the house in next to nothing. He paused and watched her hasty ascent.

Suddenly she noticed him and stopped a few steps away. Looking up into his stern face, she groaned and held a hand to her head. "Let's just ignore this, shall we?"

"No, Miss Lawson," Alex said in a grating voice. "I want an explanation of where you've been and what you've been doing."

"You won't get one," she mumbled.

Alex contemplated her silently. It was possible she had been telling the truth before, that she was indeed involved in a *tête à tête* with one of the servants. She had the appearance of it—dressed in a nightgown, barefooted, her face haggard, and her eyes dark-circled as if she were exhausted after a night of debauchery. He didn't know why the thought enraged him. Usually he didn't give a damn what others did, so long as they didn't inconvenience him. All he was conscious of was a bitter taste in his mouth.

"The next time this happens," he said coldly, "I'll pack your bags personally. In London a lack of morality is something to be admired—but it won't be tolerated here."

114

Lily held his gaze defiantly, then continued up the staircase, muttering some obscenity *sotto voce.*

"What did you say?" he asked in a soft growl.

She threw a saccharine smile over her shoulder. "I wished you a perfectly *splendid* day, my lord."

Retreating to her room, Lily requested a bath to be prepared. Efficiently the maids filled the porcelain-rimmed tub in the adjoining dressing room. One of the girls stoked the fire in the little fireplace, and set the towels on a nearby warming rack. Lily declined their assistance after that.

Easing into the tub, she idly splashed water over her chest. The walls were papered with scenery in the Chinese style, illustrated with hand-painted flowers and birds. The porcelain fireplace mantelpiece was decorated with dragons and pagodas. Outmoded. She would bet her last farthing that the wall had last been papered at least two decades ago. *If I had my way around here, there would be some changes made,* she thought, and submerged herself, head and all, in the steaming water. Coming up with dripping hair, she finally allowed herself to think about what was happening to her.

This sleepwalking business was occurring more frequently. Yesterday she had awakened in the library, this morning in the parlor, in back of the settee. How had she come to be there? How had she managed to descend the stairs without mishap? She might have broken her neck!

She couldn't allow this to continue. Frightened, Lily wondered if she should begin tying herself to the bed each night. But how would *that* appear to anyone who might discover her? Well, Raiford certainly wouldn't be surprised, she thought, and giggled nervously. He probably thought of her as the most depraved woman alive.

Perhaps she should try drinking before bedtime. If she were drunk enough . . . no, that would be the fastest course to ruin. She had seen it too many times in London, where people destroyed themselves with strong drink. Perhaps if she consulted a physician and asked for sleeping powders . . . but what if he declared her to be a madwoman? God knew what would happen to her then. Lily ran her fingers through her wet hair and closed her eyes. "Perhaps I am insane," she muttered, clenching her hands into dripping fists. It would drive any woman mad to have her child taken from her.

After an industrious scrubbing of her hair and skin, Lily rose from the bath and patted herself dry with a length of towel. She donned a white lace-trimmed shift, embroidered cotton stockings, and a cotton gown printed with tiny pink flowers. The dress made her appear nearly as young as Penelope. Sitting before the fire, Lily ran her fingers through her damp curls and considered what her plan for the day should be. "First," she said with a snap of her fingers, "I'll have to convince Raiford that Zachary is courting *me*, not Penny. That will throw him off the scent."

"Miss?" She heard a puzzled voice. The maid

was standing in the door of the dressing room. "Did you say—"

"No, no, pay no heed. I was just talking to myself."

"I came to collect the soiled linens."

"You may take my nightgown and have it washed—oh, and tell me where Lord Raiford is. I wish to speak with him."

"'E's gone to London, miss."

"London?" Lily frowned. "But why? For how long?"

"'E told Silvern 'e'd be back tonight."

"Well, that's a quick journey. What could he possibly accomplish in so short a time?"

"Nobody knows what 'e went for."

Lily had a feeling the maid knew something she wasn't telling. But Raiford's servants were close-mouthed and quite loyal to their master. Rather than press the issue, Lily shrugged indifferently.

Westfield was built on one of the three heights to the northwest of London. In good weather, it was possible to stand on the hill and obtain a view of nearly a dozen counties. The most venerable of public schools, Westfield had produced great politicians, artists, poets, and military men. As a youth, Alex had been a student there. Although he had memories of the strict discipline of the masters and the tyranny of the older boys, he also remembered the high-spirited days of close friend-ship and mischief. He had hoped that Henry would do well at the place, but evidently that was not to be the case.

Alex was shown into the headmaster's office by a sullen-looking boy. Dr. Thornwait, the headmaster, stood up from a large multidrawered desk and greeted him without smiling. Thornwait was a lean man with stringy white hair, a narrow grooved face, and bushy black brows. His tone was thin and disapproving. "Lord Raiford, I would like to express my relief that you've come to collect our culprit. He is a young man of dangerously volatile temperament, quite unsuitable for Westfield."

During this little speech, Alex heard his brother's voice behind him. "Alex!" Henry, who had been seated on a wooden bench against the wall, rushed toward him with a few quick strides, then checked himself, trying to look chastened.

Unable to prevent a grin, Alex grabbed him by the scruff of the neck and pulled him near. Then he held Henry back, regarding him closely. "Why does he say you're dangerous, boy?"

"A prank," Henry confessed.

Alex smiled ruefully at that. Henry did have a lively sense of fun, but he was a fine boy, one that any man would be proud of. Although short in stature for a lad of twelve, Henry was husky and strong. He excelled in sports and mathematics, and concealed a secret love for poetry. Usually an infectious smile danced in his intense blue eyes, and his white-blond hair required frequent combing to restrain its unruly waves. To make up for his lack of height, Henry had always been daring and assertive, the leader of his group of friends. When he was in the wrong, he was always quick to apologize. Alex couldn't imagine what Henry had done to require expulsion. Gluing the pages of a few school books, no doubt, or balancing a pail of water on top of a partially opened door. Well, he would soothe Thornwait's ire, apologize, and convince him to allow Henry to stay.

"What sort of prank was it?" Alex asked, looking from Dr. Thornwait to Henry.

Thornwait was the one to answer. "He blew up the front door of my home," he said sternly.

Alex stared at his brother. "You did *what?*"

Henry had the grace to look away guiltily. "Gunpowder," he confessed.

"The explosion might have caused serious injury to me," Thornwait said, his spidery brows drawing low over his eyes, "or to my housekeeper."

"Why?" Alex asked in bewilderment. "Henry, this isn't like you."

"On the contrary," Dr. Thornwait remarked. "It is typical of him. Henry is a boy of rebellious spirit—resentful of authority, unable to accept discipline in any form—"

"Bugger you if I ain't!" Henry shot back, glaring at the headmaster. "I took all you had to give and more!"

Thornwait regarded Alex with a *you see?* expression.

Gently Alex took the boy by his shoulders. "Look at me. Why did you blow up his door?"

Henry remained obstinately silent. Thornwait began to answer for him. "Henry is the kind of boy who doesn—"

"I've heard your opinion," Alex interrupted, giving the headmaster a freezing glance that silenced him immediately. He looked back at his brother, his gaze softening. "Henry, explain it to me."

"It don't matter," Henry mumbled.

"Tell me why you did it," Alex said in a warning tone. "Now."

Henry glared at him as he answered reluctantly. "It was the flogging."

"You were flogged?" Alex frowned. "For what reason?"

"Any reason you could think of!" A flush came over Henry's face. "With a birch, a rod . . . they do it all the time, Alex!" He threw a mutinous glance over his shoulder at Thornwait. "One time I was a minute late for breakfast, once I dropped my books in front of the English master, once my neck wasn't clean enough . . . I've been thrashed near three times a week for months, an' I'm damn sick of it!"

"I mete out the same punishment to other boys with similar rebelliousness," Thornwait said crisply.

Alex kept his face expressionless, but inside he was roiling with fury. "Show me," he said to Henry, his voice clipped.

Henry shook his head, his face reddening even more. "Alex—"

"Show me," Alex insisted.

Looking from his brother to the headmaster, Henry sighed heavily. "Why not? Thornwait's seen it enough by now." He turned, reluctantly removed his jacket, fumbled at his waist, and dropped his britches a few inches.

Alex stopped breathing as he saw what they had done to his brother. Henry's lower back and buttocks were a mass of welts, scabs, and bruises. Such treatment would not be considered usual or necessary by anyone, not even the strictest disciplinarian. The floggings had not been done for the sake of discipline—they had been done by a man who got perverse pleasure from inflicting pain on others. The thought that this had been done to someone he loved . . . Trying to control his rage, Alex raised a shaking hand to his jaw and rubbed it roughly. He dared not look at Thornwait, or he'd kill the bastard. Henry jerked up his britches and turned back to face him. His blue eyes widened as he saw Alex's cold eyes and rapidly twitching cheek.

"It was entirely justified," Dr. Thornwait said in a self-righteous tone. "Flogging is a normal part of the Westfield tradition—"

"Henry," Alex interrupted unsteadily. "Henry, did they do anything to you besides the flogging? Did they hurt you in any other way?"

Henry looked at him in confusion. "No. What do you mean?"

121

"Nothing." Alex motioned to the door with a jerk of his head. "Go outside," he said quietly. "I'll be right there."

Henry obeyed slowly, glancing back with unconcealed curiosity.

As soon as the door closed, Alex strode to Dr. Thornwait, who instinctively backed away.

"Lord Raiford, flogging is an accepted method of teaching the boys—"

"*I* don't accept it!" Roughly Alex seized him and shoved him back against the wall.

"I'll have you arrested," the headmaster gasped. "You can't—"

"Can't what? Kill you as I'd like to? Perhaps not. I can come damn close to it, though." Gripping his collar, Alex held him up until Thornwait's toes barely grazed the floor. He relished the faint choking sound coming from the headmaster's scrawny throat. Thornwait's blurring vision was filled with Alex's steely eyes and snarling white teeth. "I know what kind of perverted bastard you are," Alex sneered. "Taking out your frustrations on boys. It satisfies you to whip some poor lad across the backside until you draw blood. You're not fit to be called a man. I'll bet you enjoy the hell out of beating my brother and the other innocents in your care!"

"*D . . . discipline . . .*" Thornwait managed to gasp painfully.

"If any permanent damage results from your so-called discipline, or if Henry reveals that you've

122

abused him in other ways, you'd better flee before I can get my hands on you." Alex gripped Thornwait's throat then, pressing inward as if he were molding clay. The man writhed and gurgled in terror. Alex waited until the headmaster's face turned gray. "Or I'll have your head stuffed and mounted on Henry's bedroom wall," he growled. "As a memento of his days at Westfield. I think he'd like that." He let go of Thornwait suddenly, allowing him to collapse to the floor. The headmaster choked and wheezed. Wiping his hands on his coat in distaste, Alex opened the office door with such force that it slammed against the wall and the bolt fell from one of the hinges.

Finding Henry out in the hall, he took the boy by the arm and began walking rapidly. "Why didn't you come to me about this?" he demanded.

Henry struggled to match his long strides. "I don't know."

Suddenly the memory of Lily's accusations about his being unapproachable and unfeeling rang in Alex's ears. Was it possible there had been some truth in her words? He scowled darkly. "Did you think I wouldn't be sympathetic? That I wouldn't understand? You should have told me about this long ago!"

"Hang it," Henry mumbled. "I thought it might get better here . . . or that I could take care of it myself . . ."

"By setting off explosives?"

The boy was silent. Alex sighed grimly. "Henry,

I don't want you to 'take care of things' yourself. You haven't come of age yet and you're my responsibility."

"I know that," Henry said in an offended tone. "But I knew you were occupied with other things, like the wedding—"

"Damn the wedding! Don't use it as an excuse."

"What do you want from me?" the boy asked hotly.

Gritting his teeth, Alex forced himself to stay calm. "I want you to understand that you're to come to me when you're having trouble. Any kind of trouble. I'm never too busy to help you."

Henry nodded shortly. "What are we going to do now?"

"We're going home to Raiford Park."

"Really?" The thought nearly brought a smile to the boy's face. "My things are still at the boarding house—"

"Anything important?"

"Not really—"

"Good. We're leaving everything here."

"Will I have to come back?" Henry asked with dread.

"No," Alex said emphatically. "I'll employ a tutor. You can study with the local boys."

Giving a whoop of joy, Henry tossed his school cap in the air. It fell on the floor behind them and lay there unretrieved as they walked out of the school together.

★   ★   ★

"Shhh. I think he's coming." Having observed Raiford's carriage moving up the drive, Lily had yanked Zachary away from the music room. He, Totty, and Penelope had been happily involved in singing hymns and playing the piano.

"Lily, tell me what you are planning."

"My guess is that Raiford will come to the library for a drink after traveling all day. And I want him to see us together." Energetically Lily pulled Zachary to a heavy leather chair. She threw herself into his lap and clapped her hand over his mouth as he protested. "Quiet, Zach—I can't hear a thing." Tilting her head, Lily listened intently to the sound of approaching footsteps. A heavy, measured tread . . . it had to be Raiford. She took her hand from Zachary's mouth and wound her arms around his neck. "Kiss me. And make it look convincing."

"But Lily, must we do this? My feelings for Penny—"

"It doesn't mean a thing," she said impatiently.

"But is it necess—"

"Do it, dammit!"

Meekly Zachary complied.

The kiss was like any other Lily had ever experienced, which was to say unremarkable. Heaven knew why the poets conspired to describe something vaguely distasteful as such a rapturous experience. She tended to agree with the writer Swift, who had wondered "what fool it was that first invented kissing." But couples in love seemed fond

125

of the custom, and Raiford must be made to think she and Zachary were enamored of each other.

The library door opened. There was a scorching silence. Lily touched Zachary's fine brown hair, trying to look involved in the passionate kiss. Then she raised her head slowly, as if becoming aware of the interruption. Raiford was there, looking rumpled and dusty from his travels. A scowl was gathering on his bronzed face. Lily grinned impudently. "If is isn't Lord Raiford, with his usual cheerful countenance. As you can see, my lord, you've intruded on a private moment between—" Abruptly she stopped as she noticed the boy standing next to Raiford. A short, blond boy with inquiring blue eyes and the beginnings of a smile. Well. She hadn't counted on anyone besides Raiford witnessing her embrace with Zachary. Lily felt herself blush.

"Miss Lawson," Alex said, his expression thunderous, "this is my younger brother Henry."

"Hello," Lily managed to say.

Meeting her wan smile with an interested gaze, the boy wasted no time with small talk. "Why were you kissing Viscount Stamford if you're going to marry Alex?"

"Oh, I'm not *that* Miss Lawson," Lily replied hastily. "You're referring to my poor . . . that is, to my younger sister." Realizing she was still on Zachary's lap, she leapt away and nearly fell on the floor. "Penny and Mother are in the music room," she said to Alex. "Singing hymns."

Alex gave a curt nod. "Come, Henry," he said flatly. "I'll introduce you to Penelope."

Appearing not to hear him, Henry wandered over to Lily, who was straightening her gown. "Why is your hair chopped like that?" he asked.

Lily laughed at the description of her fashionable style. "It got in the way, hanging in my eyes when I went hunting and shooting."

"Do you hunt?" Henry stared at her in fascination. "It's dangerous for women, you know."

Lily glanced at Raiford and found he was staring at her. She couldn't prevent a teasing grin. "Why Henry, your brother said the same thing to me when we first met." Their gazes held. Suddenly there was a betraying tug at the corner of Alex's mouth, as if he were holding back a wry smile. "My lord," Lily said impishly, "don't worry that I'll be a bad influence on Henry. I'm much more of a danger to older men than to younger ones."

Alex rolled his eyes. "I believe you, Miss Lawson." Ushering Henry from the room, he left without a backward glance.

Lily did not move. She was flooded with confusion, her heart thumping irregularly. The look of him all tired and disheveled, the protective hand he had placed on his small brother's shoulder . . . all of it had made her feel strange. She was not the kind of woman who would fuss over a man, and yet she had a sudden wish that someone would smooth his hair, order a light supper for him, and make him confess what had put the troubled look in his eyes.

"Lily," Zachary questioned, "do you think he believed our kiss was genuine?"

"I'm certain he did," she replied automatically. "Why wouldn't he?"

"He's a very perceptive man."

"I'm getting bloody tired of the way everyone overestimates him," Lily said. Immediately she was sorry for sounding so sharp. It was just that she was astonished by the image that had come to mind. Her wilful imagination had conjured a picture of herself embracing Raiford, feeling his hard mouth against hers, his blond hair underneath her hands. The idea made her stomach tighten. Unconsciously she raised a hand to soothe the prickling on the back of her neck. She had been held by him only once, when she had fallen during the Middleton hunt and Raiford had picked her up and nearly strangled her. The power in his hands and the violence in his face had frightened her.

She doubted he had ever shown that side of himself to Caroline Whitmore.

Lily was immensely curious about the mysterious Caroline. Had she loved Raiford, or had she agreed to marry him because of his inordinate wealth? Or perhaps his aristocratic lineage . . . Lily had heard that Americans were quite impressed with titles and blue blood.

And what had Raiford been like around

Caroline? Was it possible he had been warm and smiling? Had Caroline made him happy?

The unanswered questions annoyed Lily. She rebuked herself silently. It didn't matter what Raiford's lost love had been like. All that was important was that she rescue Penelope from him.

Alex bid the tutor good-bye and sighed as the man left. The man, a Mr. Hotchkins, was the fourth he had interviewed for the position of Henry's tutor. So far none of them had been satisfactory. He guessed that it would take some time before he found a tutor with the right balance of discipline and understanding to suit Henry's needs. Between that and the meetings he had held for the last few days with irate tenants, Alex had been busy. The tenants were angry because of the damage done to their crops by an abundance of marauding hares and rabbits. At the same time, his gamekeeper had informed him with some distress that the amount of poaching had increased considerably. "'Tisn't bad that they poach t' rabbits, sir," the gamekeeper said. "But they's trappin' an' poachin' at night, an' they's interferin' with the pheasants breed'n. There willnae be pheasant to shoot this year!"

Alex resolved the problem by offering to compensate the tenants for their damaged crops if they would restrict their illegal poaching—which they refused to admit doing in the first place. In the meanwhile, he'd had meetings with some of the district agents for his Buckinghamshire property, discussing their rent collecting and other aspects of estate management.

"You should appoint a full-time steward," Lily had remarked to him after eavesdropping on some of the discussions. "Other men of your position do."

"I know how to manage my own affairs," Alex said brusquely.

"Of course." Lily had given him a flippant smile. "You prefer to do everything yourself. You'd probably like to go and personally collect rent from each of your tenants, if you could but find the time. I'm rather amazed you don't sweep and polish the floors in the mansion and knead the bread dough in the kitchen—why appoint a servant to do it, when you're perfectly able?"

Alex had snapped at her to mind her own business, and she had called him a medieval tyrant.

Privately, he had considered her point. Much of the work he did could be handled just as well by subordinates. But what if he did manage to make more time for himself; what would he do? Spend it with Penelope? Although they were perfectly civil to each other, he and Penelope found no great enjoyment in each other's company.

There were the options of gaming, hunting, parties, and politics in London. It all seemed a great bore. Alex supposed he could renew some old friendships. In the past two years he had avoided the company of his closest acquaintances, especially those who had known Caroline and expressed sympathy over her death. Alex hadn't been able to stand the pity in their eyes.

Frustrated, moody, Alex went to visit Penelope, who clung to her mother like a shadow. He tried to converse with them, drinking a cup of the tepid tea they offered. Shyly Penelope glanced at him while she did embroidery-work on a tambour frame, drawing colored silk through fabric using a delicate hook. She looked maidenly and refined as her soft hands moved deftly over the white muslin. After a few minutes in the cloying atmosphere, he escaped with a mutter about needing to do more work.

The sound of laughter and shuffling cards echoed from the long gallery. Curiously he went to investigate. Alex's first thought was that Henry had a friend visiting. Two small figures were sitting cross-legged on the polished floor, playing cards. One of them was clearly Henry's square-shouldered form. But the other . . . the other . . . Alex scowled as he recognized her. Not only was Lily dressed in her raspberry breeches, she had borrowed one of Henry's shirts and vests. Purposefully Alex strode to the gallery, intending to upbraid her for the wildly inappropriate attire. As he reached them, his eyes flickered over Lily, and he swallowed hard. The way she was sitting, the breeches were stretched tautly over her thighs and knees, showing the slim shape of her legs.

God help him, she was the most distracting

woman he had ever met. In his time he had known many seductive females, had seen them dressed and undressed, in sumptuous evening gowns and in gauzy wisps of nothing, naked in the bath, in French silk undergarments tied with narrow ribbons. But nothing had ever tantalized like the sight of Lily Lawson in breeches.

Alex felt his color deepening, his body tightening, filling with arousal. Desperately he struggled to bring an image of Penelope to mind. When that failed, he searched deeper for a memory of Caroline. But he couldn't see Caroline's face . . . hell, he could barely remember it . . . there were only the points of Lily's knees, the top of her curly dark head, the nimble movements of her fingers as she fanned a deck of cards. It was a battle to keep his breathing regular. For the first time he couldn't recall the exact sound of Caroline's voice or the shape of her face . . . it was all drowned in a soft haze. His traitorous senses were drawn to Lily, whose vibrant beauty was the focus of all the light in the gallery.

Lily acknowledged Alex with a brief glance. Her shoulders tensed as she waited for some negative remark. When none was forthcoming, she continued her demonstration. Expertly she cut and riffled the cards. "Now look, Henry," she said. "Just push this group of cards straight through the other group . . . and they come out the same as before . . . and you see? The ace is still on the bottom."

Henry laughed and took the deck to practice the maneuver.

Alex watched the boy finger the cards. "Do you know what they do to card cheats?" he asked.

"Only to bad ones," Lily replied, before the boy could reply. "Good ones are never caught." She indicated a space on the floor next to them, as graciously as a lady offering a chair in an elegant parlor. "Care to join us, my lord? I'll have you know I'm breaking one of my strictest rules by teaching your brother my best tricks."

Alex lowered himself to the floor beside her. "Should I be grateful?" he asked dryly. "Turning my brother into a cheat . . ."

Lily grinned at him. "Certainly not. I merely want this poor lad to be aware of the ways in which other people could take advantage of him."

Henry exclaimed in self-disgust as his fingers slipped and the cards scattered over the floor.

"That's all right," Lily said, leaning over to scoop up the cards. "Practice, Henry. You'll have it in no time."

Alex couldn't stop himself from staring at Lily's neatly rounded bottom as she industriously collected the scattered deck. A new flood of response went through him, turning the surface of his skin hot. He pulled the edges of his coat together over his lap. He should get to his feet and walk away this very instant. But instead he stayed in the sunlit gallery, sitting on the floor near the most maddening woman he had ever known.

Henry shuffled the cards together. "What about my tutor, Alex?"

Alex dragged his attention from Lily. "I haven't found anyone suitable yet."

"Good," the boy said emphatically. "The last one looked like a frig-pig."

Alex frowned. "A what?"

Lily leaned toward Henry conspiratorially. "Henry, don't use the new words Auntie Lily taught you until Alex is gone."

Without thinking, Alex caught hold of Lily's slim upper arm. "Miss Lawson, you're aptly demonstrating all the reasons I didn't want you near him." Startled by his touch, Lily glanced at him quickly, expecting a cold frown. Instead she saw a rueful, boyish smile that caused her heart to give an extra little thump. How odd, that making him smile would give her such a sense of accomplishment. Her brown eyes laughed into his, and she directed another comment to Henry.

"Do you know why your brother hasn't found a tutor yet? He won't be satisfied until he's hired Galileo, Shakespeare, and Plato, all rolled into one. I do pity you, my boy."

Henry screwed his face into an appalled grimace. "Alex, tell her it's not true!"

"I have certain standards," Alex admitted, dropping his hand from Lily's arm. "Finding a qualified tutor is taking more time than I anticipated,"

"Why don't you let Henry choose?" Lily suggested. "You could attend to your other business while he conducts the interviews. Then he would present his choice for your approval."

Alex snorted sardonically. "I'd like to see what kind of tutor Henry would choose."

"I believe he would be quite responsible in his decision. Besides, it's going to be *his* tutor. I think he should have some say in it."

Henry appeared to consider the question thoughtfully. His blue eyes met Alex's. "I'd pick a smashing one, Alex, damn me if I wouldn't."

The idea was unorthodox. On the other hand, the responsibility might be good for Henry. He supposed there would be no harm in trying it. "I'll consider it," Alex said gruffly. "But the ultimate approval will be mine."

"Well," Lily said in satisfaction. "It appears you can be reasonable at times." She took the cards from the boy, shuffled them deftly, and placed the deck on the floor. "Would you care to cut, my lord?"

Alex stared at her intently. He wondered if this was how she looked in Craven's club, her brown eyes gleaming with a mischievous invitation, her slim hand pushing back the curls that dangled on her forehead. She would never be a demure, proper wife to anyone. She would be an engaging playmate with the wiles of a courtesan, a combination of gambling sharp and hellcat . . . she was a hundred different things, none of which he needed. "What's the game?" he asked.

"I'm instructing Henry on the finer points of

vingt-et-un." A challenging grin appeared on her lovely face. "Do you consider yourself competent at the game, Raiford?"

Slowly he reached for the deck and cut it. "Deal."

CHAPTER 5

Lily discovered with consternation that Raiford was adept at cards. More than adept. In order to beat him, it was necessary for her to cheat. She used the pretext of giving further instructions to Henry in order to peek surreptitiously at the top card of the deck. Occasionally she dealt seconds, or from the bottom. Once or twice she used special shuffling to stack the deck, something she had learned from Derek after hours of practice in front of a mirror. If Raiford was suspicious he kept his silence . . . that was, until the game was nearly over.

"Now this," Lily said to Henry during the last hand, "is a two-way hand, in which the ace could either be valued at one or eleven. Your best strategy is to try for a high count. If that doesn't work, value the ace at one."

Following her directions, Henry flipped a card and grinned in satisfaction. "Twenty," he said. "No one can beat that."

"Unless," Alex remarked dryly, "Miss Lawson somehow produces a natural."

Warily Lily glanced at him, wondering if he had

caught on to her cheating. He must have. There could be no other explanation for his resigned expression. With a few flicks of her fingers, the last card was dealt and the game concluded. "Henry wins that hand," she said cheerfully. "Next time we'll play for money, Henry."

"Not a chance in hell," Alex said.

Lily laughed. "Don't get in a foam about it, Raiford. I only intended to wager a shilling or two, not bilk the poor boy out of his inheritance."

Henry stood up and stretched with a faint groan. "Next time let's play at a table, sitting on chairs," he suggested. "This floor is bloody hard!"

Alex looked at him with immediate concern. "How are you?"

"I'm fine." Henry smiled as he understood Alex's worry. "It's fine, Alex. Really."

Alex nodded, but Lily noticed the same troubled expression in his pale eyes that had been there the night before. It remained even after Henry left with a rather stiff gait. "What is it?" Lily asked. "Why did you ask Henry—"

"Miss Lawson," Alex interrupted, rising to his feet and reaching down for her. "I've never seen a woman cheat with such skill."

She was momentarily diverted. "Years of practice," she admitted modestly.

Suddenly Alex grinned, amused by her complete lack of shame. His white teeth flashed in his golden face. Taking her small hand in his, he pulled her to her feet. He slid a quick glance down her slim body. "I suppose it was necessary for you to win against a twelve-year-old boy?"

"That wasn't my purpose. *You* were the one I wanted to beat."

"Why?"

That was a good question. It shouldn't have mattered whether she won or lost a game with him. Uncomfortably Lily returned his silvery stare, heartily wishing she could stay indifferent to him. "It just seemed the thing to do."

"It might be interesting to try an honest game someday," he remarked. "If you're capable of it."

"Let's play at honesty right now, my lord. The loser must answer any question the winner poses." Deftly she cast two cards on the floor, one coming to rest faceup at his feet. A seven. The other card settled in front of her. A queen.

Alex surveyed Lily's down-bent head as she glanced at the cards. She was standing close to him. Suddenly he imagined clasping her head in his hands, dipping his face down to crush his mouth and nose into her sable curls, breathing in her perfume, her skin . . . he imagined sinking to his knees, pulling her hips forward until he was lost in the warmth of her body. Feeling himself begin to flush and tauten, he tried to banish the forbidden image from his mind. He struggled for self-discipline. When she looked up at him, he was certain she would be able to recognize the shameful turn of his thoughts. Strangely, she seemed to notice nothing.

"Another?" Lily asked. He nodded. She took the top card from the deck with exaggerated care and dropped it to the floor. A ten.

"Stay," he said.

With a flourish Lily drew the next card for herself, and grinned as she saw it was a nine. "I win, Raiford. Now tell me why you looked so worried for Henry just now—no, tell me why you brought him home from school. Was it his marks? Is he having—"

"That's three questions so far," Alex interrupted sardonically. "And before I answer, I want to know why you're so interested."

"I like the boy," Lily replied with dignity. "I'm asking out of sincere concern."

He considered that. It was possible she was telling the truth. She and Henry did seem to get along well together. "It wasn't his marks," he said brusquely. "Henry was in some trouble. Tardiness, mischief, the usual things. The headmaster 'disciplined' him . . ." Alex's jaw hardened.

"Flogging?" Lily stared at his averted face. His features were especially harsh at that angle, giving him the appearance of a golden satyr. "That's why he walks so stiffly at times. It was bad, wasn't it?"

"Yes, it was bad." His voice was gruff. "I wanted to kill Thornwait. I still do."

"The headmaster?" In spite of her loathing of anyone who could commit such cruelty against a child, Lily almost pitied the man. She suspected Thornwait would not get off lightly for what he'd done.

"Henry retaliated by lighting a pile of gunpowder underneath Thornwait's front door," Alex continued.

Lily laughed at that. "I would have expected no less of him!" Her amusement died quickly as she studied Alex's implacable face. "But you're disturbed about something else . . . it must be . . . that Henry didn't tell you about what had been happening?" She read the answer in his silence.

All at once she understood. Alex, with his unreasonable sense of responsibility for everyone and everything, would take all the blame upon himself. Obviously he doted on the boy. This would be the perfect opportunity for her to twist the knife and make him feel worse than he already did. Instead she found herself trying to ease his guilt.

"I'm not surprised," she said matter-of-factly. "Most boys of Henry's age are extremely proud, you know. Don't try to claim that you weren't when you were young. Of course Henry would try to handle things himself. He wouldn't want to run to you like a child. From what I've observed, that is the way boys think."

"What would you know about boys?" he muttered.

She gave him a chiding glance. "It's not your fault, Raiford, much as you'd like to shoulder the blame. You have too much of a conscience—it nearly matches the size of your ego."

"What I need is a lecture from *you* about conscience," he said caustically. But he looked at her without the usual animosity, and the pale gray depths of his eyes caused a strange feeling to ripple through her. "Miss Lawson . . ." He gestured to the deck she held. "Would you care to play another hand of truth?"

"Why?" Smiling, Lily flipped another couple of cards to the floor. "What question would you like to ask, my lord?"

He continued to stare at her. Lily had the startling feeling that even though they were standing apart, he was touching her. He wasn't, of course, but still she had the suffocated sensation that plucked notes of warning in her memory . . . yes, she had felt this way with Giuseppe . . . threatened . . . dominated.

Alex ignored the pretext of the cards, the game, and watched her intently. "Why do you hate men?"

He couldn't stop himself from asking. The curiosity had built with every word he had heard her speak, every wary glance she had given him, her father, even Zachary. She kept a distance between herself and every man that came near. With Henry, however, Lily was different. Alex could only surmise that Henry was too young for Lily to consider a threat. His instincts told him that Lily had been taken advantage of in the past, often enough that she had come to regard men as enemies to be used and manipulated.

"Why do I . . ." Lily's voice drifted into shocked silence. Only Derek had ever been able to disarm her so completely with a few words. Why would he ask such a thing? Certainly he had no personal interest in her feelings. He must have asked because he had sensed somehow that it would hurt her, the bastard.

And he was right . . . she *did* hate men, although she had never before put it into words, spoken or otherwise. What should she find so frigging wonderful about them? Her father had ignored her, her fiancé had jilted her, Giuseppe had abused her hard-won trust. Men had taken her child. Even her friendship with Derek, such as it was, had started as blackmail. Devil take the lot of them!

"I've had enough of games this afternoon," she said, and dropped the deck, letting it scatter. Turning quickly, she left the gallery. She heard Alex's footsteps behind her. He reached her in three long strides.

"Miss Lawson—" He caught at her arm.

She whirled around, violently flinging off his hand. "Don't touch me," she hissed. "Don't ever touch me again!"

"All right," he said quietly. "Calm yourself. I had no right to ask."

"Is that some sort of apology?" Her chest heaved with the force of her anger.

"Yes." Alex hadn't expected to hit a raw nerve with his question. Even now Lily was struggling to control herself. Usually she was so brashly confident. For the first time she seemed fragile to him, a volatile woman living with some terrible strain. "It was uncalled for."

"Bloody right about that!" Lily raked her hand through her hair until the curls fell in a wild tangle over her forehead. Her searing eyes locked onto his unreadable face. She couldn't seem to hold back a tumble of accusing words. "But here's your damned answer. I have yet to meet a man worthy of trust. I've never known a so-called gentleman with the slightest understanding of honesty or compassion. You all like to bray about your honor, when the truth is—" Abruptly she closed her mouth.

"When the truth is . . ." Alex repeated, wanting her to finish. He wanted to know at least this one small part of the complexity. God, it would take at least a lifetime to understand her.

Lily gave a small, determined shake of her head. The forceful emotions seemed to drain away magically, by a self-will that Alex suddenly understood was an equal match for his own. She regarded him with an insolent smile. "Bugger off, my lord," she said lightly, and left him there in the gallery strewn with scattered cards.

Something about that morning started a piercing ache in Lily's head that wouldn't go away. She spent the day in Totty and Penelope's company, half-listening to their ladylike conversation. In the evening she excused herself from supper and nibbled on cold beef and bread from a tray in her room. After downing two glasses of red wine, she changed for bed and lay down to rest. The silk damask bedhangings draped down from a circle overhead, shrouding her in shadow. Restlessly she changed position, shifting to her stomach and curving her arms around the pillow beneath her. Loneliness filled her chest with a cold, heavy weight.

She wanted someone to talk to. She wanted to unburden herself. She needed Aunt Sally, the only one who had known about Nicole. With her salty wisdom and unorthodox sense of humor, Sally had been able to handle any predicament. She had assisted the midwife at Nicole's birth and had taken care of Lily as tenderly as a mother.

"Sally, I want my baby," Lily whispered. "If only you were here, you'd help me figure out what to do. The money's all gone. I have no one. I'm becoming desperate. What am I going to do? What?"

She remembered going to Sally and confessing in a storm of misery and shame that she had taken a lover, and from that one night of illicit passion a child had been conceived. At the time she had thought that was the worst that could happen to her. Sally had comforted her with common sense. "Have you considered giving the babe away?" Sally had asked. "Paying someone else to rear it?"

"No, I wouldn't do that," Lily had replied tearfully. "The baby is innocent. He—or she—doesn't deserve to pay for my sins."

"Then if you plan to keep the child, we'll live quietly together in Italy," Sally's eyes had been bright with anticipation. "We'll be a family."

"But I couldn't ask that of you—"

"You didn't. I offered. Look at me, Lily. I'm a rich old woman who can do as she pleases. I have enough money to suit our needs. We won't give a fig for the rest of the world and its hypocrisy."

To Lily's sorrow, Sally had died soon after the baby was born. Lily had missed her, but she had found solace in her baby daughter. Nicole was the center of her world, filing every day with love and wonder. As long as she had Nicole, everything was all right.

Lily felt tears seep from her eyes, the pillow absorbing the hot moisture. The ache in her head spread to her throat as she began to cry silently. She had never broken down in front of anyone, not even Derek. Something about Derek wouldn't allow her to be vulnerable. Derek had seen too much suffering in his lifetime. If he once might have been moved to sympathy by a woman's tears, that ability had left him long ago. Miserably Lily wondered who was with Nicole. And who, if anyone, comforted her when she cried.

Alex stirred and groaned in his sleep, caught in the grip of a tormenting dream. Somehow he knew it wasn't really happening, but he couldn't wake up. He sank deeper into a world of mist and shadow and movement. Lily was there. Her mocking laugh echoed all around him. Her gleaming brown eyes stared into his. With a smile of wicked amusement, she held his gaze as she lowered her mouth to his shoulder and lightly bit at his skin. He snarled and tried to push her away, but suddenly her naked body was entwined with his. His mind swam with the sensation of her silky limbs sliding over him. "Show me what you want, Alex," she whispered with a knowing smile.

"Get away from me," he said hoarsely, but she didn't listen, only laughed softly, and then he grasped her head in his hands and pushed it down to where he wanted her mouth . . . there . . .

Alex awoke with a violent start, breathing in rough, unsteady gasps. He dragged his arm over his forehead. The roots of his hair were damp with sweat. His body was aching with arousal. Swearing in a guttural tone of frustration, he took a pillow, strangled and twisted it and threw it across the room. He wanted a woman. He'd never been so desperate. Trying to ignore his hammering pulse, Alex cast his mind back to when he'd last slept with a woman. Not since before his betrothal to Penelope. He felt he owed her his fidelity. He'd thought a few months of celibacy wouldn't kill him. Idiot, he told himself savagely. *Idiot.*

He had to do something. He could go to Penelope's room right now. She wouldn't like it. She would protest and cry, but Alex knew he could bend her to his will. He could bully her into allowing him into her bed. After all, they would be married in a matter of weeks.

The idea made sense. At least, it did to a man

who was dying of frustration. But the thought of making love to Penelope . . .

His mind recoiled from the notion.

It would bring him some measure of relief, of course.

No. That wasn't what he wanted. *She* wasn't what he wanted.

What the hell is wrong with you? Alex asked himself savagely, and leapt from his bed. He yanked the window hangings aside to allow the gleam of moonlight in the room. Striding to the washbasin set on a tripod stand, he poured some cool water and splashed it on his face. His thoughts had been muddled for days, ever since he'd met Lily. If only he could ease the fire inside him. If only he could think clearly.

He needed a drink. Cognac. No, some of the good Highland whiskey his father had always stocked, distinctively pale, tasting of smoke and heather. He wanted something that would set his throat on fire, burn out the thoughts that were torturing him. Pulling on a quilted blue robe, Alex strode from the bedroom. He went through the columned hall that connected the east wing to the grand central staircase.

His steps slowed as he heard the betraying *creak* of one of the steps. He stopped and tilted his head, waiting in the darkness. *Creak.* There it was again. Someone was descending the stairs. He knew exactly who it was.

A grim smile crossed his face. Now was his

opportunity to catch Lily in a clandestine meeting with one of the servants. He would use the excuse to throw her out of the house. With Lily gone, things would return to the way they had been before.

Stealthily Alex made his way to the side of the balustraded corridor. He caught a glimpse of Lily below in the domed central hall. The hem of her thin white nightgown trailed gently behind her as she drifted across the marble floor. She was going to meet a lover. Gracefully she wandered in what seemed to be a mood of dreamy anticipation. Alex was conscious of a bitter sensation seeping through him like poison. He tried to identify the feeling, but its precise nature was obscured in a mixture of anger and confusion. The thought of what Lily was about to do with another man made him want to punish her.

Alex went to the staircase and froze.

What was he doing? The earl of Raiford, renowned for his moderate, sensible ways, sneaking around his own house in the dark. Nearly wild with jealousy—yes, *jealousy*—over the antics of a little madcap and her midnight trysts.

How Caroline would have laughed.

To hell with Caroline. To hell with everything. He was going to stop Lily. He'd be damned if she was going to have her pleasure tonight. Purposefully he descended the stairs, and fumbled at the small porcelain and wood table in the entrance hall, where a lamp was always kept.

Lighting the lamp, he turned it to a soft glow. He ventured in the direction Lily had gone, toward the groundfloor kitchen. As he passed the library, the sound of whispers floated through the door, which had been left ajar. Alex's brows lowered in fury as he heard Lily murmuring something that sounded like "*Nick . . . Nick . . .*"

Alex flung the library door open wide. "What's going on?" His gaze swept the room. All he could see was Lily's small form curled in a chair. She had wrapped her arms around herself. "Miss Lawson?" He walked closer. The lamplight gleamed in Lily's eyes and cast a golden shimmer on her skin, and revealed the shadows of her body beneath the gown. She was twitching and rocking, her lips forming silent words. There were furrows in her forehead, lines that seemed to have been carved from intense misery.

A sneer pulled at the corner of Alex's mouth. She must have realized he was following her. "You little fraud," he muttered. "This playacting is beneath even you."

She pretended not to hear him. Her eyes were half-closed, as if she were caught in a mysterious trance.

"That's enough," Alex said, and set the lamp on a nearby table. With rising annoyance he realized that she intended to ignore him until he left her. "I'll drag you out of here if necessary, Miss Lawson. Is that what you're hoping for? A scene?" As she refused to even look at him, his endurance snapped. He seized her narrow shoulders, giving her a hard shake. "I said that's *enough*—"

There was an explosion of movement that astonished Alex. Lily gave an animal cry and struck out blindly, springing from the chair. She stumbled back against the table and nearly overturned the lamp. In a quick reflex Alex kept her from falling as he reached out and grabbed her. Even then her panic didn't cease. Alex jerked his head back to avoid the frantic swipe of fingers curled into claws. Although she was a small woman, her wild struggles were difficult to contain. Somehow he managed to crowd her against him, crushing her flailing arms between them. She flinched and went rigid, breathing in rapid pants. Alex slid his fingers through her thick curls and forced her head against his shoulder. He muttered a string of curses and tried to soothe her. "Christ. Lily, it's all right. *Lily*. Relax . . . relax."

The heat of his breath sank through her hair to her scalp. He kept his hold on her tight enough that only the slightest movement was possible. She was too disoriented to speak coherently. He tucked her head under his chin and began to rock her gently. "It's me," he murmured. "It's Alex. Everything's all right. Easy."

Lily regained herself slowly, as if she were waking from a dream. The first thing she became aware of was being held in an inexorable grip. Her cheek and chin were pressed against the opening of a quilted robe, where the brush of wiry hair tickled her skin. A pleasant, masculine scent stirred her memory. It was Raiford, holding her in his arms. Her breath caught in amazement.

His hand moved in a slow stroke on her back. She wasn't used to being touched so familiarly, not by anyone. Her first instinct was to wrench away from him. But the circling motion was gentle, softening the brittle tension of her body

Alex felt the shift of Lily's weight as she accepted his support. She was light and lithe against him, her small frame trembling with aftershocks. There was a tugging, twisting sensation inside him, alarming in its sweetness. The pronounced silence of the room seemed to enclose them.

"Raiford?"

"Easy. You're not steady yet."

"Wh-what happened?" she croaked.

"I forgot the old maxim," he said dryly. "Something about waking a sleepwalker."

So he had found out. Oh God, what would happen now? She must have betrayed her fear, for he began to rub her back again, as if she were an overwrought child. "This is what happened the other nights, isn't it?" His palm moved down the delicate ridge of her spine. "You should have told me."

"And give you the idea to put me in some as-asylum?" she replied shakily, making a move to push herself away.

"Be still. You've had a shock."

She had never heard his voice so gentle . . . it

didn't seem to be his voice at all. Lily blinked in confusion. She had never been held like this before. Giuseppe, with all his impetuous passion, hadn't even held her this long during their love-making. She felt uneasy, helpless. The situation was beyond her imagination. Lord Raiford, clad in a robe, no starch, buttons, or cravats anywhere in sight. The chest under her head was like the timbered side of a frigate ship, while his muscled legs were impossibly hard against hers. The beat of his heart resonated in her ear. What would it feel like to be so invincible? He must not be afraid of anyone.

"Do you want a drink?" Alex asked quietly. He had to let go of her. Either that or sink to the floor with her. He was hovering on the brink of disaster.

She nodded against his chest. "Brandy." Somehow she mustered the strength to pull away from him. She lowered herself into a leather armchair, while Alex went to the corner cupboard where the liquor was kept. He poured a small amount of cognac into a glass. In the light of the lamp, his hair shone with the gold luster of a doubloon. As she watched him, Lily bit at her lower lip. So far she had known him as a arrogant, judgmental figure, the last man in the world she would accept help from. But for one astonishing moment she had felt all his strength surround her. She had felt safe and protected.

He was her enemy, she reminded herself silently

as he approached. She must remember that, she *must* remember . . .

"Here." Alex pressed the glass into her hands and sat nearby.

Lily sipped at the drink. The brandy had a light taste, unlike the fruitier distillations Derek always stocked. The mellow liquor had a steadying effect on her. Lily drank slowly and glanced at Alex, who hadn't moved his gaze from her. She couldn't quite work up the courage to ask if he intended to tell anyone what had happened.

He seemed to read her thoughts. "Does anyone else know?"

"Know about what?" she parried.

His mouth tightened impatiently. "Does it happen often?"

Staring into the brandy glass, she swirled it in feigned absorption.

"You're going to talk to me, Lily," he said grimly.

"You may call me Miss Lawson," she shot back. "And while I'm certain you're quite curious about my nocturnal habits, it's none of your concern."

"Do you understand that you could hurt yourself? Or someone else? Just now you nearly knocked the lamp over and started a fire—"

"That was because you startled me!"

"How long has this been going on?"

Lily rose to her feet and glared at him. "Good night, my lord."

"Sit down. You're not leaving until you give me some answers."

"You may sit here as long as you wish. I'm going upstairs to my room." She walked toward the door.

Alex reached her instantly, spinning her to face him. "I'm not through with you yet."

"Take your hands off me!"

"Who's Nick?" Alex knew he had hit a vulnerable spot when he saw her eyes widen to dark pools of fear. "Nick," he repeated in a low jeer. "Some man you're keeping company with? A lover? Does your *cher ami* Craven know about Nick, or have you—"

With a muffled sound Lily threw the brandy into his face, anything to make him stop, anything to silence the stabbing words. "Don't say that name again!"

The brandy trickled down Alex's face in golden rivulets, bright drops sliding down the harsh grooves that were carved from his nose to his mouth. "Not only Craven, but a lover on the side," he sneered. "I suppose a woman like you would think nothing of crawling from one man's bed to another's."

"How dare you accuse me! At least I confine my infidelities to the living!"

His face went pale while Lily continued recklessly. "You're planning to marry my sister, even though you're still in love with Caroline Whitmore. A woman who died years ago! It's morbid, not to mention unfair to Penelope, and you know it. What kind of husband will you be to my sister, you *obstinate* brute, when you'll insist on living in the past for the rest of . . ."

Lily stopped as she realized she'd gone too far. Alex's face looked like a death mask. Once she had read a few lines that would have described him perfectly . . . *More fierce and more inexorable far, than empty tigers or the roaring sea . . .* His eyes bored into hers with an intensity that terrified her. He was going to kill her. The brandy glass dropped from her nerveless hand and fell to the thick Savonnerie carpet with a thump. The sound broke Lily's paralysis. She turned to flee, but it was too late, Alex had caught her. There was nothing she could do but writhe helplessly as he jerked her head back.

"No," she whimpered, thinking he might break her neck.

Instead his mouth came down hard on hers, his fingers gripping her nape to hold her still. Lily stiffened in surprise and pain. Her lips were ground against her teeth until the taste of blood mingled with brandy. There was no way to break free. She closed her eyes and clenched her teeth.

Suddenly Alex lifted his head with a groan. His gray eyes were hot and radiant, his tanned skin burnished with rising color. One by one his fingers unclenched from her nape. Almost tentatively, he moved his thumb over her bruised lip.

"You bloody bastard" Lily cried, childishly spiteful. She writhed as he bent his head again. "No—"

He took her lips in a savage movement, sealing off all sound and breath, suffocating her until she inhaled deeply through her nostrils. She made a move to free herself, but Alex gathered her close, tight, his hand sliding down her back and molding her hips to his. He shaped her mouth with bites and nudges, and sought the silkiness inside, his tongue delving in hot surges. Helplessly she shoved at his powerful body, dislodging the blue robe from his shoulder. Her palm came against the hair-roughened surface of his chest. Underneath her fingers, a driving pulse seemed to burn through her hand. He made a sound in his throat and cupped his hands around her head, holding her steady for the deep push of his tongue. His breath rushed hotly against her cheek.

Only half-conscious of what he was doing, Alex moved down to her throat, rubbing his mouth over her skin. His body was shaking with passion. The past years of loneliness seemed to melt away into nothing more than a dark dream. Feverishly he buried his lips against her soft shoulder. "I won't hurt you," he muttered, his breath burning through her gown. "No, don't pull away . . . Caro . . ."

The syllables fell so softly on her ears that it took Lily several seconds to realize what he'd said. She froze.

"*Let go*," she spat.

Abruptly she was set free. Her dazed eyes flew to his face. Alex looked as confounded as she was. They each backed away a step. Lily shuddered, crossing her arms over her chest.

Alex passed an unsteady hand over his jaw, wiping away the moist traces of brandy. Aroused and ashamed, he fought the urge to reach for her once more. "Lily."

She spoke rapidly, not meeting his eyes. "It was my fault—"

"Lily—"

"*No.*" She didn't know what he intended to say, she just knew that she couldn't listen. It would be disastrous. "This didn't happen. None of it. I . . . I . . . good night." She disappeared from the room in a flurry of panic.

Alex shook his head to clear the red mist of passion, and made his way to the chair. He sat down heavily. Finding his hands were clenched, he opened them and stared into his empty palms.

Caroline, what have I done?

You poor fool, he could almost hear Caroline's laughing voice say. *You thought you could hold on to me forever. You planned to marry a sweet innocent like Penelope, and then you would never have to let me go. As if the memories would always be enough for you.*

"The memories *are* enough," he said stubbornly.

Why have you always considered yourself above ordinary human weakness? Above grief and loneliness. You think you need less than other men, when the truth is you need more, much more . . .

"Stop it," he groaned, clasping his head in his hands, but Caroline's mocking shadow-voice persisted.

You've been alone for so long, Alex. It's time to go on . . .

"I am going on," he said raggedly. "I'll make a new beginning with Penelope. God help me, I'll learn to care for her, I'll make myself—"

Alex stopped suddenly, realizing he was talking to himself like some poor mad fool, holding an imaginary conversation with a ghost. He lifted his head and stared unseeing into the empty fireplace. He had to get rid of Lily, if only to preserve his own sanity.

Lily crawled into bed and pulled the covers high under her neck. She couldn't stop shivering.

How could she face Raiford after this? She could feel herself turning scarlet, even in the darkness of her room. How could he have done that to her? What was the matter with her? Grinding her hot face into the pillow, she remembered his mouth against hers, his arms locked around her body.

He had whispered Caroline's name.

Humiliated, strangely hurt, Lily rolled over and groaned. She had to settle things between Zachary and Penelope and leave Raiford Park as soon as possible. She couldn't manage Raiford as she did other men, using her sarcasm, temper, or charm. He was impervious to those things, just as Derek was.

She was beginning to understand some of what Raiford concealed behind that implacable face. From his reaction to her mention of Caroline, she knew he had never come to terms with her death.

159

He never would. All his love had been given to Caroline—she'd taken it to the grave with her. For the rest of his days Raiford would be haunted by her. He would resent every woman for not being Caroline. An innocent like Penelope would spend her life trying to please him, and find only misery in the effort.

"Oh, Penny," she whispered. "I must get you away from him. He'll grind you into dust, without even meaning to."

Contrary to his expectations, Zachary was not announced to Lily upon his arrival at Raiford Park. Instead he was shown to the library, where the earl of Raiford awaited him alone. "Raiford?" Zachary questioned, shocked by his appearance.

Alex was sprawled in a chair, his thighs spread wide. A half-drained liquor bottle was balanced on his knee. The golden copper of his skin was pallid. Dark circles rimmed his eyes. Hard, bitter lines were etched on his face. The smell of whiskey was rank in the air, as was the acrid odor of tobacco. He was smoking heavily, and had been for some time, if the thick haze in the room was anything to judge by. His fingers were curled loosely around a cigar. Zachary doubted that many people had ever seen Raiford in such a condition. Some terrible misfortune must have befallen him.

"I-is something wrong?"

"Not at all," Alex said brusquely. "Why do you ask?"

Hastily Zachary shook his head and cleared his throat a few times. "*Ahem.* No reason. I thought perhaps . . . *ahem* . . . you look a little tired."

"I'm fine. As always."

"Yes, of course. *Ahem.* I'm here to see Lily, so perhaps I'll just—"

"Sit." Drunkenly Alex waved a hand toward a leather chair.

Zachary complied nervously. A shaft of morning sunlight came through the window and brightened his ash brown hair.

"Have a drink," Alex said, blowing out a stream of smoke.

Zachary squirmed. "Actually, I make a habit of avoiding strong drink until late afternoon—"

"So do I." Alex lifted the glass to his lips and took a sloshing swallow. He studied his companion with a calculating stare. They were contemporaries, Alex thought, and yet Zachary hardly looked older than his brother Henry. The telling daylight illuminated Zachary's boyish face—the clear skin and the brown eyes filled with youthful dreams and idealism. He was so damned suitable for Penelope. Anyone with a modicum of intelligence could see it.

Alex scowled. Caroline was gone. If the fates wouldn't allow him to have the woman he loved, he'd be damned if he'd let Zachary have Penelope. Alex's alcohol-soaked brain acknowledged that his attitude was selfish, cruel, pointlessly vengeful . . . but he didn't care. He didn't care about anything.

Except maybe one thing. One little thing that had been bothering him for some reason. "Who was Miss Lawson engaged to?" he demanded gruffly.

Zachary appeared to be confused by his abruptness. "You're referring to the . . . er, episode ten years ago? When Lily was engaged to Hindon?"

"Hindon who? Lord Hindon's son Harry?"

"Yes, Harry."

"That cocky little dandy who stares into every looking glass he passes by?" Alex gave a scornful laugh. "*That* was her great love? I should have guessed she'd pick someone with more vanity than intelligence. And he was a friend of yours?"

"At the time, yes," Zachary admitted. "Hindon had a certain charm—"

"What did she do to make him jilt her?"

Zachary lifted his shoulders in a defensive shrug. "It wasn't anything in particular."

"Oh, come," Alex sneered. "She must have deceived him in some way, or publicly humiliated him, or—"

"Actually, she did deceive him. Though it wasn't intentional. Lily was quite young back then, very eager and trusting. And naive. She fell in love with Hindon for his handsomeness, without realizing that he was a man of exceedingly shallow character. In order to attract Hindon, Lily concealed her intelligence and her strong will, charming him by acting like a featherbrain. I don't believe it was a conscious plan to deceive him. She just naturally

162

adopted the qualities that she sensed he would admire."

"But eventually Hindon discovered what she was really like."

"Yes, he began to realize it in the months after he had proposed to her. Hindon behaved with utter dishonor. He jilted her not long before the wedding. Lily was devastated. I offered for her instead, but she refused me. She said she was destined never to marry. Her aunt took her abroad for a number of years. They lived in Italy for a time."

Alex concentrated on his cigar, his golden lashes lowered, concealing his thoughts. When he spoke, his voice was quieter than before. "She must have cut quite a swath across the continent."

"No, she disappeared, actually. Years passed, and no one heard from her. Something happened to her in Italy, but she's never told a soul about it. All I'm certain of is that Lily came to some sort of grief there. When she reappeared in England two years ago, I could see how she had changed." Zachary frowned thoughtfully. "There's a sadness in her eyes that never leaves. She's a worldly, unique woman, with courage that few men could match."

Zachary said something else, but Alex didn't hear. He stared at the wholesome young man sitting across from him and remembered the sight of Lily kissing Zachary in the library. A blatant attempt to convince him they were lovers. Instead, the scene had demonstrated beyond a doubt that they shared nothing more than platonic friendship. While Lily had cuddled on Zachary's lap and kissed him, he had sat there passively, his arms held stiffly at his sides. Hardly the behavior of a man embracing the woman he loved. If he had been in Zachary's place . . .

Alex dismissed the forbidden thought and pinned Zachary with a brooding stare. "Lily's a cunning little actress. But not good enough."

"I say, you're quite off the mark! Lily is genuine in everything she says and does. It's clear you have no understanding of her."

"No, it's clear *you* don't. And you're similarly mistaken about me, Stamford, if you think I've been fooled by the infantile charade you and Miss Lawson have been putting on for my benefit."

"What? I don't understand—"

"You're not in love with Lily," Alex said sardonically. "How could you be? Oh, I'll grant you have some sort of liking for her. But you're also afraid of her."

"Afraid?" Zachary turned purple. "Of a woman not half my size?"

"Let's be frank, Stamford. You're a gentleman of the first water. You're incapable of hurting anyone, save to defend your principles. Lily, on the other hand, would do anything to get what she wants. Anything. She doesn't have principles, and doesn't respect them in others. You'd be a fool not to fear her. You're her friend one moment,

164

her pawn the next. Don't think I intend any insult to you. I feel a certain sympathy for you."

"Damn y-your sympathy!" Zachary spluttered.

"Penelope, on the other hand, is what every man dreams of. A girl with an appearance and bearing that are nothing short of angelic. You freely admit you were once in love with her . . ."

"Once, but no longer!"

"You don't lie well. Stamford." Alex crushed out his cigar and smiled cruelly. "Forget Penelope. Nothing is going to stop this marriage. I advise you to attend the first few balls of the season—there you can choose from dozens of girls just like her. Pretty, innocent girls, all eager to learn of the world and its temptations. For what you want, any one of them will suffice."

Zachary shot up from his chair. He looked as if he were torn between pleading with Alex or calling him out. "Lily once said much the same thing to me. Apparently neither of you are able to see what I do in Penelope. It's true she doesn't have much courage, but she is hardly some empty-headed doll! You're a selfish blackguard, Raiford! For what you've just said, I should—"

"Zachary," Lily's voice interrupted. She was standing in the doorway, looking calm and deter-mined. Her face was drawn, her eyes just as weary and smudged as Alex's. "No more," she said to Zachary with a faint smile. "It's time for you to leave. I'll take care of this."

"I'll fight my own battles—"

"Not this one, my dear." Lily indicated the door with a jerk of her head. "Listen to me, Zach. You must leave. Now."

Zachary strode to her and grasped her hands, turning his back on Alex. He looked down at her small face. "The plan has failed," he muttered. "I have to face him, Lily. I must finish this."

"No." She stood on her toes to put her arms around his shoulders. One dainty hand came to rest on the back of his neck. "Trust me," she whispered into his ear. "I swear on my life you'll have Penelope. But you must do as I say, darling. Go home. I'll take care of everything."

"How can you say that?" he whispered back in amazement. "How can you pretend such confidence? We've lost, Lily, we've utterly—"

"Trust me," she repeated, and stepped back from him.

Zachary turned to look at Raiford who was sprawled in the library chair like a debauched king on a throne. "How can you stand yourself?" he burst out. "Doesn't it matter to you that the woman you're about to marry is in love with someone else?"

Alex smiled mockingly. "You talk as if I held a gun to her head. Penelope accepted my suit of her own free will."

"There was nothing free about it! She had no choice in this marriage. It was all arranged without her—"

"Zachary," Lily interrupted.

166

With a mumbled curse, Zachary looked from her to Alex. Turning on his booted heel he strode from the room. Soon afterward there was the sound of his horse's hooves as he rode along the graveled drive.

They were left alone. Alex's gaze flickered over Lily. With grim satisfaction he observed that she looked as exhausted as he did. The soft lavender gown with its frilly lace collar seemed to emphasize the pallor of her skin and the shadows under her eyes. Her lips were red and swollen, a testament to his roughness the night before.

"You look like hell," he commented rudely, fumbling to light another cigar.

"No worse than you. A man in his cups is always so disgusting." Lily wandered to the velvet-festooned window and opened it, letting some fresh air into the stale room. She frowned as she saw the cigar burns on the leather-lined table, an exquisite piece that was used to display rare folio books. Ruined. She turned and discovered that Alex was staring at her, his cold eyes daring her to rebuke him. "What caused this?" she asked.

He showed her a used cigar butt.

She smiled sourly. "Actually, I was asking what caused you to swill your liquor like a pig at the trough. Pining after long-lost Saint Caroline? Or is it that you're jealous because Zachary's a better man than you'll ever be? Or could it be—"

"It's you," Alex snarled, tossing the brandy bottle aside, not seeming to notice the resulting shatter.

"It's because I want you out of my home, out of my life, *away* from me. You're leaving within the hour. Go back to London. Go anywhere."

Lily threw him a disdainful glance. "I suppose you want me to throw myself at your feet and beg—'Oh please, my lord, allow me to stay'—well, you won't have your way, Raiford! I'm not begging, and I'm not leaving. Perhaps when you're sober we can discuss whatever it is that has set off this tantrum, but until then—"

"I'm fortified with a bottle of brandy, and I can barely tolerate you, Miss Lawson. Believe me, you don't want me sober."

"You pompous ass!" she exploded. "I suppose you've decided I'm the cause of all your problems, when the trouble is all in your stupid, thick, muddled-up head—"

"Start packing. Or I'll do it for you."

"Is this because of last night? Because of one meaningless kiss? Let me assure you, it held less significance for me than—"

"I told you to leave," he said with deadly calm. "I want every trace of you out of here, including your cards, your midnight rambles, your little schemes, and your big brown eyes. *Now.*"

"I'll see you in hell first!" Lily faced him, ready to stand her ground. She watched in bemusement as he left the library. "Where are you going? What are you . . ." Following him, she saw him at the foot of the grand staircase. He was heading to her bedchamber with ground-covering strides. "Don't you dare!" she screeched, and scampered after him. "You inhospitable swine, you conceited, arrogant monster . . ."

Flying up the stairs, Lily reached the bedroom at the same time Alex did. A startled housemaid was engaged in changing the linens. After one glance at the pair, she fled as if retreating before an invading army. Alex flung open the armoire and began to stuff articles of clothing into the first available valise.

"Take your paws off my things!" Outraged, Lily grabbed a delicate china figurine from the bedside table and hurled it at him. Alex ducked quickly. The figure shattered against the wall behind him.

"That belonged to my mother," he growled, his gray eyes filled with an unholy light.

"And what do you think your mother would say if she saw you now, a violent brute with a dried-up heart rattling in his chest, caring about nothing except his own selfish needs . . . *ah!*" Lily cried out in fury as Alex opened the window and tossed her valise outside. Gloves, stockings, and feminine articles fell from the half-open valise and scattered on the drive outside. Whirling around, Lily searched for something else to throw. She happened to catch sight of her sister standing in the doorway.

Penelope was staring at them in horror. "You've both gone mad," she gasped.

Soft as her voice was, it caught Alex's attention. He paused in the act of cramming a dress into a hatbox and glared at Penelope. With his contorted face and his drunken, disheveled blondness, he hardly looked like himself.

"Take a close look, Penny!" Lily said. "This is the man you've agreed to marry. A fine sight, isn't he? You can always tell a man's true character when he's pickled. Look at him, oozing meanness from every pore!"

Penelope's eyes widened. Before she could form a reply, Alex spoke to her harshly. "Your erstwhile lover won't be coming back here, Penelope. If you want him, leave here with your sister."

"She most certainly will," Lily snapped. "Pack your things, Penny, and we'll go to the Stamford estate."

"But I couldn't . . . Mama and Papa wouldn't approve," Penelope said in a faltering whisper.

"No, they wouldn't," Lily agreed. "Is that as important to you as Zachary's love?"

Alex directed a chilling stare at Penelope. "Well? What will it be?"

Looking from Lily's defiant face to Alex's ominous one, Penelope turned as white as chalk. Giving a terrified cry, she darted away and headed for the retreat of her own room.

"You bully!" Lily exclaimed. "Dog in the manger! You know very well you can intimidate the poor child into doing whatever you want!"

"She made her choice." Alex tossed the hatbox to the floor and gestured to it. "Now, should I finish your packing, or will you do it?"

There was a long moment of silence.

"All right," Lily said contemptuously. "Get out. Leave me in peace. I'll be gone within the hour."

"Sooner if you can manage."

"Why don't you explain the situation to my parents?" Lily invited with a sneer. "I'm sure they'll agree with everything you say."

"Not another word to Penelope," Alex warned, and strode from the room.

As soon as she was certain he was out of earshot, Lily took a deep breath and forced herself to relax. She shook her head, laughing quietly to herself. "Arrogant ass," she murmured. "Do you really think I'd be defeated so easily?"

CHAPTER 6

A parade of cowed-looking servants carried Lily's valises and portmanteaux out to the chaise. The closed carriage was adorned with shining lacquer and the Raiford armorial bearings. Alex had given the driver explicit instructions to deliver Lily to her terrace in London and return without delay.

Lily's allotted hour was nearly over. Mindful of the passing minutes, she wandered through the mansion in search of her father. He was in one of the small upstairs parlors, seated at a desk burdened with stacks of books.

"Papa," Lily said tonelessly.

George Lawson acknowledged his daughter with a glance over his shoulder. He straightened his spectacles. "Lord Raiford informed me that you are leaving."

"I'm being forced to leave."

"I expected that," he replied ruefully.

"Did you say anything in my defense, Papa?" Lily's forehead creased. "Did you tell him I should be allowed to stay? Or are you happy I'll be gone? Do you have a preference one way or the other?"

"I have reading to do," George said in a befuddled way, indicating his books.

"Yes, of course," Lily murmured. "I'm sorry."

He turned in his chair to face her, his expression perturbed. "There is no need to apologize, daughter. I am no longer surprised by anything you do or any commotion you cause. I ceased to be surprised a long time ago. You never disappoint me because I never expect anything of you."

Lily wasn't certain why she had come to find him—for what little he expected of her, she expected even less of him. As a child, she had bothered and provoked him relentlessly—sneaking into his office, pestering him with questions, accidently spilling ink all over his desk while trying to write with his pen. It had taken years for her to accept the crushing fact that he wasn't interested in her, not her thoughts or questions, her good behavior or even her bad behavior. She had always tried to find a reason for his indifference. For a long time she had felt it was some terrible fault in herself that caused him not to care. Before leaving home for good, she had confided her guilt to Totty, who had managed to assuage it somewhat.

"No, dear, he's always been that way," Totty had said placidly. "Your father has a quiet and withdrawn nature. But he's not a cruel man, Lily— why, there are some men who beat their children for disobeying them! You've been fortunate to have a father of such gentle disposition."

Privately Lily had considered his indifference almost as much a cruelty as beating would have been. Now she was no longer resentful, or puzzled by his lack of caring, but resigned and rather sad. She tried to find words to tell him how she felt.

"I'm sorry for being such a scapegrace," Lily said. "Perhaps if I'd been a son, we might have found some way to get along together. Instead I've been rebellious and foolish, and I've made such mistakes . . . oh, if you only knew, you'd be even more ashamed of me than you already are. But you should be sorry, too, Papa. You've been little more than a stranger to me. Since I was a child I've had to forge my own way. You were never there. You never punished or scolded me, or did anything to show you were aware of my existence. At least Mother bothered to cry." She raked her hands through her hair and sighed. "All the times I needed someone to turn to . . . I should have been able to rely on you. But you kept to your books and your philosophical treatises. Such a fine, scholarly mind you have, Papa."

George glanced at her then, his eyes filled with protest and rebuke. Lily smiled sadly. "I just wanted to tell you that in spite of everything . . . I still care about you. I wish . . . I wish you could say you felt the same."

She waited, her gaze fixed on his face, her small hands clenching into tight fists. There was only silence.

"Forgive me," she said casually. "I think

174

Mother's with Penelope. Tell them I love them. Good-bye, Papa." Abruptly she turned and walked away.

Controlling her emotions, Lily descended the majestic staircase with its multitude of landings. She realized with regret that she would never have occasion to see Raiford Park again. Surprising, how she had come to love the quiet grandeur of the place and its rich classical design. What a pity. Were it not for Alex's sour disposition, he could have offered such a splendid life to a woman. Bidding good-bye to the butler and two house-maids wearing forlorn expressions, Lily went outside to watch the last of her belongings being loaded onto the carriage. Shading her eyes with her hand, she saw a lone figure ambling along the drive. It was Henry, returning from a morning spent with his friends in the village. He held a long stick in one hand, swinging it aimlessly as he walked.

"Thank God," Lily said with relief. She gestured for him to come to her. Henry quickened his pace. When he reached her, he looked at her with questioning blue eyes. Affectionately Lily pushed a few locks of golden hair from his forehead. "I feared you wouldn't return in time," she said.

"What's this?" Henry glanced at the carriage. "In time for what?"

"For good-byes." Lily smiled wryly. "Your brother and I have had a falling-out, Henry. Now I must go."

"Falling-out? Over what?"

"I'm leaving for London," Lily said, ignoring his question. "I'm sorry I wasn't able to teach you all my card tricks, old fellow. Well, perhaps we'll cross paths again one day." She pasted a doubtful expression on her face and shrugged. "Perhaps even at Craven's. I spend most of my time there, you know."

"Craven's?" Henry repeated in awe. "You didn't mention that before."

"Well, I'm quite good friends with the proprietor."

"With *Derek Craven?*"

"So you've heard about him." Lily concealed a satisfied smile. Henry had gone for the bait, as she had known he would. No healthy, hardy boy could resist the lure of the forbidden masculine world on St. James Street.

"Who hasn't? What a life he's led! Craven knows all the richest, most powerful men in Europe. He's a legend. The most important man in England . . . aside from the king, of course."

Lily smiled. "I wouldn't exactly say that. Were Derek here, he'd most likely tell you that in the whole scheme of things, he's merely a piss in the sea. He does run quite a nice gaming establishment, though."

"At school the fellows and I all talked about the time when we'll finally be able to go to Craven's and play the tables and see the women there. It won't be for years, of course. But someday what high times we'll have . . ." Henry broke off with a wistful sigh.

"Why someday?" Lily asked softly. "Why not now?"

He gave her a startled look. "I wouldn't be allowed past the front door. At my age—"

"Of course, a boy of twelve has never seen the inside of the place," Lily conceded. "Derek has rules about such things. But he'll do anything I ask. If you were with me, you could go inside, see the gaming rooms for yourself, dine on French cuisine, and meet a house wench or two." She grinned mischievously. "You could even shake Derek's hand for luck—he claims it rubs off on you."

"You're teasing," Henry said suspiciously, but his blue eyes were bright with impossible hope.

"Am I? Come with me to London and find out. We couldn't let your brother know, of course. You'd have to stow away in my carriage." Lily winked at him. "Let's go to Craven's, Henry. I promise you an adventure."

"Alex would kill me."

"Oh, he'd be angry. I wouldn't doubt it for a minute."

"But he wouldn't thrash me," Henry said reflectively. "Not after all the breechings I got at that rotten school."

"Then what do you have to fear?"

Henry gave her a grin of incredulous delight. "Nothing!"

"*Alors*, come aboard," Lily said with a laugh. She lowered her voice. "Don't let the driver or anyone else see you, Henry. You have *no* idea how disappointed I would be if you were caught."

She was gone. Alex stared out the library window, watching the carriage round the bend of the drive. He waited for a feeling of relief that didn't come. Instead there was emptiness. He prowled through the mansion like a caged tiger, wanting to break free of something . . . something . . . if only he knew what it was. The house was unnaturally quiet. The way it had been for years, before *she* arrived. Now there would be no more arguments, no more troublemaking, no ridiculous antics. He expected to feel better any minute now.

His conscience prodded him to go to Penelope. He knew his display of drunken rage had frightened her. Mounting the stairs, Alex vowed that from now on he would be the soul of patience. He would do all within his power to please Penelope. A vision of his future with her stretched before him—long, civilized, predictable years. A bleak smile curved his lips. Anyone would agree that marrying Penelope was the right thing.

As he neared her room, he heard the sound of heartbroken weeping, and a voice so vibrantly passionate that for a split-second he thought it was Lily. But the tones were softer and higher than Lily's. "I love him, Mother," Penelope sobbed. "I'll love Zachary forever. If only I were

178

brave like Lily! Then nothing would have stopped me from going to him."

"There, there," came Totty's soothing voice. "Don't say such things. Be sensible, darling. As Lord Raiford's wife, your future—and that of your family—will be secured forever. Your father and I know what's best for you. And so does Lord Raiford."

Penelope's sobbing continued unabated, though she managed to gasp, "I don't th-think so."

"I'm right about these matters," Totty continued. "This is all your sister's doing. I love Wilhemina dearly—you know that—but she's never satisfied until she's made everyone miserable. We owe Lord Raiford an apology. That well-bred, even-tempered man . . . I can scarcely believe the state Lily has put him in! We should never have allowed her to stay."

"She was right about everything," Penelope choked. "She knew how Zachary and I love each other . . . oh, if only I weren't such a c-coward . . ."

Alex walked away, his fists clenched. A self-mocking smile crossed his face. He would have liked to blame Lily, as Totty did, but he couldn't. The fault was all his, springing from his shattered self-control, the reawakened appetite for something he could never have.

During the ride to London, Henry seemed to consider it necessary to recount every kind and selfless thing Alex had ever done for him, dating back to his infancy. As a captive audience, Lily had no choice but to listen. She endured it with what she considered to be remarkable forbearance. As he lounged on the carriage seat opposite her, Henry described the time when he had been caught up a tree and Alex climbed up to rescue him, and the way Alex had taught him to swim in the lake, not to mention the countless afternoons when they had played soldiers together, and Alex had helped him learn his numbers . . .

"Henry," Lily finally interrupted. She smiled and spoke through gritted teeth. "I have the impression you're trying to convince me of something. Is it that your brother isn't nearly the heartless brute he seems to be?"

"Yes, that's it," Henry said, looking impressed with her astuteness. "Exactly! Oh, I know how Alex comes off at times, but he's a capital fellow. Hang me if he ain't."

Lily couldn't help smiling at that. "Dear boy, it doesn't matter what I think of your brother."

"But if you knew Alex, *really* knew him, you'd like him. Tremendously."

"I don't intend to know any more of him than I already do."

"Did I tell you about the puppy he gave me for Christmas when I was seven and—"

"Henry, is there any particular reason you're so determined that I should like your brother?"

He smiled and averted his blue eyes, seeming to consider his answer carefully. "You're going to stop

Alex from marrying Penelope, aren't you?"

Lily was perturbed. Wryly she thought that she'd made the same mistake most adults did, underestimating a child's intelligence. Henry was a perceptive boy. Of course he would have grasped the situation between his brother and the Lawsons. "What gave you such an idea?" she parried.

"You're all very noisy when you argue," Henry informed her. "And the servants have been talking."

"Would you be sorry if I did stop the wedding?"

The boy shook his head. "Oh, Penelope's all right. As far as girls go. But Alex doesn't love her. Not like . . ."

"Caroline," Lily said flatly. Each time the blasted woman's name was mentioned, she felt an unpleasant stabbing sensation. What had been so bloody marvelous about Caroline that Alex had gone so mad over her? "Do you remember her, Henry?"

"Yes, quite well. Though I was just a boy then."

"And now you've reached the grand old age of . . . what is it, eleven? Twelve?"

"Twelve," he said, grinning in response to her teasing. "You're rather like her, you know. Except you're prettier. And older."

"Well," Lily said wryly, "I hardly know whether to be flattered or offended. Tell me what you thought of her."

"I liked her. Caroline was a lively girl. She never

181

made Alex angry like you do. She made him laugh. He hardly ever laughs now."

"A pity," Lily said absently, remembering Alex's brief, dazzling smile when they played cards in the gallery.

"Are you going to marry Derek Craven?" Henry asked diffidently, as if the matter were of merely academic interest.

"Good God, no."

"You could marry Alex, after you get rid of Penelope,"

A laugh burst from Lily's lips. "Get *rid* of her? Heavens, you make it sound as if I'm going to dispose of her in the Thames! First of all, my dear, I don't intend to marry anyone, ever. Second, I don't even *like* your brother."

"But didn't I tell you about the time when I was afraid of the dark and Alex came to my room and told me—"

"Henry," she said in a warning voice.

"Just let me finish this one story," he insisted.

Lily groaned and settled back, resting her head against the morocco sleeping cushion while the list of Raiford's virtues continued.

Derek and Worthy bent over the desk in the central gaming room. The mahogany surface was covered with a multitude of notes concerning preparations to be made for the upcoming masked assembly. The only thing they had agreed on was that the gambling palace should be decorated to look like a Roman temple. Derek wanted the ball to reflect the grand decadence of the Roman civilization at its zenith. Unfortunately he and Worthy had conflicting ideas on how the effect should be achieved.

"Awright, awright," Derek finally said, his green eyes glinting with exasperation. "You can 'ave the columns an' silwer swags 'angin off the walls— but that means I gets my way about the wenches."

"Painting them all white and draping them in sheets to resemble statues?" Worthy asked skeptically. "What would they do for the entire evening?"

"Stand on their bloomin pedestals!"

"They wouldn't be able to hold their poses for longer than ten minutes."

"They does what I pays 'em for," Derek insisted.

"Mr. Craven," Worthy said, his usually calm voice edged with frustration, "even if your idea were feasible, which it is not, I believe it would lend the event a tawdry and lurid atmosphere not in keeping with the usual standards at Craven's."

Derek frowned. "What the 'ell does that mean?"

"He means," Lily's laughing voice came from behind them, "that it would be outside the bounds of good taste, you lowbrow cockney."

Derek's dark face lit with a smile as he turned to see Lily standing there. Dressed in a lavender gown embroidered with silver thread, she resembled a dainty confection. Lily launched herself at him, laughing as he swung her around and set her on her feet.

"'Ere's Miss Gypsy, back from the country," Derek said. "Did you give Raiford 'is come-uppance?"

"No," Lily replied, rolling her eyes. "But I'm not through with him yet. She gave a sigh of pleasure at being in the familiar atmosphere of the club, and beamed as she caught sight of the factotum. "Worthy, you handsome devil. How have things been without me?"

The small, bespectacled man smiled. "Only tolerable. You are a welcome sight as always, Miss Lawson. Shall I order something from the kitchen?"

"No, no," Lily said immediately. "Monsieur Labarge will want to stuff me with all his latest puddings and pies."

"You needs it," Derek commented. "No bigger than a titmouse. Come 'ere." He slid an arm around her narrow shoulders and walked her to a private corner. "You looks like 'ell," he remarked.

"That seems to be the general opinion today," she said dryly.

Derek's sharp gaze detected the feverish bright-ness of her eyes and the pinched look about her a mouth. "What's the matter, lovey?"

"Raiford turned out to be impossible," Lily replied briskly. "I'm resorting to drastic measures."

"Drastic," he repeated, watching her closely.

"To begin with, I've abducted his younger brother."

"What?" Derek followed Lily's pointing finger

184

until he saw the handsome blond boy waiting at the far end of the room. The lad was turning a slow circle, viewing the opulent surroundings with wide eyes. "'Oly 'ell," Derek breathed in amazement.

"*H*oly," Lily corrected, and looked at him with a sort of sheepish defiance. "I'm setting a trap for Raiford. Henry's the bait."

"Jayzus, you done it this time," Derek marveled softly, in a tone that sent a chill down Lily's spine.

"I want you to keep Henry for me, Derek. Just for one night."

All the friendly concern faded from Derek's face. He gave her a frosty stare. "I *never* lets chiwdren in my club,"

"Henry's an angel. He won't give you any trouble."

"No."

"At least come and meet him," Lily pleaded.

"No!"

"Please, Derek." She tugged at his arm. "Henry's been so excited at the prospect of meeting you. He considers you the most important man in England, aside from the king."

Derek's eyes narrowed.

"Please," she wheedled.

"Awright," he finally said. "I says 'ello, then 'e's off."

"Thank you," Lily said, bestowing several approving pats on his arm.

Muttering under his breath, Derek allowed her

to pull him to the doorway, where Henry was waiting. "Mr. Craven," Lily said, "I would like to present Henry, brother of the earl of Raiford."

Adopting his most courteous smile, the one usually reserved for visiting royalty, Derek gave Henry an elegant bow. "Welcome to Craven's, milord."

"It's even better than I imagined," Henry exclaimed. He seized Derek's hand and shook it vigorously. "Smashing! Capital!" He left them and searched the room like an inquisitive puppy. His small hand dipped into a bowl of cribbage-counters, then traced the elaborate backs of the Empire-style chairs. He approached the hazard table as reverently as if it were a shrine.

"Does you play?" Derek asked, vaguely amused by the boy's enthusiasm.

"Not well. But Miss Lawson's teaching me." Henry shook his head in wonder. "I can't believe I'm here. Craven's. Damn and blast, what it must have taken to build this place!" He regarded Derek with an awestruck expression. "You're the most amazing man I've ever met. Only a genius could have done this."

"Genius," Derek snorted. "Not by 'alf."

"But you are," Henry insisted. "To think of starting with nothing and going so far above your buttons . . . Craven's is the most famous club in London. Hang me if you ain't a genius! Me and the fellows at school, we all admire you more than any man alive!"

Lily thought that Henry was laying it on a bit thick.

Derek, on the other hand, was warming rapidly to the boy. He turned to Lily with a pleased expression. "Certainly no cock-brain, this one."

"I'm just repeating what everyone says," Henry said sincerely.

Suddenly Derek gave him a hearty clap on the back. "Bright as a new copper," he said. "Fine boy. Come with me, you little cheeser. I 'as some comely wenches for you to meet."

"No, Derek," Lily warned. "No dice, drinking, or women for Henry. His brother would have my head."

Derek looked down at Henry with a crooked grin. "What, does she think this 'ere is, a bloody nunnery?" He dragged Henry away with him, assuming a lecturing tone. "Finest girls in England I 'as. There's no man what's ever got crinkums or the clap from my wenches . . ."

Lily and Worthy exchanged rueful glances. "He likes the boy," Worthy commented.

"Worthy, don't let anything happen to Henry. Keep him out of sight. He can amuse himself with a deck of cards for hours at a time. Make certain he's not corrupted or harmed in any way."

"Certainly," the factotum assured her. "When would you like him returned?"

"Tomorrow morning," Lily sighed thoughtfully, her forehead puckered in a frown.

In a courtly manner Worthy crooked his elbow.

"I'll escort you to your carriage, Miss Lawson."

Lily slipped her hand through his arm. "By this time Lord Raiford should be quite frantic, wondering where Henry is."

"Did you leave him a note?" Worthy inquired matter-of-factly.

"No, the earl's no fool—it won't take long for him to figure out what became of Henry. He'll be in London by nightfall. And I'll be ready for him."

Whether Worthy approved or not, he showed her the same loyalty he gave to Derek. "How may I be of assistance?"

"If by chance the earl shows up here first, direct him to my terrace. You must keep Henry hidden from him, or my plan will be ruined."

"Miss Lawson," the factotum began respectfully, "I consider you to be one of the most valiant women I've ever known—"

"Why, thank you."

"—but are you quite certain you know what you're doing?"

"Of course I do!" A smile of pure delight spread across her face. "I'm in the process of teaching Lord Raiford a lesson he'll never forget."

When Henry's absence was noted and the search for him began, one of the housemaids revealed that she had seen the young master conversing with Miss Lawson shortly before her departure. The driver returned from London, and was startled to be on the receiving end of a barrage of questions. He admitted he had not seen Master Henry entering or leaving the carriage, but Henry was an agile lad and could have maneuvered about undetected. Alex was certain his brother was with Lily. The blasted woman had taken Henry with her, in order to make him come to London. Well, he would go and take the city apart, brick by brick. He couldn't wait to reach her . . . and make her rue the day she had decided to cross him.

It was dark by the time he reached Grosvenor Square. Alex bounded out of the chaise-and-four almost before the driver had stopped the vehicle. Wearing a grimace, he strode up the steps of No. 38 and hammered on the door with his fist. After a few moments the door was opened by a tall, bearded butler. The man was impressive. He wore his dignity like an invisible mantle, his expressionless face set with authority. "Good evening, Lord Raiford. Miss Lawson has been expecting you."

"Where's my brother?" Without waiting for a reply, Alex pushed his way inside. "Henry!" he bellowed, setting the walls to trembling.

"Lord Raiford," the butler remarked politely. "If you'll come this way—"

"What of my brother?" Alex barked. "Where is he?" Not bothering to match the butler's decorous pace, Alex leapt up the stairs two at a time. "Henry? Henry, I'm going to tear you limb from limb! And as for Miss Lawson . . . she'd be wise to climb on her broomstick and escape before I reach her!"

Lily's cool, amused voice drifted to him from the hall branching off the second landing. "Raiford. After being ejected from your home, I suppose you think you have every right to barge into mine!"

Following the voice, Alex flung open the first door he came to. He discovered an empty sitting room. "Where are you?"

Her maddening laughter drifted down the nail. "In my bedroom."

"Where's Henry?"

"How should I know? Do stop that atrocious bellowing, Raiford. I doubt a wounded bear could produce more noise."

Alex charged to the next door. Flinging it open, he stepped into the bedroom. He had a brief impression of gilded beechwood and green silk hangings. Before he could turn his head, he felt a crashing blow to his skull. With a grunt of pain and surprise, he fell to his hands and knees. The scene blurred, and black mist rolled over him. Clutching at his head, he sank into the flooding darkness.

Lily lowered her arm, still holding the bottle. She stood over him, feeling a strange mixture of dismay and triumph. Alex looked like a felled tiger, his golden hair bright against the jewel tones of the carpet. "Burton!" she called. "Come here at once. Burton, help me lift Lord Raiford to the bed."

The butler came to the door of the bedroom.

For a long moment he stood there, his gaze traveling from the cloth-wrapped bottle in Lily's hand to Alex's prostrate form. He had witnessed hundreds of Lily's scrapes and escapades, but this was the first time his composure had ever been visibly rocked. He managed to school his expression into impassiveness. "Yes, miss," he finally said, and bent to heft Alex's large body over his shoulder.

"Careful, don't hurt him," Lily said anxiously. "I mean . . . not any more than I already have."

Panting with the effort, Burton lowered Alex's slack body to the bed. Then Burton stood and restored his own appearance, straightening his coat, vest, and tie. He finished by smoothing down a tuft of gray hair that was standing up from the side of his head. "Will there be anything else, Miss Lawson?"

"Yes," she said, going to sit by Alex's prone form. "Ropes."

"Ropes," Burton repeated emotionlessly.

"To tie him up, of course. We can't have him getting away, can we? Oh, and be quick about it, Burton. He might wake up soon." She regarded her prisoner thoughtfully. "I suppose we should remove his coat and boots . . ."

"Miss Lawson?"

"Yes?" She looked up from her contemplation of Alex, her brown eyes fawnlike.

Burton swallowed hard. "May I ask how long the earl will be staying with us?"

"Oh, just for tonight. Have his carriage brought to the back and lodge his driver for the evening."

"Very good, miss."

While Burton went in search of the ropes, Lily approached the slumbering giant on her bed. All of a sudden she was rather amazed at what she had done. Alex did not stir. Lying there with his eyes closed, he seemed young and vulnerable. His feathery lashes cast shadows on the highest edge of his cheeks. Without his familiar scowl, he looked so . . . innocent. "I had to do it," she said remorsefully. "I had to." She leaned over him, smoothing his tousled blond hair.

Deciding to make him more comfortable, she untied his black cravat. The silk was still warm from his skin. Contemplating him silently, she unfastened his waistcoat and the top two buttons of his white linen shirt. Her knuckles brushed the taut skin at the base of his throat. An odd, pleasant shiver went through her.

Wonderingly she touched his golden cheek, the stern edge of his jaw, the silky curve of his lower lip. The growth of his night-beard had begun to show, turning his jaw and chin into scratchy velvet against her fingertips. No fallen angel could have possessed a more compelling mixture of darkness and light. She saw the strain on his face, a tenseness that remained even in slumber. Too much drinking, too little sleep. And grief from long ago had cast its indelible shadow on his features.

"We're alike in some ways, you and I," she

murmured. "Pride, temper, and obstinacy. You'd move a mountain to get what you want . . . but you, my poor brute, don't even know where the mountain *is*." She grinned as she recalled the way he had tossed her clothes out the bedroom window.

On a sudden impulse, she bent over him, gently pressing her lips to his. His mouth was warm, unresponsive. She thought of the crudely intimate way he had kissed her in the library. Lifting her head, she stared down at him with her nose almost touching his. "Wake up, sleeping prince," she murmured. "It's time for you to realize what I'm capable of."

Alex drifted slowly into wakefulness. Irritably he wondered who was pounding on a drum nearby . . . *thump* . . . *thump* . . . reverberating in his skull. He winced and turned his aching head against a cold, soothing pressure nearby. "There," came a low voice. "There, you'll be all right." Alex squinted his eyes open, and saw the outline of a woman's face above his. He thought he must be having another dream about Lily. Those were her eyes, the spicy color of gingerbread, and her mouth, curved into a disarming smile. He felt her soft fingertips trace over his cheek. "Damn you," he mumbled, "Will you haunt me forever?"

Her smile deepened. "That's entirely up to you, my lord. No, don't move, you'll dislodge the ice. Your poor head. I tried to hit you as gently as possible. But I had to do it hard enough that a second time wouldn't be necessary."

"Wh-what?" he asked groggily.

"I hit you on the head."

Alex blinked in dawning awareness, beginning to understand it was no dream. He remembered tearing into her house, coming to her room . . . the blow to his head. He gave a muffled curse. Lily was sitting cross-legged beside him. He was stretched out full length on a bed. For all Lily's show of calm concern, there was a victorious look about her that caused his nerves to crackle with warning. "Henry—"

"Don't worry, he's fine. Absolutely fine." She smiled reassuringly. "He's staying the night with a friend of mine."

"Which friend?" he demanded. "Who?"

Her gaze turned wary. "When I tell you, don't jump to conclusions. If I had the slightest doubt as to his wellbeing, I never would have—"

He struggled to sit up. "Tell me who has him!"

"Derek Craven."

"That underworld swindler who surrounds himself with whores and thieves—"

"Henry's absolutely safe with Derek, you have my w—"

Lily broke off with a gasp, leaping from the bed as Alex reached for her with a snarl. "You *bitch!*" He was caught short by ropes that bound his wrists and ankles to the thick bedposts. Sharply his head snapped from right to left. He saw what she had done. Shock froze him from the inside out. Then he roared and began to tug in a storm of fury, causing the massive bed to tremble and creak. He fought the ropes like a wild beast experiencing confinement for the first time. Apprehensively Lily watched him. She relaxed as she saw that the sturdy bed frame would withstand the ferocious punishment. Finally Alex's struggle subsided. His lean frame was racked with labored gasps. "Why?" he demanded. "Why?"

Lily eased back onto the bed and looked down at him, her smile a fraction less confident than before. In spite of her triumph, she didn't like the sight of him bound and helpless. It seemed unnatural. And the ropes had already chafed his wrists— she could see the redness his tugging was causing. "I've won, my lord," she said calmly. "You may as well accept it with good grace. I admit my tactics lacked sportsmanship . . . but all's fair, as they say." She rubbed the sore muscles at the back of her neck and yawned. "As we speak, Zachary is at Raiford Park. He'll spirit Penelope away to Gretna Green tonight, and they'll be married. I volunteered my services for the task of detaining you. By the time I release you, it will be too late for you to do anything. I couldn't let you have Penny, not when Zachary loves her so. He'll make her happy. As for you . . . your damaged pride will soon recover." She smiled into his bloodshot eyes. "I told you that you'd never have her. You should have taken my warning seriously." Her head tilted coquettishly as she waited for his response. Perhaps he would acknowledge it had been a game wellplayed. "Well?" she prompted, wanting her victory tribute. "I'm interested to hear your opinion of all this."

It took Alex a long time to reply. When he did, his voice was nothing but a scratching rumble. "My opinion? You should start running. And never stop. And pray to God I never catch you."

Only Raiford could seem so menacing while tied hand and foot to a large piece of furniture. It was no idle threat. His words were laced with deadly purpose. Lily dismissed it blithely, deciding she could handle whatever trouble he might pose. "I've done you a great favor," she pointed out. "You're free to find someone else now. Someone far more suited to you than Penny."

"I wanted your sister."

"She never would have pleased you. Good God, you don't really want to marry a girl who would always be frightened of you, do you? If you have an ounce of sense, you'll choose someone with a little more spirit the next time. But no—you'll probably propose to another meek, gentle lamb. Bullies are always drawn to that sort."

Alex was dizzy from the ache in his head and the failed attempt to free himself and despairing, incredulous with rage. Everyone he loved had been taken away from him—his mother, his father, Caroline. He'd let himself believe that he would never lose Penelope—*that*, at least, it had seemed reasonable to depend on. He thought he would go raving mad if he had to endure any more. His jaw twitched violently.

"Lily," he said hoarsely. "Untie the ropes."

"Not to save my life."

"It's the only thing that will."

"You'll be unleashed in the morning," she promised. "Then you'll be free to collect Henry, return home, and plot your revenge. Do your worst. I don't care, now that Penny is safe from you."

"You'll never be safe," he rasped.

"At the moment I feel *quite* safe." She smiled impudently. Then she seemed to recognize the emotions that writhed beneath his fury. The wicked amusement in her eyes dimmed, replaced by something softer. "You shouldn't worry about Henry," she said. "He'll be perfectly fine tonight—Derek's factotum is making certain he stays out of trouble." She smiled wryly. "Henry filled my ears with praises of you during the carriage ride to London. A man who wins such devotion from a child can't be all that terrible." Watching his face, she put a hand on either side of his lean torso, her slight weight poised over him. "But it isn't Henry that's bothering you. What is it?"

Alex closed his eyes, trying to block out the sight of her, the sound of her voice, wishing to God this were a nightmare that would end soon. But she continued to dissect him with her soft words, heedlessly raking over raw wounds.

"No one's ever forced you to do anything before, have they?" she asked.

He concentrated on his breathing, making it steady. He tried to block out her voice.

"Why so distraught over losing my sister? You can go out and find someone else just like her, if that's what you really want." Lily paused and said thoughtfully, "If you're so intent on having someone who won't interfere with Caroline's memory." She noticed the catch of his breath. "For shame," she said softly, and shook her head. "Few men would mourn for so long. It reflects either on your capacity for love, or your remarkable stubbornness. Which is it, I wonder?"

Alex's eyes flew open. With a tingling shock, Lily saw that the depths of gray had changed from ice to smoke. She felt an odd surge of compassion. "You're not the only one who's lost someone," she said quietly. "I have too. I understand all about self-pity. It's useless, not to mention unbecoming."

Her condescension drove him wild. "If you think losing that snub-nosed little viscount is comparable to what I went through with Caroline—"

"No, I'm not referring to him." Lily stared at him in mild surprise, wondering how much he knew about her engagement to Harry Hindon. He must have gotten it out of Zach. "What I felt for Harry was infatuation. The one I loved and lost was someone else entirely. I would have died for . . . this person. I still would."

"Who?"

"That's private."

Alex lowered his head back to the pillow.

"Perhaps your temper will cool tonight," Lily remarked, delicately rearranging his collar, as if he were a plaything. She knew her careless manner would incense him further. "When you think about this sensibly, you'll realize it's the best for all concerned. Even you." Noticing his hands straining at the ropes, she touched his taut arm. "Don't. You'll only end up with blisters. You may as well relax. Poor Raiford. It must be difficult to accept the fact that you've been bested by a woman." Her dark eyes danced with sympathetic laughter. "For the rest of my life, I'll treasure this memory. The earl of Raiford completely at my mercy." She leaned over him, her smiling mouth hovering just above his. "Just what would you do if you could free yourself, my lord?"

"Strangle you. With my bare hands."

"Would you? Or would you kiss me as you did in the library?"

His eyes flickered, and a flush edged his cheekbones. "Consider that a mistake," he muttered.

Lily was stung by his contemptuous tone. Her experiences with men—Harry's desertion, Giuseppe's angry disappointment, even Derek's lack of sexual interest in her—had all taught her that she lacked whatever it was that made a woman desirable. Now Alex had joined the list. Why wasn't she like other women? What mysterious thing made her so unappealing? Some devilish impulse urged her to show Alex how powerless he was. She leaned close, her breath wafting over his chin. "You had me at a disadvantage in the library," she said. "Have you ever been kissed against your will, Alex? Perhaps you'd like to know how it feels."

Alex stared at her as if she'd gone mad. Smiling impishly, she dipped her head and pressed a light, close-mouthed kiss to his stiff lips. He jerked his head back as if he'd been touched by fire. She was doing her best to torment him. First a kiss. Next she'd probably start plucking out his chest hairs one by one.

Lily studied him in the silence. Something had made his breathing choppy. Was it anger? Or was it possible that her kiss had affected him? She was intrigued by the thought. "Should I consider that another mistake?" she whispered.

Alex stared at her, transfixed. He couldn't make a sound.

Lily moved the necessary half inch to bring her lips to his. Alex inhaled quickly. This time he didn't try to move away. Softly she brushed her mouth over his, giving him nothing more than questioning pressure. Alex tolerated her kiss with his eyes tightly closed, as if she were subjecting him to some acutely painful torture. His shoulders and chest turned rock-hard with the tension of his arms pulling on the ropes. She touched the side of his smooth, hot neck with her fingertips, and he gave a single gasp against her lips.

Astonished, Lily pulled herself higher onto his chest. She wanted more . . . something . . . but she didn't know what, or how. Then there was movement, his head turning slowly on the pillow, adjusting beneath hers. Lily curved her small hand behind his neck, instinctively pressing harder with her mouth. She felt the sleek push of his tongue, and she was shaken by a jolt of pleasure that made her want to answer the silken movement. Alex felt the way Lily shivered, her breath striking his cheek in a rush of surprise. Expecting each moment that her lips would be withdrawn, he strained upward in hunger, seeking more. But she did not pull away—she stayed against him, open and sweet.

Alex clenched his fists. He was trapped by her sinuous body and the bed and his own helplessness. Excitement flooded through him, centering in his loins. Nothing would stop the hardening rise of his flesh, coming to life in heavy, twitching surges. He ached and groaned, and damned himself. Ripping his mouth from hers, he buried his face in the perfumed curve of her throat. "No more," he said gruffly. "Either untie me or stop this."

"No," she said breathlessly. She had never felt so daring and giddy in her life. She laced her fingers into his thick hair. "I'm t-teaching you a lesson . . ."

"Get off me!" he said fiercely. He almost succeeded in frightening her away—he felt her give a little jump.

But she persisted. Still holding his gaze, she eased further over him until she was draped on him full length. He shuddered and bit his lip. The weight of her body bearing down on his aroused manhood caused him to press upward without conscious thought. It wasn't enough. He wanted more—the softness of her flesh surrounding him, the cling and pull of her body as he thrust within her. Somehow he managed to speak very quietly. "Enough. *Lily* . . . enough."

She was breathing very fast, looking as reckless as she had during the hunt, hurtling over impossible jumps. Alex couldn't fathom what was going on in her mind, until she spoke. "Say her name now," she urged in a thick voice. "Say it."

He set his jaw so hard that he felt it tremble.

"You can't," Lily whispered. "Because it's me you want, not Caroline. I can feel it. I'm a living, breathing woman, and I'm *here*. And you want me."

A thousand thoughts raced across his brain. He searched for Caroline, but she wasn't there . . . nothing but a blur of memories, faded color, muted sound. None of it was as real as the face above him. Lily's mouth remained just above his, close enough that he could feel the warmth of her lips.

He didn't answer, but she could read the truth in his eyes. Lily should have pulled away in triumph, glorying in her victory. She was right, after all. Instead she made a low sound and kissed him again. Disarmed, unable to retreat, all he could do was surrender. Her hands were on his face, his neck, exploring gently. Alex groaned with the need to touch her, hold her tight between his thighs. Instead he was spread beneath her. It was killing him slowly. The ropes tore at his wrists until they were raw.

Lily gasped at the rhythmic goading of his hips. She tried to move away, only to find that he had caught her bottom lip with his teeth. "Turn your head," he muttered, his warm breath rushing into her mouth. "Turn it . . ."

She obeyed, and he let go of her lip, his mouth opening to receive the twisting pressure of hers. Lily gave a small sob of pleasure. Compulsively she gathered tighter against him, impelling her breasts against his hard chest, her stomach flat against his. The friction between their bodies caused her gown to ride up to her knees, but she didn't care; she couldn't seem to make herself care about anything except the urgent need building inside.

There was a knock at the door. Lily stiffened at the sound. "Miss Lawson?" came the butler's muffled voice.

Weakly she dropped her head to the pillow, the puff of her breath tickling Alex's ear. He turned his head against her buoyant curls and inhaled the sweet fragrance.

Burton spoke again. "Miss Lawson?"

Lily raised her head. "Yes, Burton?" she asked unsteadily.

"A message has just arrived."

She froze. That could mean only one thing. Burton would never intrude on her privacy unless the note were from a particular source.

Alex watched Lily intently. The blush drained from her face. There was a gleam of something like fear in her eyes. She seemed dazed. "It can't be," he heard her whisper. "It's too soon."

"Too soon for what?"

The sound of his voice seemed to recall her. She wiped her expression clean and rolled away from him, jerking at her skirts. Carefully she avoided looking at him. "I must bid you good night, my lord. I th-think you'll be comfortable here—"

"Not likely, you little tease!" He watched in fury as she fumbled to restore her appearance and left the room. He shouted a few choice obscenities after her, adding, "I'll see you in Newgate for this! And as for your damn butler—" The door slammed, and he fell silent, glaring at the ceiling.

Lily faced Burton in the hall, too distracted to worry about her disheveled appearance. There was a note poised on the silver tray in his hands. The paper was sealed with a dirty blob of wax.

Burton proffered the tray. "You instructed me to deliver them to you upon their arrival, no matter what time—"

"Yes," Lily interrupted, snatching the letter. She broke the seal, and scanned the scrawled lines. "Tonight. Damn him! He must have people watching me . . . always seems to know where I am . . ."

"Miss?" Burton had never been privileged to know the contents of the letters, which arrived at the terrace on a sporadic basis. He had come to recognize them by the elaborate, untidy handwriting, and the strange appearance of the bearers. The letters were always delivered by ragged boys fresh from the street.

"Have a horse saddled for me," Lily said.

"Miss Lawson, I should like to point out the inadvisability of a woman riding alone in London, especially at night—"

"Tell one of the maids to bring my gray cloak. The one with the hood.

"Yes, miss."

Slowly she went down the stairs, keeping hold of the railing as if to steady herself.

Covent Garden was an especially unsavory area of London, where every worldly pleasure from the conventional to the unthinkable was to be had for a price. There was advertising both visible and verbal: printed bills and notices plastered on every wall, the din of swindlers, pimps, and prostitutes shouting invitations at every passerby. Regency bucks, coming from the theaters with their light-o'-loves, teetered drunkenly to the market taverns. Lily took care to avoid all of them. A drunken lord could sometimes prove as dangerous and inhuman as a professional criminal.

As she crossed through pools of gaslight and shadow, Lily felt sympathy for the parade of prostitutes trodding the thoroughfares. There were young girls and haggard old women and every age in between. They were either thin from starvation or bloated with gin. They all wore the same weary look as they rested on steps and posed on corners, producing painted smiles for any prospective customer. Surely they would never have turned to such an existence had there been any other choice.

There but for the grace of God, Lily thought, and shuddered. She would kill herself rather than turn to such a life, even the life of a courtesan wearing diamond clusters and servicing her protector on silk sheets. Her lip curled with disgust. Better to be dead than owned by a man and forced to serve his physical needs.

Traveling south on King Street, she passed the churchyard. She ignored the catcalls and jeers thrown at her from the roofed shacks that served as shops and dwelling places. Cautiously she went across the street from the market entrance. The two-story arcade was fronted with a pediment and granite Tuscan columns, an oddly regal design for a place containing such squalor. She reined in her horse and paused in a shadow. There was nothing to do but wait. Ruefully she grinned as she saw a pair of young pickpockets nimbly working the crowds. Then she thought of Nicole. Her face turned to stone. My God, what kind of existence was she leading now? Was it possible, young as she was, that she was already being used to turn vice into profit? The notion brought stinging tears to her eyes. Roughly she rubbed them away. She couldn't give way to emotion, not now. She had to be cool and self-controlled.

A lazy voice came from the darkness nearby. "So 'ere you are, then. I 'ope you bring what I want."

Slowly Lily dismounted and clutched the reins of her mount in one hand. She turned in the direction of the voice, and forced herself to speak steadily, though her entire body was trembling.

"No more, Giuseppe. Not a farthing more until you give me back my daughter."

CHAPTER 7

Count Giuseppe Gavazzi had all the striking splendor of a figure from an Italian Renaissance painting—boldly prominent features, curly black hair, rich olive skin, and lustrous black eyes. Lily remembered the first time she had ever seen him. Giuseppe had been standing in a sunlit Florentine piazza, surrounded by a group of Italian women who hung on every word he spoke. With his flashing smile and dark beauty, he had taken Lily's breath away. Their paths had crossed numerous times at social events, and Giuseppe had begun to pursue her ardently, ostentatiously.

Lily had been overwhelmed by the romance of Italy and the previously unknown excitement of being seduced by a handsome man. Harry Hindon, her only other love, had been staid and so very English, qualities that had pleased her parents. She'd thought Harry's tight grasp on propriety would influence her, save her. Instead her wildness had caused him to leave her. But Count Gavazzi had seemed to relish her impulsive glee—he had called her exciting, beautiful. At the time it had seemed as if she'd finally found the man with whom she could drop all pretenses and be herself. Now the memory of her own foolishness disgusted her.

In the past few years Giuseppe's looks had coarsened—or perhaps it was merely that her perception of him had changed. His pouting lips, praised by the Italian *signoras* for their sensuous fullness, now seemed repulsive to Lily. She loathed the way his gaze roamed greedily over her, though once she had been flattered by his attention. There was something seedy about his appearance, even in the way he stood with his hands clasped on his hips to emphasize their unusual narrowness. It made her stomach turn to look at him and remember the night they'd spent together. He had astonished and humiliated her by asking for a gift afterward. As if she were some dried-up spinster, obligated to pay a man to come to her bed.

Giuseppe reached out and pushed Lily's hood back, revealing her resolute face. "*Buona sera,*" he said in his rich voice, his fingertip extending to stroke her cheek. She knocked his hand away, making him chuckle. "Ah, still with the claws, my darling cat. I come for the money, *cara.* You come for news of Nicoletta. Now give to me, and I do the same."

"Not anymore." Lily drew in a trembling breath. "You oily bastard. Why should I give you more money when I don't even know if she's alive?"

"I promise you, she is safe, 'appy—"

"How can she be happy with no mother?"

"Such a beautiful little girl we 'ave, Lily. With the smile all the time, and the pretty 'air . . ." He touched his own ebony curls. "Pretty like mine. She call me Papà. Sometime she ask me where is Mama."

That broke her as nothing else could. Lily stared at him without blinking. She swallowed against a lump of pain, and tears sprang to her eyes. "I'm her mother," she said wretchedly. "She needs me, and I want her back, Giuseppe. You know she belongs with me!"

He regarded her with a faintly pitying smile. "Maybe I return Nicoletta before now, *bella*, but you make too many times mistake. You have men looking, asking question in the city. You do tricks on me, 'ave them follow me after we meet. You make me angry. Now I think for more years I keep Nicoletta."

"I told you, I don't know anything about that," Lily cried. It was a lie, of course. She was well aware that Derek had men searching for Nicole. Derek had informants in every part of the city, including porters, clerks, dealers, whores, butchers, and pawnbrokers. Over the past year he had summoned Lily four different times to take a look at dark-haired girls matching Nicole's description. None of them were her daughter. She couldn't afford to take them in. What Derek did with them afterward, she didn't ask and had no desire to know.

She looked at Guiseppe with hate-filled eyes. "I've given you a fortune," she said hoarsely. "I don't have anything left. Have you heard the expression 'blood from a turnip,' Guiseppe? It means I can't give you any more, because *I don't have it!*"

"Then you look to find more," came his soft reply. "Or from somewhere I take the money—there is many men asking to buy a pretty girl as Nicoletta."

"What?" Lily put a hand to her mouth to stifle a cry of agony. "How could you do that to your own child? You wouldn't sell her like that—it would kill her—and me—oh, God, you haven't already, have you?"

"Not yet. But I come close maybe, *cara*." He held out his empty palm. "You pay the money now."

"How long will this go on?" she whispered. "When is it going to be enough?"

He ignored the question and shoved his open hand toward her. "Now."

Tears slid down her face. "I don't have it."

"I give you three days, Lily. You come to bring five thousand pound . . . or Nicoletta is gone forever."

She lowered her head, listening to the sound of his retreating footsteps, the raucous noise of Covent Garden, the soft nicker of her horse. She shook with wild desperation—it took all her strength to keep it inside. Money. Her accounts had never been so depleted. This past month she hadn't turned her usual profit at Craven's. Well, her luck would have to change, and fast. She'd have to play deep. If she couldn't win five thousand in three days . . . God, what would she do?

She could ask Derek for a loan . . . No. She'd made that mistake once before, a year and a half ago. She'd thought that with his stupendous fortune, he wouldn't mind loaning her a thousand or two, especially at her promise to return it with interest. To her surprise, Derek had turned coldly cruel, and made her swear she'd never ask him for money again. It had taken weeks to get back in his good graces. Lily didn't understand why he had been so angry. It wasn't as if he were a miserly man—just the opposite. He was generous in countless ways—giving her presents, the use of his vast properties, allowing her to pilfer from his kitchens and liquor supply, helping her search for Nicole . . . but he'd never given her a farthing. Now she knew better than to ask.

She considered some of the rich old men she knew, men with whom she had gambled and flirted and maintained friendships with. Lord Harrington, she thought numbly, with his fat belly and cheerful red face and limp powdered wigs. Or Arthur Longman, a respected barrister. His face was rather unattractive—large nose, no chin, sagging cheeks—but his eyes were kind, and he was an honorable man. Both of them had hinted in gentlemanly ways about their attraction to her.

She could accept one of them as a protector. There was no doubt she would be well treated and generously provided for. But it would change her life forever. Certain doors that were yet open to her would be closed for good. She would become an expensive whore—and that was only if she were lucky. If her experience with Giuseppe was anything to judge by, she might prove so unsatisfactory in bed that no one would want to keep her.

Lily went to the horse and rested her forehead on its warm, dusty neck. "I'm so tired," she whispered. Tired and cynical. She had so little reason to hope for Nicole's return. Her life had become nothing but endless grubbing for money. She should never have wasted so much time with this business about Penny, Zach, and Alex Raiford. It may have cost her Nicole. But if not for the distraction of the past week, she thought she might have lost her sanity.

A light rain began to fall, drops pattering on her hair. Lily closed her eyes and lifted her face, letting the water trail down her cheeks in cool rivulets. Suddenly she remembered Nicole at bath time, making the discovery that she could wet her tiny fists and shake them in the air and splash them in the tub.

"Look what you can do!" Lily had exclaimed with a laugh. *"How dare you splash your mama, you clever little duck . . . water is for the bath, not the floor . . ."*

Stubbornly Lily wiped away the raindrops and

tears. She squared her shoulders. "It's only money," she muttered. "I've gotten it before. I'll get it again somehow."

The clock chimed nine times. Alex had been staring at it for nearly an hour. It was a sentimental figured bronze clock, adorned with porcelain roses and a shy shepherdess glancing over her shoulder at a nobleman proffering a bouquet of flowers. The rest of Lily's bedroom was just as feminine—the pale sea green walls decorated with delicate white plasterwork, the windows hung with rose silk, the furniture upholstered with soft velvet. Now that he thought of it, the brief glimpse he'd caught of Lily's house had been very different from this—dark, rich, and almost masculine. It was as if she had saved her private room for all the feminine indulgence she hadn't allowed herself elsewhere.

As the last chime sounded, the bedroom door opened. The butler. Burton, she had called him.

"Good morning, sir," Burton said impassively. "I trust you had a restful night?"

Alex glowered at him.

After Lily had left him, he had been alone with nothing but silent hours ahead. Until then he'd made a habit of filling every waking moment with distractions. Work, sporting, social amusements, drinking, women, countless ways he had devised to avoid being alone with his thoughts. Unwittingly Lily had forced him to face what he was most afraid of. In the quiet darkness, he hadn't been able to stop the memories from swooping down on him like vultures, tearing at his heart.

At first it had all been a jumble—anger, passion, regret, grief. No one would ever know what he had gone through in those hours of confinement. No one would ever need to know. All that was important was that the jumble had somehow sorted itself out, and things had become clear in his mind. He would never see Caroline in another woman's face again. She was part of his past, and he would leave her there. No more grief, no ghosts. And as for Lily . . . He devoted a good deal of thought to what he was going to do about her. Sometime during the early morning hours he'd drifted into a sleep of pure, dark velvet.

The butler came to the bedside bearing a small knife. "Shall I, sir?" Burton inquired, gesturing to his bound arms.

Alex gave him an incredulous look. "Oh, by all means," he replied in a sarcastic show of politeness. Deftly the butler sawed at the finely woven rope. Alex grimaced as his right arm was released. He brought it to his chest, flexing the aching muscles with a quiet groan, and watched as Burton went around the bed to the other side.

Silently Alex had to admit that Burton was impressive. He had the most authentically *butlerish* appearance Alex had ever seen. He wore a beautifully trimmed beard, and a look of intelligence and authority. All this wrapped in a package of impeccable deference. It took aplomb to approach this situation with dignity, and yet Burton was untying him from the bed in the same stoic manner with which he might have poured tea or brushed a hat.

Burton's brows twitched in what might have been dismay as he saw Alex's blistered wrists. "My lord, I will bring a salve for your arms."

"No," Alex growled. "You've done quite enough."

"Yes, sir."

Painfully Alex drew himself to a sitting position, flexing his cramped limbs. "Where is she this morning?"

"If you're referring to Miss Lawson, sir, I have no knowledge of her whereabouts. However, I have been instructed to remind you that Master Henry is at Mr. Craven's establishment."

"If anything's happened to him, I'll hold you every bit as responsible as Miss Lawson."

Burton looked unruffled. "Yes, sir."

Alex shook his head in amazement. "You'd help her with murder if she asked, wouldn't you?"

"She hasn't requested it, sir."

"Yet," Alex muttered. "But if she did?"

"As my employer, Miss Lawson is entitled to my absolute loyalty." Burton regarded Alex politely. "Would you care for a paper, my lord? Coffee? Tea, perhaps. For breakfast we can provide—"

"To begin with, you can stop behaving as if this

is a commonplace occurrence . . . or is it? Could it be the usual thing for you to offer breakfast to guests who've been tied hand and foot to Lily Lawson's bed?"

Burton considered the question carefully, as if reluctant to betray Lily's privacy. "You are the first, Lord Raiford," he finally admitted.

"What a hell of an honor." Alex put a hand to his sore head and probed gingerly. There was a tender bump a few inches above his ear. "I'll take a headache powder. She owes me that, to start with."

"Yes, sir."

"And have my driver bring my carriage around—unless you and Miss Lawson have him bound to a stable rack or hitching post somewhere."

"Yes, sir."

"Button—that's your name, isn't it? How long have you been working for Miss Lawson?"

"Since she returned to London, my lord."

"Well, whatever your salary, I'll double it if you'll come work for me."

"Thank you, Lord Raiford. However, I must respectfully decline."

Alex stared at him curiously. "Why? God knows Lily must put you through hell. Knowing her, I suspect this isn't the worst escapade she's ever involved you in."

"I'm afraid it isn't, my lord."

"Then why stay?"

"Miss Lawson is an . . . unusual woman."

"Some call it eccentric," Alex said dryly. "Tell me what she's done to merit such loyalty."

Burton's impassive facade seemed to fade, just for a moment, and there was something almost like fondness in his eyes. "Miss Lawson has a compassionate heart, my lord, and a remarkable lack of prejudice. When she arrived in London two years ago, I was in a rather difficult situation, working for an employer who was often inebriated and abusive. Once, while intoxicated, he inflicted a wound on my side with a shaving razor. Another time he summoned me to his room and waved a loaded pistol in front of my face, threatening to shoot me."

"Hell." Alex regarded him with surprise. "Why didn't you find employment elsewhere? A butler of your caliber—"

"I am half Irish, my lord," Burton said quietly. "Most employers require that their highly placed servants belong to the Church of England, which I do not. That and my Irish heritage—though not readily apparent—deem me unacceptable to butler most decent English families. Therefore I was trapped in a most intolerable situation. Upon hearing of my dilemma, Miss Lawson offered to employ me at a higher salary than the one I was earning, although she knew I would have worked for much less."

"I see."

"Perhaps you begin to, my lord." Burton hesitated and continued in a low tone, as if against his better judgment. "Miss Lawson decided I needed to be rescued. Once she takes such an idea into her head there is no way to stop her. She has 'rescued' many people, though no one seems to realize that *she* is the one most in need of—" Suddenly he stopped and cleared his throat. "I have discoursed quite enough, my lord. Forgive me. Perhaps you'll reconsider the idea of coff—"

"What were you going to say? That Lily's in need of rescuing? From what? From whom?"

Burton looked at him blankly, as if he were speaking a foreign language. "Shall I bring this morning's edition of the *Times* along with your headache powder, my lord?"

Henry perched at the long table in the cavernous kitchen, watching in fascination as Monsieur Labarge and the army of apron-clad servants worked on a bewildering array of projects. Fragrant sauces and mysterious concoctions bubbled in pots on the cast-iron stove. An entire wall was covered with a staggering collection of shining pots, pans, and molds, an assortment Labarge referred to as his *batterie de cuisine*.

The chef strode about the room in the manner of a military commander, gesturing with knives, spoons, whatever utensil happened to be in his hand. His towering white hat tilted at alarming angles in response to his vigorous movements. He barked at the second chef, who was making a sauce far too heavy for a dish of fish wrapped in pastry, and at assistant bakers who had allowed the rolls to brown a shade too dark. The fine, upturned ends of his mustache quivered in wrath as he saw that one of the vegetable maids was cutting the carrots too fine. In sudden, bewildering changes of mood, Labarge would shove tempting dishes in front of Henry and beam approvingly as Henry gobbled up the savory feast. "*Ah, le jeune gentilhomme, mange, mange* . . . our young gentleman must try some of this . . . and this . . . *c'est bien, oui?*"

"Very good," Henry said enthusiastically, around a mouthful of pastry dotted with fruit and lemon cream. "May I have some more of those brown things with the sauce?"

With fatherly pride, the chef brought him a second plate of tiny veal strips sautéed with brandy butter, onions, and mushroom sauce. "The first recipe I learned as a boy, helping *mon père* prepare supper for *le comte*," he reminisced.

"This is even better than the meals we have at Raiford Park," Henry said.

Monsieur Labarge responded with many uncomplimentary remarks about English food, calling it flavorless garbage that he would not even feed to a dog. This, on the other hand, was *French* cuisine, as superior to English food as cake was to stale bread. Wisely, Henry nodded in agreement and kept eating.

Just as Henry was forced to set his fork down because his stomach was uncomfortably full,

Worthy came to the kitchen entrance. "Master Henry," he said gravely, "your brother has arrived. He has made some, er, vigorous statements of concern for you. I think it best if you show yourself at once. Come with me, if you please."

"Oh." Henry's cornflower blue eyes turned round with dismay. He covered his mouth with his palm, suppressing a burp, and sighed as he looked around the kitchen. The staff regarded him sympathetically. "It will be a long time before I'll be able to come back," Henry said sadly. "Years."

Monsieur Labarge looked distressed, his thin mustache twitching as he thought rapidly. "Lord Raiford, he has the *grand* temper, *non*? Perhaps we shall first offer him *poularde à la Periguex* . . . or *saumon Monpellier* . . ." The chef paused and considered other delicacies he could prepare, confident that his culinary masterpieces would placate the most savage humor.

"No," Henry said ruefully, knowing that even Labarge's offering of truffled chicken or salmon in herb sauce wouldn't soothe Alex. "I don't think that would work. But thank you, monsieur. This was worth any punishment. I'd spend a month in Newgate for one of those sponge cakes with the coffee cream—or that green soufflé thing."

Obviously moved, Labarge clasped Henry's shoulders, kissed both cheeks, and delivered a short speech in French, which Henry couldn't understand. He finished by exclaiming, "*Quel jeune homme magnifique*—such a boy this is!"

"Come, Henry." Worthy gestured to the boy. They left the kitchen and walked through the dining rooms. Before they circled to the entrance hall, Worthy felt compelled to make a short speech of his own. "Henry . . . I suppose you've heard that a gentleman always behaves with discretion. Especially when it comes to discussing matters of, er . . . activity with the fair sex."

"Yes," Henry said in a perplexed manner. He stared up at Worthy with a slight frown. "Does that mean I shouldn't tell my brother about the girls Mr. Craven introduced me to last night?"

"Unless . . . you feel there is a particular reason for him to know?"

Henry shook his head. "I can't think of a single reason."

"Good." Worthy gave a great sigh of relief.

Contrary to Henry's expectations, Alex was not wearing a thunderous scowl. Actually he seemed rather calm as he stood in the entrance hall, his hands shoved casually in the pockets of his coat. His clothes were rumpled and his face was covered with heavy stubble. Henry wasn't accustomed to seeing his brother in such disarray. But strangely, Alex looked more relaxed than he had in a long time. There was something rather unsettling about his eyes, a gleam of silver fire, and a devil-may-care expression on his face. Henry frowned, wondering what had happened to him. And why he had appeared this morning, instead of arriving to take him back home last night.

"Alex," he said, "it was all my fault. I should never have gone without telling you, but I—"

Alex took him by the shoulders, surveying him critically. "Are you all right?"

"Yes, I had a splendid supper last night. I learned to play cribbage with Mr. Craven. I went to bed early."

Assured of his well-being, Alex gave him a piercing stare. "We're going to have a talk, Henry. About responsibility."

The boy nodded dutifully, perceiving that it was going to be a long ride home.

"My lord," Worthy interjected, "on behalf of Mr. Craven and our staff, I would like to say that your brother is an exceptionally well-mannered lad. I have never seen Mr. Craven—not to mention our temperamental chef—so charmed by one person."

"It's a God-given talent. Henry mastered the art of flattery at a young age." Alex glanced at his younger brother, who wore a sheepish smile, and then back at the factotum. "Worthy, is Miss Lawson here?"

"No, my lord."

Alex wondered if he were lying. Lily might be in Craven's bed right now. He felt a stab of possessive jealousy. "Then where might I expect to find her?"

"I would expect Miss Lawson to be here for the next few nights, my lord, either in the card rooms or at the hazard table. Certainly she'll be in attendance at our masked assembly on Saturday."

Worthy lifted his brows and peered at him through his round spectacles. "Shall I give her a message, my lord?"

"Yes. Tell her to be prepared for the next round." With that ominous statement, Alex bid the factotum good-bye and strode out of Craven's, Henry trotting close at his heels.

When Alex arrived at Raiford Park and strode into the mansion, he was immediately aware of the quiet alarm that permeated the air.

Henry was also sensitive to the invisible cloud of gloom. Wonderingly he looked around the silent house. "It feels like someone died!"

The sounds of subdued sniffling heralded the appearance of Totty Lawson. She crept down the grand staircase, her cherubic face drawn tight with dismay. She looked at Alex as though she suspected he might rush forward and do her bodily harm. "M-my lord," she quavered, and burst into tears. "She's gone! My darling Penny is gone! Don't blame my poor innocent child, the fault is mine. All rec-recriminations should be laid solely at my feet! Oh, dear, oh dear . . ."

A comical mixture of dismay and alarm crossed Alex's features. "Mrs. Lawson . . ." He searched his pockets for a handkerchief. He glanced at Henry, who shrugged helplessly.

"Should I get her some water?" Henry asked *sotto voce.*

"Tea," Totty sobbed. "Strong tea, with a splash

of milk. And a touch of sugar. Just a touch, mind you." As Henry scurried away, Totty continued her hiccuping soliloquy. "Oh, what am I to do? . . . I think I've g-gone a little mad! How shall I begin to explain . . ."

"No explanations are necessary." Alex found a handkerchief and offered it to her. He patted her plump back in a clumsily soothing gesture. "I'm aware of the situation—Penelope, Zachary, the elopement, all of it. It's too late to assign blame, Mrs. Lawson. Don't distress yourself."

"By the time I found the note and roused George to follow them they were long gone." Totty blew her nose daintily. "Even now he is trying to locate them. Perhaps there is still time . . ."

"No." He produced a benign smile. "Penelope was far too good for me. I assure you, Viscount Stamford will prove to be a worthier husband."

"I don't agree at all," Totty said unhappily. "Oh, Lord Raiford, if only you had been here last night. I fear your absence may have encouraged them in this terrible folly." Her round blue eyes, swimming with tears, pleaded for an explanation.

"I was . . . unavoidably detained," Alex replied, rubbing his head ruefully.

"This has all been Wilhemina's doing," Totty fretted.

He looked at her intently. "How so?"

"If she hadn't come here and put ideas into their heads . . ."

Suddenly Alex felt a smile pull at the corners of

his mouth. "I believe the ideas were already there," he said gently. "If we set aside our emotions, Mrs. Lawson, I think we might recognize that Penelope and Stamford are an ideally suited pair."

"But Stamford is nothing compared to you!" Totty burst out impatiently, wiping her eyes. "And now . . . now you are no longer to be our son-in-law!"

"Apparently not."

"Oh, my." Totty sighed dejectedly. "With all my heart I wish . . . if only I had a third daughter to offer you!"

Alex stared at her blankly. Then he began to make an odd choking noise. Afraid he had succumbed to an apoplectic fit, Totty watched in horror as he sank down to the steps, sitting with his head clasped in his hands. His whole frame shook, and he breathed in ragged gasps. Gradually she realized he was laughing. *Laughing*. Her jaw dropped, her mouth forming a lopsided oval. "My lord?"

"*God*." Alex nearly toppled over. "A third. No. Two is quite enough. Sweet Jesus. Lily's worth ten if she's worth anything!"

Totty regarded him with mounting alarm, clearly wondering if the turn of events had unhinged him. "Lord Raiford," she said weakly, "I don't think anyone would blame you for . . . forgetting yourself. However, I believe . . . I will take my tea in the parlor . . . a-and allow you some privacy." She hurried away, her plump elbows churning like cogwheels.

"Thank you," Alex managed to say, struggling to control himself. A few deep breaths and he was silent, though an open smile remained on his face. He wondered if he was all right. Oh, yes. There was a feeling of lightness inside him, a rampant surge of elation he couldn't describe. It left him a little unsteady, restless, like a schoolboy on holiday. The feeling demanded action.

He was rid of Penelope. It was more than just a relief, it was a liberation. He hadn't realized what a burden the engagement had been, an oppressive weight bearing down on him more heavily each day. Now it was gone. He was free. And Penelope was happy, at this moment probably in the arms of the man she loved. Lily, on the other hand, was completely unaware of what she'd started. Alex was filled with anticipation. He wasn't through with Lily—oh, he hadn't even begun with her.

"Alex?" Henry stood before him, looking at him closely. "They'll bring tea from the kitchen soon."

"Mrs. Lawson is in the parlor."

"Alex . . . why are you sitting on the steps? Why do you look so . . . happy? And if you weren't here last night, where were you?"

"As I recall, you have two appointments with potential tutors this afternoon. You could use a bath, Henry, as well as a change of clothes." His eyes narrowed in warning. "And I'm not happy. I'm considering what to do with Miss Lawson."

"The older one?"

227

"Naturally the older one."

"What are you thinking of doing?" Henry asked.

"You're not old enough to know."

"Don't be certain of that," Henry said with a wink, and raced up the stairs before Alex could react.

Alex swore softly and grinned. He shook his head. "Lily Lawson," he murmured. "One thing's certain—you'll be too busy with me to spend another night in Craven's bed."

Tonight was going just as last night had—dreadfully. Lily lost with grace and managed to preserve an air of confidence so that the men around her wouldn't realize she was drowning right before their eyes. She was dressed in one of the most delectable gowns she owned, a garment of black embroidered net laid over a foundation of nude silk, giving the appearance that she was covered in little more than sheer black lace.

Standing at the hazard table with a group of dandies including Lord Tadworth, Lord Banstead, and Foka Berinkov, a handsome Russian diplomat, Lily wore a calm, cheerful expression like a mask. Her face *felt* like a mask, stiff and lifeless enough to peel off like so much paste and paper. Her chances of regaining Nicole were slipping through her fingers. She was hollow inside. If someone stabbed her, she wouldn't even bleed. *What is happening?* she thought with panic. Her gambling had never been like this.

She was aware of Derek's gaze on her as he moved about the room. His disapproval was unspoken, but she was aware of it nonetheless. Had Lily seen anyone else in her position, making such disastrous mistakes, she would have advised him to try again some other night. But she didn't have time. There was only now and tomorrow. The thought of five thousand pounds nagged at her like so many sharp, tiny spurs. Fitz, the croupier, watched her actions without comment, his eyes not quite meeting hers. Lily knew she was playing too deep, too fast, taking senseless risks. Repeatedly she tried to catch herself, but it was too late. She was on the typical gambler's slide—once started, impossible to stop.

Recklessly she flung the three dice on the felt-covered table with a brisk sweep of her hand. "Come, let's have a triple!" Over and over the cubes rolled, until the numbers were up. One, two, six. Nothing. Her money was almost gone. "Well," she said with a shrug, facing Banstead's consoling smile, "I believe I'll play on credit tonight."

Suddenly Derek was at her side, his cool voice in her ear. "Come 'ave a walk first."

"I'm playing," she said softly.

"Not wivout money." He snared her gloved wrist in his hand. Lily excused herself from the hazard table, smiling at the others and promising to return soon. Derek guided her forcibly to Worthy's vacant desk, where they could talk with a measure of privacy.

"You interfering bastard," Lily said through her teeth. She smiled so that it appeared they were having a pleasant conversation. "What do you mean, dragging me away from a game? And don't you dare refuse me credit—I've played here on credit hundreds of times, and I've always won!"

"You lost the lucky touch," Derek said flatly. "It's gone."

She felt as if he'd slapped her. "That's not true. There's no such thing as luck. It's *numbers*, a knowledge of numbers and chance—"

"Call it whatewer you wants. It's gone."

"It's not. I'll go back to the table and prove it to you."

"You'll only lose."

"Then *let me lose*," she said with desperate anger. "What do you think you're doing? . . . Trying to protect me? Is this a right you've recently bestowed on yourself? To hell with you! I have to win five thousand pounds, or I'll lose Nicole for good!"

"An' if you lose more tonight?" Derek asked coldly.

Lily knew there was no need for her to answer. He was well aware of her only choice—to sell her body to the highest bidder. "You'll get your bloody money. Or your pound of flesh. Whatever appeals to you most. Nothing matters to me but my daughter, don't you understand?"

All at once Derek's accent was pristinely perfect. "She doesn't need a whore for a mother."

"Let fate decide," Lily said tautly. "That's your philosophy. Isn't it?"

Derek was stonily silent, his eyes like chips of jade. Then he produced a mocking bow and a smile, setting her free. Suddenly Lily felt lost, adrift, as she had on that night two years ago, before Derek had allowed her into the club. He was as fascinating and changeable as the tide, but once more she realized she couldn't lean on him. One small part of her had always hoped that he would be there to help her when she reached the end of her luck. Now that hope was gone for good. She couldn't blame Derek for being what he was. She was on her own, as she had always been. Turning her back on him, she walked away quickly, her skirts whipping around her ankles.

As she reached the hazard table, she pasted a smile on her face. "Gentlemen, please excuse the interruption. Now where—" She stopped with a gasp as she saw the new addition to the gathering.

Alex lounged at the table with the others. He was dressed in black pantaloons, an embroidered silk waistcoat, and a dull green coat with gold buttons that emphasized his tawny coloring. He gave her a slow, easy smile. Her senses sparked with awareness. He looked different than usual. Even in Alex's best, most impressive tempers, there had always been something a little wooden about him, some part of himself that was always kept in reserve. Now the reserve was gone. It seemed as if he were lit with an inner golden blaze.

Lily had seen gamblers wearing that same look on a lucky tear, carelessly risking entire fortunes.

Her spirits sank even lower than before. She had known she would eventually have to confront him—but why now? First losing her money, then Derek's desertion, now this. It was rapidly shaping into one of the worst nights of her life. Wearily she picked up the gauntlet. "Lord Raiford. How unexpected. This isn't your preferred sort of haunt, is it?"

"I prefer to be anywhere you are."

"A fool returneth to his folly," she quoted softly.

"You left before our last game was finished."

"At the moment I'm concerned with more important things."

Alex glanced at the table, where Banstead had just cast the dice. "Such as regaining your luck?"

So he'd heard she was having a bad night. Tadworth must have told him, or perhaps Foka, the big-mouthed ox. Lily shrugged indifferently. "I don't believe in luck."

"I do."

"And I suppose it's on your side tonight?" she sneered. "Please don't let me stop you from placing a bet, my lord."

Foka and Banstead moved to clear a place for him. Alex didn't take his eyes from Lily. "I'll wager ten thousand pounds . . . against a night with you." He watched as Lily's eyes turned wide and her throat worked silently.

The action at the table stopped.

"What did he say?" Tadworth demanded eagerly. "What?"

As the news spread around the crowd at the hazard table, the other occupants of the room became alerted to the goings-on. Rapidly a multitude formed, all pressing inward, a hundred avid gazes centering on them.

"Very amusing," Lily managed to say hoarsely.

Alex pulled a bank draft from the inner pocket of his coat and dropped it to the table. She stared at the slip of paper in astonishment, then at his face. He smiled slightly, as if he understood the panicked thoughts that whirled through her mind. Good God, he was serious.

The situation took on a dreamlike haze. Lily felt like an observer rather than a participant. She had to refuse the bet. It was the ultimate gamble, with stakes unacceptably high. If she won, the money would save her daughter. But if she lost . . .

For a moment she tried to imagine it. Turning cold with fright, she gave a tiny shake of her head. Alex's gaze dropped to her trembling lips, and the amused gleam in his eyes dimmed. When he spoke again, his tone was oddly gentle. "What if I pledge another five?"

There were hoots and cheers all around them. "It's up to fifteen now!" Tadworth called. Men began to drift in from the dining and smoking rooms. Onlookers scattered back and forth to spread the news.

Usually Lily relished being the center of attention. Her reputation for wildness had been well earned. She had laughed, danced, and cavorted, played pranks that were repeated all around London. But this wasn't a joke or prank . . . this was life or death. She couldn't throw the wager back in his face—she was too desperate for that. She needed help, and there was no one to turn to. There was only a pair of piercing gray eyes that saw through her bravado, her shamming, her fragile defenses. *Don't do this to me,* she wanted to plead. Mutely she stared at him.

"Your choice, Miss Lawson," he said quietly.

What choice? Her mind buzzed. *What damned choice?* She had to put her trust in fate. Perhaps this entire bizarre proposition was divine providence—she had to win, she *would* win, and use the money to buy more time for Nicole. "N-not with dice," she heard herself say.

"Our usual game?" he asked.

It was hard to gather enough breath for a reply. "We'll go to one of the card rooms. Th-three hands?"

Alex's eyes flickered with satisfaction. He gave a short nod.

"The wager is accepted!" someone cried.

There had never been such an uproar at Craven's. The noise of the crowd was a roar in Lily's ears. The men gathered closer in a crushing mob. Lily found herself pinned uncomfortably against the table. Those closest to her tried to withstand the pressure from outside, but the men on the fringe of the gathering were all fighting to reach the table for a good view.

Lily half-turned in confusion, wincing as the curved edge of the table cut into her side. "Stop pushing, I can't breathe—"

Alex moved swiftly. He reached out and pulled her against him, his arms forming a protective cage around her.

Lily gave a muffled laugh, her heart thudding violently. "Look what you've started. My God."

He spoke softly underneath the din of exclamations. "It's all right."

She realized she was trembling, though whether it was from shock, fear, or excitement she didn't know. Before she could ask what he meant, she heard Derek's commanding voice.

"'Ere now," Derek was calling loudly. He moved forward, pushing his way through the mass as he spoke. "'Ere now, all fall back. Let Miss Lawson 'ave a little air. Fall back, so as the game can start." The crowd loosened a little, the crush easing as Derek shoved his way to the middle. Alex let go of Lily. Automatically she turned to Derek, her eyes pleading.

Derek wore the same implacable expression as usual. He didn't look at Alex, but focused on Lily's small, tense face. "Worvy tells me we 'as a little wager."

"Three hands of *vingt-et-un*," Lily said shakily. "We . . . we need a card room—"

"No, do it 'ere." Derek's snarl of a smile appeared. "More convenient, as all of us can't 'erd into a card room."

Lily was stunned at the betrayal. Not one word of caution or concern. Derek was simply going to let it happen. He was even going to take advantage of the spectacle! If she were drowning, he would have offered her a drink.

A flare of anger braced her, gave her strength. "As always," she said coldly, "you're not above a little showmanship."

"I'm not Derek Craven for nofing, gypsy." His gaze searched the room for his factotum. "Worvy," he called, "bring a new deck. We'll see what the devil's bible 'as to say."

For the first time in the history of the gambling palace, the action at the hazard table was interrupted. Waiters scurried to bring fresh drinks. Money and markers exchanged hands until the air was filled with a clutter of paper. Voices rose as bets were made and doubled. Lily heard some of the bets with offended horror. Bitterly she realized that most of the men she had gambled with would like nothing better than to see her lose. It would put her in her place, they thought. It would serve her right, for daring to invade the sanctity of the men's club. Disgusting barbarians, the lot of them.

"Shall I deal?" Derek asked.

"No," Lily said sharply. "Worthy is the only man I trust."

Touching his forehead with a mocking salute, Derek cleared the way for Worthy.

Soberly the factotum polished his spectacles with a handkerchief and replaced them on his face. He broke the seal on the deck. The crowd settled with an expectant hush. Worthy shuffled expertly, the cards flying and snapping in his small hands. Satisfied that it was thoroughly mixed, he placed the deck on the table and looked at Lily. "Cut, please,"

She reached out and cut it with a trembling hand. Worthy took the top half she'd indicated and placed it beneath the other cards. With a precise gesture, slow enough that everyone could witness, he removed the top card and set it aside. Lily felt comforted by his steadiness. She watched every move he made, certain he was dealing a fair game. "Three hands of *vingt-et-un*," Worthy said. "Ace valued at one or eleven, at player's discretion." He dealt two cards to each of them, one faceup, one face-down. Lily's card was an eight. Alex's, a ten.

Worthy spoke quietly. "Miss Lawson?" Being the player to his immediate left, it was her lot to play first.

Lily turned her facedown card and bit her lip as she read it. A two. Looking at Worthy, she gestured for another. He placed it next to her original cards. A nine. There was an audible reaction from the gathering—whistles and exclamations. More money changed hands in the crowd. Lily began to relax, surreptitiously pressing a gloved

237

hand to her sweat-beaded forehead. Her total was nineteen. The odds were in her favor.

She watched as Alex turned his card. A seven, bringing his total to seventeen. He signaled for another card. Lily gave a quiet exclamation as Worthy dealt him a jack, which put him well over twenty-one. She'd won the first hand. She grinned as she felt a few impulsive slaps of congratulations on her back and shoulders. "Cheeky bastards, I haven't won yet." There were a few chuckles, the patrons welcoming the temporary respite from tension.

Worthy moved the cards to a discard pile and dealt a new hand. The crowd settled immediately. Lily's total was eighteen this time. It would be folly to request another card. "Stay," she muttered. She frowned as she glanced at Alex's faceup card, which was a king. He turned his card in the hole, and Lily's heart dropped. A nine. Now they'd each won a hand. She looked at Alex, who was watching her with no trace of smugness or worry, nothing but a quiet certainty that bothered her profoundly. How dare he look so composed when her entire life was poised on the fragile turn of a card?

Worthy buried the played-out hands and dealt once more. The room was unnaturally quiet, breaths held tightly. Lily looked at her card, a queen, and turned the second one. A three. She gestured for a third. Worthy dealt her a seven. Her total was twenty!

"Thank God." She grinned at Alex, silently

daring him to beat it. She was going to win. With relief and joy, she thought of the fifteen thousand pounds. Perhaps that large a sum might even be enough to bribe Giuseppe to relinquish Nicole for good. At the very least, it would buy her time. And she would be able to rehire the detective she had been forced to dismiss for lack of money. She was flushed with triumph as she watched Alex. His first card was a ten. Gently he flipped over the second.

Ace of hearts.

His gray eyes lifted to Lily's astonished face. "Twenty-one."

A natural.

There was absolute silence. Derek was the first to speak. "'Oisted with 'er own petard," he observed mildly.

Then the multitude raised a cry that sounded as if some primal jungle rite were taking place. "End of play, game to Lord Raiford," Worthy said, but his pronouncement was lost in the uproar. The guests behaved like a tribe of primitive savages rather than civilized English gentlemen. Spilled liquor and wadded paper covered the carpet. Alex was subjected to crushing handshakes and vigorous blows to his back and arms, while Foka tried to anoint him by pouring vodka on his head. He ducked to avoid the splash of liquor, then came up in search of Lily. With a muffled sound of denial she had slipped through the gathering, making her way to one of the massive doorways. "Lily!" Alex tried to follow, but the tightly packed crowd made it impossible. He swore as she disappeared from sight.

Lily fled with bone-shaking, stomach-heaving haste, too terrified to watch where she was going. Suddenly she slammed into a hard object that knocked the breath from her. She made a sick sound and gasped for air, beginning to collapse to the floor. Derek, who had blocked her mad flight with his own body, seized her and held her upright. He stared at her with eyes like green ice.

"Let me go," she wheezed.

"Women 'as no pride. Trying to cut an' run, are you? Chicken-'earted wench."

Lily grasped imploringly at his unyielding arms. "Derek, I can't do this, I *can't*—"

"You will. Nofing to it. You'll honor your bet, gypsy, if I 'as to drag you to bed myself. An' if you leaves, I'll bring you back. Now go to my apartments an' wait for 'im."

"Why here? I . . . I'd rather go to my terrace."

"You does it 'ere so I know you 'asn't welshed."

"No." She shook her head dumbly, tears ready to fall. "No."

Suddenly Derek changed, bewildering her with a tender smile. "*No?* Too late for that, gypsy. 'Tis a big lump, but you 'as to take it." His voice turned quiet and kind, as if he were speaking to a headstrong child. "If you don't honor the bet, no place in London would let you play—not Craven's, not even the lowest gaming 'ell in Thieves' Kitchen."

"Why didn't you stop me back there?" Lily burst

out, her teeth chattering. "If you cared anything about me, you wouldn't have let it happen! You should have kept me from getting into this mess—he's going to *hurt* me, Derek, you don't understand—"

"I understand ewerything. 'E won't 'urt you. All 'e wants is a little knock with you, darlin', that's all." He astonished her by bending to kiss her forehead. "Go on. Go pour a drink in yer guts, an' wait for the jack." He tried to shake her hands from his sleeves, but she clutched tighter.

"What do I do?" she choked, staring at him with huge eyes.

Derek's black brows knitted together. Abruptly his gentleness disappeared, replaced by an insolent smile. "Get into bed, an' lay flat as a flounder. Simple. Now go, an' don't ask me which side to turn up." His derisive laughter was the only thing that would have dislodged her.

Lily let go of his sleeves. "I'll never forgive you!"

Derek responded by pointing down the hall toward the stairs that led to the private rooms. She gathered the tattered remains of her dignity and squared her shoulders, striding away without looking back. As soon as she was gone, Derek's smile vanished. He plunged into the hazard room. Catching Worthy's eye, he mouthed the question *Where is he?* Worthy motioned to the edge of the mob, where Raiford was shoving a few unruly patrons aside in an effort to reach one of the exits.

★　　★　　★

Ignoring the raucous congratulations being thrown at him, Alex fought his way through the crowd to the hall. He hesitated as he glanced in the direction of the coffee rooms and libraries, wondering where Lily had gone.

"Lord Raiford?"

Alex turned to see Worthy emerge from the riot in the gaming room.

Derek Craven appeared at the same time. There was something coarse and hard in his expression that made him look more than ever like "flash-gentry," a thief who had flourished but could never escape his sordid past. Green eyes locked with gray in a challenging stare. There had been no contest between them, and yet there was a definite feeling of violent discord, masculine uneasiness.

"Milord," Derek said calmly. "I just told Miss Lawson she brung it on 'erself. Worvy dealt straight, 'e did, an' no one can say—"

"Where is she?" Alex interrupted.

"First I 'as somefing to say."

"What?"

An odd look crossed Derek's face. He seemed to search for words, as if he wanted to say a great deal but was afraid of betraying himself. "Ride 'er easy," he finally said, his voice laced with cool menace. "Nice an' easy, or I makes you pay for it but good." He made a gesture to his factotum, who waited silently nearby. "Worvy will show you to the upstairs room, milord. Lily is . . ." He paused and his mouth twisted impatiently "She's waiting there."

"Convenient," Alex said curtly. "Not only will you share your woman, you'll provide the bed as well."

Derek gave him a humorless smile. "I don't share nofing what's mine. Understand? Yes, I see you does."

Alex stared at him in bewilderment. "Then you and she aren't—"

"Narrow a once," Derek said in guttural cockney, with a shake of his head.

"But before you must have—"

"I only takes whores to bed." Derek smiled humorlessly at Alex's blank expression. "Lily's rum goods. I wouldn't touch 'er with these 'ands. She's too fine for that."

Frustration and amazement collided in Alex's chest. Was it possible that the rumors were false and there had been no affair between them? God help him if he allowed himself to believe something so implausible. But what purpose would they have for lying? It made no sense. Dammit, was he ever going to find out who or what Lily Lawson was?

Craven snapped his fingers at the factotum. "Worvy," he muttered, and walked away quickly.

Stunned, Alex watched Craven's hasty departure. "What's going on between those two?"

Worthy regarded him impassively. "Nothing, exactly as Mr. Craven told you. Mr. Craven has always felt it would be prudent to keep his friendship with Miss Lawson platonic." With that, he gestured for Alex to follow him along the twists and turns of the hall.

"Why?" Alex demanded. "What's wrong with her? Or is it him?" He stopped and grabbed the factotum's lapels, spinning him around. "Tell me, or I'll wring it out of you!"

Gently Worthy disengaged the fine worsted cloth of his coat from Alex's fists. "My personal opinion on the matter," he said quietly, "is that he's afraid of falling in love with her."

Alex's hands dropped. He felt as if he were hovering on the brink of some momentous disaster. "Oh, hell."

Worthy looked at him inquiringly. "Shall we continue, my lord?"

Alex nodded without a word. Worthy brought him to an unpretentious door that looked as though it might lead to some cellar storerooms. Instead it opened to reveal a narrow staircase that spiraled upward. Worthy ascended the remaining steps and indicated another door. He looked up at Alex with the same expression Derek had earlier, yearning to make a speech but struggling to suppress it. "Let me assure you, my lord, you will not be disturbed. If you require anything, ring for the staff. They have been chosen for their efficiency and discretion." He slipped past Alex and vanished like a shadow.

Alex found himself staring at the closed door

with a grimace. He remembered Lily's face in the gaming room as she realized she had lost. She'd been devastated. No doubt she expected the worst from him, especially after what she'd done to him. But he wasn't going to hurt her. Suddenly he was impatient to make her understand that revenge had no part of this. Grasping the doorknob, he turned and pushed.

Worthy found Derek in one of the small, seldom-used rooms in the gambling palace. It was decorated with chairs, a desk, and a chaise lounge, making it a convenient trysting spot or a place where business could be conducted with absolute privacy. Derek stood by a window, nearly hidden by a drape. Although he was aware of Worthy's approach, he remained silent, his fingers tangling restlessly in the thick folds of scarlet velvet.

"Mr. Craven?" Worthy asked hesitantly.

Derek spoke as if to himself. "Jaysus, she was white as chalk. Knees knocking fit to make 'er guts rattle. Not what Raiford expects to find, I'll wager." He gave a harsh laugh. "I don't envy the poor bastard."

"Don't you, sir?" Worthy asked quietly.

There was nothing but silence. Derek kept his face turned away. There was a peculiar sound to his breathing. After a few moments, he spoke hoarsely, making a careful effort to soften his cockney accent. "I'm not good enow for her. But I know what she needs. Someone her own kind

. . . someone who hasn't lived 'is life so long in the gutter. I think . . . I think she could've cared for me. But I 'asn't let it happen. I . . . wants better for her." He passed a hand over his eyes and gave a bitter, self-mocking laugh. "If only I was born a gentleman," he whispered harshly. "If I was born decent. Then I'd be with her now instead o' bloody damn Raiford," He swallowed audibly fighting for self-control. "I wants a drink."

"What would you like?"

"Anyfing. Just be quick about it." He waited until Worthy had left, then leaned his face in the drapes, rubbing the velvet against his cheek.

CHAPTER 8

Alex crossed the threshold of a tiny cove that served as an entrance hall. He found Lily standing in the center of a room filled with high-flown extravagance, all baroque clutter and gilt. He'd seen more tastefully decorated bawdy houses.

Lily's stillness was deceptive. Alex sensed her explosive mood. He tried to keep his gaze on her face, but he couldn't help sliding a quick glance over the black lace and nude silk of her gown, the gloves that covered her arms. He was glad she hadn't undressed. He wanted to do it. The thought caused a violent response within him, making his heart churn and his body fill with heat. He wanted to soothe the anxiety that had caused the color to drain from her face. Before he could say a word, Lily broke the silence with a nervous gasp of a laugh.

"Derek's apartments," she said, gesturing around them. She wrapped her arms tight around her middle and manufactured a wry smile. "Charming, are they not?"

Alex glanced at the room, taking in its velvet

decadence and expensive faceted mirrors and florid paintings of mythological scenes. "It suits him." Slowly he approached her. "Do you want to go somewhere else?"

"No." She hopped back, preserving the distance between them.

"Lily—"

"No. No, wait. I should like to tell you s-something first." She ducked her head and went to a small table in-laid with lapis. Snatching up a small slip of paper, she held it out to him. As soon as he took it, she backed away. "I-I've just written that out," she said rapidly. "My note for fifteen thousand pounds. I'm afraid it will take some time for me to make good on it, but I swear you'll receive it all, with interest. Any rate you want. Within reason, of course."

"I don't want interest."

"Thank you, that's very kind—"

"I want a night with you." He crumpled the paper in his fist and let it drop to the floor. "I've wanted it since I first saw you."

"You can't," she said with an emphatic shake of her head. "It won't happen. I'm sorry."

Deliberately he walked toward her. "I'm not going to hurt you."

Lily held her ground, but a visible shudder ran through her. "I can't do this with you," she cried, raising her hands to ward him off. "Not with any man!"

Her words seemed to hover in the air between

them. Alex stopped, puzzled and wary, staring at her keenly. Was the thought of taking him into her bed so repugnant to her? Was it him or all men? Was it . . . A new, startling thought occurred to him, and he felt a burning warmth creep up from his neck. In all his arrogance, there was a possibility he hadn't considered before. He took a deep breath. "You . . ." he began awkwardly. "Is it that you . . . prefer women?"

"What?" Lily regarded him with bewilderment, then turned crimson. "Oh, good God! No, it's not that."

She was driving him mad. "Then what is it?" he asked tautly.

Lily lowered her head. "Just take my pledge," she said in an agonized whisper. "Take the money. I promise I'll make good on it, just take it—"

He took her arms in a hard grip, interrupting the tumble of words. "Look at me," he said, but she kept her head down. "Lily, tell me."

She gave a dry, cracked laugh and shook her head.

"Did someone hurt you?" he asked urgently. "Is that it?"

"*You're* hurting me—"

"I won't let you go. Tell me what it is." He let her writhe helplessly, until she realized it was no use. She went still, her body trembling. His hands bit into her arms as he waited, his head bent over hers. Then he heard her emotionless voice.

"I know what men think when they look at me,

what kind of woman they—you—expect. They assume I've been with many men. But there's been only one. Years ago. I was curious and lonely and . . . oh, I have a dozen excuses. H-he was the first. And the last. I hated every minute of it. The experience was as miserable, *dreadful*, for him as it was for me. He was a great society favorite, held in high esteem as a lover, so don't assume the fault was his. It was mine. I don't have those kinds of feelings. I am the *last* woman a sane man would want in his bed." She laughed bitterly. "Now do you still want me?"

Alex slid his fingers under her chin and forced her face up. His gray eyes were filled with compassion and an underlying darkness as deep and infinite as a moonless night. "Yes."

Lily felt a tear roll down her cheek. Humiliated, she twisted away from him. "For God's sake, don't pity me!"

"Does this feel like pity to you?" Lightning-swift, he caught her hips and pulled her hard against his body. She made an inarticulate sound. "Does it?" He held her against his rigid, aroused flesh and stared into her eyes. "Why did you hate it?"

She shook her head slightly, her lips compressed.

"It's always painful the first time," he said softly. "Didn't you expect that?"

"Of course." She flushed with mortified scorn. "I would have hated it in any case."

"So you've judged and convicted all men from one experience. One night."

"He taught me all I needed to know," she agreed stiffly.

Alex pressed his hand on her lower back, keeping her against him. His voice was gently reproachful. "What if my opinion of all women were based solely on my acquaintance with you?"

"I daresay you wouldn't be so eager to get married."

"Well, you solved that particular problem of mine." He lowered his head and kissed the side of her neck. She leaned back, stiffening her arms between them. "Fifteen thousand pounds is a great deal of money," he murmured. "Are you certain you shouldn't consider spending a few hours with me instead?"

"Now you're mocking me," she said wrathfully.

"No," he whispered, the word brushing her cheek like a kiss. She turned her face away. "And you dared to call *me* stubborn." He threaded his fingers through her sable curls. "You've let the memory fester for years, probably turned it into something even worse than it was—"

"Oh, go right ahead, belittle my feelings," she cried, her temper sparking. "But you don't know the whole of the story, and I would *die* before telling you, so don't try to make me—"

"All right." He buried his lips in her hair. "I want you," he said, his voice muffled and determined. "No more talking. We're going to do this, whether or not I can find a bed in this damn place." His arms tightened and he nuzzled deeper against her scalp. "All you have to do is let it happen. Just let it happen."

Lily closed her eyes, her face wedged against his chest. His arms felt like steel around her. The jutting bulge of his loins burned through the layers of clothing between them. In spite of his urgency, he seemed to be waiting for something. His mouth moved among her curls, and his fingers splayed wide on her back. He whispered against her hair. "Lily, don't be afraid. I want to please you. I'll make it good. Trust me. You have to trust me."

A strange passiveness came over her, a weariness she couldn't withstand. She had struggled and fought for so long, using all her wiles to stay afloat in a churning sea. She had no more strength, no ideas. Nothing to lose. Finally she had come up against a will greater than her own, and there seemed to be no choice but to drift, and let herself be towed in its wake. Let it happen . . . the words seemed to echo in her ears. Hesitantly she turned her head to the doorway on the left, the direction of the bedroom. She spoke in a faltering whisper. "I believe . . . it's over there."

He picked her up easily and carried her through the next two rooms, until they came to one filled with lamplight and heavy gold-framed mirrors and an enormous bed adorned with carved dolphins and trumpets. Setting her on her feet, Alex took her face in his hands, his thumbs touching the corners of her lips. She looked at him through half-closed eyes, at his harshly perfect features

252

gleaming gold in the muted light. He bent his head, his mouth brushing against hers.

With an erotic shock, she felt the tip of his tongue against her lips, edging the smooth curve, leaving behind a trace of silken moisture. Then he pressed deep, sealing their lips together. The warmth of his mouth was mysteriously pleasant. Lily swayed, suddenly off balance as she stood on her toes. She reached around his neck to keep herself steady, and let her lips drift apart in unconscious invitation. The intrusion of his tongue was gradual, barely venturing past her teeth.

It was folly to trust him. She knew the gentleness wouldn't last. She sensed his growing tension, the way his hand shook as he took her wrist and loosened her glove and peeled the velvet from her slender arm. She could feel the raw power in him, the restraint pulling taut until it was in danger of snapping. But he removed her other glove with the same exquisite care. His fingers glided to the edge of her low-cut bodice and he toyed with the feathery border of lace. There was no other movement except for the small, restless stroke of his fingers.

Lily felt his gaze on her down-bent head, heard the deepening rasp of his breath. She wondered at the reason for his hesitation. Perhaps he might change his mind and let her go . . . the thought filled her with hope and an odd, sinking dread. Then he took her shoulders around and turned her to face away from him. He began to unfasten the row of tiny buttons at the back of her gown. The garment slipped precariously, held up only by the wispy sleeves that clung to her shoulders. Slowly the mass of silk and lace slid to the floor. He loosened the ribbon of her drawers and pushed them down, leaving her clad only in the flimsy protection of her white shift and embroidered stockings.

She felt his mouth on her shoulder, his breath wafting in a hot mist against her skin. Gently his arm came around her front, his hand passing over her chest. The floor seemed to shift beneath her feet. Leaning back against his solid strength, she hardly dared to breathe as his fingers curved underneath the slight weight of her breast. Lightly his thumb moved over the shift until he found her nipple, teasing it to a hard point. She couldn't suppress a gasp, the movement lifting her further into his hand. But the elusive wisp of pleasure was doused by a wave of self-consciousness. Her breasts were small—he must have expected more; her gowns were designed to make her look fuller. A stumbling explanation came to her lips, but before she could utter a word, his hand slipped beneath the shift to cover her naked breast. His fingertips stroked over the smooth curve, finding the dainty crest of her nipple.

"You're so beautiful," he said thickly, his mouth at her ear. "Beautiful . . . like a perfect little doll." Breathing deeply, he turned her to face him, his hands pushing her shift down until her breasts burgeoned over the top. The swollen ridge of his loins prodded against her stomach and the secret place between her thighs, and she turned hot with embarrassment. But he seemed to relish the intimate pressure, giving a soft groan, his hand clenching over her buttocks to hold her in place. "Lily . . . God, Lily . . ." Covering her mouth with his, he reached inside with deep velvet licks. She yielded to the sleek invasion, her arms wrapping tight around his neck. Suddenly he released her with a gravelly sound. He dragged at the sleeves of his coat, trying to struggle out of it, but the garment clung to him like a second skin. Muttering a curse, he lifted his head and pulled harder at the sleeves.

To his surprise, Lily's small hands crept to his lapels, spreading them open, pushing the coat from his shoulders. It dropped to the floor in a heap. Not meeting his eyes, she touched his silk waistcoat and began to unfasten it slowly. The garment was warm from his body. Alex stood motionless, his heart slamming in his chest as he felt the pluck of her fingers against the covered buttons. When the task was done, he shrugged out of the waistcoat and unwound his starched white cravat.

As Lily watched him undress, a vague recollection stirred, causing a chill to sweep through her. She had tried to forget the night with Giuseppe, but the memory swept over her—his swarthy olive skin covered with black hair, the greedy haste of his hands searching her body. She sat on the edge of the bed and willed herself to stop thinking, to swallow back the emotions rising high in her throat.

"Lily?" Alex tossed his shirt aside and knelt before her, settling his hands on either side of her hips.

As she stared into his intent gray eyes, the unpleasant memory vanished like smoke into air. Her vision was filled with him crouching there like an inquiring tiger, his skin and hair burnished gold. Tentatively she reached to his shoulder. Without conscious direction, her fingers moved lower, grazing the uneven border of springy, coppery hair. He was close enough that her calves were pressed into the ridged muscle of his stomach. He kept her at the edge of the bed, his fingers moving to the top of her thigh. Lily held her breath as he deftly unfastened her garter and began to roll her stocking down.

Something made him pause. His fingertip touched the tautness of her inner thigh, where years of riding astride had pared down a woman's usual plump softness. Bashfully she tried to pull the hem of the shift down, covering herself. "No," he muttered, brushing her hands away. His head dropped closer and closer into her lap. She tensed in astonishment as she felt his mouth against her inner thigh. The scrape of his cheek, the intimate heat of his breath, sent an electric shock through her. With a stammering denial, she tried to push his head away, but he caught her knees in his large hands and pressed them wide, holding her still.

Alex stared into the tantalizing shadow beneath the hem of the shift. He tightened his hold on her legs as she made a move to be free. His senses burned with awareness of the mysterious softness and scent before him. The protesting ripple of her voice brushed the edge of his consciousness. "Quiet," he whispered, driven forward by a clamorous beat that resonated through him. "Quiet."

Searching with his mouth, he pressed into the shadow, using his hands to crush back the delicate edge of her shift as it got in the way. Hotly he breathed into the thick cluster of curls, lured by a maddeningly sweet, carnal scent. He hunted for the source and found softness and a place of damp, trembling sensation. Delving slowly, he drew his tongue through the moisture, back and forth, discovering a rhythm that caused her thighs to quiver against his restraining hands.

Turning ruthless, he probed for the exquisite place where softness gathered into tension, and he opened his mouth to draw her in, pulling gently, gently, until he felt the resistance leave her legs. Her shaking fingers slid into his hair, tangling in the thick waves, pressing him closer. Moving upward, he dragged his mouth through the wet curls, and lifted his head from her body.

Lily was red-faced, her eyes glittering and bewildered as she stared at him. She allowed him to push her back on the bed. Rapidly he worked at the fastenings of her shift, then gave up with a curse and pushed it to her waist. He cupped her breasts in his hands and bent over her slim body, his tongue tracing the line where creamy white skin merged into the deeper color of the crest. Opening his lips over the tender peak, he tugged until it contracted to a silky point.

Lily slid her hands around him, over his broad, flexing back, using all her strength to pull him down to her. Some primitive instinct demanded his weight upon her, his heaviness bearing down on her breasts and between her thighs. With a quiet growl he left her breasts and sought her mouth. As her hips writhed upward, she skimmed the bulging ride of his loins, strained so tightly beneath his pantaloons. The slight contact made him groan against her mouth, and his kiss turned violent.

He gasped words against her neck and face while he reached eagerly between her legs. "Sweet . . . hush, I won't hurt you . . . I won't . . ." Gentle and sure, his fingers worked into her, gliding far into the wetness, teasing and sliding against the swollen inner surface. She whimpered, first trying to shrink away, then holding still underneath the gentle ministrations, her mouth falling open with a sigh of astonished pleasure. All of Alex's plans of patience and self-control crumbled into dust. Her body spread beneath him, allowing whatever he wanted, and he succumbed to a tide of greed and tenderness and lust. Fumbling at the fastenings of his pantaloons, he freed himself and climbed over her, and pushed her thighs wide. Slowly he nudged against her and pressed inside. She cried out, helplessly tightening against his entry, but it was too late; he had already sunk deep into the clinging heat of her body.

Taking her head in his hands, he sifted his fingers through her hair and scattered kisses across her mouth. Her heavy lashes lifted, and she gazed at him in tearful amazement. "Am I hurting you?" he whispered, his thumbs wiping at the trail of wetness beneath her eyes.

"No," came her low, shaken reply.

"Sweet, sweet . . ." He pulled back and drove forward, trying to keep his movements smooth and easy, while rampant pleasure threatened to overwhelm him. Lily closed her eyes and breathed deeply, her hands traveling restlessly over his back. She felt his lips on her forehead and his muscled weight settling on her and the slow rocking, the steady rhythm that drew an aching delight up from the very depths of her. "Oh," she gasped when the feeling grew more intense, and he pushed deeper in answer. She couldn't suppress a frantic sob, straining up against the hard, heavy slide of his flesh, up, and up again, grasping at his slick body.

His face was above hers, a fierce gleam of satisfaction in his eyes. Bending his head to her breast, he pulled her nipple between his teeth. The pleasure condensed into a single, unendurable spasm, and she jerked against him with a whimper. He gathered her close, his entire being focused on the flexing of her inner muscles, the wild shudders that went through her. With a few hard thrusts he found his own release, a climax of sharp, dizzying intensity.

Lily lay unmoving beneath him, her arms locked around his waist. Her body throbbed, pleasantly sore, more relaxed than she could ever remember being in her life. For a moment he was crushingly heavy, his face buried in her soft neck, and then he withdrew and lifted his weight from her. She protested faintly, wanting to keep his anchoring warmth over her. He rolled to his side, his arm curving loosely around her waist. Lily hesitated before drawing closer. His masculine scent filled her nostrils as she rested her face against the crisp hair on his chest. Had he been moved to say something, be it sardonic or kind, she would have felt too awkward to snuggle close in such a manner. But he was mercifully silent, allowing anything, everything.

His breath filtered through her hair, and his hand moved up to her head. Idly he toyed with her cropped curls, his fingers drifting through the lustrous strands, winding and unwinding. Lily was conscious of an odd feeling of abandonment, lying there naked except for the tangled shift around her waist, surrounded by an unfamiliar earthy scent. Her skin was touched with a shiver as her perspiration cooled. She was so drowsy—she felt as if she were drunk on strong red wine. The air chilled her, but her body was warm where it touched his. She should get up and dress and put herself to rights again. In a minute—soon—she would move.

She was aware of saying something groggily, something about the covers. He tugged at the front of her shift with both hands until it tore away from her. Obeying his coaxing, she crawled between the smooth linen sheets. When he joined her, he had removed the rest of his clothes. Lily was briefly startled by the sensation of his bare legs against hers. "Easy," he whispered, stroking her back. A shivering yawn overtook her, and she relaxed in his arms.

She didn't know how many hours had passed when she emerged from a deep, restful slumber. Alex slept soundly. His arm was lax as it draped over her, the other curled beneath her head. Quietly Lily absorbed the strangeness of it: the masculine body pressed against her, the feel of his breath on her neck, the silkiness of his hair against her face. The thought of the intimacy they had shared made her blush. She had considered herself wordly wise, having overheard conversations between women of the *demimonde*, praising the prowess of their lovers. But no one had ever described such a thing as Alex had done tonight. She wondered about his past, the women he had known, the particulars of his experience . . . a frown collected on her face, and a disagreeable feeling came over her.

Inch by careful inch, she disentangled herself from him. There were twinges in the secret places of her body, not pain, but reminders of what had happened—the pressures and sensations, the searing invasion. She had never dreamed it would be like that. It wasn't at all like the time with Giuseppe. It hardly seemed like the same act. She slipped from the bed, and heard a sound from Alex, an inquiring mumble. She didn't move or answer, hoping he would fall back to sleep. There was the sound of sheets rustling, a deep yawn.

"What are you doing?" he asked, his voice sleep-scratchy.

"My lord," she said awkwardly. "Alex, I thought . . . perhaps . . . I should leave now."

"Is it morning?"

"No, but—"

"Get back into bed."

For some reason, his drowsy arrogance amused her. "Spoken like some feudal lord addressing a peasant," she said pertly. "I suppose the dark ages would have been an ideal time for you to—"

"Now." He didn't want to have a conversation.

Slowly she went toward the voice in the darkness, sliding back into the warm cocoon of damask, and linen and hair-roughened masculine limbs. She lay near him, not quite touching. Then all was still.

"Come closer," he said.

A reluctant smile plucked at the corners of her lips. Shy but willing, she rolled to face him, her slim arm sliding over his neck, the tips of her breasts brushing against his chest. He didn't move to embrace her, but she heard a change in his breath. "Closer."

She flattened herself against him. Her eyes widened as she felt the full, hot brand of him on her abdomen, throbbing insistently. His hand drifted over her body in light exploration, leaving smudges of fire wherever it lingered. Tentatively she lifted her fingers to his bristled face, touching his mouth.

"Why were you leaving?" he murmured, turning his lips to her palm, her wrist, the delicate hollow of her elbow.

"I thought we were finished."

"You were wrong."

"At times I can be, apparently."

That pleased him. She felt him smile against her arm. He lifted her as if she were a toy, gripping beneath her arms and levering her over him until her breasts were at his mouth. Her heart thudded erratically as she felt the swirling stroke of his tongue against her nipple. He moved to her other breast, and then slid his mouth between them. She squirmed until he eased her down with a soft laugh. "What do you want?" he whispered. "What?"

She couldn't bring herself to say it aloud, but her mouth descended on his urgently. He smiled against her lips, his hands moving down to fondle her slender hips and the curve of her buttocks. Tenderly he bit at her lips, her chin, teasing her with nips and half-kisses. Gradually she joined in the play, her breath coming fast as she sought his wandering mouth with her own. When she caught it, he rewarded her with a deep thrust of his tongue. Unconsciously she tilted her hips forward, seeking the hard pressure of his body. She gripped his shoulders and said his name. Smiling, he turned onto his side and put his hand on her thigh, urging it high over his hip. She moved against him hungrily.

"Do you want me?" he whispered.

"Yes. Yes."

"Then you do it." He swept his hand over her slender back, encouraging her with a hoarse murmur. "Go on."

Her hands stayed modestly poised on his shoulders. "I can't," she whispered imploringly.

Alex opened her mouth with his, circling with his tongue, stirring her excitement to a higher pitch. "If you want me, you'll have to do it." He waited, his pulse racing as he felt her hand lift from his shoulder. Slowly she reached down. His breath caught, and his body stiffened at the touch of her fingers. Her hand jerked back as if she'd been burned, then returned cautiously to move in a hesitant stroke along the taut surface. With a pleasured groan he shifted to help her, feeling her guide him into place. He pushed up, sliding inside her with a smooth force that made her gasp. "Is that what you want?" He moved again. "Like this?"

"Oh . . . yes . . ." She nodded and moaned, pressing her face into the hollow of his throat. He was maddeningly careful and controlled, balancing her urgency with his own restraint.

"Not so fast," he murmured. "We have hours . . . and hours . . ." As she arched demandingly against him, he rolled her to her back with a muffled laugh, holding her down. "Relax," he said, his lips at her throat.

"I can't—"

"Be patient, you little devil, and stop trying to rush me." His hands covered hers, fingers weaving together, and he pulled her arms high over her head, until she was stretched taut underneath him. Helplessly she lay pinned underneath his surging thrusts. "This is what I thought about, all last night," he whispered, sustaining the rhythm until she groaned with pleasure. "Repaying you . . . for the most incredible . . . frustration. Making you want it . . . scream for it . . ."

She only half-understood the gently growling voice in her ear, but the veiled threat sent a tingle of fear through her. Trembling, sweating, she felt the delicious slide of his body, the measured rise and fall of his hips. There was nothing but darkness, movement, and radiant heat that clawed at her vitals until she began to struggle, breathing his name in fitful gasps.

"That's right," came his husky voice. "You'll

remember this . . . you'll want more . . . and I'll do it again . . . and again . . ."

She shuddered and cried out against his lips as the sensations raged through her in a devastating torrent. His words melted into a long purr, and he held himself deep inside her. Compulsively her body tightened around him, and he gave himself over to a climax that burst through him in fiery plenitude. He was left breathless and weary and filled with a satisfaction that sank into the very marrow of his bones.

As he held her, she fell asleep with the suddenness of a tired child, her small head resting heavily on his shoulder. Alex stroked her neck and back, unable to stop touching her. He was afraid to trust the feeling of happiness that brimmed and spilled inside him. But it seemed he had no choice. From the very first, she'd been able to find the chinks in his armor.

He was a realist, scorning to believe in things foreordained. But it seemed that Lily's sudden appearance in his life had been a gift of fate. Until then, he had allowed his grief for Caroline to overshadow everything. It had been pure stubbornness, his refusal to let go. He'd wanted to remain in bitter isolation and use Penelope as a safeguard for his solitude. Only Lily, with her twisted, tricky, haphazard charm, could have stopped it from happening.

Lily murmured in her sleep, her fingers twitching slightly against his chest. Alex hushed her with a comforting murmur and kissed her forehead. "What am I going to do with you?" he asked softly, wishing there was some way he could hold back tomorrow.

The first inkling Lily had of London's reaction to what was rapidly becoming known as "The Scandal" was at Monique Lafleur's shop on Bond Street. A dress designer who imported all the daring styles from Paris and cleverly adapted them for London tastes, Monique was always the first to know the latest gossip. Something about her lilting accent and cheerful blue eyes encouraged confidences from washwomen to duchesses, and everyone in between.

She was an attractive, dark-haired woman in her forties, kind-hearted and generous, unable to hold a grudge against anyone for longer than ten minutes or so. Her presence was so cheerfully inquisitive, her conversation filled with such understanding charm, that she had amassed a large and devoted clientele. Women trusted her to keep their secrets and dress them beautifully, knowing that Monique was that rare kind of female who never competed with those of her own sex. She never allowed herself to succumb to cattiness or jealousy.

"Why should I mind if one woman has a handsome lover, or another has great beauty?" she had once exclaimed to Lily. "I have a kind husband, my own shop, many friends, and all the gossip I can fill my ears with! It is a pleasant life, and it keeps me far too busy to covet that which others have."

As Lily entered the shop with her usual brisk stride, she was greeted by one of Monique's assistants, Cora. The girl paused with an armful of silk and muslin swatches and stared at her strangely. "Miss Lawson! . . . Wait, I shall tell Madame Lafleur you are here. She'll want to know at once."

"Thank you," Lily said slowly, wondering at Cora's unusual animation. It couldn't be that they had already heard about her wager with Alex. Not even a day had passed, for heaven's sake!

But as soon as Monique burst through the curtains that separated the front of the shop from the work area in back, Lily was certain. Monique knew.

"Lily, *cherie!*" the designer exclaimed, embracing her fervently. "Once I heard what had happened, I knew you would come here as soon as possible. There is so much work to be done—with your new status, you will need many new gowns, *n'est-ce pas?*"

"How did you find out so soon?" Lily asked dazedly.

"Lady Wilton was just here. She told me all about it. Her husband was at Craven's last night. My dear, I am so pleased for you! What a brilliantly clever move! A magnificent *coup!* They say Lord Raiford appeared to be completely besotted with you. And what's more, every man in London will surpass himself to be the next. You've been sought after for years. Now that it's known you're available, you can name any price, and any one of them will pay gladly to be your protector. No woman has ever had such a luxury of selection! Oh, think of the jewels, the carriages and houses, the riches that will be yours! If you play your cards right—no pun intended, *cherie*—you could be one of the wealthiest women in London!" She pushed Lily into a cushioned chair and dropped a pile of sketches into her lap, as well as a copy of *La Belle Assemblée*, a book containing pictures of the latest fashions. "*Maintenant*, perhaps you would like to glance at these while we talk. I want to hear every delicious detail. Trains are coming back, if you'll notice. Somewhat inconvenient, having them drag across the floor, but so picturesque. Cora? Cora, put down those samples and bring Miss Lawson some *café* at once."

"There isn't much to tell," Lily said in a strangled voice, sinking lower into the chair, fixing her eyes on the top sketch.

Monique gave her a speculative but friendly glance. "Don't be modest, dear. This is a great triumph. You're the envy of many. It was quite sensible of you to accept Mr. Craven's protection for a while—after all, he is rich enough that one can manage to overlook his commonness—but it was high time for you to make a change. And Lord Raiford is an extraordinary choice. So well-bred, so handsome and influential, so *authentic*. He descends from a true ancient landed family, not like these dandies with easily gotten titles and questionable fortunes. Have you already made an arrangement with him, my dear? If you like, I could recommend an excellent lawyer to represent you—he negotiated the 'understanding' between Viola Miller and Lord Fontmere . . ."

While Monique chatted and showed her pictures of the new, heavily ornamented style of hems, Lily silently reflected on the events of the morning. She had dressed and left stealthily at dawn, while Alex was still sleeping. He had been exhausted, his tawny body stretched out among the white sheets in a long, unguarded sprawl. Ever since then, she had been wavering between uneasiness and a strange elation. It was indecent to have such a feeling of well-being. Undoubtedly she was being gossiped about in every parlor and coffeehouse in London.

But, amazing as it was, she had no regrets. She couldn't help thinking about last night with a sense of ironic wonder. She would never have expected that Alex, with his cold eyes and remoteness, would have turned into such a tender lover, so erotic and gentle . . . even now, it seemed like a dream. She had been convinced she understood him, and now she was utterly confused on the subject of the earl of Raiford. The only thing she knew for certain was that she had to avoid him until her head was clear. Thank God Alex would probably return to his familiar life in the country, satisfied that he had received payment for his loss of Penelope.

Now she had to turn her attention to the matter of five thousand pounds, which she had to have by tomorrow night. There would be high-stakes gambling at Craven's this evening. If she didn't win the money there, she would pawn all her jewelry, and perhaps some of her gowns. She might be able to scrape enough together.

". . . Can't you tell me a little something about him?" Monique wheedled. "And without meaning to pry indelicately, *cherie*, what about the betrothal between Raiford and your sister? Does that matter stand as before?"

Ignoring the questions, Lily smiled wryly. "Monique, enough about this. I've come here to ask a favor."

"Anything," Monique said, instantly diverted. "Anything at all."

"There is a masked assembly tonight at Craven's. It is very important that I have something special to wear. I know there is no time, that you have other things to work on, but perhaps you could throw together something—"

"*Oui, oui*, I quite understand." Monique said emphatically. "This is a great emergency—your first public appearance since *le scandale*. All eyes will be upon you tonight. You must have something extraordinary to wear."

"I'll have to buy on credit," Lily said uncomfortably, not meeting her eyes.

"As much as you desire," came the immediate response. "With Lord Raiford's wealth at your disposal, you could comfortably purchase half the city!"

Lily shrugged and smiled lamely, refraining from telling her that she had no intention of being Raiford's—or anyone else's—kept woman. And that she had precious little wealth at her disposal. "I want to be wearing the most daring costume at the assembly tonight," she said. "If I must brazen this out, I'll do it with style." Her only choice was to flaunt herself without a hint of shame. Moreover, she wanted a costume so completely distracting that none of the men she gambled with tonight would be able to concentrate on his cards.

"What a clever girl. *Bien*, we'll make you a costume that will set the city back on its heels." Monique regarded her with a calculating gaze. "Perhaps . . . it would do very well if we . . . ah, yes . . ."

"What?"

Monique gave her a pleased grin. "We shall dress you, *cherie*, as the very first temptress."

"Delilah?" Lily asked. "Or do you mean Salome?"

"*Non, ma petit* . . . I am referring to the woman, Eve!"

"*Eve?*"

272

"*Bien sûr*, it will be talked of for decades!"

"Well," Lily said weakly, "it shouldn't take long to put *that* costume together."

Alex went to Swans' Court on Bayswater Road, an estate that had been in the Raiford family since it had been acquired by his great-grandfather William. The mansion was designed in the classical style, with symmetrical wings, Greek columns, and cool, wide halls of marble and white sculpted plaster. There was a large stable yard and a coachhouse that could accommodate fifteen carriages. Although Alex seldom stayed there, he had employed a nominal staff to maintain the place and see to the comfort of occasional visitors.

The door was answered by Mrs. Hodges, the elderly housekeeper. Her pleasant face, surrounded by white wispy curls, registered surprise at the sight of him. Hurriedly she welcomed him inside. "My lord, we received no word of your arrival, or I would have made ready—"

"That's quite all right," Alex interrupted. "I wasn't able to send advance notice, but I'll be staying the week. Perhaps longer. I'm not certain."

"Yes, my lord. I'll inform the cook—she'll want to stock the pantry. Will you be having breakfast, my lord, or shall I tell her to leave for market straightaway?"

"No breakfast," Alex said with a smile. "I'll have a look around the house, Mrs. Hodges."

"Yes, my lord."

Alex doubted he would be hungry for quite some time. Before he had left Craven's apartments, a housemaid had brought up a tray laden with eggs, breads, puddings, ham and sausage, and fruit. A man identifying himself as Craven's personal valet had brushed and pressed his clothes and gave Alex the most precise shave of his life. Servants had filled a hip bath with hot water and stood by with thick towels, soap, and expensive cologne.

None of them had answered his questions about where Craven had spent the night. Alex had wondered at the man's motives, and why he would make no claim on Lily when he obviously cared for her. Why would he push her into the arms of another man and even insist upon providing his own apartments for their use? Craven was an odd man—wily, crude, avaricious, and unfathomable. Alex was intensely curious about Lily's relationship with Craven. He intended to make her explain just what their strange friendship entailed.

Sliding his hands into his pockets, Alex strolled through the mansion. Owing to his sudden arrival, much of the furniture was still concealed with striped linen covers to protect it from dust. The rooms were painted in icy pastels, the floors either covered with fitted carpet or polished with beeswax. Each bedroom possessed a marble fireplace and a large adjoining dressing room, and was decorated with floral paper and chintz bedhangings. Alex's room was exceptionally large, with a ceiling painted to resemble a blue sky and clouds. The centerpiece of the mansion was an elegant gold and white ballroom with tall marble pillars, ornate chandeliers, and opulent family portraits.

Alex had lived here during some of the months of his courtship of Caroline. He had hosted balls and soirées that Caroline had attended with her family. She had danced with him in the ballroom, her amber hair gleaming in the light of the chandeliers. After her death, he had avoided the place, flinching from the memories that seemed to drift through the rooms like faded perfume. Now as he wandered through the house, the shadowy memories brought no more pain, only a barely tangible sweetness.

He wanted to bring Lily here. It was easy to imagine her presiding over a ball, moving among the guests with her sparkling smile and lively chatter, her dark beauty emphasized by a white silk gown. The thought of her invigorated him, filled him with eager curiosity. He wondered what was going on in her unpredictable mind, and what her mood had been this morning. It had been damned annoying to wake up to her absence. He wanted to see her naked body in the daylight and to make love to her again. He wanted to hear his name on her lips and feel her fingers in his hair and—

"My lord?" Mrs. Hodges had come in search of him. "My lord, there is someone here to see you."

The news caused his pulse to quicken in anticipation. Brushing by the housekeeper, Alex descended the central stairway with its wrought-iron rococo balustrade and landings illuminated by large windows topped by fanlights. Rapidly he strode through the inner hall to the entrance room with its delicately painted panels. He stopped short as he saw the visitor.

"Hell," he muttered. Not Lily, but his cousin Roscoe, Lord Lyon, whom he hadn't seen in months.

A handsome and unusually jaded young buck, Ross was one of Alex's first cousins on his mother's side. Tall, blond, blessed with wealth and charm, he was a favorite of aristocratic women with inattentive husbands. He'd had a multitude of affairs, traveled throughout the world, and accumulated a variety of experiences, all of which had served to make him excessively cynical. It was said throughout the family that Ross had been bored with life since the age of five.

"You never visit unless you want something," Alex said brusquely. "What is it?"

Ross grinned easily. "I sense a lack of enthusiasm, cousin. Expecting someone else?" Ross was fond of answering questions with questions—one of the reasons his stint in the army had been so short.

"How did you know I was here?" Alex demanded.

"Common sense. You had to be in one of two

places . . . here, or nestled in a certain pair of lovely arms, against a small but charmingly piquant bosom. I decided to try here first."

"It seems you've heard about last night."

Ross seemed unaffected by Alex's forbidding scowl. "Is there a soul in London who hasn't heard about it by now? Allow me to express my most profound admiration. I never suspected it was in you."

"Thank you," Alex indicated the door. "Now leave."

"Oh no, not yet. I've come to talk, cousin. Be congenial. After all, you see me only once or twice a year."

Alex relented and smiled reluctantly. Since childhood, he and Ross had maintained a relationship of friendly bickering. "Dammit. Come walk about the grounds with me."

They walked through the house to the parlor and opened the French doors that led outside. "I couldn't believe it when I heard about my straight-laced cousin Alex and Lawless Lily," Ross commented as they strolled across the smooth green lawn. "Gambling for a woman's favors . . . no, not our dull, conventional earl of Raiford. It had to be someone else. On the other hand . . ." He studied Alex closely, his light blue eyes glinting. "There's a look about you . . . I haven't seen it since Caroline Whitmore was alive."

Alex shrugged uncomfortably and crossed into the small but beautifully landscaped garden, with walks bordered by strawberry beds and flowering hedges. They paused at the center of the garden, where a large weathered sundial provided the necessary focal point.

"You've been a near-recluse for two years," Ross continued.

"I've made appearances," Alex said gruffly.

"Yes, but even when you bothered to attend some gathering, there was something rather hollow about you. Damned cold, actually. Refusing any condolences or expressions of sympathy, keeping even your closest friends at arm's length. Have you troubled yourself to wonder why your engagement with Penelope was received in such lukewarm fashion? People can see you don't give a damn about the poor girl, and they pity the both of you for it."

"There's no reason to pity her now," Alex muttered. "The 'poor girl' is happily married to Viscount Stamford. They've eloped to Gretna Green."

Ross looked startled, then whistled in surprise. "Good old Zachary. Did he really manage that by himself? No, he must have had help from someone."

"He did," Alex said wryly.

A long moment passed, while Ross considered the possibilities. He turned a laughing gaze to Alex. "Don't say it was Lily? That must have been the reason for your performance at Craven's last night, to even the account. *Lex talionis.*"

"That news isn't for public consumption," Alex warned quietly.

"By God, you've done the family proud!" Ross claimed. "I thought the old Alex was gone for good. But something's happened . . . you've rejoined the ranks of the living, haven't you? This proves my suspicion that Lily Lawson's charms could wake the dead."

Alex turned and leaned his weight on the stone sundial, crooking one leg slightly. A breeze rifled through his hair, lifting the lock on his forehead. He thought of Lily nestled in his arms, her lips pressed to his shoulder. Again, the absurd feeling of happiness and completeness swept over him. Staring at the ground, he felt one side of his mouth pulling upward in an irrepressible smile. "She's a remarkable woman," he admitted.

"Aha." Ross's blue eyes gleamed with a lively interest, quite different from his usual laconic boredom. "I intend to be the next to have her. What's the opening bid?"

Alex's smile vanished in a flash. He looked at his cousin with a threatening frown. "There's no auction taking place."

"Oh, really? For the past two years, every man under the age of eighty has wanted Lawless Lily, but everyone knew she was Derek Craven's domain. After last night, it's clear she's on the market."

Alex reacted without thinking. "She's mine."

"You'll have to pay to keep her. Now that word

of last night has been spread around London, she'll be neck-deep in offers of jewelry, castles, whatever bait she'll snap for." Ross gave him a self-assured smile. "Personally, I think my promise of a string of Arabians will do the trick, though I might have to throw in a diamond tiara or two. And Alex, I would like you to put a word in her ear for me. If you want to maintain her for a while, that's fine. But I'm going to be her next protector. There's not a woman in the world like her, with that beauty and fire. Any man who's ever seen her at a hunt in those legendary red breeches has imagined her riding on top of him, and that's—"

"Pink," Alex snapped, pushing away from the sundial and pacing around it edgily. "They're pink. And I'll be damned if I'll let you or anyone else come sniffing at her heels."

"You can't stop it from happening."

Alex's gray eyes narrowed, his expression turning dark and ominous. "You think not?"

"My God," Ross marveled, "you're actually angry. Livid, in fact. Hot as a Tartar. Ruffled, roiled, bridling up like a—"

"Go to hell!"

Ross smiled in wondering amusement. "I've never seen this much emotion from you before. What in God's name is going on?"

"What's going on," Alex snarled, "is that I'll strangle any man who dares approach her with an offer."

"You'll have to do battle with half the population of London, then."

It was only then that Alex saw the cool enjoyment in his cousin's eyes, and realized Ross was intentionally baiting him. "Damn you!"

Ross spoke in a quieter, more thoughtful tone. "You're beginning to worry me. Don't tell me you're beginning to have feelings for her. Lily's not the kind of woman a man keeps forever. She's hardly what one would call domesticated. Be reasonable. Don't make this interlude into something it was never meant to be."

Alex schooled his features into a pleasant, self-controlled expression. "Leave, before I kill you."

"Lily is a mature, experienced woman. She'll lead you a merry dance. I'm just warning you, Alex, because I saw what losing Caroline did to you. You've gone to hell and back—I shouldn't think you'd care to make that journey again. I don't think you understand what Lily Lawson really is."

"Do you?" Alex asked softly. "Does anyone?"

"Why don't we ask Derek Craven?" Ross suggested, watching closely to judge if the arrow had hit its mark.

Suddenly Alex astonished him with a slow, lazy grin. "Craven's no part of this, Ross. At least not anymore. All you need to know is that if you make one advance to Lily, I'll take your head off. Now come back to the house with me. Your visit's drawing to a close."

Ross strode after him quickly. "Just tell me how long you intend to keep her."

Alex continued to smile, his stride unbroken. "Find your own woman, Ross. It will be a waste of time to wait for Lily."

St. James Street was congested with a long line of carriages as people arrived for the masked assembly at Craven's. The full moon shed its bright light on the street, causing the spangled costumes of the guests to glitter and their feathered, plumed masks to cast exotic shadows on the pavement. Music, ranging from sprightly polonaises to elegant waltzes, floated outward from the open windows down the length of St. James.

Any ball would be an occasion for excess and exuberance, but the addition of masks gave the affair an exciting, even dangerous edge. People used the masks to do things they would never dream of in their everyday guises . . . and Craven's was ideally designed for uninhibited behavior. With the multitude of dark nooks and small, private rooms, with the mingling of house wenches, society women, rakes, scoundrels, and gentlemen . . . nothing was safe or predictable.

Lily stepped from her carriage and walked carefully to the entrance of Craven's. Her bare feet tingled from the friction of the pavement. She wore a dark cloak that extended from her neck to her ankles, hiding her costume—or lack thereof. She was tense with excitement and determination.

It wouldn't be difficult to win five thousand tonight, not with the amount of drinking and merrymaking going on. Not with the amount of skin she planned to expose. She would pluck the guests like pigeons ready for roasting.

Slipping past the crowd of guests awaiting admittance, Lily nodded a greeting to the butler. He seemed to recognize her despite the green velvet mask and long, dark wig that came to her hips, for he made no protest as she stepped inside.

Derek had been awaiting her arrival. As soon as Lily went into the entrance hall, she heard his voice behind her.

"You're awright, then."

Quickly she turned to face him. Derek was dressed as Bacchus, the god of debauchery. He was clad in a white toga and sandals, his head encircled in a wreath of grapes and leaves.

He gave her a searching, perceptive stare, and Lily was chagrined to feel a blush rising beneath her mask. "Of course I'm all right," she said. "Why wouldn't I be?" She smiled coolly. "Excuse me, I'm in search of a game. I have five thousand pounds to win."

"Wait." He touched her shoulder and regarded her in his old friendly, beguiling way. "Come 'ave a walk with me."

She gave an incredulous laugh. "Do you expect me to resume our friendship as usual?"

"Why not?"

Lily spoke patiently, as if explaining a situation

to an obtuse child. "Because last night I gambled with my body in a card game out of sheer desperation. And not only did you let it happen, you egged the whole thing on and used it to amuse and entertain the members of your club. That's not the behavior of a friend, Derek. It's the behavior of a pimp."

He made a scoffing sound. "If you wants a little tailtickle with someone, I don't gives a damn. I beds women all the time—it changes nofing between you an' me."

"Last night was different," Lily said quietly. "I asked you to intervene for me. I wanted you to stop it. But you didn't care enough. You *gave me away*, Derek."

Some dark emotion stirred beneath his calm, composed surface. Suddenly there was an uneasy gleam in his eyes, a betraying twitch of his cheek. "I care," he said evenly. "But you was newer mine to keep. What 'appens in a bed—that's nofing to do with us."

"Whatever I do, it's no bread and butter of yours. Is that what you think?"

"That's right," he muttered. "It has to be."

"Oh, Derek," Lily whispered, looking at him as she never had before. She was beginning to understand things that had puzzled her for two years. Derek had known for a long time about her desperate struggle for money, and yet he had never offered to help her, though it was easily within his power. All this time she had thought it was miserly greed. It wasn't greed, but fear. He preferred a mock friendship to anything real. The brutal deprivation of his youth had crippled his heart in some terrible way. "You let us all do what we wish, don't you?" she asked softly. "All you want is to sit back and observe, as if you were watching some endless puppet show. So much safer than becoming involved. Much safer than assuming risks and taking responsibility. How unchivalrous of you." She deliberately used words he couldn't understand, knowing he hated that. "Well, I won't ask for your help again. I don't need it anymore. It's strange, but after last night I feel as if I've shed all my . . . scruples." Gracefully she slipped off her cloak and stared at his face, enjoying his reaction.

The guests just arriving in the entrance hall abruptly fell silent, all gazes arrowing to her.

At first Lily's costume gave the impression of nakedness. Monique had created a gown of diaphanous, flesh-colored gauze that wrapped loosely around her. Artfully they had added large, green velvet "leaves" that in truth covered a good deal. Those patches of green velvet and the long locks of the dark wig were somewhat concealing. But there were tantalizing flashes of soft skin through the transparent fabric, and the outline of her slender, finely toned body was clearly visible. Most startling of all was the painted design of a serpent that wound around her body, starting from one tiny ankle and twisting its way up to her shoulder. It had taken three hours for a friend of

Monique's, a female artist, to paint the serpent.

With a taunting smile, Lily lifted a shiny red apple in her hand and held it under Derek's nose. "Care for a bite?" she asked silkily.

CHAPTER 9

After his initial astonishment, there was no expression on Derek's face. But Lily's sense of perception seemed to be newly sharpened. She knew there was some well-governed corner of his mind that wanted to prevent her from wearing the revealing costume in front of so many people. He would make no move to stop her, however.

Giving her a cold, speaking glance, Derek turned his back and strode away. "'Appy 'unting," he said over his shoulder.

"*H*unting," Lily muttered, watching him slink off like some betrayed lover. The sight of him made her feel guilty, responsible for some harm done to him, though she didn't know what. With a sparkling, determined smile, she handed her cloak to a waiting servant and strode in through the central gaming room. A pleased laugh escaped her as she saw how cleverly it was decorated, giving the impression of a ruined temple. The walls were hung with long blue banners to resemble the sky, while towering wood and plaster columns were painted to simulate aged stone. Statues and altars were positioned

287

in the corners and along the sides of the room. The hazard table had been moved to clear an area for dancing. Musicians were seated on the balconies above, sending sweet strains through the gambling palace. House wenches were draped in silver and gold, playing the part of Roman dancing girls as they moved among the guests with veils, gaudy lyres, and fake musical instruments.

An audible gasp went through the room as Lily appeared. She was able to go no farther as a horde of costumed men gathered around her—jesters, monarchs, pirates, and a fantastic assortment of fictional characters. Women glared discreetly from a distance as every man in the place tried to gain Lily's attention. She blinked in surprise at the multitude of urgent voices.

"It's her!"

"Let me by, I must speak with her—"

"Lady Eve, may I bring you a glass of wine—"

"I've reserved a place in one of the card rooms for you—"

"The most enchanting creature—"

At the sound of the growing tumult in the central room, Derek made his way to Worthy. The factotum was dressed as a small, bespectacled Neptune, a long trident clasped in one hand. "Worvy," Derek muttered in a seething tirade, "you plants yourself on Miss Lawson, an' don't leave 'er. A bloody miracle if she ain't raped 'alf a dozen times tonight, with every bastard in the place itching to join giblets with 'er—"

"Yes, sir," Worthy interrupted calmly, and pushed his way through the crowd, putting his trident to good use.

Derek's hard green eyes swept over the crowd. "Raiford, you bastard," he said in a quiet, biting tone. "Where the bloody 'ell are you?"

Alex arrived at the assembly shortly before midnight, when the dancing and merrymaking had gathered considerable momentum. Taking advantage of their unique opportunity to gamble at Craven's, the scantily dressed women sauntered from room to room, giving feminine squeals of dismay if they lost thousands of pounds or crowing with delight if they won. Concealed by masks and costumes, married women felt free to flirt with scoundrels, while distinguished gentlemen made overtures to *demimondes*. The charged atmosphere made it easy, almost mandatory, to engage in heavy-handed fondling, loose talk, and reckless behavior. Wine flowed like water, and the crowd became unruly with inebriated glee.

As Alex's entrance was noted, there were a few cheers and a rapid string of toasts in his honor. He acknowledged them with a distracted smile. His gray eyes searched the room for Lily, but her small form was nowhere to be seen. As he paused to stare at a weird assortment of dancing couples, a group of women approached him. They all sported alluring smiles, their eyes gleaming invitingly behind feathered masks.

"My lord," one of them purred, her voice distinguishable as that of Lady Weybridge. The young, beautiful wife of an elderly baron, she was dressed as an Amazon. Her opulent breasts were barely concealed by a flesh-colored bodice. "I know it's you, Raiford . . . those remarkable shoulders give you away . . . not to mention that blond hair."

Another of the women pressed close to him and laughed throatily. "Why does your costume seem so *appropriate?*" she asked.

Alex was dressed as Lucifer—his coat, breeches, waistcoat, and boots all dyed a glowing scarlet red. A severe, demonic mask with two curved horns concealed his face, while a scarlet cloak covered his shoulders.

You must have been hiding devilish impulses for years," Lady Weybridge murmured. "I always suspected there was more to you than met the eye!"

Frowning in bemusement, Alex nudged the clinging woman away from him. He'd been pursued by women before, been the recipient of seductive glances and pointed flirtation—but he'd never been the focus of such a direct assault. The thought that their interest was caused by his game with Lily was astonishing. They should be *repelled* by his scandalous behavior, not excited by it! "Lady Weybridge," he muttered, pulling at her hand, which had crept inside his coat and slipped around his waist. "Pardon me, I'm in search of someone—"

She flung herself at him with a brandy-scented giggle. "You're quite a *dangerous* man, aren't you?" she murmured in his ear, and seized his earlobe with her teeth.

Alex gave a perturbed laugh, quickly pulling his head back. "I assure you, I'm quite harmless. Now if you'll let me—"

"Harmless my foot," she countered seductively, pressing her lower body to his. "I heard all about what you did last night. No one knew you were such a dark, wicked, vengeful brute." Her red lips drew closer, pouting and whispering. "I could please you a hundred times more than Lily Lawson. Come to me and I'll prove it."

Somehow Alex managed to pry himself loose from her insistent grasp. "Thank you," he muttered, stepping back to avoid her possessive hands, "but I'm occupied with . . ." he floundered and finished uncomfortably, ". . . something. Good evening."

Hastily he turned and nearly knocked over a slim woman dressed as a milkmaid. He reached out to steady her, and she trembled. The blue eyes regarding him through the rosebud mask were soulful and awestruck. "My lord," she murmured fearfully. "You don't know me, but . . . I . . . I think I'm in love with you."

Alex stared at her dumbly. Before he could reply, a temptress disguised as Cleopatra—but possessing a round face and high voice that betrayed her as the countess of Croydon—threw herself into his arms. "Gamble for me!" she cried. "I'm at your mercy, my lord. Cast your passions to the whim of fate!"

With a harassed groan, Alex pushed through the room, pursued by a coterie of eager women. He headed for the door, where Derek Craven appeared. For a man who was supposed to represent the god of merrymaking, he looked rather morose, his face dark and surly underneath a crown of grapes and leaves. They exchanged a scowling glance, and Derek tugged him aside, blocking the women from following.

Derek adopted a twisted smile as he spoke to the fretful, excited ladies. "Easy, loveys. I beg your pardons, but the prince of darkness an' I wants to talk. Go on, now."

Alex watched with an incredulous stare as the women departed. "Thank you," he said feelingly, and shook his head. "After last night, they should be denouncing me as a scoundrel."

Derek's mouth twisted sardonically. "Instead you became the prize bull-beef o' London."

"That was never my intention," Alex muttered. "Women. God knows what goes on in their minds." He didn't care about any woman's opinion of him. All he wanted was Lily. "Is Lily here?"

Derek regarded him with cool sarcasm. "I would say so, milord. She's sitting naked at a table o' drooling bastards, trying to scalp five frigging fousand pounds off 'em."

Alex's face went blank. "What?"

"You 'eard me."

"And you've done nothing to stop her?" Alex demanded in explosive fury.

"If you wants 'er safe," Derek said through his teeth, "you 'as to take care ow 'er. I'm through with this 'ole crack-brained business. Keeping 'er from trouble—like trying to milk a pigeon, it is."

"Which card room?" Alex snapped, tearing off his mask and tossing it to the floor impatiently.

"Second on the left." Derek smiled bitterly and folded his arms across his chest as he watched Alex depart.

"Discard two," Lily said calmly, and picked up the necessary cards from the deck. Her luck seemed to have improved ten times over since last night. In the past hour she had accumulated a meager stash of money, which she would now begin to build on. The other five men at the table were playing clumsily, their leering gazes wandering over her transparent costume, their faces registering every thought.

"Discard one," Lord Cobham said.

Lily took a sip of brandy and studied his face. She smiled slightly as she noticed his gaze moving once more to the green velvet leaves that covered her breasts. The small room was crowded with men. Lily knew they were all staring at her. She didn't care. By now she was beyond shame or modesty—her only thought was money. If flaunting herself would help her get the money Giuseppe had demanded, so be it. She would do anything to save Nicole, even sacrifice the last few shreds of her pride. Later she would allow herself to shrink from this memory and blush fiercely at the exhibition she had made of herself. For now . . .

"Discard one," she said, flipping down a card. As she reached for another, she hesitated, feeling a hot prickling of awareness down her spine. Turning her head slowly, she saw Alex standing in the doorway of the room. No biblical angel of destruction could have looked more magnificent, his hair and skin gleaming with the rich darkness of antique gold against the blood-red garments he wore. The gray irises of his eyes smoldered wrathfully as he looked at her barely concealed body.

"Miss Lawson," he said in an utterly controlled voice, "May I have a word with you?"

The way he stared at her made Lily tense with unease. She felt pinned to her chair, and knew a sudden urge to bolt for safety. Instead she drew on every bit of her acting ability to appear indifferent. "Later, perhaps," she murmured, and returned her attention to her cards. "Your play Cobham."

Cobham didn't move, only regarded Alex in the same transfixed manner that everyone else did.

Alex's gaze remained on Lily. "Now," he said, more softly than before. There was an edge to his voice that could have cut glass.

Lily stared at him, while their audience followed the exchange with intense interest. Damn him for speaking to her in front of them as if she were his property! Well, Worthy was in the room. It was his job to ensure smooth play in the gaming rooms, and remove all sources of interference. Worthy wouldn't let Alex do anything to her. After all, she was a legitimate member of the club. She dared to give Alex a taunting smile. "I'm playing."

"You're leaving," he said curtly, and took command in a blur of motion. Lily gasped in surprise as her cards were snatched from her hand and scattered over the table. Reaching for her apple, she hurled it at his head, but he ducked it easily. Suddenly she found herself smothered in his red cloak. With bewildering swiftness Alex wrapped her until she was immobile, her arms and legs tightly bound. She shrieked and struggled violently as he bent and lifted her, slinging her over his shoulder. The long wig dropped from her head, falling to a silky heap on the floor.

"You'll have to excuse Miss Lawson," Alex advised the men at the table. "She's decided to cut her losses and retire for the evening. *Au revoir.*" Before their astonished gazes, he carried Lily out of the room, while she wriggled and shouted indignantly.

"Put me down, you arrogant bastard! There's a law against abduction! I'll have you arrested, you high-handed beast! Worthy, do something! Where the devil are you? Derek Craven, you detestable stinking coward, come help me! . . . Damn all of you . . ."

Cautiously Worthy followed Alex, offering tentative objections. "Lord Raiford? . . . er, Lord Raiford . . ."

"Someone get a pistol," Lily cried, her voice diminishing as she was carted down the hall.

Still seated at the card table, the elderly Lord Cobham closed his mouth and shrugged prosaically. "P'raps it's a good thing," he remarked. "I might play better now. Marvelous gel, but she's no good for straight thinking."

"True enough," the earl said. He scratched his white hair and mused, "On the other hand, she does my libido no end of good."

The men chuckled and nodded appreciatively, while fresh hands were dealt.

Over the lively strains of music in the ballroom, a shrill feminine voice rose louder and louder, shouting every conceivable profanity. A few of the musicians faltered, some of them staring down into the ballroom in confusion. At a peremptory signal from Derek they continued playing valiantly, but still they craned their necks to see the cause of the commotion.

Derek leaned against a statue of Mercury, listening to the wondering exclamations of the crowd. Couples abandoned their dancing and gambling and wandered out of the central room to investigate the noise. Judging from the fading sound of Lily's voice, Derek discerned that Raiford was taking her down a side corridor, toward the front entrance. For the first time in her life Lily had been rescued, though she didn't seem to appreciate it. Torn between relief and agony, Derek whispered curses under his breath that easily surpassed Lily's in foulness.

A flamboyant buck dressed as Louis XIV came back to the central room and made a laughing announcement. "Raiford's taken our Lady Eve over his shoulder—and he's carrying her outside like a deuced savage!"

The scene crumbled into bedlam. A good portion of the crowd swarmed outside to see, while the rest mobbed around Worthy's desk, demanding that the factotum take down bets. With his usual efficiency, Worthy began scribbling furiously in a large book and announcing odds. "Two to one he'll keep her for at least six months, twenty to one for a year—"

"I'll wager a thousand they marry," Lord Farmington said with drunken enthusiasm. "What are the odds on that?"

Worthy considered the question carefully. "Fifty to one, my lord."

Excitedly the throng gathered closer around Worthy to place more bets.

As Lily wriggled helplessly on Alex's shoulder, she twisted to see a few well-wishers following them. "This is a *kidnapping*, you drunken asses!" she screeched. "If you don't stop him, you'll be named as accessories when I charge him with abduction and . . . *oh!*"

She gasped with surprise as she felt a hard *thwack* on her posterior.

"Hush," Alex said tersely. "You're making a scene."

"*I'm* making a scene? I'm . . . *ow*, damn you!" She fell into a stupefied silence after another stinging blow.

Alex's carriage was brought around, and he carried her to the vehicle. A footman wearing a baffled expression opened the door. Unceremoniously Alex dumped Lily inside and climbed in after her. A good-natured cheer went up from the crowd of masked guests on the steps. The sound fueled Lily's temper to an even higher blaze. "A fine thing," she shouted out the window, "when people applaud the sight of a woman being brutalized right before their eyes!" The carriage pulled away, and the forward jolt of the vehicle toppled Lily sideways on the seat. She labored to be free of the securely wrapped cloak, nearly dumping herself on the floor. Alex watched from the opposite seat, making no move to help her.

"Where are we going?" she spluttered, wrestling with the binding fabric.

"To Swans' Court, on Bayswater. Stop shouting."

"A family property, is it? Don't bother taking me there, because I won't set one foot on the bloody—"

"Quiet."

"I don't care how far it is! I'll start walking as soon as—"

"If you're not quiet," he interrupted with soft menace, "I'm going to give you the spanking of your life."

Lily paused in her squirming to stare at him in outrage. "I've never been struck before tonight," she said in a muffled, accusing voice. "My father never dared—"

"He never gave a damn," Alex replied curtly. "And he should be shot for that. You've needed someone to spank the hell out of you for years."

"I—" Lily began hotly, but as she met his purposeful gaze, she closed her mouth with a snap, realizing he meant it. She concentrated on freeing herself from the confining cloak, but she was swaddled as tightly as a babe. Enraged, humiliated, a little frightened, she watched him in quivering silence. She'd thought that after last night she had nothing to fear from him. Now it seemed that nothing and no one would stop him from doing what he wanted with her.

He had destroyed her last chance of winning the money to pay Giuseppe. Lily blamed herself equally as much as she blamed him. If only she hadn't meddled in his affairs! If she had sensibly refused Zachary's plea for help and minded her own business, Alex would still be staying in the country with Penelope and the rest of the Lawsons, giving no thought to her existence. She thought of the way she had tied him up on her bed and a feeling of hopeless dread came over her. Alex would never forgive her for humiliating him. He would pay her back a hundredfold. He would devote himself to ruining her. She did not look at him directly, but she knew his pale silver eyes were fixed on her, and that the severe red garments he wore gave him a startling, beautiful, terrifying appearance. She doubted she could feel worse if she were trapped in a carriage with the devil himself.

Eventually the carriage lurched to a halt. One of the footmen opened the door. Scooping Lily into his arms, Alex took her from the carriage and started up the steps of Swan's Court. The footman rushed ahead of them and knocked on the door. "Mrs. Hodges," the man called urgently. "Mrs. Hodg—"

The door was opened, and the housekeeper regarded the scene before her with dawning surprise. "You've returned early, my lord. I . . ." Her eyes rounded as she saw the woman bundled in Alex's arms. "Gracious heavens . . . Lord Raiford, is she injured?"

"Not yet," Alex said grimly, and carried Lily into the mansion.

Lily twisted against him. "You can't make me stay here," she cried. "I'm going to leave as soon as you put me down!"

"Not until I make a few things clear."

Rapidly Lily glanced at her surroundings as they went through an inner hall and up a gently curving staircase with an intricate wrought-iron balustrade. The house was cool and light, decorated in a gracious but uncluttered style. It was surprisingly modern, with large windows and expensive plasterwork. She realized Alex was looking down at her, as if gauging her reaction to the mansion. "If you intended to ruin my life," she said in a low voice, "you've succeeded beyond your wildest ambition. You have no idea what you've done to me."

"Taken you away from a game? Denied you the chance to flaunt your little body in front of the *haut ton?*"

"Do you think I actually enjoyed that?" she demanded, incensed beyond all caution. "Do you think I had a choice? If it weren't for the—"

Horrified, she caught herself just in time, unable to believe what she had been about to say. He had made her so overwrought that her darkest secret was about to come spilling forth.

Alex pounced on her words immediately. "If it weren't for what? Does this have to do with the five thousand pounds Craven mentioned? What do you need it for?"

Lily stared at him in frozen terror, her face turning ghastly white. "Derek told you about the five thousand?" she asked in a raw voice. She couldn't believe it. Oh God, there was no one in the world she could trust! "I . . . I'll kill him, the traitor—"

"It's a gambling debt, isn't it," he said grimly.

"What happened to the money you inherited from your aunt? You've squandered an entire fortune at the gaming tables, haven't you? Apparently you've reduced yourself to a hand-to-mouth existence, supporting yourself through your winnings. Of all the irresponsible—" He broke off and gritted his teeth.

Lily turned her face away, biting her lip. She burned to tell him she had not been a spendthrift, nor had she foolishly gambled away the money. It had been drained away through blackmail and the expenses of a full-time investigator, all of it spent in the effort to regain her daughter. If not for Giuseppe's treachery, she would have led a comfortable life. Given any choice, she'd never set foot near a hazard table again! But she could hardly let him know that.

As he stared at her stubbornly averted face, Alex longed to shake and kiss and punish her, all at once. He sensed the terrible conflict inside her. She was afraid of something . . . she was in some kind of trouble.

He carried her into a large bedroom and closed the door. Lily was absolutely still as he set her on her feet and began to unwrap the cloak from around her. She waited with unnatural patience, keeping herself under taut control. When he pulled the binding cloak away from her, she gave a sigh of relief and flexed her arms.

Alex tossed the cloak to a chair and turned back to her. Swiftly she lashed out with all her strength and slapped him across the face with a force that turned his head to the side. The ringing blow stung her palm. As she whirled around to leave, she felt his hand clench at the back of her costume.

"Not yet," Alex muttered.

Lily wrenched away from him violently, and gasped in astonished fury as she felt the gossamer fabric of her gown ripping. The sheer material fell away from her, and she clutched at it in panic, backing up against a wall and covering her front with her arms. Alex approached her and braced his hands on the wall, leaning over her. It seemed as if he were three times her size. His searing eyes raked over her slim body, lingering on the pagan design of the serpent painted around her. The paint had been smeared in several places, leaving streaks of black, green, and blue across her white skin.

"Don't touch me," Lily said shakily. "Or . . . I'll hit you again."

"I'm not going to touch you," he replied sardonically. "I'm going to wait here while you wash that . . ." he eyed the painted snake in disgust, ". . . thing off. There's a dressing room over there, and a bathing room just beyond."

She trembled with a mixture of fear and anger. "I have some revelations for you, my lord. I'm not going to take a bath. I'm not going to sleep in your bed tonight, and I'm not going to talk with you. I know everything you're going to say. The answer is no."

"Oh?" His eyes narrowed. "What am I going to say?"

"That you find me attractive, and you desire me, and therefore you want me to be your mistress, until you tire of me. Then I'll receive a generous parting gift and be free to have a string of protectors, until my looks are faded." Lily couldn't bring herself to look at him as she finished. "You want an arrangement."

"I want you to take a bath," he said quietly.

Lily's short laugh held a tinge of hysteria. "Let me go. I've ruined everything for you, and now you've ruined everything for me. The score is settled. Just let me—" Her words were smothered as Alex bent forward and kissed her. When he lifted his head, she tried to slap him again. He was prepared this time, his hand wrapping around her wrist before her palm reached his face.

They were both still. Lily felt the scraps of her costume drop away, leaving her naked except for the streaks of paint. She flushed wildly and tried to cover herself, but he wouldn't let go of her arm. He kept it raised high, while his gaze wandered over her in a burning sweep. The pace of his breathing accelerated until it matched her own. He stepped forward, and she shrank back against the cool panelled wall, hypnotized by the silver fire of his eyes. She whispered a plea, a denial. He didn't listen. She felt his gently marauding hands touch her shoulders, the shallow sides of her breasts, her ribs. His palms slid over her breasts and cupped them, causing her to shiver as her nipples hardened against the squeezing pressure. His face turned rigid with passion, his thick lashes lowering as he stared down at the slim body he was caressing.

Lily tried to feel nothing, to ignore the devastating pleasure that ignited wherever his hands touched. But her senses ached for another draught of the rapture he had given her last night. Remembering the feel of his hard body over hers, she began to tremble with a desire she couldn't suppress. She flushed with shame. "What have you done to me?" she whispered unsteadily.

His hands slid over her skin, smearing the paint in paths of heat and color. Slowly his color-stained fingertips traced the round swell of her breast, and etched a bluish green line across her flat stomach. Lily put her hands against his chest, tensing slightly as if to push him away. But nothing would stop him from touching her, from working a pattern over her body like some erotic artist engrossed in a sensuous painting. His palm covered the serpent's head at her shoulder and smudged it down her side in a vibrant emerald trail.

Making a last desperate attempt to escape, she tried to turn away, but the solid pressure of his body crowded closer, closer, and his hot, hungering mouth found hers. Urgently his hands clamped over her bare buttocks, lifting her to him, and he groaned against her soft mouth. The force of his desire burned out reason and resolution . . . she had no hold on her own self-restraint.

Shivering with helpless excitement, Lily lifted her arms to his broad shoulders, her fingers kneading and flexing into his coat. The feel of her naked body crushed against the linen and velvet smoothness of his clothes was new and startling. Roughly he tore his mouth away from hers and pressed his lips to the tops of her shoulders in biting kisses. She turned her face into his golden hair, her breath flowing against his ear. His tongue slid over her skin and found her pulse, lingering in the hollow of her throat with a tickling stroke.

Alex drew his head back, his gray eyes filled with an engrossed expression. She felt his fingers between their bodies, touching between her thighs, tugging at his breeches, until the hard, silken heat of him throbbed against her. With an eager whimper she pushed against the tantalizing pressure, craving him inside her. His hands returned to her buttocks, and with easy strength he lifted her against the wall. Lily made an anxious sound, her hands fluttering against his shoulders.

He spoke huskily, telling her what to do, his voice laced with tender violence. "Don't be afraid . . . put your legs around me . . . that's right." She felt a heavy, invading pressure, her body stretching to accommodate his upward thrust. She drew in a sharp breath and clung to him, her legs locking around his waist while his powerful arms supported her.

Alex buried his face in her throat as he moved within her. She was making sobbing noises of pleasure . . . he felt the vibrations against his lips. Pushing steadily into her softness. Her lithe body arched, while her hands found the back of his neck and gripped hard. Understanding the silent message, he let her weight settle deeper on him, and he moved one hand to the triangle between her thighs. His fingertips searched gently through the soft curls. "As long as it takes," he muttered against her flushed skin, increasing the pace of his thrusts. "I won't stop, not until you come for me. I won't stop."

She gave a sharp cry, her body tightening around him, shuddering. Alex let himself go immediately, holding his breath as his body was shaken by powerful spasms of release. He let out a ragged sigh and pressed his forehead to hers. They rested against each other, their breath flowing together, their clenched muscles relaxing. Carefully Alex lowered Lily until her toes touched the floor. He kissed her with his hand at the nape of her neck, holding her steady. His mouth was hot and sweet, savoring the aftertaste of pleasure.

He let go of her and refastened his breeches. Lily remained propped against the wall. Slowly she brought her arms around herself, partially shielding her body from his gaze. She had the dazed expression of someone who had just endured some terrible calamity. Turning back to her, Alex frowned. "Lily . . ." Wanting to comfort her, he lifted his hand to her face, but she flinched away from his paint-stained fingers. With a wry smile, he regarded his colorful hand. "Does it wash off," he asked gravely, "or should I begin thinking of explanations?"

Lily glanced down at the rainbow of hues covering her smooth body. "I don't know." She couldn't seem to sort through her jumbled thoughts. Her heart was still clattering, as if she had dosed herself with an exhilarating, nerve-shattering drug. She felt crazy and unsteady, and ready to cry. "I'm going home," she said. "If you have a shirt I could wear, a cloak—"

"No," he said quietly.

"I'm not asking you. I'm telling you. I'm going home."

"Not when you look like that. No, I don't mean the paint, I mean the look on your face. As if you're going to do something drastic."

"I always do something drastic," she said coolly. "My life has been an unending series of predicaments, my lord, ever since I was a child. I've survived them all without your interference, and I'll continue to do so."

Alex put his hands on her body again, ignoring her reluctant protest. He toyed with her navel, the points of her hipbones, fondling her as if he were holding a priceless piece of sculpture. Lily's composure—what there was of it—disappeared at

308

his touch. Awkwardly she began to push his hands away, but her attention was distracted as he spoke calmly. "Is money the only problem?"

"I don't want money from you," she said, catching her breath as his fingers brushed the edge of the paint-gilded curls at the top of her thighs.

"Would five thousand be sufficient, or do you need more?"

"Why don't you tell me precisely what obligations would come with it?" She glared at him and nodded, "Or is this by chance a gift with no strings attached?"

He held her gaze inflexibly. "There are strings."

Lily laughed mirthlessly. "At least you're honest."

"More honest than you."

"I don't lie."

"No, you just withhold the truth."

She lowered her eyes, aware of the havoc his gentle stroking was causing within her. "That seems to be the only damned thing I've withheld from you," she muttered, and her ears burned at the sound of his soft laughter.

Linking his fingers around her fragile wrist, he pulled her away from the wall and across the bedroom. Lily sputtered in indignation as she stumbled after him. "I haven't agreed to anything!"

"I know you haven't. We're going to continue our conversation in the bath."

"If you think I'll allow you to watch me bathe—"

He stopped suddenly and spun around, sliding an arm around her and kissing her hard. She twitched in surprise, but he held her snug and compact against him, one hand clamped around her wrist so firmly that she could feel her pulse throbbing against the cinch of his fingers. He lifted his head and she remained against him, blinking in bewilderment. With a quick grin, he continued to pull her behind him until they reached the bathing room. Alex let go of her and went to the tub, adjusting the gold spigots until the pipes shuddered behind the wall. Hot and cold water came forth in tumbling streams.

Standing with her arms around herself, Lily glanced at her surroundings in wonder. It was positively decadent, outfitted with a marble fireplace and lined with white tiles painted and glazed with brilliant colors. Having seen their like before in Florence, she recognized them as rare Italian tiles more than two centuries old. The built-in tub was the largest she had ever seen, able to accommodate two.

Alex smiled sardonically as he saw her modest posture. He pried her arm away from her breasts. "After parading through Craven's in nothing more than a few scarves sewn together—"

"It wasn't as revealing as it seemed. My wig hid a great deal."

"Not enough." Forcibly he guided her into the tub. With the dignity of an offended cat, Lily sat down in the rising water. Alex began to strip off his ruined clothes. "There'll be no more of that," he said brusquely, sliding her a wary glance.

At first Lily thought he meant her sullen attitude, but then she realized he was referring to her display at Craven's. The comment annoyed her. She should have expected he would begin issuing commands. She had never accepted anyone's dictates, not even her parents'. "I'll parade stark naked up and down Fleet Street if I want to."

He gave her a derisive glance but didn't reply. Lily reached for one of the cakes of soap piled in a glass bowl on the floor. Industriously she ran the slick soap over her arms and chest and splashed water over her skin. The steam and heat gathering in the room began to relax her, and unconsciously she gave a long sigh. Out of the corner of her eye she saw Alex approach the side of the tub. Realizing he was naked, she made a move to leave the warm water. "No," she said apprehensively. "I don't want you to share my bath. I-I've had enough of your pawing for one night."

"Sit down." Clamping his large hand on her shoulder, he pushed her back into the tub. "Ten minutes ago you were quite enamored of my pawing."

Her spine stiffened as she felt him step into the water behind her. He sat down, crooking one long leg and stretching the other out beside her. There was a soft exhalation of comfort, and then his arm reached around her, extricating the soap from her hand. Lily stared at his feet and felt the brush of his bent knee against the side of her breast. His soapy hands moved over her body. Mutely she watched as he washed the paint from her breasts, the color dissolving into grayish foam.

Alex sluiced water over Lily's shoulders, rinsing until her skin was pale and shimmering. He pulled her closer between his thighs, wordlessly urging her back until her weight was settled against the sodden mat of hair on his chest. He rubbed the soap between his fingers and slid them down her body in a slippery trail, until they converged between her thighs in a slick tangle.

It was quiet in the bathing room. There was only the soft swish of water and the sound of their breathing bouncing gently from the tiles. Lily couldn't help surrendering to the soothing warmth of the bath. She felt the tension leave her spine. Half-closing her eyes, she rested her head on his shoulder while his hands wandered smoothly over her. His face turned, and his lips swept into the wet curve of her neck, the frail edge of her jaw. She leaned more heavily on him and drew in a deep breath of steamy air. Unbidden, her hand crept to his thigh, her fingers flexing into the hard muscle. Underneath the water the rough hair on his body had become soft and velvety.

At the touch of her hand, Alex went still. There was no movement except for the rise and fall of his chest beneath her. Lily squeezed her eyes closed, waiting for the moment when he would push her away and say the interlude was over. But he reached for the soap once more, lathering his hands to a foamy slickness. She felt the lambent touch of his fingers on her breasts, circling like dancing butterflies, smoothing over the tiny, hardening tips. Lifting herself higher into the teasing caress, she gave a pleasured murmur.

His hands cupped water over her, pouring liquid warmth on her breasts, leaving her nipples taut and rosy. There was another ritual with the soap as he moved it back and forth between his palms, and then he set it aside. His lubricated palms glided in circles on her stomach, pausing as one fingertip dipped curiously into the neat hollow of her navel. Lily began to breathe in irregular gasps, feeling as if she were floating in a pool of fire. Her body tensed in yearning. Relentlessly his legs hooked over her ankles and eased them wider. Sliding his hand lower, he stroked the tense line of her abdomen . . . and lower still . . . and his fingers trailed through the thatch of sodden curls, saturating them with white foam. Lily started and clutched his wrist, trying to pull him away. "I think you should stop," she said breathlessly, and wet her lips. "I think—"

"Why don't you try *not* thinking?" he whispered against her ear, sliding his middle finger deep inside her. The sweetness of his touch spread through her, quickly condensing into heavy, aching urgency. His supple stroke went deeper, and her body tightened to draw in more of the tantalizing pressure. As the water sloshed rhythmically in the tub, she realized what was happening, and she said his name weakly. He murmured to her, telling her to forget everything, to concentrate only on *this* . . . and he kept her there, cradled by the water and his body, never ceasing the exquisite manipulation, drawing pleasure from her as if he could drink it in with his fingertips. Patiently he nudged her over the edge of feeling into a climax of exquisite, infinite relief. Her muffled cry echoed from the tiles, while her glistening body arched against his restraining arms. When the pleasure ebbed, he turned her until she was draped over him, and his mouth took hers in a drugging kiss.

"You're a beautiful woman, Wilhemina Lawson," he said huskily, holding her head in his wet hands. His gray eyes stared into her dark, astonished ones. "And you're going to stay the night with me."

Had she the advantage of clothes, weapons, or even a spark of energy, Lily might have found a way to leave. But she allowed him to dry her with a thick, soft towel, and carry her to a bedroom with a luminous ceiling that looked like sky and clouds. Alex extinguished the lamps and pulled her into bed beside him. They both knew that she would take the five thousand from him, and discuss the terms of the arrangement tomorrow. The tacit agreement gave Lily a trapped, sordid feeling. The exchange of money for the use of her body could not be considered anything other than what it was. But it also brought a certain measure of peace. She would pay Giuseppe and rehire the detective to find her daughter. Perhaps the nightmare of the past two years would be over soon.

His arm curved around her, pulling her against his body. It wasn't long before his breath rifled through her hair in the slow cadence of sleep. But tired as she was, Lily found it difficult to sleep. She had the troubled awareness that in spite of her efforts to avoid this, her life had turned down a path she had never wanted to travel . . . and there was no going back.

Lily was profoundly puzzled by the man sleeping beside her. She had accused him of brutality, but in spite of his many opportunities to hurt her, he had treated her with gentleness. In fact, he had deliberately sought to give her pleasure. She had thought of him as a coldhearted man, but the truth was that he possessed unusual depth of feeling. Others might consider him as having a restrained and moderate nature, but Lily knew that she alone could provoke him into an awe-inspiring temper. Privately she admitted that she was glad of it, that something in her found satisfaction in affecting him so deeply. He'd been furious that so many men had seen her in the Eve costume. The thought brought a slight smile to her face. The smile disappeared as she reflected that it wasn't like her to take pleasure in a man's possessiveness. Perturbed, she tried to move away, but he snuggled closer with a sleepy grunt and threw an arm over her. Wryly she settled back against him and closed her eyes, relaxing into the sheltering warmth of his body.

Alex was awakened by the annoying twitch and kick of Lily's legs. Grumbling, he sat up in the darkness, rubbing his eyes. "What's the matter?" he muttered, yawning deeply. His head whipped around as he heard a low, keening cry beside him. "Lily? Dammit, what . . ." He bent over her, while she writhed against the pillow. Her body twisted, her small fists knotting around handfuls of the bedclothes. Incoherent words fell from her lips in between her agitated gasps.

"Lily." Tenderly he swept the hair back from her forehead. "Shhh. You're dreaming. It's just a nightmare."

"No—"

"Wake up, sweetheart." He would have continued to speak to her, but then he heard the name she had whispered during her sleepwalking at Raiford Park. He'd thought it was Nick, but her voice was more distinct now. It dawned on him that she was repeating a woman's name.

"Nicole . . . no . . . no . . ." She wept with dry sobs, her hands reaching out blindly, twitching against the hard muscle of his chest. She was shaking with fear, or perhaps misery.

Alex stared down at her with a mixture of compassion and wild curiosity. Nicole. He'd never heard the name from any of the Lawsons. It had to be part of Lily's mysterious past. Stroking her hair, he lowered his lips to her forehead. "Lily, wake up. Easy. You're all right."

She jerked against him, her breath stopping as if someone had thrown her to the ground. Alex gathered her close, wrapping her in his arms. Suddenly she burst into tears. Whatever he had expected, it was not this, the pitiful sobbing that expressed a grief too deep to put into words. He froze in amazement. *"Lily."* He tried to soothe her, running his hands over her trembling body. Her weeping was oddly chilling. He'd never heard such a broken, unearthly sound. He would give anything, promise the sun and moon, anything to make her stop. "Lily," he repeated desperately. "For God's sake, don't cry like that."

It was a long time before she quieted, nuzzling her wet face against his chest. Alex wanted to talk then, wring explanations from her. But she gave an exhausted sigh and fell asleep with unnatural suddenness, as if the tears had drained every last bit of strength. Dumbfounded, he stared down at the bundle in his arms. "Who is Nicole?" he whispered, though he knew she couldn't hear. "What did she do to you?"

Her small head rested heavily in the crook of his arm. Stroking her dark hair, he felt his own tension begin to recede. But it was replaced by something far more disturbing. He was amazed by the protectiveness he felt. He wanted to take care of her, this spirited woman who had made it clear that she didn't want or need anyone's help. He knew she couldn't be trusted with his heart, but somewhere along the way he had already given it to her. She had turned his life upside down. She had changed everything.

He loved her. The simple truth was astonishing, but undeniable. Fervently he pressed his lips into her hair, his body rife with uncontained, anxious joy. He wanted her bound to him with words and promises, with everything he had that might hold her. In time she might come to care for him—it was a risk worth taking. It would be wise to find out more about her, delve into her past until she was less of an enigma. But he wasn't wise, he was in love, and he wanted her as she was. He'd been careful and responsible all his life. For once he would cast aside logic, and do as his heart prompted.

Lily stretched and shivered comfortably. Blinking her eyes open, she saw a delicate blue and white ceiling illuminated by the morning light. Slowly she turned her head and found Alex's translucent eyes trained on her. His tawny shoulders rose above her as he prevented her from pulling the sheet over her exposed breasts. He said good morning with a lazy grin, and asked how she had slept.

"Quite well," Lily said warily. Last night she'd had strange, troubled dreams. She wondered if she had disturbed him in her sleep—she wondered why there were no questions and suspicious glances.

"I was afraid you'd slip away before I woke," Alex said.

Guiltily she averted her gaze, recalling her stealthy departure of yesterday morning. "I don't have anything to wear," she mumbled.

"Of course." Deliberately he inched the sheet downward. "Keeping you without clothes has definite advantages."

Uncertain of his playful mood, Lily tried to retain the sheet. "I would appreciate it if you would send someone to my terrace for a gown and some things . . . my maid Annie will know what to collect . . . and . . ." Her dignified manner collapsed as he stripped away the white linen and pressed her thighs open. "Alex," she said with a faint protest.

His hands played lightly over her body. "I like to hear you say my name."

"You can't mean to," she said breathlessly. "Not again."

"Why not?"

"It must be unhealthy, or some such thing—"

"Very," he said, cupping his hands over her delicate breasts. "Addles the brain."

"Does it really—" she began in worry, and then saw that he was teasing her. "Alex!"

His warm, smiling mouth lowered to her breasts. Lily felt him wedged intimately high against her thigh. Her senses clamored in response, and she made no protest as he pushed her arms and legs wide and mounted her. He kissed her lips and pressed forward, easing deep inside her, moving with luxurious ease. Hesitantly she flattened her hands on his back, her palms resting on the flexing of muscle beneath the taut skin. She drew her legs up higher, clasping his hips between her knees, and he plunged sharply in climax, his breath striking the side of her neck in a single exhalation. His body tensed and shuddered, and then he relaxed with a sigh.

Lily was the first to break the languid silence. She raised herself to a sitting position, yanking at a corner of the sheet and pulling it up to her neck. "There are things we must talk about right away," she said, making an effort to sound brisk. She cleared her throat. "I may as well be blunt."

"For a change," he murmured, his eyes glinting with a mocking smile. He couldn't recall a single conversation when she *hadn't* been blunt with him.

"It concerns money and obligations."

"Oh, yes." He sat up to face her, ignoring her attempt to drag the sheet over his lap. "My money, your obligations."

She nodded uneasily. He was behaving strangely, his manner oddly lighthearted, the corners of his mouth tilted in a smile that made her feel off balance. "Last night you mentioned the five thousand pounds."

"That's right."

Lily bit her lip in frustration. "Do you still intend to give it to me?"

"I said I would."

"In return for what?"

All at once Alex didn't know how to tell her what he wanted. It would have been easier if the moment were romantic. But she looked at him impatiently, her lips compressed with tension. It was clear that all the passion and adoration coursing through his veins was not something she reciprocated. He matched her businesslike tone. "To begin with, I want you to share my bed."

She nodded. "I expected that," she said gruffly. "How fortunate for me that I'm worthy of such a sum."

The sarcastic jibe seemed to amuse him. "You'll be worth even more when you've mastered a few elementary skills."

Lily dropped her gaze, but not before he saw the flash of surprise and dismay in her eyes. It hadn't occurred to her that there was anything beyond what they had already done together. He smiled slowly and reached a hand to her shoulder, smoothing over the tempting silken bareness. "It shouldn't take you long."

"I should like to be set up in a house," Lily said uncomfortably. "It should be large enough for entertaining, and in a suitable location—"

"Would you like this one?"

He was mocking her, of course, offering the use of a family estate as if lodging a mistress there was a perfectly respectable thing to do. Lily glared at him. "Well, why not Raiford Park?" she snapped.

"If you'd prefer."

Flushing, she gave him a pleading, angered glance. "Can't you see this is difficult for me? You may find this very amusing, but I wish to get on with it! Do be serious."

"I am being serious." He pulled her against his chest and kissed her, his mouth warm and savoring. She responded helplessly, her lips parting at this gentle urging. Lifting his head, he stared into her bewildered eyes, his arms locked hard around her back. "I'll make a deposit at my bank in your name—a sum I don't think you'll find fault with. I'll have a carriage made for you in any style you wish. I'll open accounts for you at any and all shops you desire. Despite my better judgment, I'll even allow you to gamble at Craven's, knowing your liking for the place. But you won't wear any gowns I consider unsuitable, and if you accept the attentions of any man but me, I'll wring your lovely neck. You'll sleep in my bed every night, and accompany me whenever I go to the country. As far as your hunting and shooting, and the other activities you enjoy—I'll allow it all to continue, as long as I'm present. No more riding alone. I'll put a stop to any behavior of yours that strikes me as reckless." He felt Lily stiffen. He knew the conditions were hard to swallow for a woman who'd never had even a marginal check on her freedom. But she offered no objections. "I won't be unreasonable," he continued more quietly. "I don't doubt you'll tell me when I am."

She spoke then, sounding choked. "You should know something . . . I . . . I'll take measures to prevent children. I don't want them. I won't have them."

He hesitated, aware of the subdued intensity of her voice. "All right."

"Don't say that if you secretly intend otherwise."

"I wouldn't have said 'all right' if I didn't mean it," he growled. He sensed the importance of the exchange, that something was significant about her insistence. With time and patience, he would dig down to the root of her fear. But if her feelings never changed, he would accept them. If he never produced an heir, Henry would continue the family line.

"And when you tire of me," Lily continued in a low, mortified tone, "you'll allow me to keep everything you've given me." From what she'd heard, that was a common understanding between a courtesan and her protector. If she were actually going to do this, she might as well look after her own interests. She was perplexed by Alex's sudden silence.

"There's something I haven't yet explained," he finally said.

Lily felt a chill of apprehension. "I can't imagine what. Is it about the money? The house? If it concerns my friendship with Derek, there's no need to worry, you already know—"

"Lily, hush. Listen to me." He took a deep breath. "What I'm trying to tell you is that I don't want you to be my mistress."

"You don't want . . ." She stared at him blankly, and began to simmer with fury. Had he been teasing her all this time? Had this been some vicious plan to humiliate her? "Then what the hell have we been talking about?" she demanded.

He pleated and smoothed a corner of the sheet, giving the task unusual concentration. Suddenly he raised his eyes and looked at her steadily.

"I want you to be my wife."

CHAPTER 10

"Your wife," Lily repeated dully, turning hot and then sickeningly cold with humiliation. So it had been a joke—a deliberate drawn out, cruel game he must have planned during the long night he'd been bound to her bed. But perhaps he still wanted her as his mistress, and this was his way of ensuring that she knew how things stood. He would be in control—she would be his to toy with and torment. She felt him watching her, and she wondered if he despised her as much as she despised herself. Her hurt went almost too deep for rage. Almost. She spoke raggedly, unable to look at him. "You and your perverse, disgusting sense of humor make me *ill*—"

He shushed her immediately, pressing his hand to her mouth. "No, no, dammit . . . it's not a joke! Hush. I want you to marry me."

She bit his hand, and glared at him as it was promptly removed. "You have no reason to propose to me. I've already agreed to be your mistress."

He stared incredulously at the impression of her

teeth marks on his hand. "I respect you too much for that, you hot-tempered bitch!"

"I don't want your respect. All I want is five thousand pounds."

"Any other woman would be flattered by my proposal. Even grateful. I'm offering you something a hell of a lot better than some scandalous liaison."

"In your conceited, self-righteous opinion I suppose it is! But I'm *not* flattered, and certainly not grateful. I'll be your mistress or nothing at all."

"You'll be my wife," he said inexorably.

"You want to own me!" she accused, trying to crawl away from him.

"Yes." He flung her down on the bed and flattened his weight on her. As he spoke, his hot breath fanned her mouth and chin. "Yes. I want other people to look at you and know you're mine. I want you to take my name and my money. I want you to live with me. I want to be inside you . . . part of your thoughts . . . your body . . . all of you. I want you to trust me. I want to give you whatever elusive, impossible, goddamned mysterious thing it is you need in order to be happy. Does that frighten you? Well, it frightens the hell out of me. Don't you think I'd stop feeling this way if I could? It's not as if you're the easiest woman in the world to—" He checked himself suddenly.

"You know nothing about me," she burst out. "And what you do know should scare the bloody wits out of you . . . God, now I *know* your brain has been addled!"

"I won't pay for Harry Hindon's failures, or the other one's, whoever the bastard is. I haven't failed you, Lily. I haven't betrayed you. I asked you once why you hate men. You're free to despise them all, every last one on earth. Except for me."

"You think my refusal is because I've been disappointed by love?" She stared at him as if he were the biggest fool alive. "I can live with your bloody conditions and rules and whims for a time—perhaps even a few years—but if you think I'd subject myself to that for the rest of my life, and give away the properties and legal rights I have to you, and for what? For the privilege of servicing you every night? It's pleasant enough, but hardly worth sacrificing everything I value."

"*Pleasant,*" he repeated grimly.

She stared at him defiantly. "You're heavy. I can't breathe."

He didn't move. "Tell me how happy you are, Lily. Do you enjoy your freedom when you're forced to spend every night gambling for your survival? Are you going to claim there aren't nights when you're lonely, when you need companionship and comfort—"

"I have everything I need." She tried to hold his piercing stare, but the intensity of his gaze made hers fall away.

"I don't," he said huskily.

Lily turned her face away. "Then find someone

else," she said with desperate determination. "There are so many women who would want to marry you. Women who need the things you have to offer, who would love you—"

"There's no one like you."

"Oh? And when did I become such an endless source of delight for you?" She looked back up at him, just in time to see a slow smile spread across his face. "What's so damned amusing?"

Relieving her of some of his weight, Alex propped his chin on his hand and regarded her thoughtfully. "We were drawn to each other from the first. We were meant for each other. I think we'd have come together even if we'd been born on different continents. You feel the attraction as strongly as I do."

"You must be reading Byron," she muttered. "To hear such romantic drivel from you—"

"You chose me."

"I did no such thing!"

"Of all the hundreds of men you've met at Craven's or at weekend hunts or soirées—young and old, dandies, intellectuals, barons and bankers and fortune hunters—I'm the only man you ever involved yourself with. You provoked an argument with me, you came to my home and interfered with every aspect of my life, plotted to stop me from getting married, lured me to London and tied me to your bed, gambled with me and staked your body against my money, knowing there was every chance you would lose . . . Sweet Jesus, do you need me to elaborate further? Have you *ever* meddled in some other poor bastard's life the way you have mine? I don't think so."

"It was all because of Penny," she said in a small voice.

He smiled derisively. "She was an excuse. You did it all because you wanted me."

"Conceited ass!" she exclaimed, turning pink.

"Is it all conceit on my part? Then tell me you want me out of your life."

"I want you out of my life," she said readily.

"Tell me the past two nights have meant nothing to you."

"They haven't!"

"Tell me you never want to see me again."

"I . . ." Lily stared at the handsome, intent face above hers, and the words could not be dragged from her throat.

Alex smoothed her hair gently. "Tell me," he whispered, gazing down at her. "And then I'll leave you alone."

Lily tried again. "I *never* . . ." Her chest hurt with the effort. She couldn't allow him to complicate her life more than it already was. But the thought of driving him away filled her with inexplicable fear. If only he would say something else, something that would convince her one way or the other. But he didn't help her; he stayed tormentingly silent. She tried to sort through her mixed-up feelings. If only he weren't so strong-willed. If only he were compliant and manageable. He could ruin what little chance she had of regaining her daughter.

Her heart thumped hard, making it difficult for her to speak. "Would you . . ." She wet her dry lips and forced herself to continue. "Would you really go away if I asked you to? As easily as that?"

Alex's thick lashes lowered as he watched the tip of her tongue sweep across the winsome curve of her lower lip. "No," he said thickly. "I just wanted to see if you would say it."

"Oh, God." She gave a frightened, wondering laugh. "I don't think I can."

"Why not?"

Lily began to shake. She had always been able to face her defeats and hardships with defiant courage, and no one, not even Giuseppe, had been able to take down her defenses. Only Alex was able to do this to her. "I don't know," she cried, and buried her face against him. "I don't know."

"Sweetheart." He spread swift, hard kisses over her small ear and neck and shoulder. His arms went around her in a crushing embrace.

"I w-would prefer to be your mistress," she said miserably.

"All or nothing. That's how it is with us." He pushed her hair back from her forehead, and gave her a crooked grin. "Besides, marrying you is the only way I can have Burton as my butler." He kissed her. "Say yes." His fingers curled into her hair. "Say it, darling," he whispered.

★   ★   ★

330

Lily managed to convince herself she was doing it for the money. She was afraid to admit to herself that there was another, even more compelling reason behind her acceptance. As Alex's wife, she would be extraordinarily rich. She would have enough money to buy back Nicole, and if Giuseppe still refused to be accommodating, she would hire some "Learies," the highly trained city officers held in such renown. The one she had employed before, Mr. Knox, hadn't been of much use, but now she could afford to hire a dozen. She'd have them pick the city apart until her daughter was returned to her. After that it didn't matter what happened. After discovering that she was the mother of a bastard child—which she intended to keep—Alex would quickly agree to an annulment, or possibly a divorce. She would move to some quiet, peaceful place with her daughter. Alex would be none the worse off, except for some justifiable anger about her deception. But he would find someone else, some pretty young girl who'd bear him a dozen heirs.

In the meanwhile, Lily intended to take pleasure in the time she had with him. There would be more nights spent in the bedroom with the cloud-and-sky ceiling. There would be time to talk, tease, and provoke him. She'd never had that kind of relationship with a man. The closest she had ever come was her odd, passionless friendship with Derek Craven. But unlike Derek, Alex was possessive of her, protective to a fault, all too willing to involve himself in her problems. Lily thought that perhaps she might secretly let herself enjoy the feeling of belonging to someone. For one brief time in her life she would know what it was like to call a man "husband."

Alex made the impossible assertion that they would be married that very afternoon. Lily knew his haste was born of his suspicion that she might suddenly change her mind. He was absolutely right. She changed her mind every ten minutes. Alex sent for her maid Annie and arranged for her to be brought to Swans' Court, bearing the necessary clothes and toiletries.

Lily fretted while she dressed in a soft yellow cotton gown with multipuff sleeves. The modestly high neckline was bordered with embroidered openwork lace. "I look like a country maid in this gown," she muttered, staring at herself in the mirror while Annie fastened the silk loops in back. "And all of fifteen years old. Why didn't you bring something more sophisticated?"

" 'Tisn't the dress that makes you look young, miss," Annie said, smiling over her shoulder. " 'Tis your face."

Lily sat in front of the rectangular gilt-framed mirror at the dressing table, and peered at her reflection curiously. With annoyance, she realized that Annie was right. The natural pink of her lips was a deeper shade than usual, slightly swollen from Alex's ravaging kisses of the night before. Her face was different, soft and luminous and vulnerable. Even a brushing of powder couldn't tone down the rosy color of her skin, which had always been so fashionably pale. She didn't look at all like the bold woman who rooked all the pigeons at Craven's. Her cynical, mocking stare, which she had used to such satisfying effect, had lost all its potency. Her eyes were as guileless and open as Penelope's. As she stared at herself, she remembered the carefree days of her teens, when she had been a passionate girl wildly infatuated with Harry Hindon. Not since then had she felt such stirrings inside herself.

The changes she saw in the mirror made Lily uneasy. "Did you bring any of my *bandeaus?*" she asked, running her hands through her dancing curls. "My hair is falling into my eyes." Efficiently Annie brought them to her, and Lily chose a ribbon of gold adorned with topaz. She tied it around her forehead and scowled as she saw that the exotic band contrasted oddly with the girlish style of the dress. "Damn!" Ripping the ornament from her head, she pushed her hair back impatiently. "Please, bring some scissors and cut some of this mop off."

"But miss," Annie protested. "It looks so pretty and soft around your face."

"Then let it be." She buried her head in her hands and groaned. "I don't care. I can't go through with this, Annie."

"Go through with what?" the maid asked in confusion.

"This sham of a . . . oh, you don't need to know. Just help me get away from here and tell Lord Raiford . . ." She paused in indecision.

A new voice entered the conversation. "Tell Lord Raiford what?" Alex wandered into the room, having returned from a brief excursion through the city. From the satisfied expression on his face, Lily knew he'd been successful in finding a minister who would marry them at such short notice. Heaven only knew what he'd told the man.

Annie regarded Alex with rapt admiration, never having seen a man allowed to intrude on Miss Lawson's privacy without asking permission. She retreated to the corner of the room and fussed with a light silk shawl, watching with discreet delight as Alex went to stand behind Lily.

He slid his hands over Lily's shoulders and bent low to her ear. "Little coward," he whispered. "You're not going to run away from me."

"I wasn't planning to," she lied with an air of dignity.

"You look beautiful in that gown. I can't wait to take it off you."

"Is that all you ever think about?" Lily asked in a low tone, mindful of Annie's pricked ears.

He smiled and kissed the side of her neck. "Are you almost finished?"

"No," she said with an emphatic shake of her head.

"We have to leave soon."

Lily slipped away from him, standing up from

the chair and striding about the room. She paced back and forth, passing by him repeatedly. "My lord," she said in agitation, "I've been thinking about the folly of decisions made in haste, and in the last few minutes I've come to the conclusion that I was reckless in agreeing to—"

One long arm reached out and caught her to him, like a cat interrupting the frantic scurrying of a mouse. His mouth came swiftly upon hers, and she inhaled sharply, her mind reeling with surprise. Behind her back, Alex waved his hand in a gesture for Annie to leave the room. With a grin and a bobbing curtsey, the maid departed with discreet haste. Alex kissed Lily long and hard, until he felt her lean heavily against him, her knees wobbling. He lifted his head and stared into her drowsy dark eyes. "Marrying me is the least reckless thing you've ever done."

She plucked fitfully at the lapels of his coat and smoothed them. "I . . . I just wish I had some sort of guarantee."

"Will this do?" He kissed her with raw passion, parting her lips and setting her nerves ablaze with a slow search for her tongue. Lily's hands crept around his neck, and her breath became labored, her body turning light and hot. When he dragged his mouth from hers, she kept her arms around him to preserve her balance.

"Alex," she said unsteadily.

"Hmm?" His lips played at the sensitive corner of her mouth.

"I won't be the usual sort of wife. I couldn't even if I wanted to."

"I know."

She slanted a suspicious upward glance through her lashes. "But how can I be certain you won't want me to change?"

He smiled sardonically. "Into what?"

"You'll want me to become respectable and leave off riding astride, and begin collecting recipes for cow-heel jelly and shoe-blacking, and sitting in the parlor with an embroidery frame on my lap—"

"Hush," he said with a laugh, cradling her face in his hands. He brushed his lips over hers. "No wonder you've avoided marriage for so long. Burn every embroidery frame in the house, if you want. Let Mrs. Hodges bother with the cow-heel jelly—whatever the hell that's for—no, don't tell me, please." His fingertips slid up and down her slender neck, toying with the fine curls at her nape. "I don't want to change you, sweetheart. Just rein you in a little."

As he had intended, the comment nettled her. "You're quite welcome to try," she said pertly, and he laughed.

Giving her time only to find her gloves, he guided her downstairs to the phaeton outside. After helping her up, Alex nodded to the groom to release the horses, and they headed south in the direction of the river. Lily found herself almost enjoying the ride. Perched on the high seat of the phaeton, she watched with amusement as Alex worked to control the beautifully matched horses. The animals were fresh and filled with explosive energy, requiring all his attention. Lily made certain to give Alex enough room on the seat to allow sufficient arm movement. Finally the horses evened their pace enough to allow conversation.

"Why haven't you had their tails docked?" Lily asked, gesturing to the horses' long black tails. Surgically removing the animals' tails, including several of the vertebrae, was a popular custom, for the sake of both fashion and practicality. "They could become tangled in the reins."

Alex shook his head, replying in a mumble she couldn't quite hear.

"What?" she asked. "What did you say?"

"I said it's painful for the horses."

"Yes, but the pain doesn't last long, and really it's safer with them docked."

"Their tails are their only protection against flies," he said, not looking at her.

"Adores children and animals," Lily murmured, feeling a kindling of warmth toward him. "You're not living up to your coldhearted reputation, my lord. Here, let me drive the phaeton." She stretched her hands out for the reins.

Alex gave her a blank look, as if the concept of a woman guiding the horses were completely foreign.

Lily laughed and chided him gently. "I'm quite good at it, my lord."

"You'll ruin your gloves."

"What's one little pair of gloves?"

"I've never let a woman take the reins before."

"Afraid?" she asked sweetly. "Apparently the trust in this marriage is to be one-sided."

Reluctantly Alex handed over the reins. Her firm, expert grip seemed to reassure him, and he sat back a little.

"Relax," Lily said with a laugh. "You look as though you intend to snatch them back at any moment. I've never overturned a phaeton, my lord."

"There's a first time for everything." He glanced at the reins longingly.

"So it seems," she said with perfect demureness, and flicked the horses to increase the pace.

After about a mile, Alex complimented Lily on her driving. He took pride in the sight of her small hands exerting such confident pressure on the reins. Not that he was entirely comfortable with being her passenger—it was not in his nature to relinquish control easily. But Lily's pride in her own skill was as exciting as it was attractive. She would never be easily cowed by him or anyone. She would be an ideal wife for him, a woman capable of matching his passion, strength, and stubbornness with her own.

The phaeton progressed toward Brompton and Chelsea, and Alex retrieved the reins the last part of the way. He took them down a side street to a small stone church with arched wooden doors. A soberly dressed lad in his teens waited outside the church entrance. "Hold the horses," Alex murmured, tossing him a coin. "We won't be long."

The boy caught the coin in his fist and grinned cheerfully. "Aye, m'lord."

Alex descended from the phaeton and reached up for Lily. She was frozen in place, looking down at him with wide eyes. The sight of the church had been like a bucket of cold water thrown in her face, making her realize exactly what was about to happen. Alex spoke casually. "Give me your hand, Lily."

"What am I doing?" she asked in a small voice.

"Let me help you down."

Lily put her hand to her thrashing heart as she stared at him. His manner was easy and unthreatening, but deep in his eyes there was a steely gleam, and his voice contained a thread of warning. Now that she had allowed him to bring her this far, there would be no escape. Feeling as if the situation weren't quite real, she placed her hand in his and alighted from the carriage. "After H-Harry jilted me," she stammered, "I promised myself . . . I vowed . . . I'd never marry anyone."

Alex looked at her down-bent head, realizing how much her fiancé's desertion had hurt her, enough that the memory of the humiliation still lingered after ten years. He slid an arm around her and kissed the top of her head. "He didn't deserve you," he whispered into her hair. "He was a weak, cowardly fool."

"Intelligent enough to s-save himself. And some might call you even more of a fool for doing this—"

"I have my faults," Alex said, gently kneading her shoulders, turning his back to shield her from the curious gazes of passersby. He smiled ruefully. "Many faults, and you've managed to become acquainted with most of them. But I'd never leave you, Wilhemina Lawson. Never. Do you understand?"

"I understand," she said with a smothered, hopeless laugh, "but I don't believe you. You think you know the worst about me, but you don't." She didn't dare say more than that. Holding her breath, she waited to see if it would be enough to make him change his mind.

"I know all I need to," he said quietly. "The rest will keep for later." Keeping his arm around her, he walked with her into the church.

The inside of the little building was touching in its simplicity, filled with the light filtering through quaint stained-glass windows. The glow of candles caused the polished oak pews to gleam. An elderly vicar waited for them inside. His face was weathered and kindly. Although he was no taller than Lily, he possessed a strong and vibrant presence. "Lord Raiford," he said with a serene smile. His clear blue eyes moved to Lily's apprehensive face. "And this must be Miss Lawson." He surprised Lily by taking her shoulders in his hands and studying her appraisingly. "I've known Raiford for quite some time, my dear. Almost since the day of his birth."

"Oh?" Lily returned with a wan imitation of her usual saucy smile. "And what's your opinion of him, vicar?"

"The earl is a good man," he replied thoughtfully, his eyes twinkling as he glanced at Alex, "though at times he is apt to be somewhat prideful."

"And arrogant," Lily added, her smile widening.

The vicar smiled also. "Yes, perhaps that too. But he is also responsible and compassionate, and if he follows the family tradition, he'll prove to be an unusually devoted husband. The Raiford blood, you see. I am glad that the earl has chosen a woman of strong mettle as his companion. Throughout the years he has been given many burdens to carry." The vicar glanced at Alex's averted face, and returned to Lily's attentive expression. "Have you ever been on a sea voyage, Miss Lawson? You may have heard the word 'marry' as a nautical term. It refers to the sailors' practice of matching two ropes together to give them greater strength as one. I pray this will be true of your union."

Lily nodded, touched by the quiet atmosphere of the church, the vicar's kind face, the sight of the color creeping up from Alex's collar. Alex did not look at her, only kept his gaze on the floor, but she sensed that he was as affected by the moment as she was. "I hope so," she whispered.

The vicar gestured to both of them, and walked toward the altar at the front of the church. Lily hesitated, her heart racing with emotion. Slowly she removed her gloves and handed them to Alex. He put the white kid gloves in his pocket and took her hand, folding her fingers between his. Lily looked up at him with a tremulous smile. But there was no smile on his face, only a grave expression and a flash of heat in his gaze.

They stood before the vicar with their hands linked. Lily only half-heard the clergyman's measured voice as it drifted in and out of her consciousness. It was like a dream—a blurred, bewildering dream. Of all the twists and turns her life had taken, this was the most unexpected. She was marrying a man she barely knew, but somehow it seemed she had known him for a lifetime. The feel of her hand in his, turning warm and damp, was oddly familiar. The sound of his even breathing, the quiet timbre of his voice as he spoke the vows, all of it called to something deep within her, soothing the restless fear that had been a part of her for so long. She repeated her own vows carefully, trying to make her faltering voice steady. Alex brought her hand up and slid a heavy, carved gold ring on her finger. The band, a little too loose for her finger, was adorned with a large ruby that glowed as if a flame were trapped in the brilliant depths.

The vicar pronounced them man and wife, and sealed the marriage with the blessings of God.

They signed the church register and affixed their names to a marriage certificate and special license. With one last stroke of the pen, Lily gave a trembling sigh, knowing it was done. There was a sound at the back of the church as an elderly couple entered, some of the vicar's parishioners. Excusing himself, the vicar went to talk to the pair, leaving Alex and Lily alone in front of the heavy register book. They looked down at their two names and the date inscribed below. Lily glanced at her ring, twisting it around her finger. The ruby, and the duster of diamonds that surrounded it, was almost too large for her small hand.

"It belonged to my mother," Alex said gruffly.

"It's beautiful," Lily replied, raising her eyes to his. "Did you ever . . . did Caroline . . ."

"No," he said swiftly. "She never even saw it." He touched her hand. "I wouldn't ask you to wear something tainted with memories of another woman."

"Thank you." Lily couldn't prevent a shy, pleased smile.

His hand tightened on hers until it almost hurt. "I did care for Caroline. Had she lived, I would have married her, and . . . I believe we would have been content."

"Of course you would have," Lily murmured, puzzled by the short speech.

"But with you it's different . . ." Alex stopped and cleared his throat awkwardly.

Breathlessly Lily waited for him to continue,

feeling as if she were poised at the brink of a dizzying height. "What do you mean, different?" She stared at his golden face, wreathed in shadows and candlelight. "Different in what way?"

But the vicar interrupted them just then, returning from his brief conversation with the elderly couple. "Lord and Lady Raiford. I have a matter to attend to. Counsel to offer to some parishioners—"

"Yes, of course," Alex said smoothly. "Thank you."

The shock of being addressed as Lady Raiford caused Lily to forget her question. Dutifully she said good-bye to the vicar as she walked to the door with Alex. "I'm a countess," she said, and gave an incredulous laugh once they had left the church. She stared up at Alex's amused expression. "Do you think my mother will be pleased?"

"She'll faint," Alex replied, helping her into the phaeton, "and then she'll ask for a cup of strong tea." He grinned as he saw her reach for the reins. "Don't touch those, Lady Raiford. I'll be the one to drive us home."

At Lily's request, Alex took her to the bank of Forbes, Bertram, and Company, and withdrew five thousand pounds from the venerable institution. Lily was surprised that Alex didn't bully her with questions about her obligation. She knew he assumed it was a gambling debt. Perhaps he thought she owed the money to Derek. "Will it be enough?" was all he asked, pulling her to a private corner as his banker headed toward the vaults and security boxes in the next room.

Lily nodded with a guilty blush. "Yes, thank you. I'll need to take care of some things this afternoon." She hesitated almost imperceptibly. "I would prefer to do them by myself."

Alex looked at her a long time, his face impassive. "Are you going to see Craven?"

Lily was tempted to lie to him, but she nodded. "I want Derek to be the first to know about the marriage. He deserves that much from me. Oh, I know it's obvious he has no morals or scruples, but in his own peculiar way he's been kind to me, and for some reason I think he would be hurt if I didn't explain this to him."

"Don't explain too much," Alex advised. "That would be just as hurtful." At her bewildered expression, he smiled without amusement. "Are you really so unaware of how he feels about you?"

"No, no," she said in a rush, "you don't understand how it is with Derek and me—"

"Oh, I understand." He looked at her speculatively. "So it's necessary that you go out alone this afternoon."

Already it had begun, the strangeness of accounting to someone for her activities. Lily hoped he wouldn't make it necessary for her to lie to him. "And perhaps the early part of the evening."

"I want you to take a groom and a pair of outriders with the carriage."

"Certainly," she said with an agreeable smile. She wouldn't mind riding to Craven's in a closed carriage and a whole army of outriders. But she would have to be unaccompanied for her meeting with Giuseppe in Covent Garden. She would simply borrow one of Derek's mounts and sneak away alone.

Alex looked torn between pleasure and suspicion at her easy acceptance of his request. "While you're gone," he said, "I'm going to call on Lord and Lady Lyon."

"Your aunt and uncle?" Lily guessed, having heard her mother mention the names before.

He nodded ruefully. "My aunt is well respected, and experienced in matters requiring extreme diplomacy."

"You think she'll be able to help us avoid the appearance of scandal? After our card game at Craven's and the scene last night and Penny's sudden elopement and our hasty marriage?" She made a comical face. "Don't you think the damage has already been done, my lord?"

"She'll consider it a challenge."

"A *disaster*, more likely," Lily said, suddenly tickled by the idea of a society matron trying to delicately smooth over their brazen antics. Her flurry of giggles caused a multitude of offended gazes to turn to them as the soberfaced clerks and clients noticed the undignified behavior of the couple standing next to the gray marble column.

"Hush," Alex said, though a grin flicked across

his face. "Behave yourself. Every time we're in public together, we cause a scene."

"I've been doing it on my own for years," Lily said airily. "But you're concerned for your reputation, I see. Eventually you'll be reduced to *begging* me not to make scenes—"

She started with astonishment as Alex bent and kissed her right in front of the assembled crowd at the bank. The somber room resounded with quiet exclamations of disapproval and gasps of amazement. Pushing at the heavy muscles of her husband's chest, Lily strained to escape him, feeling herself turn hot with mortified dismay. He persisted until she forgot where they were, and she gave a shiver of pleasure. Then he lifted his head and smiled down at her, his eyes glinting with challenge and enjoyment. Flustered, Lily stared at him, and suddenly she laughed in admiring surprise. "*Touché*," she said, raising her hands to her flushed cheeks.

Lily found Derek in one of the private rooms at the gambling palace. He had pushed two tables together and piled them high with account books, bank drafts, promissory notes, and money—piles of coins and thick wads of bills tied with white string. In the past Lily had observed him count money with dazzling speed, his thin dark fingers rifling through notes until they were a blur. But he seemed strangely clumsy today, combing through his profits with exaggerated care. As she

347

approached the tables, Lily caught the bittersweet smell of gin. She saw a glass of it on the table, surrounded by splashes that would ruin the fine wood. She regarded Derek in surprise. It was unlike him to drink heavily, and especially gin, the liquor of the poverty-stricken. He hated gin. It reminded him of his past.

"Derek," she said quietly.

He raised his head, his green eyes traveling over the yellow gown and the heightened color of her cheeks. He looked like a jaded young sultan. The hard bitterness of his face was especially pronounced today. Lily thought objectively that he might have lost a little weight. The edges of his cheekbones were as sharp as knife blades. And he was strangely untidy. His cravat was undone, and his black hair spilled over his forehead.

"Worthy hasn't been looking after you," Lily said. "Just a minute, I'm going to the kitchen to have them send up someth—"

"I'm not hungry," he interrupted, pronouncing his *h* with mocking care. "Don't bother. I told you I'm busy."

"But I came to tell you something."

"I don't have time to talk."

"But Derek—"

"No—"

"I married him," Lily said bluntly. She hadn't meant to blurt it out so suddenly. She gave a sheepish, self-conscious laugh. "I married Lord Raiford this morning."

Derek's face went blank. He was very quiet, taking his time about finishing his drink. His fingers exerted unnecessary pressure on the glass. His face was unreadable as he spoke in a flat voice. "Did you tell 'im about Nicole?"

Lily's smile vanished. "No."

"What do you expect ow 'im when 'e finds out you 'as a bastard daughter?"

She lowered her head. "I expect he'll seek an annulment or divorce. I wouldn't blame him for hating me when he discovers how I've deceived him. Derek, don't be angry. I know it seems a foolish thing for me to have done, but really it makes sense—"

"I'm not angry."

"With Alex's wealth, I'll be able to bargain with Giuseppe—" She gasped with surprise as Derek moved suddenly, scooping up a handful of coins and scattering them at her feet. Frozen amid the gleaming puddle of coins, she stared at him with wide eyes.

"You didn't do it for that," he said, his voice gentle and cool. "It wasn't for money. Tell me the truf, gypsy—it's all we've ewer 'ad, you an' me."

"The truth is that I want my daughter back," she said defensively. "That's the only reason I married him."

He raised an unsteady hand and pointed to the door. "If you wants to lie to me, then leave my club."

Lily looked down at her feet and swallowed hard.

"All right," she mumbled. "I'll admit it. I care for him. Is that what you want me to say?"

Derek nodded, seeming to calm down. "Yes."

"He's good for me," Lily continued with difficulty, twisting her hands together. "I didn't believe someone like him could exist, a man without a trace of malice or dishonor. He says he doesn't want to change me. When I'm with him, there are moments when I know what it's like to be happy. I've never known such a feeling before. Is it wrong to want that, even for a little while?"

"No," he said softly.

"You and I can still be friends, can't we?"

He nodded. Lily sighed and smiled in relief.

Derek's face was strangely blank. "I 'as to say somefing. You—" He stopped and made a careful effort to speak in the way that pleased her. "You needs—need—a man like Raiford, and you'll be a bloody fool if you loses him. The life you've been at would of brought you low gypsy. It was making you hard. He'll keep you respectable, and take care of you. Don't tell him about your bastard babe. There may be no need."

"He'll have to know eventually, when I find Nicole."

"You may newer—*never*—find her."

Anger flared in her eyes. "Yes, I will. Don't be petty and horrid, Derek, just because I've done something that's displeased you."

"It's been two years." The quiet urgency of his voice unnerved her more than mockery would have. "Not me or your bloody Learie man 'as been able to find her, and I've had my people look in ewery flash-house and gin shop, question ewery fence in Fleet Market and Covent Garden . . ." He paused as he saw the color drain from her face, and then he continued resolutely. "I've had them look in prisons, inn yards, workhouses, at the docks . . . she was dead or sold away from London, gypsy, a long time ago. Or . . ." His jaw tensed. "It's too late to save 'er from what she's become. I know what they do to chiwdren, things they make them do . . . I *know*, gypsy, because . . . some ow it was done to me. You'd rather 'ave 'er dead." The cold green of his eyes seemed to glitter with the remnant of some long-ago torment.

"Why are you doing this?" Lily asked hoarsely. "Why are you saying this to me?"

"You deserves a fair chance wi' Raiford. You 'as to leave your past behind, or it will bring the future tumbling down around you."

"You're wrong," she said in a thin, shivering voice. "Nicole is still alive. She's somewhere in the city. Don't you think I would know if she were dead? I would feel it, something inside would tell me . . . you're wrong!"

"Gypsy—"

"I won't discuss it anymore. Not another word, Derek, or our friendship is over for good. I'm going to get my daughter back, and someday I'll watch in pleasure as you eat your words. Now, I'd like to borrow a horse from you, just for an hour or two."

"You're going to give that Italian bastard the five thousand," Derek said grimly. "I should follow you an' kill 'im."

"*No.* You know that if anything happens to him, my only chance of finding Nicole will be gone."

He nodded with a sullen scowl. "Worvy will arrange for the horse. An' after this, I 'ope to God Raiford can find a way to keep you 'ome at nights."

Lily reached the meeting place at twilight. A light rain had begun to fall, temporarily washing away the smell of garbage, rotten food, and manure that always permeated Covent Garden. She was surprised to see that Giuseppe was already there. Approaching Giuseppe slowly, she noticed that his usual cocksure manner was absent. There was an edginess to his posture. The dark, well-cut clothes he wore seemed shabby. She wondered why, with all the money she had given him, he had not invested in new garments. As he saw her, his swarthy face turned eager.

"*Hai il denaro?*"

"*Sì, l'ho,*" Lily answered, but instead of placing the satchel in his outstretched hands she held it to her midriff, her arms wrapped around it.

His full-lipped mouth curved downward as he surveyed the wet darkness. The rain had quickly dissipated into a cool mist. "*Come piove,*" he remarked sullenly. "Always the rain, always the gray sky. I loathe this England!"

"Why don't you leave?" Lily asked, staring at him without blinking.

Giuseppe shrugged moodily. "The choice is not mine. I stay because they want me 'ere." He shrugged. "È così."

"That's how it is," Lily translated softly. "Who are 'they,' Giuseppe? Do 'they' have something to do with Nicole and this extortion?"

He looked annoyed, as if he had said more than he should have. "Give the money to me."

"I won't do this anymore," Lily said stiffly, her white face framed by the hood of her dark cloak, her eyes bright with strain. "I can't, Giuseppe. I've done everything you've asked. I came to London when you told me to. I've given you everything I have, without one shred of proof that Nicole is alive. The only thing you've ever given me is the little dress she was wearing when you took her."

"You doubt I still 'ave Nicoletta?" Giuseppe asked silkily.

"Yes, I doubt it." Lily swallowed painfully. "I think she may be dead."

"You 'ave my word she is not."

"Well." Lily gave a contemptuous laugh. "Forgive me if I don't find your word all that reliable."

"You are wrong to say this to me, *cara*," Giuseppe said with an insufferably smug expression. "Some'ow I t'ink to myself tonight, I should bring with me proof that Nicoletta is safe. I do not wish you to doubt me. I t'ink maybe I show you somet'ing, that make you believe my word." He glanced back over his shoulder, toward the twisted maze of alleys.

Puzzled, Lily followed his gaze. He called out something in Italian, using a dialect so obscure that even she, with all her fluency in the language, couldn't follow it. Gradually a dark, shrouded shape appeared several yards away, seeming to materialize from nothing. Lily stared at the strange apparition, her lips parting in wonder.

"*È lei*," Giuseppe said complacently. "What do you 'ave to say now, *cara?*"

Lily's body quaked as she realized the distant figure was a man, holding up a small, doll-like form. His hands were hooked underneath the child's arms. He raised her a little higher, and the little girl's black hair glowed like polished onyx against the lavender-gray sky. "No," Lily croaked, her heart pounding in a frantic drumbeat.

The child stared at Giuseppe and called out in a tiny, questioning voice. "*Papà? Siete voi, Papà?*"

It was her daughter. It was Nicole. Lily dropped her satchel and staggered forward. Giuseppe caught her hard against him, clamping his hand over her mouth to smother her agonized scream. She fought wildly, flailing against his restraining arm, her eyes flooding. Whimpering behind his hand, she blinked to clear the tears that blurred her vision. Giuseppe's voice was a quiet hiss in her ear. "*Sì*, that is Nicoletta, our baby. *È molto carina*, yes? Such a pretty child."

At Giuseppe's nod, the man disappeared with the child, melting into the darkness. Giuseppe waited for half a minute before releasing Lily, until all chance of following her daughter through the convoluted streets and alleys was gone. His arms withdrew from around her.

Lily relaxed slowly, still crying. "My God," she sobbed, wrapping her arms around her middle, her shoulders hunched like an old woman's.

"I tell you I 'ave her," Giuseppe said, picking up the satchel of money, lifting the flap to view the contents. He sighed in satisfaction.

"Sh-she spoke in Italian," Lily gulped, staring at the place where her daughter had been.

"She speak in English too."

"Are there other Italians where you're keeping her?" she asked unevenly. "Is that why she still knows the language?"

He regarded her with a gleaming black stare. "You make me angry if you try again to look for 'er."

"Giuseppe, we could make an arrangement, you and I. There must be an amount that would satisfy you enough to . . ." Lily's voice wavered dangerously. She fought to keep it under control. "To give her back to me. You know this can't go on forever. You s-seem to care about Nicole. In your heart you must know she would be better off with me. That man who held her . . . is he a partner of yours? Are there more like him? You wouldn't have come here alone from Italy, without some cadre or group to associate with. I think . . ." She reached out a beseeching hand to him. "I think you're involved in some underworld gang, or conspiracy, whatever you wish to call it. That's the only conclusion that makes sense. The money I've given you . . . they've taken a great deal of it, haven't they? If anything I've heard about these gangs is true, then you're in a dangerous situation, Giuseppe, and you can't wish to expose Nicole to harm—"

"You see for yourself that I 'ave kept 'er safe," Giuseppe exclaimed sharply.

"Yes. But for how long? How safe are *you*, Giuseppe? Perhaps you should consider making an arrangement with me, for your own sake as well as hers." Her hatred of him was thick in her throat, nearly choking her, but she managed to keep it from showing. Seeing the interest in his eyes, she continued quietly. "We could agree on an amount that would satisfy your needs. The three of us would be better off—you, me, and most importantly our daughter. Please, Giuseppe." The word was bitter on her tongue, but she repeated it softly. "Please."

He did not reply for a long time, his avid gaze wandering over her. "For the first time you ask me somet'ing like a woman," he commented. "So soft, so sweet. Per'aps you 'ave learn this in Lord Raiford's bed, no?"

Lily froze. "You know about that?" she whispered painfully.

"I know you 'ave become Raiford's whore," he murmured, his voice silky. "Maybe you change since our time together. Maybe now you 'ave something to give a man."

Her soul revolted against the note in his voice. "How did you find out?"

"I know everything you do, *cara*. Every place you go." He touched her face, sliding his hot fingers beneath her chin.

Passively she accepted his caress, but inside she shrank with revulsion. The brush of his fingers on her skin was sickening. She suppressed a shiver of disgust. "Would you consider what I've said?" she asked unsteadily.

"Per'aps."

"Then let's talk about the amount you require."

He chuckled at her bluntness and shook his head. "Later."

"When? When will we meet again?"

"*Fra poco*. I send you a note to say."

"No." Lily reached for him as he drew apart from her. "I must know right away. Let's agree on something now—"

"Patience," he drawled, evading her hand, and grinned tauntingly. "*A più tardi*, Lily." With a gesture of farewell, he left quickly.

"It's been a real pleasure," she said, bitterly wiping away her welling tears. She felt like falling to the ground, screaming and kicking in furious grief. Instead she stood like a statue, her fists clenched. Beneath her bleak despair, there was a flicker of exhilaration. She had seen her daughter, and there was no doubt it had been Nicole. Hungrily she remembered the beautiful little face, the doll-like fragility of her child. "God, keep her safe, keep her safe," she whispered.

She walked back to the small Arabian gelding Derek had loaned to her, and stroked the horse's shining chestnut hide. Her mind raced with frenzied thoughts. Blindly she swung onto the mount and arranged her skirts and cloak. On impulse she walked the horse along the route Giuseppe had taken, deeper into the no-man's land where police never dared to patrol, night or day. The dark streets of the rookery were lively with gaming, whoring, and every criminal offense from pickpocketing to murder. With its multitude of hideaways, blind alleys, and shadowed corners, it was the perfect breeding place for corruption. This was the world her child was living in.

At the sight of the fine horse and richly cloaked figure, vagrants began to approach Lily, reaching their grasping hands toward her. As one of them gripped her riding boot, she recoiled in fear and spurred the horse to a trot. What a fool she was, venturing into such a place without weapons or protection, courting danger for no reason. She wasn't thinking clearly. Turning the chestnut gelding down a side street, she headed back to the relative safety of Covent Garden.

The sounds of a violent tumult came to her ears, growing stronger as she approached the end of the street. Small groups of men, some of them in rags and some finely dressed, wandered between the rickety wooden buildings. They seemed to be attending some sort of exhibition. Lily frowned as she heard the muffled barking and snarling of dogs. Animal baiting, she thought in disgust. Men were fascinated and excited by the bloodthirsty sport, putting animals in a pen with vicious dogs and watching them destroy each other. She wondered what kind of beast was being slaughtered for tonight's entertainment. The latest craze was to throw badgers to the dogs. The tough-skinned badgers, with their vicious bites and fierce resistance to death, provided an enjoyable spectacle for the brutish audience. Cautiously she cut between two buildings to avoid the spectacle, knowing that the men who attended such events were easily incited to violence. She wouldn't care to be discovered by any of them.

The wild bellowing of the men at the animal baiting blasted through the wooden walls of a converted stable yard. Amid a crowded lot of carts, wagons, and empty stalls, a small boy crouched on the ground, his head resting on his bent knees. His shoulders trembled, as if he were crying. Against her better judgment, Lily eased her horse to a halt. "Boy," she said, a questioning lilt to her voice.

He looked up at her, revealing a dirty, tear-streaked face. He was thin and pale, his features pointed. It was possible he was the same age as Henry, eleven or twelve, but his growth had been stunted by malnourishment or disease. At the sight of her on the gleaming horse, his tears stopped and his mouth fell open.

"Why are you crying?" Lily asked softly.

"I ain't crying," he returned, smearing the wet grime on his face with a ragged sleeve.

"Has someone hurt you?"

"Naw."

"Are you waiting for someone in there?" She gestured to the wooden wall, which reverberated from the noise within.

"Aye. They're coming soon to take 'im." The boy pointed to the back of a painted wagon. The rickety vehicle bore the name of a traveling circus. A dappled gray nag was hitched in front of the wagon, a scrawny, wiry animal that did not look at all healthy.

"Him?" Lily asked in bewilderment, dismounting from her horse. The boy stood up, keeping a respectful distance from her, and led her to the side of the wagon. Lily gasped as she saw the bars on the side of the wagon, and the matted, furry face of a bear. "Damnation!" she couldn't help exclaiming.

The bear rested his great head on his paws. His brows quirked at her, giving him a mournful, questioning expression. "'E won't hurt you," the boy said defensively, reaching in and rubbing the creature's head. "'E's a good old fellow."

"Old, indeed," Lily said, staring at the bear in fascination. His fur was rough and filthy, liberally strewn with gray. There were several large bald patches on his neck and body, gleams of whiteness among the dark fur.

The boy continued to rub the bear's head. "You can touch 'im."

Cautiously Lily reached between the bars, ready to snatch her hand back at any second. The bear breathed placidly, his eyes half-closed. She gave his broad head a gentle stroke, and regarded the massive creature pityingly. "I've never touched a bear before," she murmured. "Not a live one."

The boy sniffled beside her. "Not for long, 'e won't be."

"You're from the circus?" Lily asked, reading the side of the wagon.

"Aye. My father is the animal master. Pokey don't remember 'is tricks no more. My father told me to bring 'im 'ere and sell 'im for ten pounds."

"So they can bait him?" Lily asked, her indignation rising. They would chain him to the floor and let the dogs tear him to pieces.

"Aye," the boy said miserably. "First they start with rats and badgers, to whip the dogs up. Then it's Pokey's turn."

Lily was outraged. "There'll be no sport in it. He's too damned old to defend himself!" She stared at the bear and realized that the bald patches were shaved spots, indicating the vulnerable areas where the dogs would be drawn to attack and tear with their teeth. He had been prepared for slaughter.

"I can't go 'ome without ten pounds," the boy sobbed. "My father would beat me."

Lily looked away from his miserable face. There was nothing she could do, except hope the dogs would make short work of the bear, so that his suffering wouldn't last long. "What a night," she muttered. The world was filled with brutality. It was useless to try and fight against it. The sight of the defeated, helpless animal filled her with bitterness. "I'm sorry," she said in a low voice, and turned back to her horse. There was nothing she could do.

"'Ere's the gundiguts now," the boy muttered.

Lily stared over her horse's back at a huge, slovenly man approaching them. He had the neck of a bull and arms the size of tree trunks. His face was covered with black bristle and his thick lips opened to reveal broken teeth clamped on a cigar. "Where are ye, little rumper?" he demanded in a booming voice. His eyes slitted in curiosity as he saw the fine Arabian horse. "What's this?" He strode around the animal, staring at Lily. His gaze took in her elegant cloak, the soft folds of her yellow skirts, the lustrous sable curls that fell over her forehead. "What a fine bit o' fluff," he said, setting his lips. "Are ye a giver, milady?"

Lily gave a crude reply that made him laugh

uproariously. His gaze alighted on the boy. "Brung the meat, did ye? Give us a look." The sight of the docile bear huddled inside the wagon caused his thick lip to curl disdainfully. "Big lump o' dog paste . . . looks like he's already been *through* a baiting! And yer father asks a tenner for *this?*"

The boy's face quivered with repressed emotion. "Yes, sir."

Lily could tolerate no more of the man's bullying. There was enough cruelty and needless suffering in the world. She'd be damned if she'd let him torture a tired old bear. "I'll pay ten pounds for him. It's obvious the poor animal wouldn't be of use to you, Mr. Gundiguts." With a businesslike expression that matched her crisp tone, she fished discreetly in her bodice for a small money pouch.

"'Is name is Rooters," the boy said beneath his breath. "Nevil Rooters."

Lily winced, realizing that *gundiguts* was a gutter-cant insult.

The man's sneering laugh cut through the sound of the roaring crowd inside the makeshift arena "We got more than two hundred men in there," he said, "and they's already paid for the sight o' blood. Keep yer mumper's brass, milady. I'm taking the bear."

Lily glanced quickly around the area. Her gaze lingered briefly on a length of heavy chain piled on top of some stacked crates. "If you say so," she murmured, and let the money pouch slip through her fingers. It fell to the ground with a rich-sounding clink. "Oh, dear, my gold and jewelry!" she exclaimed.

Rooters stared at the pouch with patent greed. "Gold, is it?" He licked his lips and bent low to the ground, reaching a meaty hand toward the pouch.

There was the brief clatter of metal and the muffled jangle of a heavy blow. Rooters gasped and dropped neatly to the dirt, his mammoth form unmoving. Lily dropped the massive chain and dusted her hands together with satisfaction. The boy's jaw dropped as he regarded her in amazement. Swiftly Lily scooped up the pouch and gave it to him. "Take that home to your father. It will more than compensate him for the horse and wagon."

"But what about Pokey—"

"I'll take care of him," she promised. "He won't be mistreated."

The boy's eyes glittered, and he gave her a wobbling smile. Daringly he reached out and touched a fold of her fine woolen cloak. "Thank you. Thank you." He scampered away into the darkness. Lily watched him go, then hastened to tie her Arabian to the back of the bear wagon. Aware of the activity outside the iron bars, the bear mustered a half roar sending the horse into nervous fidgets. "Quiet, Pokey," Lily muttered. "Don't ruin your own rescue." Gingerly she climbed into the wooden seat of the rickety vehicle and reached for the reins.

She started as she felt something close around her ankle. Looking down, she saw Rooters's enraged, bristled face. Clasping her leg in his meaty hands, he dragged her bodily from the wagon. She fell on the hard ground with a shocked cry, her rump smarting from the impact.

"Steal my bear, will ye?" He stood over her, his face crimson with rage, flecks of spittle falling from his mouth. "Come here from yer high-kick mansion, riding on your fine horse, looking for trouble . . . Aye, you'll get it, milady!" Dropping over her, he began to paw roughly at her bodice and pull at her skirts.

Lily screamed and tried to wriggle free of him, but he had pinned her down with his bulky weight, crushing the breath from her. She felt her ribs compress from the pressure of his body, and she thought they might break. A curious ringing began in her ears. "No," she wheezed, struggling to breathe.

"Fancy thieving West End bitch," he said viciously. "Ye gave me a frigging hard knock on my head!"

A new, eerily calm voice interrupted the scene. "A bad habit of hers. I'm trying to break her of it."

"Who's this—her pimp?" Rooters stared at the newcomer threateningly. "Ye'll have her when I'm done with her."

Lily turned her head. With disbelief she saw the blurred shape of her husband. But it couldn't be. It was an illusion. "Alex," she whimpered. She heard his low, deadly voice through the dull roaring in her ears.

"Get the hell off my wife."

CHAPTER 11

Rooters stared at Alex as if trying to assess how much of a threat he presented. The bear moved restlessly inside his cage with grumbling whines, stirred by the palpable fury in the air. But the animal's disquieting noise was nothing compared to the odd, frightening snarl that came from her husband as he lunged at the man on top of her. Suddenly the punishing weight was gone, and Lily gasped in relief. Pulling in lungfuls of air, she clasped her hand to her sore ribs. She tried to comprehend what was happening.

The two men grappled and fought a few yards away, moving so quickly that all Lily could detect of Alex was the flash of blond hair. With murderous grunts, he smashed his fists into Rooters's face and sank his fingers into the bull-like neck, closing off his windpipe. Rooters's jowls puffed with scarlet rage. He reached up to grab Alex's collar and kicked up with his legs, flipping Alex over his head. At the sound of her husband hitting the ground with a heavy thud, Lily shrieked and tried to scramble over to him. He was up before she could reach him. Ducking underneath a swinging fist, Alex seized Rooters and threw him against the stack of crates. The wood cracked and splintered beneath him.

Lily's mouth fell open. Her eyes were dark and round as she watched Alex. "My God," she breathed. She hardly recognized him. She would have expected a little civilized boxing, some articulate insults, the brandishing of a pistol. Instead he had turned into a bloodthirsty stranger, intent on tearing his opponent apart with his bare fists. She had never dreamed he was capable of such violence.

Staggering to his feet, Rooters lunged at Alex again, who sidestepped, twisted, and buried his fist beneath the man's ribs. He finished him off with a solid blow to the back. Rooters collapsed to the ground with a bellow of pain. He spat out a mouthful of bloody saliva, tried to rise again, and crumpled with a moan of surrender. Slowly Alex unclenched his fists. He turned his head and looked at Lily.

She fell back a step, half-frightened by the savage gleam in his eyes. Then the harsh lines of his face seemed to soften, and she ran to him without thinking. She flung her arms around his neck, trembling and laughing wildly. "Alex, Alex—"

He folded her in his arms and tried to soothe her. "Take a deep breath. Another."

"You came just in time," she gasped.

"I told you I'd take care of you," he muttered.

"No matter how difficult you make it." Pressing her close against his large, sheltering body, he murmured against her hair, alternating between curses and endearments. His hand pushed beneath the muddied cloak to the tense line of her back, and he kneaded her rigid spine. Lily was more overwrought than he had ever seen her. More wild laughter bubbled up from inside her.

"Easy," he said, afraid she would fly apart in his arms. "Easy."

"How did you know? How did you find me?"

"Lady Lyon wasn't at home. I went to Craven's and discovered that although the carriage and driver were still there, you were gone. Worthy admitted that you had left unaccompanied for Covent Garden." He nodded to the open end of the alley, where the driver, Greaves, waited with a pair of horses. "Greaves and I have been combing the streets to find you." He eased her head back, his gray eyes penetrating as they stared into hers. "You broke your promise to me, Lily."

"I didn't. I took outriders a-and a groom to Craven's. That was all you asked of me."

"We're not going to play at semantics," he said grimly. "You know what I meant."

"But Alex—"

"Hush." Alex stared over her head at a pair of burly men who had just come from the arena. They glanced from him to Rooters's unmoving form on the ground.

"What the bloomin 'ell . . ." one of them

369

exclaimed, while the other scratched his head in befuddlement. "Get the bear—the dogs're near done with the badger."

"No!" Lily cried, jerking around to face them. Alex kept his arm around her front. "No, you f-frigging butchers! Why don't you throw your-*selves* into the pit? I'm certain the dogs wouldn't stand a chance!" She turned back to Alex, gripping his shirt. "I-I bought the bear. He's mine! When I saw what they were going to do—the poor beast looks so pathetic—I couldn't help myself. Don't let them take him away, he'll be torn to pieces—"

"Lily." Gently he cupped her face in his hands. "Calm down. Listen to me. This happens all the time."

"It's cruel and barbaric!"

"I agree. But if we manage to rescue this animal, they'll only find another to take its place."

Her eyes began to water. "His name is Pokey," she said thickly. She knew her behavior was irrational. She'd never been so emotional, clinging to a man for comfort and help. But after the shock of seeing her daughter, and the bewildering events of the past days, she seemed to have temporarily lost her sanity. "I won't let them have him," she said desperately. "I want him as a wedding present, Alex."

"A wedding present?" Blankly he stared at the battered wooden wagon. The moth-eaten, rheumy-eyed old bear nosed against the unevenly spaced bars. The damn thing didn't have long to live, baiting or no baiting.

"Please," Lily whispered into the folds of his shirt.

With a low curse, Alex pushed Lily aside. "Go to Greaves and get on one of the horses," he muttered. "I'll take care of this."

"But—"

"Do it," he said with quiet finality. Averting her eyes from his hard, uncompromising stare, Lily obeyed. She walked slowly to the corner. Alex approached the two men. "The animal is ours," he said calmly.

One of them stepped forward, squaring his shoulders. "We needs 'im for the baiting."

"You'll have to find another bear. My wife wants this one." He smiled slightly, his eyes cold and dangerous. "Do you care to take issue?"

The men looked apprehensively at Rooters's prone body and at Alex's threatening stance. It was clear that neither of them wished to suffer the same fate as their crony. "What the bloomin' 'ell should we give to the dogs, then?" one of them demanded plaintively.

"I have a number of suggestions," Alex replied, staring at them steadily. "But none that you'd like."

Faced with his ominous gaze, they backed away uneasily. "I s'pose we could make do with more rats 'n badgers," one of them murmured to the other.

The other frowned unhappily. "But we promised 'em a *bear* . . ."

Unconcerned with their dilemma, Alex gestured to Greaves.

The driver came quickly. "Yes, milord?"

"I want you to drive the wagon home," Alex said matter-of-factly. "Lady Raiford and I will return on the horses."

Greaves looked far from happy about the prospect of driving the ursine passenger to Swans Court. To his credit, he offered no protest. "Yes, milord," he said in a subdued voice. He approached the garish wagon gingerly, made a great show of spreading a handkerchief over the wooden seat, and sat with great care to avoid getting dirt on his fine livery. The bear watched the proceedings with a mild expression of interest. Alex smothered a grin and strode to the corner where Lily was waiting.

Her face creased with a worried frown. "Alex, do you think we might be able to fashion a pen or cage for him at Raiford Park? Or perhaps set him free in some forest—"

"He's too tame to be set free. I have a friend who keeps exotic animals on his estate." Alex gave the bear, who hardly came under the category of "exotic," a dubious glance. He sighed tautly. "With any luck, I might be able to persuade him to give Pinky a home."

"Pokey."

With a speaking look, he swung up on his mount.

"Do you have another escapade planned for tomorrow night?" he asked. "Or is it possible we might have just one quiet evening at home?"

Lily lowered her head meekly and didn't reply, although she was tempted to point out that she had warned him she wouldn't be the usual sort of wife. Glancing sideways at his dark, disheveled form, she tried to suppress the waves of giddy nervousness that swept over her. She wanted very much to thank him for all he had done, but she was strangely tongue-tied.

"Let's go," he said curtly.

She paused, biting her lip. "Alex, I suppose you must already regret having married me." There was an anxious lilt in her voice.

"I regret that you disobeyed me and placed yourself in danger."

At any other time, the concept of wifely obedience was something she would have debated hotly. But with the memory of his rescue so fresh in her mind, she answered with uncustomary mildness. "It couldn't be helped. I had to resolve matters on my own."

"You didn't owe the money to Craven," he said flatly. "You gave the five thousand to someone else." At her slight nod, his mouth tightened. "What are you involved in, Lily?"

"I wish you wouldn't ask," she whispered miserably. "I don't want to lie to you."

His voice was low and grating. "Why not confide in me?"

She wrapped the leather reins around and around her hand, keeping her face turned away.

Alex paused with his hand on the brandy bottle, staring through the semidarkness of the library. Lily was upstairs, preparing for bed. It was obvious she was afraid of something that no amount of time or patience would make her reveal. He didn't know how to make her trust him. Each time he looked into her eyes he sensed a shortening of time, a danger that was drawing her deeper into a coil. He knew the problem wasn't money. He'd made it clear that she could have any part of his extensive resources, and yet that hadn't helped. Foolishly he'd hoped that after clearing her debt, the panic that surfaced so often in her gaze would magically disappear. But it was still there. What had happened tonight was not to be dismissed as a charming scrape—it was a wild rebellion against some burden that was dragging her down like a millstone. He knew all the signs of someone trying to escape from grief. He'd spent two years doing the same.

He set the bottle down without pouring a drink, and rubbed his eyes. Suddenly he was still, knowing she was there. His senses burned in immediate awareness. The soft sound of his name on her lips made his body hard with a ravening appetite.

He turned to face her. She was dressed in thin layers of white cambric nightclothes, her hair an unruly mass of sable curls. She looked hesitant and small, utterly beguiling. Her dark eyes flickered to the liquor bottles behind him. "You're having a drink?"

"No." He raked his hand through his hair, his voice threaded with tired impatience. "What do you want?"

Her breath caught in the prelude to a laugh. "It's our wedding night."

The statement diverted him, dispelled all thoughts except the need to have her again. He knew the shape of her beneath the delicate cambric, the feel of her body beneath his, the soft clasp of her flesh around him. Excitement shimmered along his nerves, but he forced himself to stand there with an appearance of indifference. He wanted the words from her, wanted her to admit why she had sought him out. "So it is," he said neutrally.

She fidgeted a little, raising a hand to her neck, toying with a curl in a gesture that held an innocent, maddening allure. "Are you tired, my lord?"

"No."

Gamely she persisted, though her voice was shadowed with increasing embarrassment. "Do you intend to retire soon?"

He pushed away from the table and approached her. "Do you want me to?"

She lowered her eyes. "I wouldn't mind if you decided to—"

"Do you want me in bed with you?" He took

375

hold of her, his hands sliding beneath her arms.

Lily felt herself flush. "Yes," she managed to whisper in the second before his mouth closed over hers. She gasped softly and relaxed against him, linking her arms around his waist. The yielding promise of her body inflamed him; he wanted to hold her close, close, until he crushed her. Instead he carried her upstairs and undressed her carefully, and allowed her to help him with his own clothes. Unfamiliar with a man's garments, Lily had difficulty in locating the flat, invisible buttons on the inside of his trousers. Gently he showed her how to unfasten them, his breath whisked away as the back of her hand brushed intimately against him.

Pressing her back to the bed, he covered her body with slow, hot kisses, nudging his face against her downy skin, loving the pale softness of her breasts and waist and stomach. Lily was more abandoned than she had been the other nights they'd been together, her hands wandering over him more freely, her limbs twining around his. Her cool fingers threaded through his hair, toying languidly in the golden locks, stroking his nape.

The lithe, slender body arching beneath him caused a groan to escape his lips. Breathing hard, he sealed his mouth over hers. His hand reached down and cupped over her, trapping her damp heat against his palm, momentarily flattening the soft thatch of curls. Shivering, she parted her knees and pushed upward, craving more of the delicious pressure. His fingers rubbed slowly, and then entered her in a gentle, flexing thrust.

With a helpless moan, Lily hugged herself closer to him, writhing in time to the compelling movement of his fingers. He kissed her neck and shoulders and withdrew his hand, using his palms to push her thighs apart. "Open your eyes," he whispered fiercely, staring into her face, holding her knees wide. "Look at me."

Her dark lashes lifted, and she held his intense gaze. Deliberately he pushed forward. Her eyes dilated as she felt the heavy, stimulating force of him within her. Grasping her hips, he wedged himself deeper, moving in an insistent rhythm. Lily stroked the smooth surface of his back, and as her pleasure mounted, her fingers dug into the hard plane of muscle. Her face turned against the shaven scrape of his cheek. She heard him whisper to her then, in broken phrases he couldn't seem to hold back—how beautiful she was to him, how much he wanted her . . . that he loved her. Confused, disbelieving, she felt the silken pleasure explode within her, around her, and she was drowning in feelings she could never have found words for. He drew in his breath and held it at the moment of climax, his body taut and shaking against hers.

The most pressing silence she had ever known settled over them. Lily kept her eyes closed, though her mind was spinning with questions. *I love you* . . . He couldn't have really said it, she thought. And if he had, he certainly couldn't have meant it. Her Aunt Sally had once warned her never to pay heed to the things a man said in passion. At the time, she hadn't understood the full significance of the advice.

After a minute, she felt Alex move slightly, as if he intended to roll away from her. Pretending to have fallen asleep, she kept her arms locked around his neck, her limbs heavily entangled with his. When he attempted to disengage her, she affected a drowsy murmur and wrapped herself tighter. To her relief, he settled back, his chest rising and falling rapidly beneath her head. She wondered at the reason for his disturbed breathing. He must know what he had said. He must regret it.

But dear Lord . . . she wanted it to be true.

Alarmed by her own thoughts, she somehow managed to stay relaxed against him. He deserved someone far better than her, someone pure, innocent, untarnished. If he did care for her, it was only because he still didn't know what she truly was. Once he knew about her bastard child, he would leave her. And if she allowed herself to fall in love with him, her heart would shatter into a thousand jagged pieces.

"You don't need me to remark on what a hopelessly vulgar mess this is," Lady Lyon said sternly, regarding the newlywed pair in the manner of a governess having caught her charge kissing in the corner with an ill-bred peasant. An elegant woman with gleaming silver-white hair and direct blue eyes, she possessed a strong, flawless bone structure that had made her a renowned beauty in her youth.

Alex shrugged apologetically. "But Aunt, the truth is—"

"Don't attempt to tell me the truth, you impetuous boy! I've heard the rumors, and that is quite enough."

"Yes, Aunt," Alex replied humbly for the tenth time, sliding a sideways glance at his wife. They were in the gold and green parlor of Lord Lyon's mansion on Brook Street. Lily was huddled in a nearby chair, her gaze fixed on her folded hands. He struggled to suppress a grin, never having seen her look so chastened. He had warned her what to expect. True to his predictions, his elderly aunt had lectured them in her imperious way for at least a quarter-hour.

"Gambling, nudity, promiscuity, and the merciful Lord knows what else," Lady Lyon continued sharply, "all carried out in the public forum, which places the two of you quite beyond redemption. I hold you just as accountable as your wife, Raiford. Your part in this is no less reprehensible. In fact, it is *more* so. How dare you wantonly cast aside your sterling reputation and sully the family name in such a manner?" She shook her head and regarded them severely. "The only wise step you have taken is to come to me with this. Although I can't help but think it is too late to pluck the two of you from the jaws of social ruin. It will be the greatest challenge of my life, gaining you entrée."

"We have absolute faith in you, Aunt." Alex said in a penitent murmur. "If anyone can accomplish it, you can."

"Indeed," Lady Lyon replied sourly.

Lily raised a hand to her lips, wiping away the twitch of a smile. She relished the picture of her husband being scolded like a troublesome schoolboy. In spite of the old lady's enthusiastic dressing-down, it was clear she adored Alex.

Lady Lyon regarded her suspiciously. "I fail to understand why my nephew married you," she announced. "He should have wedded that well-behaved sister of yours, and made you his paramour."

"I couldn't agree more," Lily said, speaking up for the first time. "I was perfectly willing to be his mistress. It would have been a far more sensible arrangement." Smiling sweetly at Alex, she ignored his sardonic stare. "I believe he compelled me to marry him out of some mistaken idea that it was possible to reform me." She rolled her eyes dramatically. "Heaven knows where he got *that* notion."

Lady Lyon regarded her with new interest. "Hmm. Now I begin to understand the attraction. You're a spirited chit. And I don't doubt you've a quick wit. But all the same—"

"Thank you," Lily said demurely, interrupting

before another round of scolding began. "Lady Lyon, I appreciate your willingness to exert your influence on our behalf. But gaining us admittance into respectable circles . . ." She shook her head decisively. "It can't be done."

"Indeed," the elderly woman said frostily. "Then let me inform you, my impertinent miss, that it can and *will* be done. Provided you manage to keep from making any further scandalous exhibitions of yourself!"

"She won't," Alex said hastily. "And neither will I, Aunt."

"Very well." Lady Lyon gestured for a housemaid to bring her lap desk. "I shall begin my campaign," she said, in a tone that must have resembled Wellington's at Waterloo. "And you, of course, will follow my instructions to the letter."

Alex strode to his aunt and kissed her wrinkled brow. "I knew I could depend on you."

"Fustian," she replied rudely, gesturing for Lily to approach her. "You may kiss me, child."

Obediently Lily pressed her lips to the old woman's proffered cheek.

"Now that I've had a look at you," Lady Lyon continued, "I am assured that *all* of the rumors about you can't be true. Decadent living always shows in the face, and you look far less degenerate than I expected." Her blue eyes narrowed. "In the right clothes, I suppose we could pass you off as a woman of reasonably good character."

Lily gave her a small curtsey. "Thank you," she

said with a meekness that bordered on burlesque.

"We'll have a problem with the eyes," Lady Lyon said disapprovingly. "Dark, heathenish, full of mischief. Perhaps you could find some way to restrain the expression in them—"

Alex interrupted with a protest, sliding his arm around Lily's waist. "No more talk about her eyes, Aunt. They're her best feature." He glanced down at his wife caressingly. "I'm rather partial to them."

Lily's silent amusement faded as her gaze was imprisoned by his. She felt a peculiar warmth blossom inside of her, making her warm and unsteady, her heart beating swiftly. Suddenly the hard support of his arm seemed to be all that kept her standing. Conscious of the interested regard of Lady Lyon, Lily tried to look away, but she was unable to do anything except wait helplessly for him to release her. Finally he gave her waist a squeeze and let go.

Lady Lyon spoke, her voice less sharp than before. "Leave us alone for a moment, Raiford."

He frowned. "Aunt, I'm afraid we don't have time for any more talk."

"Don't worry," Lady Lyon said dryly. "This old dragon will not chew your pretty young bride to bits. I merely want to give her some advice. Come here, child." She patted the space beside her. Without looking at her husband, Lily seated herself on the sofa.

Giving his aunt a warning glance, Alex left the room.

Lady Lyon seemed to have been amused by her nephew's glowering frown. "It's clear he can't abide any criticism of you," she remarked with a throaty chuckle.

"Unless it's given by himself." Lily was surprised by the way the *grande dame's* entire manner had softened.

That caused Lady Lyon to laugh again. "My favorite nephew, you know. The most exemplary man the family has ever produced. Far more praiseworthy than my own charming, spoiled, good-for-nothing son Ross. You'll never fully appreciate your own good fortune in landing Raiford. How you did is a mystery to me."

"To me also," Lily said feelingly.

"No matter. You've wrought quite a change in him." Lady Lyon paused reflectively. "I don't think I've seen him so lighthearted since he was a boy, before his parents passed away."

Unaccountably pleased, Lily lowered her gaze to hide the effects of the elderly woman's words. "But surely when he and Caroline Whitmore were affianced—"

"Let me tell you something about that American woman," the elderly woman interrupted impatiently. "She was a beautiful, carefree creature, prone to romantics and follies. Certainly she would have made Raiford an adequate wife. But Miss Whitmore didn't understand the depth to him, nor did she care to." Her blue eyes turned soft and thoughtful, almost sad. "She never would have appreciated the kind of love he is capable of giving. The Raiford men were unique in that regard." She paused and added, "They allow their women such terrible power over them. Their love tends toward obsession. My brother Charles willed himself to death after his wife passed away. The thought of living without her was intolerable to him. Did you know about that?"

"No, ma'am," Lily said, startled.

"Raiford is no different. Losing the woman he loves, through death or betrayal, would have the same effect on him."

Lily's eyes widened. "Lady Lyon, I think you are exaggerating the case. His feelings for me do not tend to that extreme. That is, he doesn't—"

"You are not as sharp-witted as I thought, child, if you haven't realized that he loves you."

Caught in the grip of dismay and some deeper, perplexing emotion, Lily stared at her in silent astonishment.

"Young people are far more thickheaded now than in my day," Lady Lyon observed tartly. "Close your mouth, child, you'll catch flies."

The acerbic tone in Lady Lyon's voice reminded Lily of Aunt Sally, although Sally had certainly been far more outlandish than this elegant matron. "Ma'am, you said you have advice for me?"

"Oh, yes." Lady Lyon pinned Lily in a meaningful stare. "I've heard all about you and your wild ways. In truth, you remind me of myself when I was young. I was a comely, high-spirited girl with quite a good figure. Before my marriage I left a string of broken hearts in my wake, long enough to make my mother exceedingly proud. I felt no pressing urge to accept some man as my lord and master. Not when I had all of London at my feet. Flowers, poetry, stolen kisses . . ." She smiled reminiscently. "It was delightful. Naturally I regarded it as a dreary prospect to sacrifice all of that for the sake of matrimony. But I'll tell you something I discovered when I married Lord Lyon—the love of a good man is worth a few sacrifices."

Lily hadn't talked so frankly with a woman since Sally had died. She dared to unburden herself a little, leaning forward as she spoke earnestly. "Lady Lyon, I had no desire to marry anyone. I've been independent for too long. Raiford and I will be at each other's throats constantly. We're both too strong-willed. It's a classic *mésalliance*."

Lady Lyon seemed to understand her fear. "Consider this . . . Raiford wants you enough that he is willing to expose himself to the possible censure and ridicule of his peers. For a man who values his pride so highly, that is a great concession. You could do worse than marry a man willing to make a fool of himself over you."

Lily frowned in concern. "He won't be made to appear foolish," she said emphatically. "I would *never* do anything to embarrass him." Just then the recollection of the spectacle in Covent Garden concerning an old circus bear flashed before her, and she colored. She hadn't waited even one day after their wedding before behaving scandalously. "*Damn*," she whispered, before she could catch herself.

Surprisingly, the elderly woman smiled. "It won't be easy for you, naturally. You do have a struggle, a worthwhile struggle, ahead of you. I believe I speak for a great many people in saying it will be quite interesting to watch."

Lady Lyon arranged for the two of them to attend a series of private soirées, at which their marriage was announced in a quiet and seemly manner. There was no way to avoid the appearance of scandal, not when the details of their "courtship" were being bandied about London. But at least Lady Lyon had managed to water down the disgrace somewhat. At her insistence, Lily wore modestly becoming gowns to these affairs, and took care to associate mostly with dowagers and respectable married women.

To Lily's surprise, the men she had gambled with, traded friendly insults with, drank and joked with at Craven's treated her with unexpected deference at these gatherings. Occasionally one of the elderly gentlemen would give her a surreptitious wink, as if they were engaging in a pleasant conspiracy. Their wives, on the other hand, were only marginally friendly. But no one dared to cut her openly, since Lady Lyon and her revered cronies were always at her side. It also helped that

Lily possessed an impressive title and the backing of an even more impressive fortune.

With each gathering she navigated through successfully, Lily became more "established." She couldn't help noticing the change in the way others regarded her, the courtesies and attentions they paid her. In fact, some of the aristocrats who had been only coolly polite to her for years were now complimentary, even affectionate, as if she had always been a great favorite. Privately she denounced this entire procedure of becoming respectable as a great indignity, which amused Alex greatly.

"I'm being trotted forth for their inspection," Lily told him while they pored over a list of invitations in one of the upstairs sitting rooms. "Like some pony with ribbons braided through her tail. 'Look, everyone, she isn't quite as heathenish and vulgar as we feared' . . . I sincerely hope this is all worth the effort, my lord!"

"Is it really such a trial?" he asked sympathetically, his gray eyes gleaming with laughter.

"No," she admitted. "I want to succeed. I'm terrified of what your aunt will do to me if I don't."

"She likes you," he assured her.

"Oh, really? Is that why she's always making remarks about my behavior and my eyes and my gowns. Why, the other day she complained that I was flaunting my bosom—Good God, I hardly have one to speak of!"

His brows drew together. "You have a beautiful bosom."

Wryly she glanced down at her small, pert breasts. "When I was a girl, Mother always made me splash cold water on my chest to make them grow. They never did. Penelope's bosom is much better than mine."

"I never noticed hers," he said, shoving the pile of invitations to the floor and reaching for her.

She evaded him with a quick laugh. "Alex! Lord Faxton will be here momentarily to discuss the bill he wants to propose."

"Then he'll have to wait." Catching her around the waist, he pulled her beneath him on the sofa.

Lily laughed and wriggled in protest. "What if Burton shows him upstairs and he discovers us like this?"

"Burton's too well trained for that."

"Really, my lord, the pride you take in him makes me wonder." She shoved at his shoulders and twisted under him. "I've never seen a man so attached to his butler."

"Best damn butler in England," he said, and pinned her down, enjoying her energetic grappling. For a woman of her diminutive size, she was remarkably strong. She giggled uncontrollably as she tried to fend him off. He let her nearly succeed in pushing him away, but then he collected her wrists in one hand and stretched them over her head. His other hand roamed boldly over her slender form.

388

"Alex, let me up," she said breathlessly.

He pulled her sleeves down and tugged at her bodice. "Not until I convince you how beautiful you are."

"I'm convinced. I'm beautiful. Ravishing. Now stop this at once." She gasped as she heard the sound of delicate fabric ripping and stitches popping.

Staring into her eyes, Alex continued, to pull away the dress until her breasts were exposed. His fingers brushed against her bare skin, sending tingles of delight through her. Gently he traced around the delicate peaks with a fingertip, his gaze smoldering as it fell on the slight curves of her breasts. Her playfulness vanished, and she began to breathe deeply. "My lord, we can wait until later. It's important that . . ." Her mind swam with sensations, and she almost lost her train of thought. "Important to see Faxton when he arrives."

"Nothing's more important than you."

"Be sensible—"

"I am being sensible." His mouth opened over her nipple, drawing the taut bud tightly inside.

Lily trembled as he held her down and kissed her breasts with leisurely sensuality. Her head turned listlessly to one side, then the other, her wrists flexing within his firm grip. Alex pulled her skirts up, the warmth of his hand seeping through her fine silk stockings as he caressed her legs. "I've never wanted any woman as much as I want

389

you," he murmured. His mouth played over the side of her neck, and he licked the inside of her ear. "I could devour you. I love your breasts, your mouth, everything about you. Do you believe me?" When she refused to answer, he rubbed his lips over hers, coaxing a reply. "Do you believe me?"

Through the tumult of her passion, she heard a knock upon the closed door of the sitting room. Her pleasure-drugged mind refused to accept the sound, but Alex paused, lifting his head and controlling his breathing. "Yes?" he demanded, his voice amazingly steady.

Burton's sedate voice came through the closed door. "My lord, a number of visitors have just arrived, all at once."

Alex frowned. "How many? Who is it?"

"Mr. and Mrs. Lawson, Lord and Lady Stamford, Master Henry, and a gentlemen he identified as his tutor."

"My entire family?" Lily squeaked.

Alex sighed tautly. "Henry wasn't supposed to arrive until tomorrow . . . was he?"

She shook her head dumbly.

Alex raised his voice so that Burton could hear him clearly. "Show them all to the downstairs parlor, Burton, and tell them we'll join them right away."

"Yes, my lord."

Lily clutched at Alex's shoulders, her body aching with unfulfilled desire. "No," she moaned.

"We'll continue this later," he said, stroking her flushed cheek with his fingertip. Frustrated beyond her ability to bear, she caught at his hand and urged it to her breast. With a laugh, he pulled her body close and nuzzled against her hair. "They'll want to stay for dinner."

She gave a protesting groan. "Send them away," she said, although she knew it wasn't possible. "I want to be alone with you."

Alex smiled crookedly and rubbed her back. "There'll be thousands of nights for us. I promise."

Lily nodded silently, although inside she was filled with despair. He couldn't make such a promise when he didn't know what she had kept hidden from him, the secret that would separate them forever.

Idly Alex investigated the torn edges of her bodice, dropping his head to kiss the shallow vale between her breasts. "You'd better change your gown," he murmured, his breath collecting in the damp hollow and causing her to shiver. "Although I find you utterly charming like this, I'm not certain your mother would approve."

Lily entered the parlor dressed in her favorite gown, a close-fitted garment made of dark red silk and trimmed with filmy embroidered net. The gauzy sleeves revealed flashes of her slender arms, while the slightly flared skirt moved gently around her legs as she walked. It was the gown of a temptress, hardly a style that Lady Lyon would have approved of. But it showed her to her best advantage, and Lily had decided to keep it as an at-home gown. Alex, who couldn't take his eyes from her, most definitely approved.

"Lily!" Totty cried eagerly. "My favorite, darling daughter, my lovely child, I had to see you at once. You've made your dear mother so happy, so pleased and proud that I'm moved to tears of joy every time I think of you—"

"Hello, Mother," Lily said wryly, hugging Totty and making a face at Penelope and Zachary. She was filled with satisfaction as she saw the two of them standing together. Penelope's face was radiant with love as she stood nestled against Zachary's side.

Zachary looked similarly happy, though he regarded Lily with a patent question in his eyes. "We could hardly believe the news," he commented meaningfully, moving forward to embrace Lily. "We had to come, to see if you were all right."

"Of course I'm all right," Lily said, blushing self-consciously as she met her old friend's gaze. "It happened rather quickly. Lord Raiford has an overwhelming style of courtship, to say the least."

"It must agree with you," Zachary replied slowly, contemplating her rosy face. "I've never seen you look more beautiful."

"Mr. Lawson," Alex said, moving forward to clasp his father-in-law's hand. "You can be assured I'll take care of your daughter and provide for her every need. I'm sorry there was no time for me to ask your permission. I hope you'll overlook our unseemly haste, and give your blessing to the union."

George Lawson regarded him with a wry twist to his mouth. Both of them were aware that Alex didn't give a damn if he approved or not. Perhaps George was compelled by Alex's hard gray eyes to observe the formalities with grace. Whatever the reason, he replied in an unusually warm fashion. "You have my blessings, Lord Raiford, and my sincere wish that you and my daughter will have a life of contentment together."

"Thank you." Alex reached for Lily and drew her close, forcing father and daughter to confront each other.

Lily eyed her father warily. "Thank you, Papa," she said in a subdued manner. She was surprised when her father reached out and took her hands, one of the few spontaneous gestures of affection he had ever shown her.

"I do wish you well, daughter, no matter what you may think to the contrary."

Lily smiled and returned the pressure of his grip, her eyes becoming suspiciously moist. "I believe you, Papa."

"My turn," a boyish voice interrupted. Lily laughed with glee as Henry launched himself at her. "You're my sister now!" he exclaimed, crushing her with a hearty hug. "I couldn't wait another day to see you. I knew Alex would marry you. I had a

393

feeling about it! And now I'm going to live with you, and you'll take me to Craven's again, and we'll go riding and shooting together, and you'll teach me how to cheat at cards, and—"

"Shhh." Lily put her hand over his mouth and glanced at Alex, her eyes gleaming wickedly. "Not another word, Henry, or your brother will begin proceedings to divorce me."

Heedless of the shocked gazes of her family, Alex tangled his fingers in her curls and kissed her cheek, drawing his head back to smile down at her. "Never," he said firmly, and for one heart-stopping moment Lily allowed herself to believe it.

"Lord Raiford," Burton interrupted sedately, presenting a white card. "Lord Faxton has arrived."

"Show him in," Lily said with a laugh. "Perhaps he would like to stay for dinner."

They all partook of a long and enjoyable dinner, with conversation that ranged from the merits of Lord Faxton's proposed bill to the accomplishments of Henry's tutor Mr. Radburne, a sober but amiable man with an affinity for history and language. Lily was the perfect hostess, giving the conversation gentle nudges when it dawdled, effortlessly drawing a spell around the group to make each guest feel comfortable and included. Alex watched her from the other end of the table with dawning pride. For tonight, at least, the inner tension had faded away, leaving behind a woman so lovely and charming that she dazzled his eyes like sunlight. She faltered only once, when she met his eyes and a searing awareness passed between them.

While the gentlemen were having their port, Penelope drew Lily aside for a private conversation. "Lily, we were so shocked when we heard you had married Lord Raiford, of all people! Mama nearly fainted. My word, we all thought you hated him!"

"I thought so too," Lily said uncomfortably.

"Well, what happened?"

Lily shrugged and smiled lamely. "It's difficult to explain."

"Lord Raiford seems a completely different man, so kind and smiling, and he stares at you as if he adores you! Why did you marry so suddenly? I don't understand any of this!"

"No one does," Lily assured her. "Least of all me. Penny, let's not talk about my marriage. I want to hear about yours. Are you happy with Zach?"

Penelope sighed ecstatically. "Beyond anything I could have imagined! I wake up every morning afraid it's all going to end like some miraculous dream. It sounds ridiculous, I know—"

"Not at all," Lily said quietly. "It sounds wonderful." Suddenly she smiled wickedly at her younger sister. "Tell me about the elopement. Was Zach terribly masterful, in the mode of Don Juan, or did he play the shy, blushing bridegroom? Come, don't keep the thrilling details all to yourself."

"Lily," Penelope protested, turning scarlet. After a brief hesitation, she leaned forward and spoke with her voice lowered. "With the servants' help, Zach stole into the house after Mother and Father had retired. He came to my room, threw his arms around me, and told me that I was going to be his wife, and he wouldn't allow me to sacrifice my happiness for my family's sake."

"Good for him," Lily cheered.

"I put a few things into a valise and went with him to the carriage waiting outside—Oh, I was so terrified we would be caught, Lily! At any moment Mother and Father might have discovered my absence, or Lord Raiford might have returned unexpectedly—"

"No," Lily said dryly. "I made certain that Lord Raiford was indisposed for the evening."

Penelope's eyes turned round with curiosity. "What in heaven's name did you do to him?"

"Don't ask, dearest. Just tell me one thing—did Zach play the gentleman and wait until the night you reached Gretna Green, or did he waylay you at the coaching house?"

"What a dreadful question," Penelope said reprovingly. "You know very well that Zachary would never dream of taking advantage of a woman. Zachary slept in a chair by the fireplace, of course."

Lily made a face. "Hopeless," she said with a laugh. "The two of you are hopelessly honorable."

"Well, so is Lord Raiford," her sister pointed out. "In my opinion he is even more staid and conventional than Zachary. Had the two of you been in our situation, I'm certain Lord Raiford would have conducted himself with all decency and decorum."

"Perhaps," Lily mused and then grinned. "But no matter what you suppose . . . he wouldn't have slept in a chair, Penny."

The guests all left at a late hour, and finally Henry and his tutor were settled in their respective rooms. After running back and forth to confer with the household staff, Lily was assured that everything was in order. She went up to the bedroom with Alex, exceedingly pleased by the way the evening had turned out. Alex dismissed the maid and helped Lily undress, while she gloated over her sister's happiness.

"Penny is radiant," she said as Alex unfastened the back of her gown. "I've never seen her so happy."

"She looks well," Alex admitted grudgingly.

"*Well?* She absolutely glows." Lily took off her dress and sat on the edge of the bed in her under-garments, extending a leg for him to roll off her stocking. "The sight of her now makes me realize how truly miserable you made her, with your grim face and gruff manners." She smiled provocatively, reaching out to unbutton his shirt. "It was the best thing I ever did, getting her away from you."

"Nearly killing me in the process," Alex said sardonically, holding up one of the embroidered silk stockings and viewing it with interest.

"Oh, don't be dramatic. It was only a little tap on the head." Contritely Lily smoothed his golden hair. "I did hate the idea of hurting you. I couldn't think of any other way to stop you, though. You're an impossibly obstinate man."

Alex scowled as he stripped off his shirt, revealing his broad, muscled chest. "You could have thought of a less painful way to keep me away from Raiford Park that night."

"I could have seduced you, I suppose." A smile lingered at the corners of her mouth. "But at the time the idea didn't hold much appeal."

Alex regarded her with a speculative gaze as he removed the rest of his clothes. "I still haven't paid you in kind for that night," he commented. There was a gleam in his eyes that she didn't trust.

"Paid me in kind?" she repeated. Modestly she slipped out of her chemise and sought to climb beneath the sheet. "You mean you'd like to knock me on the head with a bottle?"

"Not precisely."

He joined her on the bed and pushed her to the pillows with playful roughness, taking care not to hurt her. Lily laughed and struggled, while he used his strength to hold her down and steal swift kisses from her. She enjoyed the mock wrestling match, until suddenly she felt her arm being stretched and neatly secured to the bedpost with one of her stockings. A startled laugh burst from her. "Alex . . ." Before she could gather her wits, he fastened her other arm in the same manner. Abruptly her laughter died away, and she tugged at her wrists in astonishment. "What are you doing?" she asked rapidly. "Stop this. Untie me, right away—"

"Not yet." He levered himself over her, gazing down at her.

An erotic, fearful thrill shot through her. "Alex, no."

"I won't hurt you," he said, a faint smile touching his lips. "Close your eyes."

She hesitated, staring into his hard golden face, the sensual promise in his eyes. His powerful body was poised just over hers, while his fingertips rested lightly on the thrashing pulse in her throat. Slowly her lashes fell, and she surrendered with a moan. His hands and mouth began to move over her, eliciting a burning pleasure that she was help- less to return. He tormented her with gentle caresses until she was rigid beneath him, waiting blindly for the torture to end. She lifted herself to him as he joined their bodies in a slow, splendid thrust. The weight and force of him drove deep within her, while his mouth brushed over hers with sweetly flirting kisses. Trembling, she drew tightly around him, using her legs and body to hold him to her. Abruptly the diffuse sensations converged in a burst of rapture and white heat. She jerked against him with a low cry and fell back gasping as he took his own pleasure inside her.

In the slow, surging aftermath, she fought to catch her breath. Alex loosened the bonds at her wrists. Blushing fiercely, she slid her arms around his neck. "Why did you do that?"

His hands moved slowly over her body. "I thought," he replied softly, "you'd like to know how it feels."

Vaguely she recalled having once said the same thing to him, and she choked on a mortified groan. "Alex, I-I don't want to play games with you anymore."

She felt his lips press into the warm space between her neck and jaw. "What do you want?" he asked huskily.

Lily grasped his head in her small hands. "I want to be your wife," she whispered, and urged his mouth back to hers.

As the days passed, Lily found herself craving her husband's touch, his smiles, his nearness. She had feared that life with him might be confining and dull. Instead it held an excitement she had never known. Alex challenged and bewildered her, making it impossible to know what to expect from him. Sometimes he treated her with the same brisk, masculine manner he accorded his friends while drinking and arguing politics over several hands of cards. He showed no hesitancy about taking her riding or shooting with him, and he even brought her to a boxing match, laughing as she alternated between cringing at the violent action in the ring and leaping up to cheer her favorite. Alex took pride in her intelligence, making no effort to hide his surprise at her skill in managing her household accounts. She told him dryly that her uncertain income over the past two years had made her expert at scrimping and economizing.

It was pleasant to have him praise her accomplishments, and she was gratified by his respect for her opinions. She even enjoyed the way he provoked her at times, spurring her into unladylike behavior and then mocking her for it. But there were other times when he disconcerted her by treating her like a rare, easily bruised flower. Some evenings when she was in the bath, he would wash her hair and dry her with soft towels as if she were a child, and rub perfumed oil over her body until her skin glowed.

Lily had never been so thoroughly indulged and spoiled in her life. After years of fending for herself, it was a constant surprise to have someone take her side in all things. She had only to wish aloud for something and it was hers, whether it was more horses in the stable, tickets for the theatre, or just the comfort of being held by him. When she had nightmares, he awakened her with kisses and soothed her back to sleep in his arms.

When she sought to please him in bed, he was lovingly patient as he guided her in erotic lessons that aroused and fulfilled them both. His love-making was infinitely varied, ranging from savage plundering to gentle seduction that took hours to unfold. Whatever his mood, she was always left completely satisfied. Day by day he was stripping away her defenses, leaving her soft, open, and frighteningly vulnerable. Yet she was happier than she had ever thought she could be.

Alex could change from arrogance to gentleness in the blink of an eye, luring her to confide private things she had never thought anyone would want to know about her. He saw through her with terrifying clarity, understanding the shyness beneath her facade. Countless times she was tempted to tell him about Nicole, but she held back in fear. The time with him was becoming too precious. She couldn't lose him yet.

She waited in vain for word from Giuseppe, warning Burton privately to bring her any messages from him. Although she had considered the idea of rehiring the Leary officer, Mr. Knox, to look for Nicole, she was afraid he might inadvertently jeopardize her chances of regaining her daughter. All she could do was wait. Sometimes the strain caused her to lash out irritably at those around her, even at Alex. On one occasion he responded with a sharpness that nearly moved her to tears, and they had a bitter argument. She was hardly able to meet his eyes the next morning, embarrassed by her outburst. She was also afraid that he would demand an explanation for her unreasonable behavior. Instead Alex behaved as if nothing had happened, his manner gentle and warm. Lily realized that he made allowances for her that he would make for no one else. He was the kind of husband she had never imagined existed—generous, quick to forgive, concerned more for her needs than his own.

But as she discovered, Alex did have his faults. He was overprotective and jealous, scowling at any man he perceived to be staring at his wife too closely or taking her hand too long. It amused Lily, his attitude that every man in London must be lusting after her. He took special pains to warn her away from his own cousin, Roscoe Lyon, who made charmingly outrageous overtures to her every time they met. At a magnificent ball they attended, Ross made her laugh by seizing her hand and bestowing a multitude of kisses on the back, as if he were a starving fox in the company of a delectable hen. "Lady Raiford," he sighed eloquently, "your beauty is so luminous that we have no need of moonlight. It fairly humbles me."

"*I'll* humble you," Alex interrupted grimly, retrieving his wife's hand in short order.

Ross encompassed Lily with a beguiling smile. "He doesn't trust me."

"Neither do I," she murmured.

He affected a wounded look. "All I wish for is

a waltz with you, madam," he protested, and added with a seductive grin, "I've never danced with an angel before."

"She's promised this one to me," Alex said darkly, and began to pull his wife away.

"What of the next?" Ross called after them.

Alex answered over his shoulder. "She's promised *all* of them to me."

Laughing, Lily tried to warn him as he led her toward the waltzing couples. "Alex, there's something I should tell you. Mother always tried to teach me to glide gracefully, but it was no use. She said my style of dancing is comparable to the romping of an unbroken horse."

"It can't be that bad."

"I promise you, it can!"

Alex thought she was jesting, but to his amusement he discovered that it was true. It took all of his skill to restrain his athletic wife's vigor upon the dance floor, not to mention several firm maneuvers to keep her from trying to lead. "Follow me," he said, slowing his pace and guiding her through the steps.

Despite the strong guidance of his hand, Lily kept moving in the wrong direction. "This might be easier if you just followed *me*," she suggested impishly.

He bent his head and whispered in her ear, telling her to think of the last time they made love. The unorthodox advice caused her to giggle, but as she stared into his eyes and concentrated on being together with him, it was suddenly easy to allow him full control of their movements. She relaxed enough to allow something approaching a glide. "Why, we're very good at this!" she exclaimed. Grinning at her expression of pleased surprise, Alex claimed her for several more waltzes, causing more than a few raised eyebrows.

It was unfashionable for a husband to dote openly on his wife, but Alex didn't seem to care. Lily was amused by the sophisticated society women who mocked enviously behind their fans at the close attention Alex paid to her. Their own husbands spoke indifferently to them, if at all, and spent every night in their mistresses' beds. To Lily's surprise, even Penelope remarked on Alex's possessiveness, declaring that Zachary never sought out her company the way Alex did with Lily.

"What do you talk with him about all the time?" Penelope asked curiously during the intermission of the most recent play at Drury Lane. "What do you say that interests him so?" The two sisters stood together in a corner of the domed foyer on the first floor, fanning themselves. Before Lily could answer, they were joined by Lady Elizabeth Burghley and Mrs. Gwyneth Dawson, both of them respectable young matrons Lily had begun friendships with. Lily especially liked Elizabeth, who had a lively sense of humor.

"I must hear the answer to this," Elizabeth declared with a laugh. "All of us have been wondering how to keep our husbands planted firmly by our sides as Lily does. What do you say that he finds so enthralling, dear?"

Lily shrugged, glancing at Alex. He was standing with a group of men across the room, all of them involved in idle conversation. As if he felt her gaze, he glanced back at her and smiled slightly. She turned her attention back to the women. "We talk about everything," she said with a grin. "Billiards, beeswax, and Bentham. I never hesitate to give him my opinion, even when he doesn't like it."

"But we shouldn't talk to men about politicians such as Mr. Bentham," Gwyneth said, puzzled. "That's what they have their friends for."

"It seems I've made yet another *faux pas*," Lily said with a laugh, pretending to cross the subject off an invisible list. "No more improper discussions of politicians."

"Lily, don't change a thing," Elizabeth hastened to tell her, her eyes twinkling. "It's clear Lord Raiford likes things just as they are. Perhaps I should ask *my* husband his opinions of beeswax and Mr. Bentham!"

Smiling, Lily let her gaze wander over the crowd in the foyer once more. She was startled by a glimpse of inky black hair, a flash of familiar features. A shudder of uneasiness went through her. Blinking hard, she searched again for the vision, but it was gone. She felt a soft hand on her arm.

"Lily?" Penelope questioned. "Is something wrong?"

CHAPTER 12

Lily continued to stare absently at the crowd. Recovering herself, she pasted a smile on her face and shook her head. It couldn't have been Giuseppe. Over the course of the past years he had become too seedy to mingle in a gathering such as this. Aristocratic bloodlines or not, he wouldn't be allowed to associate with the guests in here, only with the lower classes outside. "No, Penny, it's nothing. I thought I saw a familiar face."

She managed to dispel the dark feeling enough to enjoy the rest of the performance, but she was definitely relieved when it was over. Reading the expression on her face, Alex refused several invitations to gather with friends after the play, and he took Lily back to Swans' Court.

Lily stared hard at Burton as he welcomed them inside and took Alex's gloves and hat. It was the same look she gave him whenever she asked if a particular message had arrived for her that day. In response to her silent question, Burton shook his head slightly. The negative motion sent her heart plummeting. She didn't know how much more she could take, how many more silent nights of waiting for news of her daughter.

Although Lily made an effort to chat lightly about the play, Alex sensed her bleak mood. She asked for brandy, but he told the maid to bring up a glass of hot milk instead. Lily frowned at him but didn't argue. After downing the milk, she undressed and climbed into bed, nestling in Alex's arms. He kissed her, and she pressed against him willingly, but for the first time she couldn't respond when he made love to her. Gently he asked what was wrong, but she shook her head. "I'm tired," she whispered apologetically. "Please just hold me." Alex relented with a sigh, and she rested her head on his shoulder, desperately willing sleep to come.

The image of her daughter floated around her, dancing before her in darkness and mist. Lily cried out her name and reached for her, but she was always a few steps away, just out of her grasp. Eerie laughter echoed around her, and she recoiled from an evil, mocking whisper. *"You'll never have her . . . never . . . never . . ."*

"Nicole," she called out in despair. She ran faster, her arms outstretched, she stumbled and fought against vines that crept around her legs, pulling her down, keeping her from moving. Sobbing with anger, she screamed out for her daughter, and then she heard a child's frightened wail.

"Mama . . ."

"Lily." A calm, quiet voice cut through the mist

and darkness. She swayed dizzily, flailing with her arms. Suddenly Alex was there, holding her steady. She relaxed and leaned against him, breathing unevenly. It had been a nightmare. Pressing her ear against his solid chest, she listened to the strong beat of his heart. As she blinked and wakened fully, she realized they weren't in bed. They were standing by the wrought-iron balustrade at the top of a long flight of stairs. She exclaimed softly, her brow furrowing. She had been sleepwalking again.

Alex tilted her head back with his hand. His face was remote, his voice almost detached. "I woke up and you weren't there," he said flatly. "I found you at the top of the stairs. You almost fell. What were you dreaming about?"

It wasn't fair of him, asking questions when he knew she was disoriented. Lily tried to dispel the grogginess that still clung to her. "I was trying to reach something."

"What?"

"I don't know," she said unhappily.

"I can't help you if you won't trust me," he said with quiet intensity. "I can't protect you from shadows, or keep you safe from dreams."

"I've told you everything . . . I . . . I don't know."

There was a long silence. "Have I ever mentioned," he said coldly, "how much I hate being lied to?"

She averted her gaze, looking at the carpet, the wall, the door, anywhere but his face. "I'm sorry."

She wanted him to hold and cuddle her as he always did after her bad dreams. She wanted him to make love to her, so that for a little while she could forget everything but the powerful warmth of him inside her. "Alex, take me back to bed."

With impersonal gentleness, he eased her away and turned her in the direction of the bedroom. "Go on. I'm going to stay up for a while."

She was surprised by his refusal. "And do what?" she asked in a small voice.

"Read. Drink. I don't know yet." He went downstairs without looking back at her.

Lily wandered to the bedroom and crawled beneath the rumpled covers, feeling guilty and annoyed and worried. She buried her head in a pillow, making a new discovery about herself. "You may hate being lied to, my lord," she muttered, "but not half as much as I hate going to bed alone!"

The slight chill between them persisted the next day. Lily took her morning ride in Hyde Park without him, accompanied by a groom. Later she busied herself with correspondence, a chore she detested. There were piles of calling cards, announcing at-home times at which she would be welcome to call, and lightly penciled requests for when *she* planned to receive visitors. There was a stack of invitations to balls, dinners, and musical evenings. They had been asked to join the Clevelands in Shropshire for autumn grouse shooting, to stay at the Pakingtons' shooting lodge on the moors, and to visit friends in Bath. Lily was at a loss to know how to respond to the requests. How could she accept invitations for a future she wouldn't be part of? It was tempting to let herself pretend she would always be with Alex, but glumly she reminded herself that it would all end someday.

Putting the invitations aside, Lily shuffled through a sheaf of paper on Alex's desk. He had penned a few notes that morning, before leaving at midday to attend some meeting concerning parliamentary reform. She smiled as her eyes moved across his decisive handwriting—strong, bold marks made with a forward slant. Idly she read a letter he had addressed to one of his estate agents, declaring his wish that the tenants be allowed multiyear leases that would be more beneficial to them instead of the more expensive yearly tenancies. Alex had also instructed the agent to install new ditching and fencing on the land at his own expense. Thoughtfully Lily set the letter down and smoothed the corner with her fingertip. From what she knew of most wealthy landlords' selfish greed, she was aware that Alex's sense of honor and fairness were rare. Another letter caught her eye, and she skimmed over it quickly.

. . . regarding your new tenant, I will assume responsibility for all of Pokey's monthly expenses for the duration of the animal's lifetime. If any particular

item for his diet is required, please inform me and I will do what is necessary to ensure a steady supply. With all assurance and respect for your excellent care of him, occasionally I would like to visit and ascertain the bear's condition myself . . .

Lily smiled thoughtfully, recalling the scene a few days ago when they had gone to Raiford Park to send Pokey to his new home. Henry had sat in front of the cage in the garden all morning, looking as dejected as the servants were relieved.

"Must we give him away?" Henry had asked when Lily came out to join him. "Pokey's no trouble at all—"

"He'll be so much happier at his new home," Lily replied. "No more chains. Lord Kingsley described the pen they've constructed for him, cool and shady, with a little stream running through it."

"I guess he'll like that better than a cage," Henry conceded, rubbing and scratching the bear's head. Sighing peacefully, Pokey closed his eyes.

Suddenly they were interrupted by Alex's quiet voice. "Henry. Get away from that cage—slowly. And if I catch you with him again, I'll thrash you until your experiences at Westfield are a pleasant memory by comparison."

Henry stifled a grin and obeyed at once. Lily also repressed the urge to smile. As far as she could tell, Henry had been threatened with dire beatings for years, and so far his older brother hadn't once laid a finger on him.

"He's not dangerous at all," Henry mumbled. "He's a nice bear, Alex."

"That 'nice bear' could take your arm off with one snap of his jaws."

"He's tame and too old to be a threat."

"He's an animal," Alex replied flatly. "One that's been subject to mistreatment from humans. And it doesn't matter that he's old. As you'll eventually learn, boy, age does little to soften anyone's temperament. Think of your Aunt Mildred, for example."

"But Lily pets the bear," Henry protested. "I saw her do it this morning."

"Turncoat," Lily muttered, giving him a damning glare. "I'll remember this, Henry!" She faced Alex with apologetic smile, but it was too late.

"You've been petting that damn animal?" he asked, advancing on her. "After I made it clear that you were not to go near him?"

Pokey lifted his head with a grumbling whine as he watched them.

"But Alex," she said contritely, "I was feeling sorry for him."

"In a minute you're going to be feeling sorrier for yourself."

Lily grinned into his stern face and made a sudden dodge to the left. Catching her easily, he swung her in the air, and she shrieked with laughter. Alex lowered her to the ground, clasping her snugly against his body. His gray eyes flickered with amusement as he stared at his rebellious wife. "I'll teach you what it means to disobey *me*," he growled, and kissed her in front of Henry.

Remembering it now, Lily finally understood the feeling that had rushed over her that day, the feeling that had taken root with startling insistence and permanence since the first moment she had met him. "God help me," she whispered. "I do love you, Alex."

Lily dressed with care for the ball they were attending that night, a celebration of Lady Lyon's sixty-fifth birthday. There would be six hundred guests, many of them coming from their summer estates in the country for the occasion. Knowing that speculative gazes might turn her way, Lily decided to wear a new gown from Monique's, modest but delicately beautiful. The garment, with all its intricate stitchery, had taken days of ceaseless labor by two of Monique's talented assistants. It was made a filmy material of the palest pink, thickly embroidered with gold. The layered skirts of the gown, cut long enough to form a slight train, seemed to float behind her as she walked.

Alex waited for her in the library, leaning over the papers on his desk. His golden head lifted as she entered the room. Lily smiled at the expression on his face, and turned to show him the rest of her ensemble. Golden pins adorned with diamond clusters were fastened in her hair, glinting among the dark curls. On her feet were small, flat gold slippers with ribbons that tied around the ankles. Alex couldn't resist reaching out and brushing his hands over her slender body. She was exquisite and perfect, as if she were made of porcelain.

Lily came close and leaned against him temptingly. "Will I do?" she murmured.

"You'll do," he said gruffly, and planted a chaste kiss on her forehead. Any more than that would unravel his self-control.

The ball, held at the Lyons' London home, was even more elaborate than Lily had anticipated. Built on medieval foundations and enlarged over several centuries, the cavernous home was filled with light and fresh flowers and expensive decorations of crystal, silk, and gold. A large orchestra sent rich melodies outward from the ballroom. The moment they arrived, Lady Lyon took Lily under her wing. Lily was introduced to great numbers of people—cabinet ministers, opera singers, ambassadors and their wives, and distinguished members of the peerage. She despaired of ever remembering more than a handful of names.

Smiling and chatting, Lily sipped from a glass of punch and watched as Alex was dragged away by Ross and a number of men. They were demanding that he arbitrate some wager. "Men," Lily remarked dryly to Lady Lyon. "I have no doubt the wager is over how quickly a particular raindrop will roll down the window pane, or how many glasses of brandy a certain lord can drink before he topples over!"

"Yes," Lady Lyon replied, a teasing glint in her eye. "It's astonishing what some people will do for a wager."

Lily held back a mortified laugh, knowing the elderly woman was referring to the infamous evening at Craven's. "That bet," she said with an unsuccessful attempt at dignity, "was entirely your nephew's suggestion, ma'am. I hope I may live long enough to put the entire episode behind me."

"When you're my age, you'll tell your grand-children all about that episode, in order to shock them," Lady Lyon predicted. "And they'll admire you for your lurid past. Time has given me great understanding of the old saying 'If youth knew, if old age but could.'"

"Grandchildren . . ." Lily mused, her voice soft with sudden melancholy.

"There's still plenty of time for that," the elderly woman assured her, misunderstanding the reason behind her sadness. "Years, in fact. I was thirty-five when I bore Ross, forty at the birth of the last, my Victoria. You still have a great deal of fertile ground, child. I suspect Raiford will sow it very ably."

"Aunt Mildred," Lily exclaimed with a quick laugh, "you're shocking me!"

Just then a servant approached Lily discreetly. "Milady, I beg pardon, but there is a gentleman in the entrance hall without identification. He claims to be here at your request. Perhaps you would deign to come and testify as to his credentials?"

"I invited no . . ." Lily began in surprise, but her mouth snapped shut as an ugly suspicion entered her mind. "*No,*" she whispered, causing the servant to regard her with confusion.

"Milady, shall we compel him to leave?"

"No," Lily gulped, and manufactured a fake smile, conscious of Lady Lyon's sharp gaze fastened on her. "I believe I'll go and investigate this little mystery." She stared directly at the elderly woman and forced herself to shrug blithely. "Curiosity has always been my downfall."

"Killed the cat," Lady Lyon replied, looking at her speculatively.

Lily followed the servant through the handsome house to the entrance hall with its ceiling of intricate plaster-work and painted rondels. A flow of guests came in the front door, each one individually greeted by the Lyons' efficient staff. Amidst the incoming crowd, a still, dark figure was clearly distinguishable. Lily stopped abruptly, staring at him with horror. He smiled at her and made a shallow, mocking bow, accompanied by an elaborate flourish of his dark hand.

"Can you vouch for this guest?" the servant at her elbow inquired.

"Yes," Lily said hoarsely. "He's an old acquaintance, a-an Italian nobleman. Count Giuseppe Gavazzi."

The servant eyed Giuseppe dubiously. Although he was dressed in the manner befitting a nobleman—silk breeches, sumptuously embroidered coat, a starched white cravat—there was something about Giuseppe that betrayed the crudity of his character. Compared to him, Lily thought silently, Derek Craven had the bearing and gentility of a prince.

Once Giuseppe had mingled freely with the nobility, had unquestionably been one of them. It was obvious from his smug expression that he still considered himself to be. But his charming smile had deteriorated into an oily smirk, and his striking handsomeness had turned hard and common. The black eyes that had once been so soft now contained an offensive rapaciousness. Even dressed in fine clothes, he was as distinct from the other guests as a raven would be in a company of swans.

"Very well," the servant murmured, and left her quietly.

Lily stood still at the side of the hall as Giuseppe sauntered toward her. He smiled and gestured to himself proudly. "It remind you of the days in Italy, no?"

"How could you?" she whispered, her voice shaking. "Get away from here."

"But 'ere is where I belong, *cara*. I come to take my place now. I 'ave a money, blue blood, every-t'ing to belong. Like when I meet you first in Florence." His black eyes narrowed insolently.

419

"You make me very sad, *bella*, not to tell me you 'ave marry Lord Raiford. We 'ave many t'ings to talk about."

"Not here," she said through her teeth. "Not now."

"You take me in there," he insisted coolly, gesturing to the ballroom. "You introduce me, you become my, ah . . ." He paused and searched for the word.

"Sponsor?" she asked disbelievingly. "My God." She put her hand over her mouth, struggling to maintain her composure, aware that people were glancing at them curiously. "Where is my daughter, you insane bastard?" she whispered.

He shook his head tauntingly. "There are many t'ings you do for me now, Lily. After, I bring you Nicoletta."

She choked back a frustrated, hysterical laugh. "You've said that for twenty-four months." She couldn't stop her voice from rising. "I've had enough, *enough*—"

He hissed at her to be quiet and touched her arm, making her aware that someone was approaching them. "This is Lord Raiford?" he asked her, noting the man's golden hair.

Lily glanced over her shoulder and felt her stomach throb sickly. It was Ross, his handsome face alert with curiosity. "No, his cousin." She turned to face Ross, masking her torment with a bland social smile, but not quickly enough.

"Lady Raiford," Ross said, looking from her to

Giuseppe. "My mother sent me to inquire about your mysterious guest."

"A friend of mine from Italy," Lily replied easily, though inwardly she was humiliated at having to introduce him. "Lord Lyon, may I present Count Giuseppe Gavazzi, a recent arrival in London."

"How fortunate for us," Ross said with such overdone blandness that it was an insult.

Giuseppe preened and smiled. "It is my 'ope we will both profit from our acquaintance, Lord Lyon."

"Indeed," Ross replied in a regal manner reminiscent of his mother. He turned to Lily and asked politely, "Are you enjoying yourself, Lady Raiford?"

"Immensely."

He regarded her with a thin smile. "Have you ever considered a career on the stage, Lady Raiford? I believe you may have missed your calling." Without waiting for a reply, he strolled away in no apparent hurry.

Lily swore under her breath. "He's going to my husband. Leave, Giuseppe, and put an end to this farce! Those seedy rags won't fool anyone into thinking you're an aristocrat."

That infuriated him—she could see the malevolence flaring in his ebony eyes. "I t'ink I stay, *cara.*"

Lily heard her name being called in greeting as more guests arrived. She threw them a smile and a little wave, and spoke quietly to Giuseppe.

"There must be a private room nearby. We'll go somewhere and talk. Come quickly, before my husband finds us."

Idly rolling a snifter of brandy in his hands, Ross stood by Alex, who had gathered with the other men in the gentlemen's room. They were all engrossed in arranging objects on a table to illustrate points as they disputed military tactics. "If the regiments positioned themselves here . . ." one of them was saying, sliding a snuffbox, a pair of spectacles, and a small figurine to the corner of the table.

Alex grinned and clamped the end of a cigar with his teeth as he interrupted. "No, it's easier if they split and move here . . . and here . . ." He positioned the snuffbox and figurine so that they trapped the enemy, represented by a small painted vase. "There. Now the vase doesn't stand a chance in hell."

Someone else spoke up. "But you've forgotten the scissors and the lampshade. They're in a prime position to charge from behind."

"No, no," Alex began, but Ross interrupted, pulling him away from the table.

"You have an interesting strategy," Ross said dryly, while the others continued the battle. "But there is a flaw, cousin. You should always leave a path for retreat."

Alex glanced back at the table assessingly. "You think I should have left the snuffbox where it was?"

"I'm not talking about the deuced snuffbox, cousin, or any sham battle." Ross lowered his voice several notches. "I'm referring to your clever little wife."

Alex's face changed, his gray eyes freezing. He removed the cigar from his mouth and heedlessly stubbed it out on a silver tray nearby. "Go on," he invited gently. "And choose your words with care, Ross."

"I told you Lawless Lily isn't the kind of woman a man keeps forever. It was a mistake to marry her, Alex. She'll make a fool of you. She's making a fool of you at this very moment."

Alex regarded him with cold fury. He was going to beat Ross to a pulp for speaking of Lily so cuttingly, but first he had to find out what was going on. She might be in some kind of trouble. "Where is she?"

"Hard to tell," Ross said with a slight shrug. "Just about now I would imagine she's found a private corner, to share a passionate embrace with an Italian good-for-naught masquerading as a count. Gavazzi was the name, I believe. Sound familiar to you? I didn't think so." Ross's confidence was shaken as Alex gave him a look so darkly promising that it could have come from the devil himself. Then Alex left with silent swiftness. Ross leaned back against the wall indolently and crossed his legs, assured once more that whatever he wanted in life would be his—as long as he had the patience to wait. "As I predicted," he murmured pragmatically, "I'll be the next to have her."

"You'll never put an end to this, will you?" Lily railed in the privacy of a small upstairs parlor. "It will go on forever. I'll *never* have her back!"

Giuseppe crooned softly, trying to pacify her. "No, no, *bellissima*. It is over soon, very soon. I bring you Nicoletta. But first, you make me welcome to these peoples. You make me friends 'ere. This, *this* is what I work for all these years, to get the money for making me an important man in London."

"I see," Lily said dazedly. "You weren't good enough for Italian society—Good God, you're a wanted criminal there—and so now you want a place *here?*" She stared at him in furious disgust. "I know how your mind works. You assume that you'll be able to marry some wealthy widow or some foolish young heiress and play lord of the manor for the rest of your life. Is that your plan? You want me to become your sponsor and gain you entrée? And you think these people will accept you on *my* recommendation?" She exploded with a bitter, mocking laugh, and then fought to control herself. "My God, Giuseppe, *I'm* barely respectable. I don't have a thimbleful of influence!"

"You are the countess of Raiford," he said in a hard voice.

"It's only out of respect for my husband that these people tolerate my presence!"

"I tell you what I want," he said inflexibly. "Now you do it for me. Then I give you Nicoletta."

Lily shook her head wildly. "Giuseppe, this is ridiculous," she burst out desperately. "Please, just give me my daughter. Even if I wanted to, I couldn't do anything for you. You aren't meant for the *haut ton*. You use people, and you have contempt for everyone—do you think they can't see it in your face? Don't you realize that they'll find out exactly what you are?"

She started in repulsed shock as Giuseppe came to her, putting his wiry arms around her, the flowery musk of his cologne wafting in her face. He touched her chin with his hot, damp hand, and moved it to her throat. "Always you ask me, when do I bring back your baby, when do I make an end to this," he said silkily. "Now I tell you, it will end. But *after* you 'elp to make me part of this world."

"No," she said, giving a disgusted sob as she felt his hand slide to her heaving breast.

"Remember what we 'ave together?" he whispered, confident in his powers of seduction, his body becoming aroused against hers. "Remember the way I teach you love? The way we move together in the bed, the pleasure I bring to you as we make our beautiful baby—"

"Please," she said in a strangled voice, straining away from him. "Let me go. My husband will come soon to find me. He has a jealous temper and he won't . . ."

Suddenly a terrible, agonizing coldness came over her. She stopped speaking and began to tremble. With slowly dawning horror she turned her head to find Alex in the doorway. He was staring at her in disbelief, his face stark white.

Giuseppe followed Lily's unblinking gaze and made a slight exclamation of surprise. "Lord Raiford," he said smoothly, dropping his hands from Lily. "I t'ink you 'ave per'aps a little misunderstanding. I leave now, and allow your wife to make the explaining, *si?*" He winked surreptitiously and left with a smug smile, certain Lily would smooth everything over with a few glib, wifely lies. After all, she had a great deal to lose.

Alex's gaze did not move from his wife. They were both silent, forming a frozen tableau in the midst of the elegant room. The laughter and music of the assembly floated up to them, but it might as well have been a universe away. Lily knew she should speak, move, do something that would take the dreadful expression from his face, but all she could seem to do was stand there and shiver.

Finally he spoke. His voice was low and so raw that it was unrecognizable. "Why were you letting him hold you like that?"

In a whirl of panic Lily tried to think of a lie, something that would convince him he was mistaken, some clever story. Once she might have been able to. But she had changed. All she could do was stand there stupidly. She knew exactly how a fox felt when it had been run to ground—stiff and cowering, waiting helplessly for the end to come.

When she didn't answer, Alex spoke again, his face contorted. "You're having an affair with him."

A trapped, terrified look came over Lily's features, and she stared at him mutely. Her silence was answer enough. With a hoarse sound of pain, Alex turned away from her. A moment later, she heard his ragged whisper. "You little whore."

Lily's eyes brimmed with tears as she watched him stride to the door. She had lost him. Lady Lyon had been right . . . only death or betrayal could destroy him. Her secrets didn't matter now. Somehow she managed to croak his name pleadingly. "Alex."

He stopped with his hand on the closed door, keeping his back to her. His shoulders lifted and fell rapidly, as if he were trying to master emotions too violent to contain.

"Please stay," she said brokenly. "Please, let me tell you the truth." Unable to bear the sight of his still form, she half-turned, wrapping her arms around herself. She took a tormented breath. "His name is Giuseppe Gavazzi. I met him in Italy. We were lovers. Not recently . . . five years ago. He was the one I told you about." She bit her lip until it ached sharply. "It must disgust you, having seen that contemptible man and knowing that he and I . . ." She broke off with a harsh sob. "It disgusts *me*. The experience was so dreadful that he wanted nothing more to do with me, nor I with him. I thought I was rid of him forever. But . . . that wasn't quite true. My life changed forever after that night, because I found out . . . I found out . . ." She shook her head impatiently at her own stammering cowardice, and she forced herself to continue. "I was pregnant." There was no sound from Alex. She was too afraid and ashamed to look at him. "I had a child. A daughter."

"Nicole." His voice sounded thick and odd.

"How did you know that?" she asked in dull amazement.

"You spoke it in your sleep."

"Of course." She smiled with self-derision, tears running down her face. "I seem to be quite active in my sleep."

"Go on."

Lily wiped at her cheeks with her sleeve, and steadied her voice. "For two years I lived with Nicole and Aunt Sally in Italy. I kept my baby a secret from everyone but Giuseppe. I thought he had a right to know, that he might take an interest in her. He didn't care, of course. He didn't come to see us. Sally died during that time, and all I had left was Nicole. Then one day I came back from the market, and . . ." Her voice faltered. "She was gone. Giuseppe had taken her. I knew he had her, because later he brought me the dress she was wearing that day. He kept my baby in hiding and refused to give her back. He asked for money. It was never enough . . . he wouldn't let me see her, and he kept demanding more. The authorities couldn't find her. Giuseppe was involved in other illegal activities, and he was forced to leave Italy to avoid prosecution. He told me he was bringing my daughter to London, and I followed him here. I hired a Learie officer to search for Nicole. All he managed to discover was that Giuseppe had become part of an organization, an underworld that has taken root in many countries."

"Derek Craven knows about it," Alex said tonelessly.

"Yes. He's tried to help me, but it's impossible. Giuseppe holds all the cards." She tried to get control over herself. "I've tried everything, I've done what he asked, but it goes on and on. Every night I wonder if Nicole is sick, if she's crying, if she needs me and I'm not there. If she's forgotten me." Her throat clenched in agony, and all she could force out was a whisper. "He showed Nicole to me just the other day . . . I'm certain it was her . . . but he wouldn't let me touch her, or speak to her . . . I don't think she recognized me." The words dried in her throat. Lily felt as if she would shatter at the slightest touch. She needed to be alone . . . she had never been so defenseless in her life. But as she managed to break her paralysis and step away, she felt his hands close over her upper arms. Suddenly she began to shudder with the force of incoherent sobs torn from deep within her. Swiftly he turned her, and held her against his broad chest as she crumpled against him, crying with wretched, uncontrollable gasps, with the force of emotions that had been pent up for years.

Hot fears flooded from her eyes onto his shirt. Clutching at him, Lily crawled into his arms, the only safe haven in the world. She writhed frantically to get closer, but slowly she comprehended that there was no need to struggle, he was not going to let go of her. One of his hands cupped the back of her head, securing it against his shoulder. "It's all right, darling," he whispered, stroking her dark curls. "It's all right. You're not alone anymore."

She tried to stifle the agonized sounds that seemed to be ripped from her throat, but the convulsive sobs wouldn't stop. "Easy," he murmured in her hair, stroking her trembling body as she gave in to her shattering grief. "I understand now," he continued hoarsely, his own eyes stinging. "I understand everything." He would have willingly given his life to spare her such suffering. He kissed her hair, her wet face, the small hands that clung to his shoulders. Wishing fiercely that he could draw her pain into his own body, he held her hard against his sheltering strength. Finally she wilted against him, her tears abating. "We'll find out what happened to her," he said roughly. "We'll get her back, no matter what it takes. I swear it."

"You should hate me," she said brokenly. "You should leave me—"

"Hush." His grip tightened, just short of bruising her. "Do you think so little of me? *Damn* you." He crushed his lips in her hair. "You don't understand anything about me. Did you think I wouldn't want to help you? That I would abandon you if I knew?"

"Yes," she whispered.

"*Damn* you," he repeated, his voice choked with anger and love. He forced her face upward. The hopelessness in her eyes caused a cold pressure to squeeze around his heart.

Alex summoned a servant to show him a way they could discreetly leave the house without being witnessed by the guests. He bid the same servant to give a message to Lady Lyon that Lily was ill with a headache and had left the ball precipitately. Leaving Lily alone to rest for a moment, Alex took a quick, determined tour through the Lyon mansion, but wisely Giuseppe had taken his leave.

Lily was so drained that she was forced to lean on Alex as they left. He scooped her up in his arms and carried her to their enclosed chariot, declining to give explanations to the surprised footmen. Once inside, he reached for her, but she warded him off gently, telling him in a queer voice that she was fine. They headed home at a rapid pace, while Alex struggled with overwhelming thoughts and emotions.

It devastated him to know what Lily had gone through. She had chosen to endure it alone, she had chosen to withdraw and build up defenses on that foundation of secrets, she had willingly chosen every moment of solitude . . . but knowing all that didn't stop the grief he felt on her behalf. He couldn't give her back the years. He couldn't even be certain of giving her back Nicole, though he would move heaven and earth in the effort. Burning rage spread through him, as if it were seeping out from the marrow of his bones. He was angry at her, at Derek, at the damned useless detectives, at the Italian bastard who had caused such misery, and he was angry at himself.

Another part of him was terrified. Lily had sustained her hope for so long . . . if the source of it was taken away, if Nicole could not be returned to her, she would never be the same. The vibrant laughter and passion that he loved might vanish for good. He had seen people lose what they loved most, and the way it had changed them. His own father had become an empty shell of a man, longing for death because life had lost all power to entice him. Alex wanted to beg Lily to be strong, but he could see that she had no more strength left. Her face was pinched and tired and her eyes were dull.

They arrived in Swans' Court and Alex escorted Lily to the front door. Burton greeted them with instant concern, staring at Lily questioningly. He looked at Alex. "You've returned early, my lord," he remarked.

Alex didn't have time to explain anything. He urged his wife forward. "Have her drink a glass of brandy," he told Burton curtly. "Force it down her throat if necessary. Don't let her go anywhere. Tell Mrs. Hodges to prepare her a bath. And have someone with her at every moment until I return. Every moment, do you understand?"

"You needn't worry, my lord."

Alex exchanged a glance with him and relaxed slightly, reassured by the butler's calmness. It moved Alex, the realization that Burton, in his own quiet way, had done his best to take care of Lily during the nightmare of the past two years.

"Good God, there's no need to carry on," Lily said in a ghost of her usual pert voice, pushing past them into the house. "Make the brandy a double, Burton." She paused to look back at her husband. "Where the devil are you going?"

The flicker of spirit she showed made Alex feel slightly better. "I'll tell you when I return. I'll be home soon."

"There's nothing you can do," Lily said wearily. "Nothing that Derek hasn't already tried."

In spite of all his sympathy and devotion, Alex found himself giving her a cool, caustic stare. "Apparently it hasn't occurred to you," he said pleasantly, "that I have influence in places where Craven doesn't. Go have your brandy, darling."

Annoyed by his condescension, Lily opened her mouth to reply, but he had already turned and gone down the steps. He paused at the last step and spoke to her once more. "Tell me the name of the man you hired."

"Knox. Alton Knox." She smiled bitterly. "A top-notch Learie officer. The best that money could buy."

Sir Joshua Nathan had come to prominence as a chief magistrate of the city a few years before, when Alex had used his influence to sponsor and pass a bill creating several new public offices. The political battle had been vicious and bloody, facing opposition from a number of corrupt "trading justices" who were in the habit of altering sentences for gifts of money, women, and even liquor. It had taken Alex months of debating, making speeches, and asking for personal favors in order to push the bill through. Alex had done it not only because of his own belief that the bill was worthy, but because Nathan, a man of integrity and courage, had been a close friend from his school days.

Nathan's name was always paired with that of Donald Learman, the fiery young magistrate who served at the Westminster office. The two of them shared the same unorthodox beliefs in the method of policing, considering it a "science" that needed to be reformed and improved. Together they had worked to train their officers as meticulously as military squadrons. At first they had been ridiculed by a society accustomed to only the meager protection of aging watchmen. Despite their lack of popularity, the results of their efforts had quickly become apparent, and other precincts were beginning to follow their lead. The members of Nathan and Learman's crack foot patrols, known as "Learies," were often privately hired by banks and wealthy citizens.

A lean, well-groomed man with an unassuming presence, Nathan greeted him with a calm, friendly smile. "Hello, Alex. A welcome face from the past."

Alex reached out to clasp his hand. "I'm sorry to visit at such a late hour."

"I'm quite accustomed to late hours. The nature of my work. As my wife observes, her only hope of seeing me is in the middle of the day." Nathan led Alex to his library, and they sat in dark leather chairs. "Now," he said quietly, "enough pleasantries. The sooner you tell me the problem, the sooner we may set things to rights."

Alex described the situation as succinctly as possible. Nathan listened thoughtfully, occasionally interrupting with a question. The name of Gavazzi was not recognizable to him, but the mention of Alton Knox seemed to be extremely significant. When Alex concluded his monologue, the magistrate leaned back in his chair, forming a triangle with his thumbs and forefingers as he thought. "Child-stealing is a thriving business in London," Nathan said cynically. "Attractive little boys and girls are a profitable commodity, efficiently harvested from shops and parks and sometimes right from the nursery. Often they're sold to buyers in foreign markets. It's a convenient business—easily dismantled at the first sign of trouble and just as easily resurrected when the scene is clear."

"You think Gavazzi may be involved in such a scheme?"

"Yes, I'm certain he's part of a rookery gang. From your description, he doesn't seem the kind who could manage this on his own."

The following silence seemed to spin out endlessly, until Alex couldn't stand it anymore. "Dammit, what is it?"

Nathan smiled sardonically at his friend's impatience, and then his thin face turned somber. "I'm considering some disquieting possibilities," he finally said. "The man your wife hired, Mr. Knox, is the pride of Learman's Westminster office. Lady Raiford was not at fault for believing him to be trustworthy."

"Is he?" Alex asked tersely.

"I'm not certain." Nathan gave a long sigh. "In the course of their duties, Alex, my officers become quite familiar with the underworld and its workings. Sometimes they are tempted to use this knowledge in evil ways . . . trading innocent lives in return for money, and therefore betraying every principle they are pledged to uphold. I'm afraid your wife and her daughter may have been victims of this devil's bargain." He frowned in disgust. "Knox has earned a large amount of 'blood money' this year, in the form of rewards for recovering stolen children. His unusual success leads me to suspect he could be in collusion with the criminals who are responsible for the abductions. Feeding them information, warning them when to change locations, helping them to avoid arrest. Knox may actually be partners with this Gavazzi."

Alex's jaw hardened. "What the hell are you going to do about it?"

"With your permission, I would like to set a trap, using Lady Raiford as our front."

"As long as she won't be exposed to danger."

"No danger of any kind," Nathan assured him.

"What about her daughter?" Alex asked tersely. "Will this help to find her?"

Nathan hesitated. "If we're fortunate, it will lead to that."

Alex rubbed his forehead and closed his eyes. "Dammit," he muttered. "That's not much to take home to my wife."

"It's all I can offer," came the quiet reply.

CHAPTER 13

"Mr. Knox was *helping* Giuseppe?" Lily demanded in outrage. "While he was working for me?"

Alex nodded, taking her hands in his. "Nathan suspects Giuseppe may be part of a rookery gang, and that Knox is in collusion with him. Recently Knox has been making a large amount of 'blood money' in addition to his regular salary."

"Blood money?" Lily asked in confusion.

"Rewards given him by private citizens for finding and returning stolen children. Knox has collected rewards for resolving several such cases this year."

Lily's eyes widened with surprise and anger. "Then the gang abducts children . . . Mr. Knox returns them . . . and they all divide the reward money amongst themselves? Why has he returned everyone's child except mine? Why not Nicole?"

"Giuseppe may have persuaded him that they'd make more by keeping Nicole and draining you of everything you had."

Lily was still. "He was right," she said numbly. "I handed over several fortunes to him. I gave him whatever he wanted." She dropped her head into her hands. "Oh, God," she muttered. "What a naive, blind fool I've been. I made it so damned easy for them."

While she remained hunched over, his hand settled over her head, his long fingers sifting through her curls in an easy, repeated stroke. Until now she had winced away from his attempts to embrace her, but she allowed the soothing massage, the tense muscles in her neck loosening.

"Don't blame yourself," Alex said gently. "You were alone and frightened. They took advantage of that. It's impossible to look at things objectively when you're afraid for your child."

Lily's mind seemed to spin with questions. What did he think of her now that he knew all about her past? . . . Did he feel pity or censure? . . . Was he only being kind until he felt she was strong enough to face his rejection? She told herself that she couldn't make a move toward him until she had the answers. She would rather die than force herself on him . . . but rational thought was becoming impossible with his fingers playing softly in her hair. A surge of need rose inside her, and she couldn't stop herself from lifting her head with a quiet plea. She didn't care if it was pity. She just wanted him to hold her.

"Sweetheart." Alex gathered her into his lap, cradling her tenderly as she buried her face against his neck. He seemed to read her thoughts easily, as if she were a treasured volume he had paged through a thousand times. By telling her secrets, she had given him that power over her. "I love you," he said against her temple, brushing back her hair with his fingertips.

"You can't—"

"Quiet. Listen to me carefully, Wilhemina. Your mistakes, your past, your fears . . . none of it will change how I feel about you."

She swallowed hard, trying to absorb the statement. "I-I don't like that name," she faltered.

"I know," he said gently. "Because it reminds you of when you were a girl. Wilhemina is frightened and eager, wanting to be loved. And Lily is strong and brave, and would tell the world to go to hell if she wanted to."

"Which do you prefer?" she whispered.

He nudged her chin upward, staring into he eyes. He smiled slightly. "All of you. Every part of you."

Lily trembled at the assurance in his voice, but as he lowered his mouth to hers, she flinched. She wasn't ready for sensual kisses or embraces . . . her inner wounds were raw . . . she needed time to heal. "Not yet," she whispered pleadingly, afraid he would be angry at her refusal. Instead he gathered her close again, and she rested her head on his shoulder with a weary sigh.

It was ten o'clock in the morning. At the East End of London shops had been open since eight, the streets filled with the noise and bustle of vendors, wagons, fishermen, and milkmaids as they all went about their work. Here in the West End, the populace awakened in a far more leisurely fashion. Having arrived early at the corner of Hyde Park, Lily watched the world outside the carriage window. Milk women, chimney sweeps with their soot bags, newsmen, and bakery boys rang at the doors of fine homes, greeted by maidservants. Children walked along the streets with their nannies to take the morning air, while their parents would not stir from bed and partake of breakfast until early afternoon. In the distance was the drumbeat and music of the guards marching from their barracks toward Hyde Park.

Lily's gaze sharpened as she saw a lone figure come to stand by a timber post next to the street corner. It was Alton Knox, garbed in the traditional Learie uniform—black breeches and boots and a gray coat studded with shiny brass buttons. A low-crowned hat topped his head. After taking a steadying breath, Lily leaned out the carriage window and beckoned with her handkerchief. "Mr. Knox," she said in a low voice. "Over here. Please come to the carriage."

Knox complied, exchanging a brief, pleasant word with the footman before climbing into the privacy of the enclosed vehicle. Removing his hat, he smoothed his salt-and-pepper hair, and murmured a greeting. A solidly built man of medium height, he had a nondescript face that could have belonged to a man much younger than his forty years.

Lily sat in the opposite seat, giving him a nod of welcome. "Mr. Knox, I appreciate your willingness to meet here instead of at my residence. For obvious reasons, I cannot allow my husband, the earl, to discover that I have conducted any business with you. He would insist on explanations . . ." She let her voice trail off and looked at him helplessly.

"Of course, Miss Lawson." Knox paused and corrected himself with a faint smile. "But of course, it is Lady Raiford now."

"My marriage was an unexpected turn of events," Lily admitted self-consciously. "It has altered my life in many ways . . . except one. I still am determined to find my daughter Nicole." She lifted a money pouch and jangled it slightly. "Fortunately I now have the means to continue the search. I would like your help in this matter, as before."

Knox's gaze riveted on the money pouch, and he gave her what was intended to be a reassuring smile. "Consider me reinstated, Lady Raiford." He reached out his hand, and she gave him the small but hefty bag. "Now, tell me how matters stand with Gavazzi."

"My communications with Count Gavazzi have not ceased, Mr. Knox. In fact, he boldly confronted me last night, making entirely new demands."

"Last night?" he questioned in surprise. "*New* demands?"

"Yes." Lily gave a distraught sigh. "Before, as you know, Giuseppe wanted only money. *That* I was able and willing to supply, as long as I believed there was hope I would regain my child. But last night . . ." She broke off and shook her head with a sound of disgust.

"What sort of demands?" Knox asked. "Forgive my bluntness, but did he ask for your personal favors, my lady?"

"No. Although he did make advances that I found intolerable, it was even worse than that. Count Gavazzi threatens everything I have, my home, my marriage, my social position, because of some ludicrous ambition of his to become a member of the *beau monde!*" Lily hid her satisfaction as she saw that Knox's face was wiped clean with astonishment.

"I can scarcely credit that," he managed to say.

"It's true." She lifted a lace handkerchief to the corner of her eye, pretending to blot a tiny tear. "He approached me at Lady Lyon's birthday celebration last night, arrayed like a straggly peacock, in front of hundreds of people! He demanded that I introduce him, and become his sponsor so that he would become accepted into the elite circles. Oh, Mr. Knox, you should have seen the dreadful spectacle."

"The fool!" he burst out angrily, paying little heed to how odd his sudden fury must have seemed.

"He was witnessed by several people, including

Lord Lyon and my own husband. When I managed to coax him to a private corner, he revealed his bizarre ambitions. He said that he would return my daughter back to me soon, but first he wants my influence to gain him a position of social consequence. The idea is quite unsupportable. He's known in Italy as a scoundrel, a criminal! How could he *imagine* he would be well-received here?"

"He's nothing but foreign scum," Knox said grimly. "And now it seems he's not only worthless but unstable."

"Exactly, Mr. Knox. And unstable men tend to betray themselves—and their schemes—with foolish mistakes. Is that not so?"

"You're correct," he said with a sudden and unnatural calmness. "In all probability he will become a victim of his own greed."

There was a cold flatness to his gaze that chilled her. His grave face had taken on a reptilian expression—sinister and predatory. There was no doubt, Lily thought, that he intended to put an end to Giuseppe's dangerously unrestrained behavior. If Knox truly was involved with Giuseppe and some rookery gang, his fortunes were tied to theirs, and the wagging of loose tongues was untenable.

Earnestly Lily leaned forward and touched his arm. "I pray you will find my Nicole," she said softly. "Mr. Knox, I can promise you a significant reward if you succeed in this." She placed a delicate emphasis on *significant*, and he visibly savored the word.

"This time I will not fail you," Knox said firmly. "I shall resume my investigations this very morning, Lady Raiford."

"Please, use discretion in notifying me of your progress. My husband . . . the necessity of secrecy . . ."

"Of course," Knox assured her. Replacing his hat, he bid her good day and left the carriage, his weight causing the vehicle to lurch slightly. He walked away with the brisk stride of a man with a destination in mind.

Lily's appealing expression vanished as soon as he turned away, and she watched him through the carriage window with cold, dark eyes. "Go to hell, you bastard," she whispered. "And while you're at it, take Giuseppe with you."

After telling Alex and Sir Nathan the details of the meeting with Knox, and placing every possible construction on his words, there was nothing to do but wait. Henry had gone to the British Museum with his tutor to study Greek vases and antiquities. Although none of the servants understood what was going on, they were all subdued, aware of the tension that permeated every room of the mansion. Lily longed to go for an invigorating ride, but she was afraid to leave the house in case something occurred while she was away.

Half-wild with the need to do something, she attempted a bit of needlework, but she kept accidentally pricking her fingertips until the handkerchief she was embroidering was spotted with blood. She couldn't understand how Alex remained so maddeningly calm, attending to paperwork in the library as if this were any other day.

Drinking endless cups of tea, she paced, read, and endlessly shuffled cards in a rhythm that had become second nature to her. The only reason she managed to swallow a few mouthfuls at dinner was because of Alex's bullying and his sardonic comments that she would be of no use to anyone if she starved herself.

Finding the privacy of her room unendurable, she seated herself in the corner of one of the settees in the parlor, while Alex read aloud from a book of poetry. Lily thought he had deliberately chosen the most tedious passages. His deep voice, the ticking clock, and the wine she'd consumed at dinner combined to make her eyelids heavy. She settled deeply against the brocaded cushions of the settee, and felt herself drifting into the quiet gray mist of sleep.

What could have been minutes or hours later, she was aware of Alex's voice close to her ear, and his gentle but urgent hand on her shoulder, shaking her awake. "Lily. Sweetheart, open your eyes."

"Hmm?" She rubbed her eyes and murmured groggily. "Alex, what are you—"

"Word from Nathan," he said, picking up her slippers from the floor and shoving them onto her feet. "The men Nathan planted on Knox have followed him to the St. Giles rookery. Nathan and a dozen officers have cornered him in a nethersken. We're to go there immediately."

"St. Giles," she echoed, snapping awake. It was arguably the most dangerous place in London, a slum riddled with thieves' kitchens and nicknamed the "Holy Land." Even police officers did not dare venture past its borders of Great Russell and St. Giles High streets. They knew it as a criminal stronghold, where thieves and murders could mine the riches of the West End and escape into the murky network of yards, narrow alleys, and crooked lanes. "Did the message say anything about Nicole? About any children—"

"No." Alex fastened a dark cloak around her. He led her outside to the waiting carriage before she had time to ask more questions. Lily swept a quick glance at the half-dozen armed outriders, realizing that Alex was taking no chances with their safety.

The carriage hurtled through the streets with a violent clatter. Two outriders traveled far enough ahead to clear the way of pedestrians or slow-moving vehicles. Clenching her hands together, Lily tried to calm herself, but she could feel her pulse throbbing in panic. The streets and courts they passed became older and progressively filthier, the buildings crammed together so tightly that they allowed no air or light between them.

The people slinking around the decaying areas were withered and ghostly white. Even the children. The rank smell of thousands of uncovered cesspits drifted inside the carriage, causing Lily to wrinkle her nose in disgust. She caught a glimpse of the distinctive spiral tower of St. Giles-in-the-Fields, a church which had begun as the chapel of a medieval leper hospital.

The carriage stopped in front of a nethersken, an old, crumbling lodging house. Alex got out of the carriage and conferred with one of the outriders and the driver, telling them to guard his wife carefully. If necessary, they were to drive the carriage away at the first sign of danger.

"No!" Lily exclaimed, trying to leave the vehicle, but Alex barred the doorway with his arm, preventing her from climbing out. "I'm going in there with you!" Her blood rushed with agitation and excited fury. "You wouldn't dare leave me outside!"

"Lily," he said quietly, giving her a hard stare. "I'll give you leave to come in soon. But first I'm going to make certain it's safe. You're more precious to me than my own life. I won't risk you for any reason."

"The place is swarming with officers," she pointed out heatedly. "At the moment it's probably the safest place in London! Besides, it's *my* daughter we're searching for!"

"I know that." He swore underneath his breath. "Dammit, Lily, I don't know what we're going to find in there. I don't want you to see something that may hurt you."

She stared at him steadily and made her tone very soft. "We'll face it together. Don't protect me, Alex. Just let me stand by your side."

Alex looked at her a long moment. Abruptly he slid his arm around her waist and swung her from the carriage. She slipped her hand in his as they walked to the doorway of the nethersken, where a battered door had been removed from its hinges and set aside. Two officers waited for them, greeting Alex respectfully. They looked askance at Lily. One of them murmured that there had been some deaths during the invasion of the building. Perhaps she wouldn't care to go inside.

"She'll be all right," Alex said curtly, and preceded Lily into the nethersken, still retaining her hand. The air in the building was stifling and fetid. They climbed a few broken steps and proceeded down a narrow, garbage-littered hall. Insects crept busily up and down the walls. The repulsive odor of burnt herring came strongly from one of the rooms they passed, where someone must have toasted fish in the blackened fireplace. There was little furniture except a few bare tables and pallets strewn on the floor. Straw was stuffed in between the shards of glass at the windows. As they went deeper into the nethersken, toward the sound of voices, Alex felt Lily's hand clench tighter on his until her fingers had formed a crushing vise.

They approached a large room crowded full of officers. They were engaged in subduing outraged suspects and reporting information to Sir Nathan. Wailing children were ratted out from the corners of the building and brought to him. Nathan stood in the center of the room, surveying the scene calmly and giving soft-voiced orders that were obeyed with alacrity. Alex paused as he saw three piled-up bodies before them in the hall, ragged men from the rookery that must have been killed in the fray. He heard Lily's soft gasp, and he looked more closely at one of them. Nudging the lifeless body with his boot, he turned it over. Giuseppe's glassy eyes stared up at them.

Lily recoiled from the sight and whispered his name.

Alex surveyed the blood-soaked body without emotion. "Knife wound," he observed with detached interest, and pulled Lily with him into the crowded room.

Upon seeing them, Nathan signaled for them to stay there, and he made his way to them. "My lord," he said, and gestured to the bodies behind them. "The plan worked only too well. Knox made his way here as soon as night fell. It was only through the efforts of our man Clibhorne, a specialist on the rookery, that we were able to follow him through the area—roof, yard, and cellar. By the time our forces arrived, Knox had already killed Gavazzi out of fear that he would betray the entire scheme. Knox has confessed to us that afterward he intended to return the child to Lady Raiford and collect the reward money she had promised." Nathan gestured to the sullen Knox, bound and seated on the floor in line, his back to the wall. He was lined up with four other men, all of them captured gang members. Knox glared at Lily with hatred, but she was too anxious to notice. Her gaze traveled frantically over the half-dozen children in the room.

"What of these children?" Alex asked Nathan.

"All belonging to well-heeled families, according to Knox. We'll try to return them to their parents—*without* accepting reward money, since these crimes were perpetrated with the aid of an officer." Nathan glanced at Knox with cold disdain. "He's brought shame on all of us."

Lily stared at the gathered children. Most of them were blond and fair, sniffling tearfully and clinging to the officers who tried in vain to comfort them. The little group was a heart-wrenching sight. "She's not here," Lily said dazedly, her face white with panic. She wandered forward, trying to see through the crowd of men. "Are these all the children?" she asked Sir Nathan.

"Yes," Nathan replied quietly. "Look again, Lady Raiford. Are you certain none of these is your daughter?"

Lily shook her head violently. "Nicole has dark hair," she said desperately, "a-and she's younger than these children. Only four. There must be more, she must be here somewhere. Perhaps in

451

one of the other rooms. I know she's afraid. She's hiding from all these people. She's very small. Alex, help me look for her in some of the rooms—"

"Lily." Alex's hand clenched on the back of her neck, silencing her frantic babble.

Trembling, she followed the direction of his gaze. A Learie's bulky form crossed before them, blocking her view. Then she saw the small figure in the corner, half-hidden in shadow. Lily froze, her heart thumping so hard that it seemed to drive the air from her lungs. The child was a wrenchingly perfect little replica of her mother. Her eyes were dark and somber in her small face. Her tiny arms were clutched around some rags that had been knotted to resemble a doll. Standing in shadow, she solemnly watched the milling adults before her. No one had noticed her because of her quietness, like that of a mouse peeping from a secret corner.

"Nicole," Lily said in a choked voice. "Oh, God." Alex let go of her as she moved forward. But the little girl shrank back, staring at her cautiously. Lily's throat ached, and she wiped clumsily at the tears that slid down her face. "You're my baby. You're my Nicole." She crouched before the child. "*Sono qui,*" she said in a voice that shook with suppressed emotion. "I've waited s-so long to hold you. Do you remember me? It's your mama. *Io sono tua mama, capisci?*"

The child looked at her alertly, responding to the Italian. "Mama?" she repeated in a tiny voice.

"Yes, *yes* . . ." Sobbing uncontrollably, Lily rushed forward and snatched her up, holding the child's precious weight against her. "Oh, Nicole . . . you feel so good, so good—" Crooning against the tangled black hair, she ran her hand over the small head, the frail length of her daughter's spine. Nicole rested passively in her arms. Lily heard herself speaking in a frayed voice that didn't seem to be her own. "It's over now. It's finally over." She drew her head back and looked into the brown eyes so like her own. Nicole's little hand came up to Lily's cheek, then moved curiously to her forehead and the shining dark curls that dangled at her temples.

Lily tried to stifle her sobs as she pressed tearful kisses against her daughter's dirt-smudged face. All at once the waking nightmare was gone. The icy stranglehold on her heart had melted away, softly, magically. Lily had never known such peace. She hadn't remembered what it felt like to be free of bitterness and grief. All she had ever wanted in the world was here—the warmth of her daughter's body, the pure, perfect love that could exist only between mother and child. For the moment, nothing existed but the two of them.

Alex watched them until his throat was uncomfortably tight. He'd never seen Lily's face so tender, so maternal. It was a side of her he had never seen before, nor yet imagined. His love for Lily was suddenly altered by a depth of compassion he hadn't been capable of until now. He had never suspected it would be like this, that someone else's happiness would mean so much more to him than his own. Awkwardly he turned to hide his own emotions.

Nathan stood nearby, observing the scene with satisfaction. "Alex," he said in a businesslike manner, "this seems a good opportunity to mention Lord Fitzwilliam's new crime bill, which proposes the opening of three new city offices I'm in dire need of—"

"Anything you want," Alex said hoarsely.

"The bill is facing great opposition in the House—"

"You'll have them," Alex vowed, his face averted. He passed his sleeve over his damp eyes and continued huskily. "If I have to twist every arm in Parliament, I swear you'll have them."

CHAPTER 14

Alex looked up from the newspaper in surprise as Burton announced the arrival of Mr. Craven. They had spent a pleasant morning so far, Alex reading the Times and occasionally joining Lily and Nicole on the parlor floor as they stacked wooden building bricks into precarious towers.

"Oh, do show him in," Lily said to Burton, and threw Alex an apologetic smile. "I forgot to mention that Derek intended to call this morning. He wanted to allow us a few days of privacy before he came to see Nicole."

Frowning slightly, Alex stood up from the sofa, while Nicole went to chase the baleful cat, Tom, around the room. Whenever the poor animal settled in a patch of sunlight, Nicole was drawn to the inviting flick of his tail. Lily gathered some of the toys that were scattered across the parlor floor. She thought with a rueful smile that Alex had bought too many toys, a multitude that would have overwhelmed any child. The sight of the pitiful knot of rags that served as Nicole's doll had been too much for him. He hadn't rested until he had bought every kind of doll available at the Burlington Arcade shop ... dolls with real hair and porcelain teeth, dolls made of wax and china, complete with their own tiny trunks and trousseaus. The nursery upstairs was crammed full of toy theatres, a rocking horse, a grand doll house, balls, musical boxes, and to Lily's dismay, a painted drum that could be heard throughout the mansion.

It had not taken long for them to discover Nicole's disconcerting habit of playing hide-and-seek, spontaneously disappearing and then grinning at their anxious faces when she was found beneath a sofa or end table. Lily had never encountered a child who could move so stealthily. Alex would sit down at his desk in the library and work for an hour, and discover that at some point she had quietly crept underneath his chair.

Gradually Lily's fears that Nicole might have been abused in Giuseppe's care subsided. Although she was a cautious child, she was not fearful, and in fact possessed a sunny nature. With each day that passed she became more vocal, and soon her enchanting giggles and ceaseless questions, spoken in garbled Italian and English, rang through the house. She developed a particular attachment to Henry, frequently demanding to be held by him, yanking at his thick blond locks and gurgling with laughter at his reproving frowns.

Derek came to the parlor, his green eyes falling

upon Lily. She rushed to him with a pleased laugh, discomfiting him with a quick embrace. "Here now," he said in a mock reproof. "Not with your husband looking on, gypsy."

"What marvelous *h*'s," she observed with a grin.

Derek moved forward and shook hands with Alex. "Good morning, milord," he said, smiling sardonically. "Quite a day for me. I'm not usually received in such high-kick parlors."

"You're welcome any time," Alex said pleasantly. "Since you were so hospitable in allowing me the use of your apartments."

Derek grinned at that, while Lily turned crimson. "Alex," she protested faintly, and jerked at Derek's arm to divert him. "Mr. Craven, I'd like to introduce you to someone."

Derek's gaze settled on the little girl, who was standing next to the sofa. Nicole peered at him curiously. "Miss Nicole," Derek murmured. Slowly he sank to his haunches and smiled at her. "Come say 'ello to your Uncle Derek."

Hesitantly Nicole started for him, then changed her mind and ran to Alex, clamping her arms around his leg. She gave Derek a bashful grin.

"She's quite shy," Lily said with a soft laugh. "And she has a decided attachment for blond men."

"No luck for me there," Derek said ruefully, fingering his dark locks. He stood up and regarded Lily with an odd expression. "She's beautiful, gypsy. Like her mother."

Alex struggled to suppress a sharp twinge of jealousy. He reached down and smoothed Nicole's hair, dislodging the huge pink bow that was tied on top of her head. He knew there was no reason to be jealous of Craven. Although Craven loved Lily, it was clear by his actions in the past that he would never be a threat to her marriage. Still, it would never be easy for Alex to stand by silently while another man looked at her that way.

He gritted his teeth in frustration. It would be easier to bear if he and Lily had resumed their marital relationship. The last time they had slept together was before he had found her alone with Giuseppe Gavazzi. Since that night, Lily had been completely absorbed in her child. A tiny bed had been moved into the room next to theirs. Several times each night Lily awakened to check on Nicole. He saw Lily's outline in the darkness, hovering over the peacefully sleeping child, guarding her as if she feared her daughter would be spirited from the bed. The child was seldom out of Lily's sight. Alex offered no objection, knowing that as time passed, Lily's fears would gradually subside. And after all the emotional turmoil his wife had been through, Alex was hardly going to force himself on her . . . although it might soon come to that. He had never wanted anyone this much—having her so near, seeing her soft and utterly happy, her skin and her hair so beautiful, her lips warm, smiling . . . Sternly he forced himself to stop thinking about her, feeling his body beginning to react to the stimulating images.

The truth was, he didn't know what the hell Lily wanted. She seemed so content with the way things were. He was desperate to know if she needed him, if she loved him, but he remained stubbornly silent, deciding she could make the next move, and if it took a hundred years of silence, suffering, and celibacy, so be it. He cursed her every night as he retired to his solitary bed. When he fell asleep, he dreamed of her all night. Sighing grimly, he turned his attention back to the visitor.

". . . I'm going to take my leave," Derek was saying.

"No, you must stay to supper with us," Lily protested.

Ignoring her pleas, Derek grinned at Alex. "Good day, milord. I wish you luck with these two. You'll need it."

"Thanks," Alex replied dryly.

"I'll see you out," Lily said, accompanying Derek to the entrance hall.

As they stood alone in the doorway, Derek folded his hands over hers and gave her a brotherly peck on the forehead. "When are you coming back to Craven's?" he demanded. "It isn't the same without you."

Lily lowered her eyes. "Alex and I will visit some evening."

There was an awkward silence between them,

while they each contemplated a multitude of words better left unspoken.

"So you have her back now," Derek observed.

She nodded, gazing into his dark face. "Derek," she said softly. "I never would have survived the last two years without you." She knew they were saying good-bye to their friendship as it had been. There would never again be the conversations before the fire, the shared secrets and confidences, the odd relationship that had sustained them both in different ways. Impulsively she leaned up and kissed his cheek.

Derek flinched as she took her mouth away, as if the touch of her lips had hurt him. "Good-bye, gypsy," he muttered, and left, striding rapidly to the carriage that awaited him.

The cat stared at Nicole with slitted eyes as she approached him with a winning smile. Reaching out slowly, she grasped his flicking tail. Hissing with annoyance, Tom whirled around and struck out with his paw, leaving a scratch on her hand.

Nicole's mouth opened as she regarded him with surprise and hurt. She began to wail piteously. At the sound of her crying, Alex came to her swiftly, scooping her up as she ran toward him. He patted her back and jostled her comfortingly. "What happened, sweetheart? What is it?"

Still crying, Nicole showed him her hand.

"Did Tom scratch you?" he asked with soft concern.

"Yes," she sobbed. "Naughty, naughty."

"Let me see." Alex scrutinized the faint pink line on the back of her hand. With a sympathetic sound, he kissed the tiny scratch to make it better. "Tom doesn't like his tail pulled, sweetheart. When he comes back I'll show you how to pet him, and he won't scratch you ever again. Here, give me a hug, my brave girl." Amid his light talk and soothing, Nicole promptly forgot about her scratch and beamed at him, her little arm clutched around his neck.

Silently Lily stood watching from the doorway, an ache of love gathering in her chest until it became painful. Unaware that he was being observed, Alex carried on a conversation with Nicole, setting her down and searching beneath the sofa for her misplaced doll. The sight made Lily smile. She hadn't known until this moment if he would truly want to be a father to her child. She had no right to expect it. But she should have realized he had more than enough love to give both of them. He was not the kind of man who would blame an innocent child for her unfortunate beginnings. He had so much to teach her, she thought, about love and trust and whole-hearted acceptance. She wanted a lifetime of being with him and giving him all the joy one man could possibly endure.

Out of the corner of her eye Lily saw a passing housemaid, and she beckoned discreetly. "Sally, please look after Nicole for a while. It's time for her nap, so if you gathered up a doll or two and took her to the nursery . . ."

"Yes, mum," the maid said with a smile. "A good little girl she is, mum."

"She won't be," Lily replied wryly, "after a few years of Lord Raiford's spoiling."

Giggling softly, Sally went into the parlor and began to sort through some toys. "Mine!" Nicole cried, wriggling to be let down, and she went indignantly to rescue her dolls.

"My lord," Lily said demurely, though inside she was filled with giddiness and anticipation. Alex looked at her questioningly. "I wondered if we might have a word in private?" Without waiting for an answer, she headed to the stairs and ascended them gracefully, her hand lightly touching the lacy iron balustrade at measured intervals. A frown worked between Alex's tawny brows, and he followed her slowly.

When they reached the blue and white bedroom, Lily closed the door behind them and turned the key. Suddenly the silence became electric. Alex watched her but didn't move, conscious of his body swelling and thickening, his skin turning hot and sensitive beneath his clothes. His breathing became shallow, and he strove to control it.

She came to him, and he felt the touch of her fingers on his vest, her movements deft and light as she unfastened the intricately carved buttons. The vest hung loose, and she moved to his cravat, unknotting the warm silk and pulling it free from his throat. Alex closed his eyes.

"I've neglected you terribly, haven't I?" she whispered, starting on his shirt.

He was stiff and straining with arousal. He knew she could see the flush creeping over his skin. The touch of her breath sinking through his shirt to his chest nearly caused him to groan. "It doesn't matter," he managed to say.

"It matters very much." She pulled his shirt from his trousers and slid her arms around his lean waist, rubbing her face against the rough hair on his chest. "It's hardly the way to show my husband how much I love him."

Suddenly his hands came up and closed around her wrist in an unconsciously brutal grip. "What?" he asked numbly.

Her dark eyes gleamed with emotion. "I love you, Alex." She paused as she felt a tremor in his powerful hands. "I love you," she repeated, her voice vibrant and warm. "I was afraid to say it until now. I thought you'd send me away once you knew about my daughter. Or worse, that your sense of honor would make you keep us, when you secretly wanted to be rid of us and the scandal we'd cause."

"Be rid of you," he repeated thickly. "*No*, Lily." He let go of her hands and caught her face between his palms. "It would kill me to lose you. I want to be a father to Nicole. I want to be your husband. I've been dying slowly over the past days, wondering how to convince you that you need me—"

She laughed throatily, her eyes bright with tears of happiness. "You don't need to convince me of that."

He buried his mouth in her throat. "I've missed you . . . Lily, my love . . ."

Her breathless laugh dissolved into a moan. His body was hot and demanding against hers, his muscles taut beneath her palms as she caressed him. Hastily he undressed her, and stripped off his own clothes. She reclined on the bed as she watched him, wanting to cover herself but knowing that he took pleasure in the sight of her. Lowering himself to the bed, he pulled her smooth, naked body against his and cupped her buttocks in his hands, urging her hard against him. "Tell me again," he muttered.

"I love you," she whispered. "I love you, Alex."

His hand slid deep between her thighs, while his mouth possessed her in a long kiss. She touched her tongue to his, and they slid together in a mingling of silken heat and fire. "Again . . ." he said, but this time all she could do was sigh brokenly and writhe in time to the invading push of his fingers. As she arched against him, the tips of her breasts dragged through the springy hair on his chest. He bent his head and wet her nipples with his tongue, stroking and circling until the rosy peaks ached exquisitely.

Turning her face, she pressed her lips to his

shoulder, drawing in the scent and taste of his golden skin. Moving lower, she searched with her tongue until she found the flat, silken point of his nipple, and he groaned with pleasure. Inquisitively her fingers combed through the thick, inviting hair and over the tautly delineated muscle of his abdomen, following the narrow tracing of hair that led to a denser thatch. Her palm slid over him, lightly gripped the silken hardness, and she caressed him once, twice, before he moved, pulling back and spreading her wide, easing inside her soft body with a guttural moan.

Intoxicated by the sensation, she wrapped her arms and legs around him, urging him deep within her supple strength. He nudged upward, driving high and slow, lost in an intense enchantment. He pulled back and she grasped at him hungrily, using her legs to press him inside her once more. He repeated the movement, taking fierce delight in the way she worked to pull him back. The smooth, controlled motion drove her wild, and she felt herself sliding helplessly into a trembling state of madness, existing only to feel him pushing and thrusting, his back turning as hard as oak beneath her hands, his hips driving with relentless force until the torment ended with a soaring, shattering burst of pleasure.

Afterward she moved her fingertips idly over his face, tracing each beloved line, the texture or his shaven cheek, the lush crescents of his lashes. Filled with contentment, Alex took her hand and pressed his lips fervently to the delicate palm.

"I've been afraid of so many things for so long," Lily mused absently. "And now . . . now there's nothing left to be afraid of."

Alex propped himself up on an elbow and looked down at her with a lazy smile. "How does it feel?"

"Strange." Her warm brown eyes stared lovingly into his. "It feels strange to be so happy."

"You'll get used to it," he assured her gently. "Soon you'll take it for granted."

"How do you know?" Lily whispered with a smile.

"Because I'll make certain of it." He lowered his head over hers, while her arms slid lovingly around his neck.

EPILOGUE

The coolness of autumn blew in from the partially opened window, causing Lily to snuggle deeper into the warmth of her husband's arms. They were in Wiltshire for a hunting weekend hosted by Lord and Lady Farmington. Gazing at the dark sky outside, Lily sighed regretfully as she realized it would be time for the hunting party to rise soon in order to attend the early-morning meeting.

"Tired?" Alex asked.

"We didn't sleep much last night," she murmured.

He smiled against her hair. "No one did." Together they had rested in bed and listened to all manner of nocturnal sounds—feet creeping down the hallway, doors quietly opening and closing, whispers of inquiry and assent as the weekend guests sought out bedpartners for the night. Lily had made Alex chuckle by pointing out that they were one of the few married couples who actually desired to share the same bed instead of someone else's. To demonstrate just how much he appreciated her company, he had kept her awake for most of the night with his lovemaking.

The discreet tap at the door by Alex's valet alerted them to the fact that it was time to get dressed. Stretching luxuriously and grumbling, Alex left the bed and picked up the clothes that had been laid out for him. Lily, who usually prepared for a hunt with lively anticipation, was strangely slow to move. She propped herself up and watched him from the bed with a slight smile. Her hair, a thick cloud of curls that reached her shoulders, spread across the downy pillows.

Alex paused and regarded her questioningly.

"Darling," she said slowly. "I don't think I'll hunt today."

"What?" Fastening his breeches, he came over to her and sat on the edge of the bed. His face darkened with a frown. "Why not?"

She seemed to choose her words carefully. "I don't think I should."

"Lily." He took her shoulders and pulled her to him gently. The unanchored sheet fell to her waist, baring her slender body. "You know I'd rather you didn't hunt—I can't stand the thought of a single scratch or bruise on you. But I don't want to deprive you of anything that makes you happy. I know how you love to hunt. As long as you're careful, and walk the horse around the more difficult jumps, I don't have any objections."

"Thank you, darling," she replied with a tender smile. "But I still don't think it's advisable."

His eyes became shadowed with concern.

"What's the matter?" he asked quietly, his fingers tightening on her shoulders.

Lily returned his searching stare and traced the curve of his lower lip with her delicate fingertip. "It's just that women in my condition should avoid strenuous activity."

"Women in your—" He broke off in astonishment, his face becoming blank.

She smiled in the silence. "Yes," she whispered in response to the question in his eyes.

Suddenly he crushed her against him, burying his face in her hair. "Lily," he muttered in an aching whisper of joy, while she laughed softly. "How do you feel?" he demanded, pushing her away so that his gaze could wander over her. His large hand searched gently over her body. "Are you all right, sweetheart? Are you—"

"Everything's perfect," she assured him, lifting her face as he scattered kisses over her cheeks.

"*You're* perfect." He shook his head in bemusement. "Are you certain?"

"I've been through this before," she reminded him with a smile. "Yes, I'm certain. What do you want to wager that it's a boy?"

Alex bent his head to murmur in her ear.

Lily laughed throatily. "That's all?" she teased provocatively. "I thought you were more of a gambler than that." Smiling, she drew him down to her, her hands clasping his broad back. "Come closer, my lord," she whispered, "and we'll see if we can't raise the stakes."